**Project: Shadow Walker**

# Project: Shadow Walker

Dalin Moss

Published by Tablo

Copyright © Dalin Moss 2021.
Published in 2021 by Tablo Publishing.

**All rights reserved.**

This book or any portion thereof may not be reproduced or used in any manner whatsoever without the express written permission of the author except for the use of brief quotations in a book review.

Publisher and wholesale enquiries: orders@tablo.io

20 21 22 23 LSC 10 9 8 7 6 5 4 3 2 1

# PROJECT: SHADOW WALKER

# THE TIME BEFORE

A melody of chaos lilted through the open window, singing with a wail of sirens and the flashes of red and white lights. The streets below had grown vacant as terrified citizens hurried into the safety of their homes, hoping that the spreading stories of Death's return were nothing but rumors and hearsay. But the man above knew the truth, knew that in the coming hours millions would be dead and even more would be dying. He knew that the endangerment of humanity was, once again, irrefutable, and the fragile balance that had once controlled the world would return.

Those working on the floors below believed that the next few hours were critical. They hoped, prayed, and wept to find a solution, a cure that would allow humanity to conquer this newest threat and continue their paradisiacal reign. But their efforts would only lead to failure, for that was the will of their savior, of a god, of the man who listened to their tireless work from the top floor of the Elden Laboratory, the man whose name was Dom.

Dom contemplated at the sound of their struggles, remembering a time when the panic that now consumed the workers below had driven him to near madness. That had been a millennia ago, before he had uncovered the secret of cellular regeneration, before he had introduced immortality into the human population, before the Death Cure. Those days of hysteria, of fear and doubt and exhaustion, had led to his greatest inspirations and his most desperate discoveries and, within the span of mere hours, he had been placed in a position of near-divinity. Now there were songs sung in Dom's name, prayers whispered at the base of his tower, stories told of his miraculous works and creations, all due to that single act.

But, they were wrong to praise him; Dom could see that now. It had taken years, centuries even, but the clarity of his error had bloomed with each passing day. The world had grown monotonous and dull. The safety of life had halted the necessity of discovery. He had limited the potential of humanity, blocked the answers of both scientific and religious query, by ridding the world proper motivation. *Humans have a need for death.*

After countless years and millions of attempts, Dom was correcting his mistake. A virus, both elegant and effective, was coursing through the living population, countering his Death Cure and reintroducing the death that humanity had feared so long ago. A final creation, a damning act of regression from the man who had been a savior.

The door to Dom's lab opened. Marcus, a senior member of his staff, stepped on to the gleaming white tiles. His breath was ragged, his clothing wrinkled and disrupted. Marcus was a drowning man looking for a life preserver, but while reaching out he had found the slick scales of a shark.

"Do you know what's going on?" Marcus's voice was hoarse and dripped with fear. "People are dying, Mr. Elden, actually dying." His voice wavered for a moment, trying to comprehend the meaning of what he had just said. "Dom you need to fix this. You have to...." Marcus began coughing, lightly at first, but the coughs grew violent. He aimed his mouth into the crook of his elbow, trying to force himself to breathe and end the barrage of spittle and blood.

Dom remained quiet through Marcus's outburst of fear and illness. He was never the kind of man to falsely comfort in a dire situation. He believed in being forthright, never withholding the information that had become socially acceptable to deny. So, Dom remained silent.

Marcus pulled away from his elbow, his coughing fit finally yielding. He glanced at his blood-covered sleeve and then stared into Dom's eyes, his fear growing. Dom could see the different stages as Marcus's fear manifested into shock, causing the poor man to tremble in uncontrollable panic.

"Please...." Marcus's gaze drifted back to his bloody elbow, contemplating his own inevitable demise. "If you can't fix this...." His breaths came slow and deliberate, his chest showing signs of struggle as it pulled oxygen into his lungs. "I'm going to die. If you can't fix this Dom, I'm going to DIE!" Marcus's fear had advanced into angry terror as he shouted towards his only hope of salvation.

It was time for Dom to talk. He knew that. Marcus had been a loyal partner in the past. Dom had even considered him a friend—almost. The occasional groveling and obsequious nature of respect that Marcus showed him grew old quickly. It was something Dom had had difficulties dealing with since his Death Cure was proven. Too many people tried to get into his good graces, though they had difficulty articulating why.

"This is right, Marcus." Dom's words were calm and methodical, each syllable contemplated individually. He was telling this man that he was doomed; he was pronouncing Marcus dead. "You will not understand it, and you will never forgive me." Marcus was studying Dom's words with an educated understanding. "Things are finally progressing as they should have before I interfered. It's the way that Life intended."

Marcus stared blankly at Dom. His emotions were obvious on his face: confusion, concern, fear and finally, revelation. Marcus's face changed from desperation to rage. The man before him, his chosen god, had betrayed him.

"So, this was you?" The accusation was posed as a question. Marcus was still too careful around Dom to risk a false statement. "You revived Death?"

Dom thought briefly. He'd never imagined death as an actual physical being. It had been one of the rumors that led the religions that worshiped him. *Dom killed Death and gave humanity a true dominion over their lives.*

"Yes, Marcus, this was me."

Marcus shook at the distressing truth. His hopes were gone. His beliefs were shattered. His life was over.

"Should I even bother asking why?" The malice in Marcus's voice sank into Dom's mind like quicksand pulling at a defeated animal.

"You won't agree with me, Marcus. You see eternal life as a right, as something we humans have earned, but this is a choice I had to make. There was a need that death fulfilled, and I destroyed its role. I have found the need, and I have integrated it once again."

Marcus's coughing fit returned, but he made no move to cover his mouth. He coughed into the air, displaying all his discomfort and pain openly. The coughs turned violent and a bloody foam began oozing from Marcus's mouth.

"You've...killed me... Dom." Marcus's final words pushed through his coughs and gags. Leaning over, Marcus began to vomit blood, trying to clear his airway enough to breathe. His chest was heaving slower as his stomach was trying to push harder. The foam continued to flow from his mouth, becoming thick when Marcus tried to breathe at the same time. With an intense effort, Marcus raised his eyes toward Dom. Stories of anger, fear, betrayal, and family all screamed through the dying man's gaze. Then, in an instant, the stories fell silent and their creator went still.

"I suppose I have." Dom's words fell on the corpse of a man that had, almost, been a friend.

The virus took an ugly route. Dom had tried to design a subtler and less painful way to rid the human body of his cure, but none would take. This was the first, the only successful method of returning death to humanity, and it was brutally effective. To see it make a victim of the man who had worked beside him, was as marvelous as it was vicious.

Dom walked out of his lab, stepping over the dead man blocking his doorway. It was time for a change of scenery. His joints felt stiff as he walked and, though he had not yet contracted a cough, the tickle in his throat told him of the virus's advancements within his body.

Dom meandered through the hallways toward the elevator at the center of the building. His personal apartment, which gave access to only him, and the few partners whom he deemed worthy to drink with, was at the top floor. It was where Dom had always felt the most comfortable, a place where all his thoughts could entangle in solitude. There, he surrounded himself with the music and books he'd collected throughout decades.

*You've killed me, Dom.* Marcus's voice rang through his head. He knew it was an awful way to die, but to experience the effects in front of him, to know he'd be feeling them soon, gave Dom a momentary shiver of hesitation. *My insides were on fire. I was drowning in my own blood. Each breath I took became a dagger that cut into my chest. And YOU did that, Dom.*

The elevator chimed, and the doors opened revealing Dom's apartment. Calling it an apartment sometimes felt like an insult. The size alone made it feel more like a cathedral, with dozens of rooms holding lifetimes of memories. Dom walked through the entrance and down the hallway. Each room he passed gave him pause, a moment to relive one of his realizations that eventually lead towards discovery. He saw the rooms as a brief glance into the past, looking back in time with an eye of envy at the man who still had the world to discover, who was still oblivious to the error of his creation.

The crooked silhouette of the scientist walked towards the large chair in the center of his library room. The red velvet beckoned to him, demanding Dom sit and enjoy the comforts that it would bring. He had spent countless hours in this chair, reading, thinking, looking out over the city. So, Dom sat.

The chair faced a large window, giving Dom a view of the city. He took in the beauty of the skyscrapers, the intricately laid streets, the sun painting dusk onto the buildings below. This could be the last thing he would ever see. Ironically, now that the cults were dying, it was the first time he really felt like a god.

Dom reached into his pocket, fumbling slightly with the small remote he had placed there. One touch of the button would ensure that all he had created would be destroyed. He placed his thumb over the switch, delicately rubbing the smooth metal. So much power restrained in such a small device. He pressed, the remote gave a happy click, and the world became light.

This was Dom's final gift. It was given to the force that he had thwarted so many years ago. *To: Death, From: A Foolish Scientist.*

Dom watched the city. Everything electric began vibrating and buzzing. Then, like fireworks celebrating the end, it all exploded.

Dom was washed in heat and smoke as everything around him became fire. The chaos was beautiful, Dom's final contribution to this dying world. Now all he needed to do was wait. Wait for the virus to destroy his body, wait for the fire to destroy his building, wait for all of this to become a distant dream and all the screaming to finally end.

Dom sat through the flames and waited, but as the heat began searing the flesh from his bones, Death refused to take him.

# 1: BANDITS AND BUTTERFLIES

"Let's go over it again." Colter said, unfolding the contract and clearing his throat. "A ring of significant value has been located in the Father Tower of the Eastern city Elodin. The tower currently houses a gang of Southern rebels, all human – from what our informants say. You'll know the ring by its onyx color and golden markings. An image in the shape of a phoenix is engraved on its face and the interior of the ring has an unknown inscription. The buyer is unsympathetic to the South and would not mind if bloodshed became necessary to fulfill the contract."

"It won't." Jim said, sharply.

Colter nodded. "Good."

The contractor fetched another parchment from his jacket pocket. As his nimble fingers smoothed out the creased paper, Jim saw the grip of a pistol peer from his beltline. The Hero was undisturbed, knowing that Colter always kept a near armory on his person, but was surprised at his old friend's carelessness in revealing the weapon. *He's usually more careful. Something has him nervous.*

Colter pointed to the faded blueprint of the Father Tower. "It's safe to assume that the ring will be on the top floor – that's sixty-four stories in total. I'm told...."

"There are vines that grow as high as the tenth floor and a shaft from a dumbwaiter that reaches from the master suite – on the sixty-fourth floor- all the way down to the kitchens on floor twenty-seven." Jim finished. "I don't mind repetition Colt, but there's something you're not telling me."

Colter let out a huff, allowing his professional persona to dissolve. The simple act made the room feel brighter as the meeting went from one between contractor and thief, to one of friends.

"I don't think you should take this one." Colter said, looking at the floorboards. "There's something…off. This contract is easy, yet it was terribly expensive."

"We've had easy contracts before, Colt." Jim reassured.

"But none that involved Southerners."

Jim was quiet for a time, searching for understanding in his friend's unease. "I can handle my own people."

"Can you?" Colter took a step forward. "If a man from your faction ran at you with a knife, would you be able to cut him down before he warned of your arrival? Or what if you're spotted, what then? They'll know who you are, there's already rumors whispered in every city about that mission you botched in Forge. What was that? Eighty years of hiding? All for naught due to a single night."

"It won't come to that."

"You're sure?"

"I am."

"You're a liar."

Jim shrugged. "I'm a thief."

"Fine." Colter pulled a knife from his belt and held it out for Jim to take. The thief dutifully took the blade and ran it across the tip of his thumb. Then, he placed the wound in the upper corner of the contract. "With your blood, this contract is yours."

Jim moved to the door. "Three weeks. I'll meet you in Indrasmos." He said, then exited the room.

○ ○ ○ ○ ○ ○ ○

Elodin was a city of sparsity: the few houses were tall and separated by long stretches of road, the market was comprised of less than a dozen merchants, and the wall that surrounded the city was plain and stone. In the darkness of night, Jim wandered down the vacant streets, moving ever closer to the East edge of Elodin where the three towers looked down upon the sleeping city.

The towers were the only real thing of significance in this place. Each structure was rumored to have been built during The Time Before, and each was now worshiped individually by the followers of Vlour. The tower on the Northern point was known as the Spirit Tower, the one to the South was called the Child Tower, and the one in the center, the tallest of the three, was named the Father Tower. They were dangerous places to hide; a sure way to earn the title of *enemy* to the masses that followed the Vlour's teachings. But the few bandits that Jim had known, cared little of enemies and friends.

The thief stalked outside the three towers, looking through the hundreds of windows for any signs of life. *Quiet. Nothing. Asleep.* Jim sprinted forward, quick and soundless, covering the long stretch of empty road in a few, short steps. He pushed his body up against the Father Tower, trying to blend into the dark shadow at its base. Then he waited, listened, using all of his fine senses to ensure he was safe and unnoticed.

After a full minute of silence, Jim crouched around until he spotted the tall, sturdy vines that crawled along the Father Tower. He took a handful of the foliage and pulled hard. When the vines remained attached to the wall, the thief hoisted himself off the ground and began the ten-story climb.

The window was locked, but, prying with a knife, Jim was able to snap the delicate metal lock and enter the Father Tower. Inside, the floorboards were covered in a layer of heavy dust. The walls were covered in ripped paper and decorated by unlit sconces. A small plaque with the word *stairs* pointed to a door at the opposite end of the hallway.

As he moved, Jim searched the dust for indications of footprints and recent movement but found none. He silently opened the door to the stairwell and began his ascent to the twenty-seventh floor.

As Jim approached his destination, the clank of metal rang from the doorway ahead, followed by the sound of angry voices. Jim pressed his ear against the door and listened. The voices of two men sounded as hushed shouts, their words distorted but their emotion obvious. Jim slowly turned the door handle and cracked the door open.

"...mone had heard you, we'd be marked and convicted by the church. You need to be more careful!" One man chastised.

"It slipped!" Another defended. "The handle was all greasy from *your* breakfast this morning! It's you that needs to be more careful!"

"Me?" The first man chuckled. "If it weren't for *me* the whole stack of pots would've tumbled! If I hadn't...." He stopped abruptly.

Another voice, light and songlike, mumbled from farther ahead, too quiet for Jim to properly hear.

"I'm sorry angel, we didn't mean to wake you. Uncle Supe and I were just cooking up some roasted onions. Would you like some?"

The quiet voice mumbled again.

"No, no, it's alright! We're not angry at each other." The second man said, kindly. "Just a bit tired."

"Let's get you back to bed." The first man said. "I could tell you the story of Dinny again. Her stories always help you have happy dreams."

The quiet voice sounded in a delighted chirp.

"Dinny was one of our guardian Heroes. She was known to hunt game, using a bow crafted from the four trees of the Hero people." The man's voice grew distant as he spoke. "She was kind, even to us humans, and defended our villages when our walls were torn to splinters after the...." The sound of a door opening and closing ended the man's story.

Jim moved then, squeezing through the door and easing it closed with a barely audible click. He stayed low, observing the hallway and the many doors that led to varying rooms. At the end of the hall was a shimmering, silver kitchen, lit by a faint fire and accompanied by a lone man. The man stared at the dancing flames, humming softly and cooking fragrant vegetables in a metal pan. At the far end of the kitchen, Jim saw a small door, placed precariously above one counter, *the dumbwaiter.*

Jim crouched to the bar, keeping his head lower than the table's surface. To reach the small door he'd have to distract the man. Jim pulled out a handful of copper coins and jingled them just loud enough for the man to hear. The man's humming stopped as he listened intently. Jim shook the coins louder and more persistent than before.

The man stood and cleared his throat. "Hello?" He asked. "Who's there?"

Soft footfalls told of the man's careful approach. Jim dropped the coins, ensuring they scatter messily where he waited. As the man came nearer, Jim pivoted around the bar, using the solid surface as a barrier from the man's sight.

"Huh?" The man grunted. "What's this?" He bent down to inspect the spread of coins. "Father, bless." He whispered after a moment, then began noisily collecting the small sum.

Jim snuck to the dumbwaiter and lifted the door with a quiet resonance. The thief stopped for a breath, then, noting that the man had not heard the small noise, he slunk into the shaft and slid the door closed.

The inside of the dumbwaiter was small and cramped. The smell of dust and copper hung heavy in the stale air, making the dark shaft feel ancient and confined. Jim reached above the mobile box for the thick wires that stretched up to an unseen destination. Then, he climbed.

The feeling of strain in his arms and hands gave Jim a small exhilaration. With each pull of his body he rose above countless stories and came closer to another successful mission. When he reached the circular gear that served as the dumbwaiter's pulley, the thief brushed his hand against the wall until he found the inner latch that released the door to the master suite on the highest floor of the Father Tower.

The soft moonlight was almost blinding to Jim's sensitive eyes. He lifted a hand to shield his vision and squinted to observe the elegant suite.

The floors were covered in a red, velvet rug, a chandelier made of clear crystal hung from the center of the ceiling, and on each wall were paintings of religious figureheads. Sitting against one wall was a table, covered in jewelry and a scattering of papers, and, against the farthest wall, near a large window adorned in purple drapes, was the largest bed that Jim had ever seen.

Jim walked to the table, searching for the ring, for the totem that would mark his success. But, while there were many rings that seemed to hold incredible value, there was none that fit his desired description. He moved then to the bed, tossing the pillows and blankets in search of hidden treasures, but found nothing but dust and yellowing sheets. A chest rested at the bed's foot, but, searching through the contents, Jim only found more papers and a few, motheaten cloaks.

As he stood, Jim felt the hairs on his neck rise as he heard a muffled click. The thief dove to the bedside as an explosion and the smell of gunpowder erupted in the room. Fiery heat radiated from Jim's shoulder where a bullet had pierced his flesh.

"Jimmy!" The voice of a man shouted, sounding far too delighted. "How unexpected to see you here!"

Jim knew the voice, knew the arrogant tones and the nauseating smell of tobacco. He'd had the displeasure of working with a man as vile as he was clever and as cruel as he was conniving, the same man who this voice belonged to.

"Floydd," Jim said, harshly, "you caught me by surprise, so I'll forgive your attack. But be smart about this. Me owing you a favor can be more valuable than any contract you'll ever accept."

"Oh, bargaining?" Floydd chuckled. "It's like you don't even know me, Jimmy! Like…like we aren't even friends."

Another gunshot rang through the suite and a pebbling of debris rained on Jim from the wall behind him.

"You know I'm a professional," Floydd continued, "and when I accept a job, I complete it. Now, why don't you peak that pretty Hero head of yours over the bed so we can be done with this?"

"This is a job?" Jim asked. "You're after a ring?"

"A ring?" Floydd said, bemused. "Oh, yes, the ring."

Floydd flicked something into the air, the object tumbling to where Jim was crouched. Jim picked up the onyx ring, an engraving of a phoenix covering its face. On the inside of the ring, a fine inscription read *"The Death Killer, a true and living God"*.

"Most of us have wanted you dead for some time now, Jimmy." Floydd taunted. "But you are a slippery vermin. It took me a few years to set this all up, but my payment is well worth it. You're making me a near legend, Jimmy; killing a Hero is no small feat. Now, why don't we get this over with? It's time to accept your fate, stand up and..."

Jim stood suddenly and threw a knife at the arrogant bastard. Floydd's expression went from overconfident to surprised in an instant. Then, he began to smile. Tendrils of lightning sprouted from his waist, catching Jim's soaring blade and stopping it midair.

Now was Jim's turn to be surprised. *A lightning belt? Where did he get a lightning...?*

Floydd shot again, catching Jim in the side, the pain forcing him to fall backwards.

"Do you like it Jimmy?" Floydd taunted. "A small piece of my payment. A small piece of what your death is giving me." He lifted his gun and shot again.

Pain erupted from Jim's arm and his vision began to fade.

Floydd rushed to the fallen thief, lifting him by the throat and shoving him against the window. "Keep my place in Hell warm for me, Jimmy." Floydd placed the gun against Jim's chest and pulled the trigger.

The sound of gunfire and shattering glass became Jim's reality. He felt the sensation of falling and saw the distant stars as he fell from the Father Tower.

*Be careful when you climb, Jim. Even one of us can die if we fall far enough.*

Brisk wind flew by Jim as he fell, and the feeling of butterflies danced in his stomach. As he watched the Father Tower grow above him, he knew that the ground would meet him and end the life of the traitorous man. He closed his eyes, accepting his offering to Death.

Only...Death never came. Instead, when Jim opened his eyes, he found that the world had turned dark. No stars, no Father Tower, no death. Only falling, wind, pain, and the feeling of butterflies.

## 2: A NAME LEFT UNSPOKEN

*"You are wrong."*

Jim opened his eyes, feeling the pain in his chest and abdomen that had caused him to lose consciousness. He looked around, hoping to see something other than darkness, smoke, and shadows, but gave a shaky and discouraged breath when the sight that taunted him was the same, dismal blackness.

The air no longer whooshed past his ears, yet Jim still floated in the empty space, suspended by an unknown abeyance. The blood on his shirt felt chilled and caused the garment to stick to his skin uncomfortably.

Above him, a formation of fog drifted back and forth, following the floating man with similar patterns of suspension. Jim watched it, reveled in the distraction of the smoke. He felt like a child looking at clouds, pleased with himself for seeing the shapes of animals and landmarks in the ethereal vapor. This time, the shape of the fog formed a man, rubbing at his chin in study.

*"You see me. You live?"* Jim both heard and felt the vibrations of the voice, which seemed to emanate from nothingness. *"Many see, but rarely do any live. You are wrong."* The man made of smoke tilted his head and drifted closer. *"You see smoke because you do not understand."*

"Understand what?" Jim asked.

*"That I am what remains."* The smoke moved around Jim like a spider studying a fly that had become trapped in its web. *"You do not understand, because you are what we were, and you are wrong."*

Every word spoken by the swirling being sent rumblings through Jim's chest, reawakening the pain in his wounded body. He tried to shift, to ease some of his discomfort, but only succeeded in escalating his aggravation.

"*Floating does not suit you?*"

The smoke moved its arm and made a quick motion. All at once, gravity returned to Jim. He plummeted a few inches and landed on invisible ground. Pain ruptured through his body, causing flashes of red to interrupt the familiar darkness and dropping him to his knees. Jim felt rivulets of cold blood drip down his body.

"*He kneels?*" The smoke said with obvious indignation. "*How formal. How annoying. You kneel to worship, and you worship because you do not understand what I am. None do. None will. You only see me as your perception of a deity. Yet, here I am, in the same purgatory as....*" The smoke reached his hand forward, nearly touching Jim's trembling form. "*Oh.*" It said, embarrassed. "*I apologize. You kneel due to pain, and pain is much preferred to worship.*"

The man crouched before Jim and hovered his hands over the many wounds. Jim's chest tingled and itched, and he wanted nothing more than to scratch at the incredible irritations. But when he moved his arm, the itching stopped, as did the pain.

Jim was in a state of amazement. He was used to the quick healing of injury that came with his kind, but what he had just experienced was instantaneous. One moment he was on the brink of death, the next he could move and breathe with no sign of the torment that had threatened to end his existence.

Jim looked at the smoke man's face. "Thank you." He said and stood.

"*There is no need to suffer, not here.*" The smoke said, drifting as he spoke. "*Death uses pain as a motivation for life. But life has no purchase here, so pain is useless.*"

"Where is *here*?" Jim asked, gesturing towards the dark plane.

"*Where?*" The smoke chuckled. "*Below, Hell, purgatory, eternity: there are too many names for a place as disappointing as the afterlife. What you should be asking is 'How'. How are you here, living amongst the deceased? How did God mistake you as a man who belonged in a place such as this? How is it* that you can leave when none else who reside here can? 'Where' is not nearly as important as 'How', and 'How' is a question that I have asked for millennia."

"I can leave?" Jim asked, finding hope in the small rant that the smoke had uttered.

The smoke-man tilted his head, quizzically. "Of course, you can leave. You are wrong, you do not belong amongst the souls of former life. But you will return; I know your kind. Your leave will be temporary, but your stay will be eternal. Just as mine has been."

Hope elated Jim, "Can you show me how to leave?"

"Of course, I can." The smoke said, plainly. "But, in return, you must show me how you came here."

The man drifted forward and hovered his hands over Jim's temples.

"How do I..." Jim began to ask, but never finished his question.

Memories began to flood through Jim's mind, overcoming his existence within the darkness. He saw the tower that he had fallen from, felt the bullets tear through his skin. He heard the twang of the elevator cable and felt the strain in his muscles as he hoisted himself in the air.

Then, he was with Colter, receiving contracts from his trusted companion for a price that compared to governors and Leaders. He felt Colter's grip on his shoulder. *We're gonna be rich, Jim! With you in the frontline and my negotiation skills, we'll never want for anything!*

Jim found himself suddenly in a forest; he was younger than he remembered. Winter was harsh and deadly. Wisps of frigid air snuck through the cabin's walls and diminished the comfortable heat of the fire. A knock came from the door and Jim undid the latch, allowing more cold to enter his haven.

In an instant, Jim was outside. Winter was only starting, but his cloak was made for concealment, not heat. He shivered, grasping to the trunk of the pine as monsters stumbled below him.

Then, he was home. Walls reached high above him offering their protection with dutiful resilience. His family was here: his father, mother, and... and?

No. Only he was there, staring at the green that would never see again. There was too much blood; she looked so small. There was nothing he could do. He was alone. She was gone.

Jim screamed.

Tears blurred the smoky landscape before him. He was still screaming and, it seemed, that the world was screaming back. A vortex of smoke swirled around him, releasing a deafening roar of wind and wails.

The man made of smoke moved close to Jim. *"You must be quiet! You must be still!"*

Jim listened, hearing the urgency in the man's voice, and calmed his terrified shout. As he quieted, the vortex mimicked his mood. It was slow to settle but became still and silent as Jim soothed his shaky breathing. Once the motion around him stopped, Jim saw the forms of dozens, if not hundreds, of smoke-made people standing around him. The sight was unsettling. Jim crouched low, his instincts telling him that danger was all around.

*"They can feel your life."* The man said, *"They know you are wrong, just as I do, and they wish to use you to return. But it's not that simple, things rarely are. They have become carnal in their desire for life and they cannot control what you will see. But…perhaps I can."*

Jim stayed crouched, listening to the man while keeping his eyes planted on the crowd of fog.

*"I can help you return."* The man of smoke said, as the mist around him shimmered and began to dissipate. *"But you may lose yourself to my touch."* A form was becoming revealed beneath the concealing smoke. Jim squinted his eyes, trying to see the details of the man who had been speaking with him. *"Only one has ever lived through my life. But madness is the first step towards magnificence."* The smoke vanished completely, and Jim shuddered at the man who had taken its place.

Arms covered in blisters and blackened flesh connected to a thin torso which moved with agonized breaths and showed its exposed ribcage. No clothing covered the man, though there was barely enough flesh on his body that would have required coverage. His face was made of charred skin, his lips burned away long ago to reveal his gaping mouth. Jim had heard stories of this man, who shrouded himself in shadows and harbingered those of life to the underworlds and beyond: Death.

"*Do you fear me?*" Death asked, stepping close to the crouching man. "*Do you wish for me to hide the truth of my form?*"

"Should I fear you?" Jim asked, calming the shudder that rippled through his chest.

"*Ahh, a question of a man who knows that truths are often deceiving.*" Death took another step. "*When you return, will you seek revenge?*"

"Yes."

"*Excellent. It seems our intertwinement may continue. Your revenge and my imprisonment have a commonality. If I return you to life, will you promise to seek out one from my time? There is much that I wish to ask him, answers that he has discovered that may lead to my true salvation.*"

"If you return me to life, I'll do anything you ask."

Death chuckled. "*Never make that sort of promise. This is how evil men become exalted and deceivers receive immortality. No. What I ask of you, Hero, is a contract. Your payment will be life, given to you preemptively by me, and your mission will be to find the answer of my freedom. Do you accept?*"

Jim studied the decrepit figure for a moment. "If I cannot find the answer, will you return me here?"

"*Eventually.*"

"Then tell me, where should I go?"

Death's gaping maw crooked into a smile. "*There is a city in the West called Salix, do you know of it?*"

"The Willow capitol?"

"*Precisely. The man who killed you has residency there. He also has a friend, a priest that has shared a similar fate as you. This is the man that you must find, this is the man who holds the key to my shackles.*"

"I'll find him."

"*Good.*" Death reached a hand forward formalizing the contract with a shake. "*I am sorry for my death. I do hope that you recover from it.*"

"What do...?" Jim started, but, before he could finish, his world faded into heat.

■ ■ ■ ■ ■ ■ ■ ■

*My name is.... No. Not now. My life is not important, but my death will return you.*

*Fire. That's what I remember most. Flames licked at my flesh and boiled the marrow in my bones: they split like logs beneath a carver's ax. Can you feel it? I was screaming. I could hear the moisture of my body escape through my pores in whistles of steam. I couldn't see, the flames had eaten my eyes and taken my sight. I needed reprieve.*

*I reached forward searching for...something. What was it? Does it matter? No. Maybe. I...no. But I found it. My hand tingles with wonderful distraction. The pain was gone from my fingertips, so I continued to reach forward, numbing my arm and shoulder with the same, beautiful escape. Then, I immerse myself completely, and my world goes dark.*

*I can see darkness, smoke, shadows. Only now do I realize that the fire was bliss, and this darkness is torture.*

*We are all connected.*

■ ■ ■ ■ ■ ■ ■ ■

Jim gasped, pulling drafts of cool air into his lungs. The world around him was bright, colorful, beautiful. The greens of the forest had never looked so wonderful; the darkness was gone. He examined his hands and arms and saw no burns or blisters. He was back; He was alive.

## 3: DEAD MAN'S REQUEST

Jim placed the onyx ring on the table for Colter to examine. The contractor studied the ornate jewelry with a practiced eye, a look of admiration unmistakable on his face.

"This is it." Colter said, pocketing the ring. "How do you want your payment?"

"Coin this time." Jim said.

"Not sticking around?" Colter asked.

"No."

Colter shrugged then uncinched the purse from his belt. He pulled thirteen gold coins from the pouch, placing them carefully on the table as he counted. But, when Jim reached forward, Colter covered the neat pile.

"I heard...something." The contractor said, looking away. "A few days back one of my...colleagues passed through here. He told me about a contract that he had priced for some outrageous sum for a buyer richer than the Elken God. A contract that he'd sold to Floydd."

Jim nodded. It had taken him far longer to get to Indrasmos than he'd first expected. When he awoke, it had taken him days to find his bearings. Somehow, after his fall from the Father Tower, after the world made of smoke, he had wound up in the foothills of the Eastern Mountains, more than twenty miles away from the city of Elodin.

Still sore and confused, he'd stumbled around the foothills until he finally found a thin passage that led to a small river. It was there that he thought, thought about the world that he had been forced to experience, thought about his fall, his death. It was there that Jim realized that all that he had run from was nipping at his heels. And, it was there, that Jim decided that Floydd would be his final contract.

"I'm sorry if I worried you." Jim said.

"Worried?" Colter exclaimed. "Jim, I thought you were dead. I heard you'd been shot half a dozen times and thrown from the highest floor of the tallest tower. The way Floydd tells it, he stripped you of your Hero blood and danced upon your lifeless corpse."

Jim stayed quiet.

"Well?" Colter pushed. "Nothing you want to tell me? Jim...I thought I'd lost my friend. And when you showed up this morning...."

"I died, Colt." Jim said, in barely a whisper. "Floydd caught me off-guard. He shot me and...and I fell."

"You...?" Colter started, but stopped suddenly. "You're serious?"

"Yes."

"Jim...." Colter started, but his words faltered.

Jim looked at his friend. "I'm going to Salix. Floydd has a home there." From the contractor, Jim could feel his questions radiating, but he continued without explanation. "I could use your help."

Without hesitation, Colter answered. "You have it." He turned, grabbing at some loose papers and reading through them rapidly. "I don't know much about Salix, but I'll send feelers out immediately. It'll be an expensive ask...but I'll make it work."

"Thanks." Jim said, turning to exit the room. "I'll scout the city for a few days – lay low, stick to alleys and rooftops – that sort of thing. I'll reach out to you when I'm ready - our usual parameters?"

"I'll be there." Colter said with a smile. "Just...don't keep me waiting this time."

Jim returned the smile. "Wouldn't dream of it." He said, then opened the door and entered the streets of Indrasmos.

It would take a few days to get to Salix, Jim knew, so he stopped to fill his water pouch at a decently clean and cheap pump. He visited a few shops, restocking his tinderbox and snagging a piece of dried meat to settle his grumbling stomach. Then, he left, leaving through the Western gate and wandering toward the forest that he'd once called home.

## 4: EMERALDS AND GOLD

A calm breeze swept through the forest, causing the treetops and grass to sway and dance. The smell of pine and soil mingled in Jim's nose. It brought cold memories to the surface of his mind. Cowering behind boulders and large trees for shelter; he had needed to rely on his sense of smell and sound in the black of night. It was the first time Jim had been forced to struggle and it was the first time he had chosen to live.

Walking here, in the middle of an unforgiving forest, felt right to Jim. He had struggled, fought through a hellish world of smoke, and emerged in a place that had tried to kill him before. But often the places that had tried to kill him only succeeded in shaping him, honing his body and mind into a razor sharp enough to survive. *There is a pattern to places, Jim. You will either succumb, or you will overcome and be all the better for it.*

Is that what he had done? Overcome Hell, climbed through the surface of the world to wake beneath the sun once again? That place, with its shadows and screams, had it molded him into a stronger being simply by allowing him to live? And the man who hid himself in shadows, had he....

A crack from behind sent Jim's reflexes to work. Crouching low, he found the hilt of a dagger in each hand. His eyes swept the forest, scanning the trees and ground for signs of people or husks. Another crack rang from his left, and Jim let his dagger fly towards the noise. The dagger sliced at a cloaked figure hiding behind a tree. The blade caught the hood of the cloak, forcing it off and pinning it to the trunk.

A girl stared at Jim, her eyes and face contorted in a fierce expression of rage. She seamlessly shed the cloak and sprinted forward, closing the gap between them in moments. A thin sword extended from her hand, angled to sweep at Jim's throat. Jim easily caught the sword with his own blade, redirecting it to the ground.

The girl moved quickly, jabbing a small knife from her other hand at Jim while her sword soared. Jim stepped past the blade, allowing it to brush against the fabric of his shirt but never allowing it to contact his body. He kicked at the girl's leg, trying to force her off balance to gain a quick victory. His foot made contact, and she began to fall.

The girl leaned into her fall and, using her hand to push off the ground, smashed both feet into Jim's chest. Unprepared for the attack, Jim staggered backwards. The kick was faster than he had anticipated. No human could match the speed and grace that had caught him off-guard. She had to be a Hero.

Jim knew the fight just got dangerous. To fight another Hero meant he would have none of the advantages that he had relied on so heavily in the past years. He slowed his breathing and reached for the calm place that would allow him to win. The girl rose to her feet, breathing heavily. She looked up at Jim, locking eyes.

A panic began to grow in Jim as he stared. Her eyes were green, emeralds contrasting her dark hair. She was no Hero, only a human. A human that moved so quick that a Hero couldn't avoid an attack. The panic continued to bloom, moving into Jim's arms and legs. If he didn't do something, cut down his opponent now, the panic would consume him. He needed to move, to attack, to be rid of this girl. Now.

Jim and the girl lunged forward at the same time, each adjusting to the other's course. Metal screeched as weapons collided, each threw their entirety into their attacks. The girl's sword came fast and often, forcing Jim to parry and defend. *I need to end this quickly!* Jim attacked back, putting a force into each swing that sent a ripple through the girl's arms and into her chest. *I'm getting tired. My attacks are slowing.*

Jim continued to catch each attack, predicting the next with practiced precision. The girl's breathing had quickened, and a sheet of sweat had formed on her forehead. Jim pushed forward with a sweep, his blade catching the girl's arm. She allowed herself a glance at the wound, the bright crimson stained through her shirt. The cut was long but shallow, starting at her shoulder and working its way towards her elbow.

A desperation overtook Jim. He wanted to run but knew that by turning his back he would ensure his death. So, Jim began another onslaught, forcing his blade to contact and overcome his enemy. He drove down, using his desperation as strength with each blow. The girl parried, and Jim found one of his daggers stuck in the ground at her feet. He let go of the hilt, forgetting the weapon immediately, and attacked with his single blade. *My arm is killing me.*

Jim saw an opening as he jumped towards an attack. His blade sang against his opponent's while his foot kicked at her outstretched leg. The girl fell again, trying to replicate the kick she had landed once before, but this time Jim was ready. He sidestepped quickly, grabbing at the girl's ankle. With her leg in his grip, he pulled her up into the air and slammed her against the trampled soil.

Jim's head suddenly became clear and calm, the desperation and panic disintegrating in an instant. The lack of fear and emotion caused him to stop and evaluate his fight. Constantly, the battle was in his favor. There was no reason behind his fear. There was no reason to panic. Victory was always his.

Confused, Jim looked down at the girl. She lay dazed. Sweat had mixed with dirt from the fall, covering her face in a muddy sheen. She lay so still, so calm, no panic or fear anywhere in sight. Why had he attacked her with such fierce intent?

Jim retrieved his dagger from the ground a few feet away and polished the steel on his cloak. He looked towards the unconscious girl. The sun would set within the hour, and the night that followed would no doubt be cold and harsh. If she was left here alone, she would freeze before she awoke, even if she was a Hero. Or, her blood would attract wolves and husks. She would be dead by sunrise.

Jim looked up at the sunlit canopy. More memories began to play through his mind. On freezing nights, he had huddled in the tops of trees, the only safe places from the packs of wolves pawing at the trunks below. He would shiver as he hugged the rough bark close to his cheek, but the shivers were never from fear—until the wolf pack would run, and the ground below grew silent. He would often hear footsteps and ragged breathing as the true terror walked nearby. Then, when those footsteps grew louder, and the figures appeared in the opening below, that is when his shivers turned to shakes and his eyes would close tight.

No one deserved to wake in a night like that, not even this girl who had tried to kill him.

Jim walked back to the still figure in the grass. He picked her up, slung her over his shoulder, and retrieved her cloak from the nearby tree. The night was going to be long, but less lonesome than it had been all those years ago.

■ ■ ■ ■ ■ ■ ■ ■

The darkest part of the night had passed before Emma began to stir. Every inch of her hurt; the slightest movement sent torrents of pain cascading through her chest and into her bursting head. But she was alive, somehow. After that Hero tossed her to the ground, and her world went dark, he had kept her alive. Emma opened her eyes, allowing the rude light to assault her senses and magnify the throbbing inside her skull.

A bright, warm fire illuminated a small makeshift barricade. A narrow exit between two boulders led towards the blinding shadows of the long night. At her back, Emma sat against three large trees. Their trunks had grown close together, forming a natural wall against the darkness and elements beyond. Next to the fire lay a charred rabbit, a spit sticking through its torso and into the soft earth.

Emma sat up. A quick examination revealed she had no broken bones, all her weapons had been sheathed in their proper places, and her arm had been bandaged prettily. Attempting to move her shoulder too quickly resulted in a flash of red pain that made her wince and gasp sharply.

A rustling came from the entrance to the barricade. Emma instinctually grabbed for the sword that she kept on her back. The blade felt like an extension of her arm as she held it against the noise. Two golden eyes peered at her from the narrow opening, then the Hero entered the sanctuary.

The man who emerged was tall, causing him to crouch low as he came to the place where the two boulders met. His brown hair shagged past his ears, bouncing as he awkwardly stepped and sat next to the fire. Emma watched, unblinking, at the average looking man sitting quietly a few feet away. The man stared intently at the fire, keeping his eyes as hidden as possible with a practiced ease.

Emma understood now why she hadn't feared to fight him at first. He knew the advantages that came with his kind, so he knew that a more cautious approach would be taken if his opponents knew what he was. In the fight, he refused to look her in the eyes until she was too close to back down. Emma shivered, remembering the panic that threatened her when he showed her what he was. Sure, she had fought Heroes before, but never up close, and never alone. It was a miracle that he had allowed her to last for more than a moment.

The man sat perfectly still, never reaching for his weapons or acknowledging the pointed metal Emma held. Emma inched backwards. The coarse bark scratched against her wounded arm, forcing her to acknowledge the fiery pain with a blink. The Hero's eyes snapped at the movement, an odd concern showing in the brief motion.

"Sorry, about earlier." Sympathy lay heavy on his tired voice. "I don't know what came over me."

His eyes darted to Emma's bandaged shoulder, then drifted back to the flames.

He gestured towards the rabbit at Emma's feet, "You should eat before your watch."

Emma gently laid her sword on the ground and reached for the crisp rabbit. She poked at its belly and her fingertip turned black after touching the burnt flesh. She smelled the animal; the sour scent of smoke filled her nostrils.

"You're not much of a cook, are you?" The vibrations from Emma's voice reverberated through her whiplashed neck, a reminder that the Hero in front of her was an enemy.

A genuine smile grew on the Hero. His face and body seemed to relax, causing Emma to also relax before she realized and tensed her shoulders again.

"I gave you the better one. My hare was mostly ash. I ate half of the spit before I realized the wind had carried away the good parts." The Hero's smile grew.

Against her will, Emma smiled. She was sitting next to a man who had nearly killed her, who had thrown a knife at her head, yet she was smiling. Her body still rang with sore disdain, but she had been spared from the freezing night, so she allowed the smile to stay.

Emma's stomach grumbled, so she bit into the rabbit. The foul-tasting meat caused her eyes to water. She wanted to spit onto the ground, but she needed the sustenance. Her face must have spoken of the onslaught on her taste buds, because the Hero let out a low laugh.

Despite the horrendous taste, Emma continued to eat. She picked at her teeth with its bones once her meal was finished. The Hero stayed still and silent as she ate, his golden eyes staring at the flames between them.

The crackling fire served as entertainment as a silence grew. The Hero's heavy eyes blinked rapidly as sleep threatened to take him.

"Do you really want me to take a watch?" Emma asked the Hero.

He looked up, slightly startled at the disrupted silence. "More than anything."

The Hero stood and began to clear an area of twigs and rocks. Did he truly trust her, an armed stranger, to take watch while he slept? He would be helpless; it would be so easy to leave or cut his throat while he dreamt. But the Hero continued to sweep at the soft grass.

He sat upon the area he had cleared, bunching his cloak into a pillow and leaning his head into the cloth. And then, he closed his eyes.

Emma stared in disbelief at the vulnerable man. One motion, one quick slip of her sword, and he would belong to Death. It would be so easy—too easy. Emma's body tensed.

"Why shouldn't I kill you?" Her voice betrayed her thoughts, acknowledging what must be a trap.

The Hero shifted onto his side, putting his back towards Emma and the fire. "You wouldn't be the first." His reply was soft and groggy, as if sleep had already taken him. "I'm Jim, by the way. There are a few extra logs by the entrance, if the fire gets too low."

Then, he was asleep. His chest heaved slow and deep, exhaustion overtaking him completely. His breath puffed in clouds of dragon smoke, reminding Emma of the frigid fate that the slumbering Hero had spared her from.

Emma stared at the fire as the Hero lay in the depth of unconscious dreams. Only leaving once to retrieve a few logs, she moved slow and silently so she wouldn't disturb her companion of the night.

The Hero only awoke once, grasping at his chest with wide and fearful eyes. He looked towards Emma, the fear morphing back into calm exhaustion.

"My name is Emma." She kept her voice low, barely more than a whisper.

Jim blinked, each movement of his eyes growing slower. A few seconds later he was asleep again. And still, through the remaining hours of the night, Emma watched.

## 5: THE SOUNDS OF THE FOREST

A bright morning sun greeted Jim as he woke from his restless sleep. The fire's glow was low, merely embers surrounded by smoldering ash and charcoal. And the girl, Emma, was gone.

Jim rubbed the sleep from his eyes. He couldn't blame her for leaving. A person traversing the forest obviously had a destination in mind. It was only natural for her to be on her way the moment the dangers of the night were banished.

Jim got to his feet, stretching dramatically as he prepared to leave his comfortable shelter. He took inventory of his weapons, patting at hidden places in his cloak and shirt where knives lay unseen. Everything seemed in order. Emma hadn't robbed him in his sleep. A lifetime ago he would have offered a prayer of thanks for this good fortune. But now, he shrugged off the welcome happenstance and exited through the boulders.

A vibrant world stretched in every direction. A lush maze of trees and bushes helped conceal the little shelter from peering strangers. That was exactly why Jim had built it here, years ago. The walls were strong, good for protection against the elements, and the foliage was thick, good for protection against the living. It was one of the many pieces of paradise that had kept him safe through the long winters.

"Oh, you're up." A voice sang from Jim's left. He turned slowly, recognizing the melodic tones from his brief conversation the night before.

Emma stood near an outcropping of trees. She was holding her cloak like a basket between her outstretched arms. A smile threatened the corner of her mouth. *She's not sure if she made the right choice by staying.* Jim offered a smile at the cautious look, attempting to ease her inner quarrels into a sense of delight.

The girl walked forward, a pleasant expression now radiating from her face. "I was hoping to have a rabbit or two for breakfast this morning. But," she gestured at her cloak, "this will have to do." She opened her arms revealing the contents she held: a handful of black berries, wild mushrooms, and one crisp apple.

The duo sat, sharing the crunchy berries and earthy mushrooms. Emma threw the apple into the air and, in a swift motion, sliced it in half with her rapier. She caught the halves and handed one to Jim, a boastful quiet speaking for her while they ate.

"I need to thank you." Emma broke their silent, happy eating. "You could have killed me yesterday or left me to die in the night. But...." She stared intently at the ground, drawing circles in the dirt with her boot. "Thanks."

Jim nodded. He understood the confusing circumstance that brought them here. It was always peculiar acts that made enemies turn into allies.

"How is your arm?" Jim asked. The bandage he had placed around her was peeking out from under her shirt collar.

Emma rubbed at her shoulder. "Barely more than a scratch, really." Her smile faltered. "I suppose I'm lucky, because most Heroes wouldn't have left me an arm to bandage."

The truth of the statement made everything still. Emma's words rippled through the world, hushing the wind and halting the trembling trees. Most Heroes saw humans as a necessary nuisance, mere stones to be trampled on by the boots of their betters. It wasn't uncommon for a Hero to cut a man down for less reason than a squinted look.

Jim's thoughts wandered into the forest, thinking back to that perfect place with its perfect people. A place he had called home through his childhood. Home, until She shattered the facade. Her eyes were green too, emeralds in a sea of gold.

Emma tapped Jim's shoulder, waking him from his daylight memory. "Did you hear me?" Jim's face remained blank in expression.

"I said, it's time I get moving. There are only a few good hours of light left."

"Right." Jim stood, shaking the dullness from his mind that he often got when reminiscing.

"I suppose you'll be heading back to Paradise?" Emma's eyes brightened at the name of the Hero city.

Every human wondered at what majesties lay hidden inside the ancient city of the Heroes. Jim had heard all the rumors: there was no hint of disease, fields of fresh fruits stretched beyond what the eye could imagine, every person who drank from the Ever-Flowing Fountain gained life eternal. So many wonderful stories, so many disappointing realities.

"No." The firmness in Jim's voice erased the childlike wonder from Emma's eyes.

"So, where will you go?"

"Salix." Jim replied.

"Salix?" Emma paused, looking suddenly shy and uncertain. "Could...could I travel with you? Just for a time? I've got a camp in the West; their waiting for me and...well, I'm already late." She stared again at the circles she had drawn in the dirt. "Traveling with a Hero is sure to be faster than going alone."

Jim thought. It would be nice to have someone who could watch his back while he slept in the punishing forest. Plus, he felt partially responsible for Emma's safety. If she were to be killed due to her injured arm Jim would carry the blame wholeheartedly.

So, seeing his choice mingle with guilty responsibility, Jim said, "Alright."

The pair finished their portioned breakfast, packed their few loose belongings, and began their journey through the woods.

□ □ □ □ □ □ □

Emma spoke of the destination. She had friends waiting for her near the edge of the forest. Apparently, she had lost track of time, and a good amount of coin, at a tavern in the city of Snow and decided to make up the time by cutting through the ancient woodland.

The way she spoke of her party made Jim think of family. Each of them had history and sacrifice that resulted in a tight knot of emotion, strong enough to withstand ages and arguments. They were in no way related, but that didn't stop the group from gathering together each month for drinks and songs.

Emma assured Jim that he would be welcome to stay until the festivities ended. They would all part ways, each going to a different corner of the Protected Lands. But, once the month came to an end, they would gather again and speak of the ever-interesting lives they all sought.

When Jim asked where Emma intended to travel, she shrugged her shoulders and watched as the treetops swayed. She stayed silent for a while, closing her eyes and breathing deeply, before saying, "Wherever Life wants me."

Jim closed his eyes, listening as the wind rustled leaves and soared through the vast forest. It sounded different here. In the cities the wind always carried a hint of dread and disdain. But here, it sang of relief and joy. It sang of touching the highest clouds and playing on the limbs of towering trees. It sang of freedom.

Jim had been listening to the wind his entire life. Its song was too beautiful for him to ignore. He had followed it over a wall and through a deserted plain. He had shivered on the snow-covered peaks of the Eastern Mountains and swam through the Life-Giving Lakes, searching for dragons and other fairytale creatures – all just to follow the direction that the wind had whispered as it flew past his listening ears.

They walked in silence for a while. Neither wishing to interrupt the reverence that had waded into their thoughts. The sun began to descend as night quickly approached. The time for travel had ended.

Jim scanned the canopy, looking for branches high and thick enough to offer a suitable place to sleep. Emma gathered sticks and splintered an old fallen pine for firewood.

"I'm going to hunt us some dinner. I owe you a lesson on how to cook properly," she said, smiling, "for the next time you decide to throw me to the ground." Emma blushed, not realizing the innuendo until she had finished speaking.

"I look forward to the lesson." The Hero offered a smile and a smooth wink, adding color to Emma's face that seemed to make her glow.

Jim continued to search for sturdy branches while Emma hunted, settling on a branch high in the air that was wide enough for him to comfortably fit while lying on his side. He started a fire beneath the large oak with the collected tinder, making it large enough to last through most of the night and hot enough to cook thoroughly through meat and fat. And then he waited for Emma to return.

He counted the minutes. At first, it was due to a meditated boredom. But, as the minutes grew, and the sun began to hide, his boredom became concern. Emma should have been back, even if she hadn't caught anything, she should have returned to the safety of the fire. Something felt wrong.

Jim got up and ran in the direction he had seen her travel. She wouldn't have gone far to hunt, maybe a mile if she had lost track of her distance. *She can't fully use one of her arms.* Jim began to sprint, twigs snapping as he noisily searched for his companion.

First, he heard the snarl. Low and rumbling, the threatening sound pushed through Jim's teeth. Then, he felt panic, not the usual panic that came so rarely to the Hero. This panic came abruptly; it forced Jim to stop and take a breath and search for his calm. The panic began to waver. The emotion receded into Jim's mind, far enough away for his sanity to take control. If he reached for the feeling, it would consume him again, forcing him to stop and push it back into his near-unconscious.

"Whoa. Easy. Easy. No need to get bitey." Emma's voice cut through Jim's thoughts. Her words sounded calm and soothing, but they were tainted with a cold fear.

Jim slowed his pace, carefully avoiding the dried leaves and rocks that would loudly crunch if disturbed by his footsteps. Emma's figure appeared from behind a large evergreen. Frozen in place, she whispered her soothing words to the large wolf that was baring its teeth at her.

The panic behind Jim's mind dropped to an icy dread. He pushed the emotion back again and crept towards the terrifying beast. He unsheathed his longest dagger. It wouldn't do any good against the towering canine, but it made him feel a bit more secure.

The fear had made the Hero clumsy. A bush rustled as Jim stepped past it. The noise was enough for both Emma and the wolf to notice his added presence. He stopped in place, for moving too quick would spook the wolf into attacking. So, Jim inched forward, wanting, needing, to get in front of Emma. If the wolf attacked her, she would be dead before Jim could react. She was his responsibility.

Emma sniffled and the wolf focused on the new noise. The claws on its padded paws extended into the soft soil. The beast was ready to pounce, the hair on the back of its neck stuck high in the air.

"Hey bud, over here." Jim kept his voice low as he got the wolf's attention away from Emma. "Wouldn't you rather attack a Hero? I'm much older than this tiny human. *Aged to perfection* is what my father used to say." Jim continued to inch forward. He was close enough to Emma that he could hear her shaky breathing. "My death will be one you can brag about to all your wolfy friends." Jim could grab Emma's cloak if he dared reach out his arm. "Just be a good boy and let the nice…"

A loud snap came from behind the wolf. The beast leapt towards Jim and Emma, drool spilling from its mangled mouth. Jim grabbed Emma's cloak and threw her to the ground, extending his dagger towards the beast in the same motion. Emma hit the ground and the wolf collided with the sharp metal.

The dagger slid easily into the wolf's underbelly. Hot blood dripped down Jim's hand, steaming in the cold night. But the blade didn't stop the beast as it jumped again into the air. The dagger was torn from Jim's hand as the wolf pounced and landed behind him and…ran. The wolf ran into the dense trees, fading into darkness.

*That was odd* . Wolves in these woods were vicious and difficult to scare. In all his encounters, this was the first time a wolf had actually run away after Jim stuck it with a dagger. He stared in the direction the wolf fled. *Must be my lucky night.* He allowed himself a coy look at Emma.

Another snap came from in front of Jim. His head swiveled, and he squinted to try and see farther into the darkness. Emma climbed to her feet, brushing dirt from her hair and testing the movement in her shoulder.

"That was clo..." Jim's eyes never left the source of the snap as he slapped a hand over Emma's mouth.

He began to back away, pulling Emma with him as silently as he could. Another snap, closer this time. Jim moved faster, his grip unintentionally tightening on the girl's face. Emma pulled his hand away, but he forced a finger over her lips. No speaking, only listening.

Emma followed Jim's stare into the thick darkness. Another snap and then... Jim's eyes went wide. Three husks were stumbling through the foliage. The creatures walked with a careless pace. They stopped for a moment, but Jim knew if he could see them, it was only a matter of time before they spotted him. He took another step backwards.

All at once the husks turned in the direction of the terrified duo. Everything was still for a heartbeat, two, and then they howled.

Jim grabbed Emma's shoulder and shoved her in front of him. "Run!" He yelled.

The Hero grasped at his fallen dagger as he ran, Emma only a footstep ahead. They flew as they sprinted into the dead of night. Hot breath and the sound of rapid footfalls forcing them to quicken their pace. Death was wildly approaching from behind.

## 6: THREE MILES

Twigs snapped against the soft flesh of Emma's face, leaving stinging red marks as she flew through the prying fingers of the forest. She could hear Jim behind her, though she didn't dare look for him. He could get past her, Emma knew that. He could run beyond what she was capable and leave her as bait for the drooling husks that trampled through the forest behind them. But he never made the move, never even attempted to deny her the small protection of an extra body between her and the husks.

They had been running for nearly an hour through the shadowy brush. Emma's legs and lungs burned in protest of the repeated motion, but fear and adrenaline allowed her to continue forward. How many miles had they run? How many miles were left until she collapsed and allowed the husks to tear her apart?

"I have a plan." Jim's voice cut through her labored breathing.

Emma couldn't reply. Couldn't use her precious energy to form words and acknowledge the Hero.

"There should be a Hero patrol about three miles North. If we can get to them, we might have a chance." Jim was breathing hard. Even with the beyond human stamina that every Hero possessed, he was beginning to show signs of wear.

*Three miles* , Emma repeated in her head. *Only three miles* . Her vision faded for a moment, and she tumbled through the air. Before she hit the ground two strong hands were around her waist, keeping her on her feet and pushing her forward. *Three miles.*

"Dammit," Jim whispered under his breath.

He must have seen that she was on the brink of collapse. Emma felt his hand on her shoulder, his grip was firm, protective. He was at her side, keeping his hand on her to ensure she kept running.

Jim pointed forward, "North. Three miles, Emma." He took a breath. "Say it to me."

Emma looked at the Hero. His face was merely an arm's reach away, but his golden eyes felt so far to her tunneled vision.

"North…three miles…." Her voice was shaky.

Jim's grip tightened. "Good." He backed away, returning to his spot behind her. "When you get there, tell the Heroes the husks will be coming from the East." He fell even farther behind, "I'll take them a long way. You can slow, but don't stop." Jim changed directions suddenly, pivoting to his right.

"*Inside a mountain weathered and old there rests a city made of stone.*" Jim was singing. "*And in that place, there lives a door that never has been opened before.*" The husks were following him. Emma could hear their staggering stomps fading with the song. "*Gods and men and Life have tried, but only Death has seen inside.*" He was giving her a chance to make it, possibly sacrificing his life so she could get to the patrol. "*Until your final breath is drawn, the door will stay closed, safe, and strong.*"

Jim's words fell into the distance, leaving Emma running in silence. *I won't let you down. I'll make it to the patrol. We'll live through this night,* Emma silently promised and pushed herself forward.

North. Three miles.

■ ■ ■ ■ ■ ■ ■ ■

The sounds of the husks were growing closer with each, passing minute. Jim's body ached angrily, but he kept going. He should be able to see Paradise's wall any moment. He'd follow the wall West, hopefully to the waiting Heroes.

This wasn't his first time dealing with husks. He was usually able to hide or avoid them altogether, but not always. He remembered the words his father had said. '*You must remove the head. If it's touching at all, the bastards will regenerate. Do you know that word? Regenerate? How about bastards? Don't tell your mother I said that one.'* He made it sound so simple, but, from his experiences now, Jim knew it was nearly impossible to accomplish alone.

Husks roamed and hunted in packs and pairs. But even if you were fortunate enough to catch one hobbling by itself, it was best to duck and run before it caught your scent. They had the speed of a Hero with an endless stamina. Their reflexes were beyond human, beyond Hero even. Their talons were sharp and long enough to cut a person in two with a single swipe. But their true terror came from what happened when a man was touched. Fear would bubble and boil beneath the skin, petrifying their prey. Jim had felt it once, been touched by one of those demons. The fear that had manifested still haunted him in his deepest dreams.

When he was young, Jim heard the stories and songs about Heroes who had managed to kill one of the monsters. They were revered as legends; their names were sealed in the History Hall and song books. Jim idolized those brave men, risking their lives to vanquish the monsters that bred nightmares. But tonight, Jim didn't care for the stories or songs. All he cared about was making it out alive.

In the distance, a large wall peaked over the tops of the trees. Paradise, the ancient Hero city. He was close to his former home, his family.

Jim turned to his left, following the distant wall West. The husks were growling, and near-human screams escaped their wretched mouths. Only a little farther; the patrol was so close.

■ ■ ■ ■ ■ ■ ■ ■

Emma had been running towards the wall for a few minutes. The moment it peered over the towering trees, she recognized it was not just any wall but THE wall. The wall that protected the magnificent city beyond, Paradise. She didn't realize how close she had been to the mystifying city. She had heard so many stories, but this was the first time she had laid her eyes upon its giant barrier.

The girl only allowed herself a breath of amazement before she started to run again. Running North, towards the wall, towards salvation. The light of a fire danced on the trees ahead. Emma quickened her stride, throwing all her remaining energy at the beacon of light and then bursting into the small camp. Emma's heart sang as she stared at five Heroes, their eyes shocked at the panting girl that had just interrupted their dinner.

The Heroes moved quickly, reaching for weapons and taking a defensive stance. Emma fell to the ground, trying with all her might to pull air into her lungs and speak of the news she so desperately needed to tell.

"Husks." She forced the word from her lips and the Heroes' faces went grim. "East."

■ ■ ■ ■ ■ ■ ■ ■

Jim ran along the forest's edge so close to the Barrens that the guards atop the wall had surely seen him and signaled a silent warning to their troops on the ground. As the husks continued to gain on him, his care for stealth and subtly around the Hero city diminished and even ground of the Barrens provided him with less need to concentrate on his coordination.

*Where are they?* The last time he had monitored the Hero patrols they had stopped just ahead, but Jim saw no indication of fire or smells of cooked meat. *Must be a slower group, farther ahead.*

A gnarled root grabbed at Jim's foot, stealing the ground from beneath him, and he fell. One husk was closer than Jim anticipated, it lurched over his fallen body and collided with the ground in a tangle of limbs and fury.

The creature before him was grotesque. Grey, leathery skin covered the monster's entirety. Two legs shot from its stretched torso with talon-like feet that dug through soil and flesh. Its arms were long and wiry. On the husk's hands were five sword-like claws, tipped in barbed coils, searching for blood and life with deadly ease.

Jim jumped to his feet as the creature staggered into a gaited sprint. The husk grabbed at Jim, its claws skimming his neck and chest. Terror enveloped him.

Every piece of guilt mingled with each moment of desperation, threatening to swallow him whole.

The creature's claws continued to slip down Jim's body, disconnecting from his wounded flesh for only an instant. The instant was all Jim needed. The stupefying paralysis fled from his rigid muscles, and he was free to run again.

The rampant feelings of freedom, and warm blood dripping from his wound, fueled Jim as he ran. He didn't know how much longer, how much farther, he could keep the husks behind him. But the faint glow of firelight informed him of life lingering in the distance. He forced his legs to move faster, pushing the Hero quickly towards exhaustion.

■ ■ ■ ■ ■ ■ ■ ■

One Hero gave Emma a drink from his canteen. She had dropped hers while running, needing to relieve herself of the small weight. She offered a nod to the dark-haired man and drank deeply. The rejuvenating waters helped slow her breathing and calm her pounding heart.

Emma handed the canteen back to the jolly looking man. "Thanks, um?" She tried to think if he had told her his name.

"You won't remember a name in the heat of a husk attack. And if you're lying about the attack, you'll be thrown in the darkest prison pit we can find. So, names won't be given tonight." He gave a big toothy smile.

"Oh, okay...." Emma looked the Hero up and down, focusing on the double-sided ax that was sheathed on his back. "Lumberjack."

A rumbling chuckle erupted from Lumberjack. "That's a good one!" He clapped Emma on the back, "You're Fencer then, eh?"

Emma gave a smile and nodded. She looked over the other Heroes.

Two of them looked East. One was very tall and heavily muscled; he had a burly brown beard and a scar that ran from chin to chest.

*Grizzly.* The other, an equally muscled woman, had dark hair chopped just below her ears and bangs that tickled her forehead. *Helmet.* Grizzly and Helmet held spiked shields that reached a head above them, the metal looking as thick as Emma's outstretched arm. *They must weigh a ton.*

One Hero was staring down the sights of a rifle. Emma had seen a few guns like that before, mostly in the hands of Heroes that passed through her childhood town. *He'll be Scope.* Scope prodded at the sight of his gun, adjusting circular dials on the sides minutely.

The final Hero was an easy one. She had two identical, and deadly, looking swords strapped to her back. Emma was sure the Hero had them specially made to mirror each other. *Twin.*

Helmet made a small coughing noise, and the others began to move. Scope loaded a cartridge into his weapon, pulling the slide back with the slick sound of metal on metal. Twin and Lumberjack picked up heavy crossbows from nearby the fire, placing bolts in front of the taut bow strings. Helmet and Grizzly stood shoulder to shoulder, planting their heavy shields into the dirt. Emma squinted towards the East and took a step back at the sight she saw.

There was Jim, sprinting for his life as the three husks nipped at his cloak only a few feet behind. The husks were even more terrifying than Emma had imagined. From this distance they almost looked human. They were bipedal, and their arms and legs looked to be similarly proportioned. But as they came closer their human façade decayed.

Remnants of hair, from lives millennia ago, stuck to their graying flesh. At each end of their fingers, foot-long talons threatened any who dare stand in their way. But, Emma decided, the most disturbing thing about them was the way they ran. Instead of smooth and fluid movements, the creatures seemed to twitch and skip. It reminded her of the puppet shows that she had loved as a girl.

Jim grew closer. She could see the strain in his face and…the blood. So much blood soaked his clothes and his shirt was barely more than tatters. Emma's eyes teared. He did this for her, had got hurt for her, and he still might die. All for her.

"Ready." Helmet raised her voice. "Fire!"

The sound of thunder and the feeling of rain washed over Emma as Scope released a bullet into a husk. The shot hit the creature, tearing its arm from its body and throwing it to the ground.

"Get another shot ready," Helmet commanded. "Crossbows...now!"

Lumberjack and Twin pulled their triggers and the bolts tore into the second husk just below its knees. The monster fell but continued to crawl after Jim.

"No time for another crossbow!" Helmet shouted, "Unsheathe and get ready." Twin and Lumberjack threw their crossbows onto the ground and did as Helmet commanded. "Final rifle. Now!"

Scope released another shot, flinging the final husk into the dirt. Emma gave a breath of relief. Jim kept running, quickly gaining ground towards her and the Heroes.

Then, Emma watched in terror as the first husk was back to its feet, muscle and synapse twining together where its arm had been removed. Emma watched in curious horror as the arm stitched itself together and the monster began to run again. Then, like flowers budding from the dirt, the other two husks rose from the ground. All three were running again, quickly gaining on Jim.

Helmet and Grizzly tilted their shields away, opening a gap between them. Jim flung himself through the gap and the shields slammed together with a twang the moment he passed. Jim landed hard on his side; he took a brief glance at the small patrol. His eyes paused, his expressions growing with relief, when he saw Emma. But the moment was short-lived. Jim got back to his feet and put his body against the shields, just as the three husks smashed into the waiting wall.

The Heroes grunted with effort as the massive force pushed against their protection. Lumberjack and Twin stood slightly behind, their weapons ready to strike. Scope stood next to Emma and held a long pike pointed towards the incoming enemies.

"Get ready!" Helmet yelled. "Release!"

Helmet, Jim, and Grizzly jumped backwards, throwing their shields at the enemies beyond. The shields fell away, the husks on the other side staggering due to the sudden weight. The Heroes pounced at the small opening, swiping their weapons at the husks' legs and torsos. Emma looked in awe at the beauty the Heroes each had while fighting. Every movement, every attack, every parry, seemed coordinated between the never-speaking fighters. When one attacked, the other would take a defensive position for the attacker. When one was forced to dodge or parry, another would move to protect their flank and strike back. It looked like a dance, only with much more blood and many more weapons.

But, for every attack, the husks seemed ready. They moved with erratic and sudden speeds, blocking every blade that searched for their necks with unnatural ease. They stepped past the fallen shields and began to advance, forcing the Heroes to step back farther and farther. Emma shook away the fear that had kept her planted in place and stepped into the fray.

Emma had to focus on defending. She kept her position behind an attacking Hero, her weapon guarding their sides. The beasts were moving too fast for her attacks. She had tried a swipe at a husk's neck, but its claws deflected her blow easily and it swiped for her exposed chest. Grizzly's blade caught the claws just before they impaled her and ripped her in half. She decided then that her skills were better set on defending the rest of her group.

The seven people fought against the three husks. They outnumbered the creatures two-to-one, but the fight never felt in their favor.

Emma heard Jim scream "Wait!" as Grizzly attacked at an open husk.

Grizzly's sword seared the air and connected with the monster's exposed shoulder. The husk fell back, pulling Grizzly with it out of position. The other husks were waiting, they pounced on Grizzly in an instant, shredding his flesh from his face and belly. The bearded Hero fell, dead, little more than a pile of clothes and gore.

Emma saw a fury manifest in Jim, the same fury she had seen just before he threw her to the ground the day before. The night seemed to grow even darker as he began a rage-induced offensive. He pushed two of the husks back with his blows, knocking one off balance as it retreated a step. The third husk tried to attack Jim's flank, but Scope was there waiting. His pike stuck into the husk's chest and pinned it to the earth below. Jim took a step to the side and sliced at the fallen husk's neck, and its head rolled into the crimson-soaked dirt.

Hope surged through Emma's core. There was a chance of victory with one of them dead, all they had to do was keep coordinating their attacks.

Twin screamed from Emma's left and she felt sticky warm droplets pebble her arm. Helmet shoved Twin into the middle of their circle and Emma caught the wounded Hero. She looked at Twin's chest: crimson with four gaping wounds. Blood pooled and spilled upon the already stained ground. In less than a minute, Twin was dead. Emma decided to grieve over this loss of life later.

Jim lurched at one of the remaining husks. The fiend ducked, predicting the attack, and lurched its talons at Jim's side. Emma stepped in. Her blade missed the decimating claws, but her forearm caught the deadly attack.

Pain hit Emma; however, it was despair that began to choke her. The world had gone dark, and everyone around her became shadows and fog. She felt like she was falling deep within her own body. She tried to scream, but her voice had no sound. She tried to move, but her muscles refused the order. She tried to think, but the all-consuming fear strangled her mind. She was so empty. She must be nothing. From eyes that seemed to belong to someone else, Emma watched as Scope fell to a husk's attack. The claws had struck straight through his eyes, a silent scream permanently plastered on his face.

Emma just watched, so empty, so nothing, as the husk jumped at her. Jim appeared from nowhere, pushing the demon back. Jim truly was a hero. He had saved her so many times already. It was a shame that he had given so much to someone so undeserving.

Jim was staring into her eyes. "Snap out of it!" His scream was far away. He pushed back another attack from a husk. "We need to move!" His voice felt like a whisper tittering on the wind. "Emma, now!" Jim reached his hand back and slapped Emma across the face.

Waves of the world rushed back to her. She gasped for breath at the sudden emotion and pain that anchored her to reality. Her face stung, and pain oscillated in her arm, but she was happy to feel anything. She was no longer empty, no longer nothing.

Helmet and Lumberjack were standing back to back, defending each other from an attacking husk. Emma and Jim followed their lead. Each duo fought a monster, and each duo felt their time coming to an end.

It took all of Emma's concentration and honed skill to keep up with the husk, because its movements were so unpredictable. It would feign attacks and follow up with a rapid barrage of flurry. It would allow her blade to pierce its flesh in order to gain an opportunity to strike. This was an enemy that knew its own strengths and its opponents' weaknesses.

Emma could feel Jim's muscles as he parried or struck from her other side. She felt his cold blood against her bare neck. His arms moved in a succession of swings. He was trying to finish off the husk and end this torment.

She turned to help, absorbing some hits with her rapier that were meant to pierce Jim's vulnerable sides. The husk moved back, preparing for another attack. But Jim and Emma moved as one. They pushed against the demon's bloody razors, continually forcing it backwards. The pair were waves of water splashing against a battered stone, slowly breaking the ageless body into mud.

Jim thought he saw an opening, but Emma saw the feign as his daggers flew. She tried to move and help her Hero, but she was not fast enough. The husk's claws slipped under Jim's arm, stabbing deep into his chest.

Emma screamed as she saw Jim's face grow pale.

■ ■ ■ ■ ■ ■ ■ ■

Everything was cold. The world around him was smoke and shadow. Far in the distance he could hear the screams of a girl he recognized from a far-off dream. But there were no dreams here, only cold. Ice grew up his legs, keeping him planted on the invisible ground.

The ice traveled into his chest. His breaths were coming slower, more difficult to pull into his frozen body. The world had gone dark.

But, somewhere in the distance, he felt a familiar thread. It was unusual, a thread from a memory that didn't belong to him. He reached for the object and his mind began to soar.

He stared at a Hero. He hated the foul monsters that wandered his land. His nails had discovered a soft place under the Hero's arm. The Hero had moved fast, nearly overtaken him so many times. But here he stood, ready to die by his foe.

Then he saw the girl. She was no Hero, but still she was trespassing. She had to die too. He just needed to squeeze his hand, finish off this Hero, and then he would move to her.

*Emma.*

He paused at the name, whispered in his mind by someone else.

The girl was moving towards him. He needed to be rid of the Hero now. He needed to defend himself and throw down this human. Her green eyes stared into his with a storm of enraged passion. She wanted to kill him, he wanted to kill her. But he couldn't move his hand. He couldn't defend his neck as the girl's thin blade cut into his flesh and removed his head.

Jim opened his eyes. The husk fell to the ground, Emma's blade stained by its dark blood. Her gaze was fixed on him, mouth gaping in a mixture of fear and confusion.

■ ■ ■ ■ ■ ■ ■ ■

The husk went still the moment it contacted Jim's flesh. Jim's eyes closed, and he shivered as his blood ran down the monster's arm. But the husk didn't move.

Emma placed her hand on Jim's shoulder. Steam wafted from where she touched. No, not steam, smoke. Black and billowing smoke rose from the Hero's flesh. She took a surprised step back.

The husk stared at her, its eyes looking into her own. It didn't' move, only stared as she walked towards the frightening beast. The world had grown so dark, darker than any night she had ever lived before.

She pulled back her blade, aiming for the exposed neck of the beast. She had tried many times to hit the monster, each time failing against the superior fighter. But, this time, her blade struck true. She cut through the husk's neck, its eyes continually staring as its head toppled onto the grass.

To her left, Emma heard Lumberjack's deep voice exclaim, "What in the hells?" And she saw their husk fall as well. The world became lighter again. It was still night, but the darkness that had nearly suffocated them seemed to evaporate.

Jim gasped, and his eyes opened. He looked at the fallen husks and a large smile grew on his face.

"You saved me, Ellie," he whispered, and then collapsed.

# 7: ASH

Jim woke, rising quickly to a sit and grasping for the knife that he kept on his arm. As he reached, a pain seared in his chest, halting his movement and driving the breath from his lungs. Emma was at his side in an instant, muttering calming words to the heavy breathing Hero. He could feel his heart pounding through his skin, feel the husks mean claws still gripping beneath his flesh.

He fingered his healing wounds. Large, crude, stitches held together the remaining skin and muscle that covered his heart. He could feel warm blood seeping from between the stitched areas. A shock of pain surged when his digits wandered too far down his throbbing side. He could already feel his inner body repairing the damaged tissue. The strike that caused the wound should have killed him; however, by the divine miracle of his genetics, all he would have in the end is another scar.

Jim's eyes wandered over the ravaged battlefield. Four large pyres burned, raining grey ash from the sky and dusting the battered landscape in a snow-like perfection.

"They burned the bodies. A pyre for each fallen Hero, and one for the monsters." Emma said with a reverence that rivaled the Divine Priests.

Jim closed his eyes. "Through the fire, they are cleansed. Through the smoke, they will be tested. Through the wind, they shall live again." He whispered the prayer for the Heroes who had fought with him and died in his stead.

Emma placed her hand over Jim's.

"And through their stories, they will be immortal." The prayer was complete.

They allowed the still, small quiet to permeate the mourning. Hero and human, hand in hand, watched as the flames turned the fallen into ash. The air stayed somber until the last of the pyres had changed to charcoal and embers.

The female Hero stood, addressing Jim and Emma. "Thank you for your respect."

Jim nodded and moved his hand. He pushed himself to his feet, testing his body. Standing was easily done, but pain constantly showered down his spine. With some difficulty, he was able to take small steps and hop from foot to foot. Each minute he healed more, and the pain slowly dissipated. But these wounds would take him a few days to fully heal, even with his Hero advantages.

"Glad to see you're still alive," the male Hero said.

He had a round face with slightly pudgy cheeks. His dark hair blended with the night sky, hiding the stars from directly above his head.

*Low born, unknown chosen faction.*

A crude, double-sided ax was strapped to this Hero's back. Its blade was clean and freshly sharpened. The man cared for his weapon.

Jim nodded at the man. "Thank you for believing my companion. Not many would have listened to a human."

The man let out a rumbling chuckle. He said, "There wasn't much to believe." He clapped Emma on the back. "Between gasping for breath and drinking all my water, Fencer here could barely say two words. And 'husks, East' would make for a poor lie." He gave a large, toothy smile. "We've got some extra portions if either of you are hungry."

They followed the large man to a makeshift camp. The female Hero was picking at the meal she held, tearing off pieces of discolored meat and dehydrated corn and greedily plopping them into her mouth. Jim studied the meal as well as the eating Hero. She had raven colored hair that shaped her face and sat on her head almost like a hat. Her golden eyes glowered behind a hooked nose. Jim's practiced eye knew her faction, knew her name. *She's a Willow.*

Jim took a place by the fire and partook of the offered food. He devoured the maroon meat and crunchy corn in minutes. These meals were made for easy travel and multiple-day storage. They usually tasted of salt and stale flour. Flavor was a commodity rewarded to Hero patrols after a successful night beyond the wall, not during one. Jim ignored the taste and dwelled on the full feeling in his stomach. Emma sat beside him, her hand resting on her satisfied belly.

"So," Jim said, "Your true name is Fencer?"

The Willow Hero sat stoically, her eyes never leaving the flames, as if fascinated by them. She waited for the meal to end before speaking. "I've made a decision." Jim noticed the jolly Hero stiffen at her words. "At sunrise, Captain Blackthorne and I will escort the two of you to Paradise." Jim stared in disbelief at the woman. "You will be our official guests, and you will be guarded at all times while within the city walls.

Emma's eyes went wide. She glanced at Jim to see his reaction, which he did not give.

The Hero continued. "You assisted us in the cleansing of three husks. Your names will be added to the History Hall, and you will be rewarded with the same glory as any Hero."

Captain Blackthorne, looked in awe at the Willow woman. "Brig, Fencer is a human. It's been nearly a decade since the last human entered Paradise's wall as a guest. The Twenty-Four will be irate and...."

She cut him off. "I will deal with the Twenty-Four, Captain. Emma earned the right while fighting the husks, same as we did tonight."

Emma beamed, her excitement erupting into the night. This was her dream, the dream of most humans. She would be an honored guest in the city of the Heroes. Jim fondly remembered when he first laid eyes on the History Hall. All the names chiseled into golden bricks; it was a marvel that had no equal. Emma would be allowed to add her name. But...

*Go back inside the Hero city? See the fountain and the halls? Could it be so bad?*

Emma cheerfully asked the Blackthorne what the inside of Paradise looked like. What wonders would she see, and what melodies would she hear? He replied with exhilaration. A smirk populated even the Willow's face.

Emma turned her attention towards Jim, his turmoil unknown to the ecstatic girl. He could return, watch as the first human in a decade entered the scarred gates—the towering walls closing him in the city. He could allow Paradise to suffocate and strangle him, walk those wicked and winding streets that led towards....

"No." Jim's word cut through the palpable joy.

"Excuse me?" the Willow woman raised an eyebrow. "You would deny the riches of a husk killer?"

"Yes, I would." Emma's confused stare bit into Jim's side. "We have a camp waiting for us. We will need to leave at sunrise."

"I'm afraid you may have misunderstood." The Willow's voice stayed cool and piercing. "My invitation was more of a command than a request. We will enter Paradise and inform the Elders of what we encountered."

"No." Jim's word threatened to snap the fragile friction that lingered in the air.

Emma spoke, "Jim, we can be a little late. The festivities usually last a few days. We could...."

"No, Emma. I will not step foot in the False City." Jim's voice came out colder than he intended.

The Willow Hero stood, one hand resting on the hilt of her sword. "I don't think you know who I am. You would not insult our great city if you knew who I serve." Her voice dripped with venom.

Jim stayed seated. "You are Brigadier General Willow. Your faction is charged with defending the Western Walls. And you mistake my denial for ignorance." Emma was standing behind him, her hand gripped tightly around her rapier.

The Brigadier's mouth fell agape. "But, to have your name in the History Halls is the highest honor and to deny the chance would be...."

"My name is on its walls," Jim cut in again, emotion steeping his voice. He could not allow her claims to continue. She was so lost in her thinking, so blinded by the ideals of glory and gold.

Her grip tightened on her hilt. "Which is your faction?" Her voice was low and blunt.

Jim stared into her eyes. He knew the power in his name, knew of the danger and the outrage that came when it was ironically praised in songs and whispered in brothels. The forbidden faction of wretched killers. Most Heroes forsook the faction's name once Jim left the city walls, his faction ruined by his most traitorous act.

"My name is James." He spoke each word with deliberation, feeling the power in every syllable. "My faction is my birthright. I am the first born of the Southern guardians. I am the Heir of Ash."

In a blink, the Willow had her sword unsheathed and dashed towards the traitor. Jim's dagger was ready to intercept her blade. Emma gasped. Lumberjack wrapped his arm around Jim's torso and threw him backwards.

Pain exploded from Jim's aggravated wounds, but he jumped to his feet and prepared to defend an onslaught. To his surprise there was no need. Where Jim sat a moment ago, Lumberjack now stood. His ax blade pressed tightly against his commanding officer's sword.

"Brigadier General Willow," Lumberjack said, his voice apologetic but firm. "Jim and Fencer fought with us. They have earned the right of friend and ate beside us. We may not take action against them until the sun rises, an agreement which you signed when you accepted the rank of Brigadier." Lumberjack's face was contorted from exertion. "Even as an Ash, he has earned his life for tonight."

The angry woman glared at Jim, but she pushed her sword into the dirt. And, instead of speaking, she screamed at the thief just beyond her reach. Then, she walked away from the fire and into the darkness of the trees.

"She is honor bound," Lumberjack spoke, "and will not attack you tonight. You will be free to leave at sunrise." His burning eyes betrayed his defending action. "But, if I have the misfortune of seeing you again, Heir of Ash, I will not fight by your side." His gaze fell to the dark earth. "My time of serving your faction is over."

"Thank you, Captain Blackthorne," Emma said softly.

"Good luck, Fencer." For once, the Hero left without a smile.

Emma's gaze shifted to Jim, and he held her stare. In her eyes he saw so much confusion, so much new uncertainty. If she asked, he would tell her everything, anything. He only hoped that, someday, she would.

## 8: A TRAITOR'S STORY

The morning was uneventful, and Emma was grateful for it. The remaining group rose with the sun, had a small breakfast of cold portions and hot tea, and decided to part ways. Helmet hadn't returned from storming into the forest, but Lumberjack assured them that she was fine and would return once she cooled off. And then Emma was alone with Jim, with the Heir of Ash, walking towards the Southern edge of the dense forest.

She had heard stories, so many stories, about the Ash faction. They held the strongest of the Hero forces and guarded the Southern territories. But devious intentions were buried beneath their good doings. They killed the heir of one of the Pure Families, the Dogwood's, if Emma remembered correctly, an act that began the Southern War.

The humans of the Southern colonies, and the few Heroes who remained loyal to Ash, struck a devastating blow inside Paradise's wall, and chaos threatened the balance. The war lasted a few years, the bodies of the fallen could be piled halfway up the wall.

In the end, the Northtrees rallied most of the Pure Families and successfully defended their great city from the Ash deceivers. The South was given to the Dogwoods as penance for their initial loss in the war, and the Ash faction was dismantled and disgraced. The Ashes who remained in the city were stripped of their purity but were allowed to remain inside Paradise's walls.

Every child, human or Hero, was taught the downfall of the Ash faction. The riots in the South grew too out of hand for the Dogwoods to handle alone. So, the Northtrees sent their forces and burned those who stood in their way. The Northtrees proved to be the most powerful faction, and the riots quickly stopped.

Emma shook. Those tragedies, that war, it had all started by the action of the Heir to the Ash family. The man who she had been traveling with, Jim. Knowing his title, knowing his past, changed everything she thought she knew. Jim had caused so many deaths, had shattered the ever-growing alliance of the humans and Heroes, all for a petty gain of power for his faction.

"I've been able to feel your hesitation since last night." Jim said, pulling Emma from her thoughts. "And your disdain grows with each step you take with me." His tone was sad, pathetic almost, Emma thought. "Just…don't believe the stories…not all of them."

Emma blinked. Her prejudice towards the Hero made every word he spoke feel like nails piercing her eardrums.

"How should I be feeling, Heir of Ash?" she asked unkindly, "The man I've been traveling with turns out to be the most notorious rebel in recent history. My mother was loyal to the Ash faction, Jim." Emotion harshened her voice. "She died fighting for what you did. You might as well have killed her yourself." Angry tears streamed down Emma's face, blurring her vision.

Jim slowed, but she kept her pace. Emma didn't dare look in the Hero's direction, didn't let him see the hot vulnerability that escaped her eyes. She could hear the subtle rustle of his cloak as he jogged to catch up to her.

Emma's tears caused her to miss a root that tangled with her foot and caused her to trip. She fell but felt the Hero's hand grab her shoulder to bring her back to stability. Emma recoiled at the Hero's touch and punched where she knew his face would be.

Fist contacted cheek, and Jim stumbled backwards. But that wasn't enough. She moved towards the stunned man, throwing her fists in a barrage of blind fury. Tears flowed heavier with each hit Emma landed on the Hero. He never made a sound, never tried to defend himself from her punches, never tried to stop the barrage of attacks that rained from the angry girl.

Jim's face was bruised, and his lip was bloodied, but he just stared at the canopy above. "Are you finished?" he asked.

The Hero's words filled Emma with boiling rage. She pulled the rapier from her sheath, gripping its pommel until her knuckles turned white. Jim made no move to stop her, just kept staring at the leaves and sky above. He wouldn't defend himself; she could cut him and rip the bones from his body, and he would just speak to her in an arrogant voice and condemn her with words.

"Damn you." Emma whispered, attempting to steady her angry grip.

She couldn't look at him, couldn't talk to him, couldn't kill him. He was the cause of the worst thing to ever happen to her, but she felt powerless against him. She stared at the ground, trying to find the ability to slay the Heir of Ash.

They stood in silence for a while.

Her hand cramped painfully before Jim finally spoke. "What they say about my faction isn't true." He needed Emma to believe him, needed her to hear what he had to say, "They weren't trying to gain power or bring Paradise to its knees. It was all an accident, my accident. I killed the Dogwood Heir, and I ran." He paused at the painful memory, "I was young, and I was angry. But afterwards, I was just afraid."

Emma listened intently to the story that she had heard hundreds of times throughout her childhood. Some of what the Hero said sounded familiar, but many of his recollections seemed to be distorted from her taught truths.

"We always treated our colonies, and the humans who lived there, as equally as we could. We protected them from husks and laid down our lives for their families. Many of the Pure Families hated the way we treated humans, thinking that we should be harsher on those we ruled. But we saw humans as our younger brothers and sisters and continued to strive towards humanity becoming part of the Hero world.

"Our faction was strong, but Paradise is full of powerful families and full of hatred towards humanity. They decided to teach us a lesson and began to attack our colonies by pretending to be husk hoards. We could never bring concrete evidence to the Twenty-Four, so we sent more of our fighters to the colonies for protection." Jim paused. "When our forces were the weakest inside the walls, they struck.

"There was a...an outsider who lived with my family. She was a loyal member of our faction, but many of the Pure Families wished for years that she would be banished from their city." Jim hid his emotions well, so Emma was shocked to hear the stone-faced Hero sniffle. "They took her when I wasn't watching. I was supposed to be guarding her, but..." Jim cut off his words.

Emma looked at the Hero's face, saw the torment that the repressed memories caused him. She placed her hand on his cheek and rubbed at a tear with her thumb. This was a tale much different from what she had been taught, and the monster in her stories was nothing but a frightened boy.

Jim cleared his throat. "They killed her. They beat her in the streets, and nobody stopped them. I held her while she died." Jim sniffled again. "And then I was angry. My world became red and my thoughts tasted of blood. I found the one responsible, and I killed him. I killed him and crippled the Heroes that tried to stop me." Jim's hands were clenched, his fingernails biting into his palms. "The Lord of Northtree, Lye, found me and pulled me from the pulp of the Dogwood Heir.

"He told me to run. He said that if they saw what I did they would convict my father for my crimes and have him exiled. So, I ran. And when I got to the wall, I climbed. And then I jumped into the forest and just kept on running." Jim held his hands in the sky, clenching his fingers into fists, "They used me. I was too young to see it then, but I see it now. They framed me and my family, and they killed her to make me angry. They used her...." Light glinted from Jim's tear-soaked face. His mouth moved as he prepared to speak again, but all that escaped was a wrathful scream that caused the Hero to shake.

"Ellie?" Emma's voice was dwarfed compared to Jim's scream, but his reaction to the name felt even more violent.

Jim looked into Emma's eyes, stared for a long moment before he turned and began to walk. He looked back and waved at Emma, motioning for her to join him.

He said, "We need to keep moving. Let's make it past the trees in the daylight."

Emma met his stride, following his lead through the thick bushes and trees. The sounds of twigs snapping and branches bending filled the air. The wind's songs were so quiet now as they marched through the brush.

A mile passed before Jim spoke again. "You remind me of her sometimes, of Ellie." The tender sweetness he held in his voice when he spoke her name spread a warmth into Emma's chest and nearly erupted from her fingertips. "She was fierce and strong, and her eyes were the most beautiful things I had ever seen. She was..." Jim shook his head as emotion made him verklempt again.

"Sounds like she was a hell of a girl," Emma offered with a broad smile.

"She was." Jim smiled back.

They walked for a few hours, allowing the comfortable silence to return between them. Emma decided to trust the Heir of Ash, believe his story against what she had been taught. So, her disdain dwindled, and her hesitation vanished, and she walked with Jim towards the forest's edge.

## 8: PROMISE

The tree line opened, revealing a lush field of tall grass and wildflowers. Dusk was beginning to flare in the sky, changing the clear blue of day into a collage of dark purple and red. The dangers of the forest stayed behind, trapped by the thick wall of trees and bushes. The safety of the open field promised a restful sleep for Hero and human.

The emotion in the back of Jim's mind had receded to a mere content after he told Emma about the Dogwood boy. Her contemplation seemed to heavily influence her quiet mood, but at least Jim sensed no hatred.

Emma turned left, following the forest's edge West, toward the Willow territory. She was deep in thought as the duo walked. She stared into the distance, never focusing on what her eyes observed, but always seeing something in her mind and listening intently to what it implied.

Jim rubbed the tender flesh beneath his armpit and rotated his shoulder to test his healing wound. Needles and fire greeted the movement, but the response was far from agonizing. Truth-be-told his face hurt much more than his side. He was sure an impression of Emma's knuckle had imprinted itself just below his eye.

Emma's voice broke the silence, "They are going to hate you."

Jim stared at the girl.

"They'll probably hate me too, for bringing you." She shrugged. "But, after a few drinks, I'll be forgiven. Easy enough."

She was talking about her friends, the group that was celebrating in their traditional get-togethers. Anyway, it didn't matter to him. For Heroes and humans, hatred crashed like rain over rooftops. It was a way of life, a stubborn stallion that pulled against his bit.

"I'm sure I'll charm them without much trouble." Jim offered. "All I have to do is knock them to the ground and force-feed them charred rabbit."

Emma's return smile ran over Jim's body like crystal water on smoldering coals. Relief steamed from his unconscious as the girl who had the emerald eyes offered him her smile.

"No." Her voice was playful. "They will definitely hate you." She looked forward again and began to walk.

Jim hesitated before catching up. "If you want me to leave...."

"No," she cut in. "You should stay. It would be good for them to see a Hero up close, without fear. Just...." She paused and looked into Jim's eyes. "We shouldn't tell them who you are."

It was an odd request for Jim, not because he didn't agree with the logic of it, but because nobody had ever really known his history to request such a thing in the first place. He wanted to brush it off as an obvious plan, but her tone chilled him. These friends of hers would hate him as a Hero, but their true contempt would come from being an Ash.

"I understand," he said.

They continued West as the sun fell beneath the horizon. A cloudless night illuminated a freshly worn trail that Emma meandered down. They followed the winding trail as the smell of smoke rose from close ahead.

"We met because of the Southern War," Emma whispered. "I was orphaned, and their colony was decimated by the Northtrees. They were the only family I could find." She took a breath. "They are going to hate you, Jim, but please stay."

As they rounded a corner of particularly dense trees, Jim spotted a raging bonfire. He could see the outlines of people sitting and dancing in the fire's light. Now would be the time to leave, turn around and head into the forest. He had secured Emma's safety, but she seemed to have secured him in a way of her own. He knew that she had made it to her loved ones. He could leave, his conscience clear of guilt. But....

"I'll stay." he promised the girl, and himself.

## 9: THE BOY AND THE MAN

The silhouettes around the bonfire grew clear as Jim and Emma moved closer to their destination. The outlines of two wagons and five horses also became evident, though they sat a few yards from the fire's light. Emma's pace had quickened, nearing a jog. An elated smile was shining from her face, so happy and excited, as the fire's heat brushed her cheeks. The group ahead had noticed them and gathered into a tight semi-circle in case the new arrivals tried to attack.

Emma raised her hand and gave an exaggerated wave. "Sorry I'm late! You better have saved me some ale!"

At once, the group sprinted towards the familiar voice. Emma was charged by a wave of hugs and happy faces.

"Emma!"

"Your hair has gotten so long!"

"I've had three drinks already. You need to catch up!"

"How was the journey? You must be exhausted!"

Jim did his best to put on the kindest expression for the strangers that had swallowed his companion. *They are going to hate you.* The dreaded moment was close, and Jim could feel it. The excitement was dropping from a chaotic torrent, becoming more manageable by the second. He closed his eyes, savoring the pure bliss that tickled the depths of his mind.

"How rude of us! Who is your guest, Em?" A male voice asked.

Jim took a breath. It felt like such a shame to ruin the beautiful reunion. He opened his eyes and smiled.

From a combination of instinct and reflex most of the strangers reached for their weapons and the man to his left gave an audible gasp. Jim knew how jumpy humans were around Heroes, and he knew that these humans would see his eyes and immediately mark him as a threat. So, he made every movement careful and obvious, showing his full intent behind each action. There would be no mistaking his offered handshake or nod of the head as anything other than friendly.

"My name is Jim," he said, tightening the skin around eyes and widening his smile.

A man stepped forward and apprehensively took Jim's hand. "Davey." His voice told Jim that he had become used to stepping forward in times of distress. "Umm, Emma," Davey started to say, his eyes glued on the Hero, "can we talk with you for a moment?"

Emma's voice came from behind Jim. "Of course!" Her hand squeezed Jim's arm as she moved passed him.

Davey and one other woman walked towards a traveling wagon with Emma on their heels. The others, two men and two women, awkwardly stood around Jim, rubbing at their arms and staring at the ground. Three of them slowly excused themselves from the Hero, claiming to have a tent to finish setting up, or an item to recover near the fire.

Jim was left alone with one of the girls. She had brown eyes and hair that reached past her ears and neared her shoulders. Her head was raised as she looked over the strange man that Emma had brought. He stayed still and silent, allowing her eyes to wander over his entirety.

The girl nodded and smiled. "Hello, Jim, I'm Aisley." She offered her hand and Jim shook it delicately. "First time anyone's brought a Hero to one of these."

"I figured as much," Jim lightly replied, keeping his voice kind.

Aisley put her arm around Jim in an attempt to lead him closer to the fire. His body tensed at the stranger's touch, but he allowed her arm to stay.

"I need to get back towards our meal for the night. And, since Bren is gone, I could really use some help." She stepped in front of Jim, facing him with an incredibly serious look. "Would you please be my Second?"

Jim felt a small amount of relief from her offer. "Of course." This time, his smile was genuine.

"Gods bless!" Aisley took Jim's hand and rushed towards the fire.

Getting to the cooking supplies took them through the small camp. Aisley gave a quick introduction of each of the others as they passed the remainder of the group.

She pointed at a handsome, dark-skinned man lounging by the fire. "That's Prince. He's pretty and he knows it, so don't give him too much attention." She smiled and pointed at a blonde girl who was brushing one of the knots from her horse's mane. "She's Belle. One minute she will be laughing at your joke, the next she'll be sticking a fork into your thigh. My mother used to call girls like her 'very eccentric'." She pointed towards the last man who was singing next to Prince. "Bazzer, his real name is Sett, but I didn't tell you that." She winked at Jim. "He's loud, and he's always moving."

They stopped by one of the wagons. Its walls were filled with spices and various plants. Fruits and vegetables were stacked in crates which surrounded a large wooden salt box which, Jim knew, would be hiding various meats.

Aisley suddenly stopped. "Oh ya! You met Davey, and Shell is the one who ran off with him. They aren't married, but they may as well be, because they're always tied at the hip." Her eyes wandered as she entered a memory. "They took care of most of us after our...." She blinked back to the present and gave Jim a happy smile. "Well, I'm sure you know."

Jim didn't, but he could feel her distress from the memory. So, he nodded his head in feigned understanding. Now wasn't the time to dig into each other's past. Jim wasn't even sure if he would be welcome to stay once Davey and Shell were finished speaking with Emma.

Aisley clapped her hands together. "Jim," she started to say, jumping into the wagon, "would you rather have stew or roasted hen?"

"It has been a while since I've had hen," Jim said ponderously. "So, let's go with...."

"Wait!" Aisley cut him off. "Say stew!" Her look was worrisome, almost frantic.

Jim stuttered. "Umm... what?"

"Say stew!" she pressed urgently.

"Alright then. How about stew?" Jim's bewilderment grew as Aisley sighed in relief.

"Thank the Gods!" She reached into the salt chest and pulled out a large slab of beef. "Someone has gotten into my meats. Probably Prince, that smooth-mouthed bastard. He loves hen, so it must have been him." Aisley met Jim's in cautious expression. "This was your first responsibility as my Second, and I almost set you up for failure! It is a sacred bond we now share, Jim, and the first responsibilities are always the most important! Everyone knows that!" Her voice was soaked in sarcasm and she gave Jim another wink.

He chuckled before snapping his arm into a salute. "Thank you for saving me from that fatal error!" Jim said dutifully.

Aisley laughed, deep and pure, and Jim joined her after failing to keep his soldier façade. She dropped the beef onto a nearby table and clapped happily while sustaining her laugh and letting a rumbling snort escape her mouth. Jim laughed harder at the embarrassment she tried to hide on her face.

"Now there's a sight I never thought I'd see." Jim and Aisley turned to see a stern-faced woman, a deer carcass draped over her shoulder. "A Hero laughing with a human. The world must be ending again."

Aisley let out a happy and incredibly high-pitched scream and ran towards the stranger. "Bren! You're back early!" She kissed the woman briefly on the lips.

"This is Jim. Emma brought him for some drinks and stew." Aisley motioned at the Hero, and he walked forward with his hand extended.

But Bren didn't take it. She just looked at him, with hatred burning in her eyes, and dropped the deer onto the ground. "I'll be with the others. Call for me if you need a new Second," she said to Aisley.

"Oh, alright." Aisley said somberly.

Bren gripped Aisley's rear, eliciting a yelp from the girl, before walking towards the fire. Aisley's eyes fixated on Bren's swaying hips as she walked away and let out an adoring sigh. When the girl was no longer in earshot, Aisley whispered, "Amazing."

Jim hoisted Bren's deer on to a wooden table near the food wagon. Aisley shook the love from her head when the body slammed against the table's surface.

"Umm," Aisley said bashfully. "Sorry about Bren. She'll warm up to you once she gets some ale in her belly."

Jim flashed a grin. "I think it might take a bit more than ale. Do you have anything stronger in that magic salt box?"

She walked towards the table and studied the animal it held. "No, Jim, trust me. Ale will work for that one. It's all I used the first night I slept in her bed, and now.... well, she's stuck with me." She winked, and laughter erupted again.

■ ■ ■ ■ ■ ■ ■ ■ ■

"A Hero, Em? You thought it would be alright to bring a Hero!" Davey's whisper felt like a shout in the wagon's hollow cabin. "We are supposed to be celebrating the day we rid ourselves of their reach."

"He's different," Emma tried to explain, but her voice was drowned by Shell.

"This is going to be a disaster! How many of his friends do you think are out there waiting for his signal to rob and kill us?" Shell's paranoid eyes darted towards the canvas flap.

Emma tried again. "Jim and I have been...."

Davey interrupted. "I knew it felt wrong this month. I told you, Shell, something was interrupting the wind. We should have called it off, maybe skipped next month too." Davey was beginning to absorb Shell's paranoia.

Emma had to put a stop to their ramblings. The usual calm and careful attitudes of her chosen parents had become warped by the mere sight of a Hero. She couldn't blame them. When she had first seen Jim, she had felt a similar fear. But she knew better now, and it was important for them to see who he really was.

So, Emma put on the most stern and angry face she could muster and said, "Davey, shut up. Shell, calm down. Both of you, listen." To her amazement, they both stopped talking. "Jim found me in the woods.

I fell from a tree and hit my head, out cold, and dusk had already set. I had earned my death, and there was nothing I could do. But, somehow, I woke up next to a fire. There was food and warmth and walls. And, there was Jim." Emma hoped she would always remember the bafflement on Davey's face. "He saved me, even bandaged my arm, and told me I could leave if I wanted. He fell asleep, in front of me!" Shell had placed a hand over her mouth in amazement. "It was difficult to move my arm the next morning, so I asked him if he would escort me here. He was kind enough to oblige."

The two sat in front of Emma in a stunned silence. She could see the thoughts working through their minds. She had told a devastating lie that she knew would convince them to let Jim stay, and she still had one more card to play.

"Em," Davey said, giving her his parenting look. "People can pretend. You know that. We can't let every good-doer into our lives just because they acted kindly one day. It's not how the world works. He's a Hero. Eventually he will remember that you are a human and be rid of you the moment...."

"He saved me from a Husk, Davey." Shell actually gasped. "It caught us off guard. It was able to tear into my arm, but Jim threw me back and killed it. He was hurt badly. But he didn't leave me."

Davey and Shell shared a look, and Emma knew she'd won. Their expressions softened, and they both nodded and turned back towards her.

"A husk?" It was Davey, wonderfully calm, who finally responded. "I'm sorry we weren't there to help." He looked down in shame. "Jim can stay. But if there is any piece of him that smells of threat, I will kill him without a thought."

"I would expect nothing less," Emma said with a delighted smirk.

They sat in understanding for a few minutes before Emma decided it was time for her to leave the wagon. She rose to her feet and parted the canvas flaps.

"Oh, Em!" Shell called. "Aisley has found religion, again."

Emma smiled. "I'm sure we will be hearing all about it tonight. Any extravagancies I should be excited for?"

Shell's mouth twisted in mock contemplation. "Umm. This time it's something about a Shadow God, or maybe it's a world made of smoke, or was it the ancient tribes of the mountain?" Shell stuck out her tongue. "It's all blending together now."

Emma chuckled with Shell. "I'd better go save Jim, before Aisley decides to save him herself." And with that, she left the wagon.

■ ■ ■ ■ ■ ■ ■ ■

Jim inhaled the delicious scent from the concoction boiling in the iron pot. Aisley had insisted on a private fire so the others wouldn't try and get to her food before it was ready. He thought it was a bit of an extreme measure but, with the smell that lingered in his nostrils, now understood her concerns.

He carved the freshly killed deer into fine cubes for the stew. Aisley had made the executive decision to swap the stale, salted beef for the fresh, gamey venison as the main ingredient in the dish. And, as her Second, Jim offered to slaughter the carcass. His blade shone with crimson and his hands reeked of blood. It was a sight he had seen so many times, and it gave him a small feeling of comfort.

"I wonder what it's like to die." Aisley pulled Jim from his thoughts.

"Whoa. You don't' beat around the bush with life's greatest mysteries, do you?" Jim lightheartedly teased.

Aisley smiled and shook her head. "I've heard that death isn't the end. When you die, you go to some magical place and relive the lives of the forgotten people." She looked far into the distance. "Can you imagine? All the beauty other people have seen, Jim? It sounds amazing."

Jim thought on her words. He had felt what must be death. He had gone to a place that shredded his soul and forced him to his knees. He shook remembering the boney hand that gripped his arm.

He chose his words carefully. "I've been around a lot of death. More than most people can even imagine. But I wouldn't want to live through any of the lives that I've seen end. It's much better to live as you and fight to keep on living." Jim refused to look into Aisley's eyes, but he could feel her gaze rest upon him.

"Hmm. You're probably right." Aisley paused in thought. "But my priest has been telling me about what is waiting beyond. Now, he's not a Divine Priest, but he is very holy. You can feel his spirit's radiance from across the room. He says that we never truly live until we die. And that the only way...."

"What in the hells are you doing!" Emma stomped angrily towards Aisley. "Did you allow this man to touch our food?"

Aisley's eyes grew from an unknown fear. She looked at Jim, trying to find an explanation, but he shook his head in confusion.

"Y-yes, Em. I...I did." Aisley trembled. "He only cut some of the deer. I was going to let him stir in some spices but...."

"Allowing this man," Emma said, pointing a finger at Jim, "near any food is a crime against all of humanity. I've been poisoned before, Aisley, you know that. But the things that he has forced me to eat made me wish for the poison's sweet torment." She looked at Jim and immediately lost all signs of anger.

Jim couldn't hold back the laugh from his stomach. Emma had Aisley so terrified that she didn't realize it was an absurd joke until Emma began laughing along with him.

"I thought humans only ate dirt and grass," Jim said, shrugging his shoulders. "I didn't know you were so weak stomached."

Aisley glanced from Jim to Emma, confusion clearing from her face. "Oh, you." She walked towards Emma and enveloped her in a warm embrace. "I've missed you, Em."

Emma returned the hug. "Missed you too, Aisley." She gestured at Jim. "Mind if I steal your new Second? I'd like to get him drunk before he realizes this is all a trap and he is the one we are going to eat tonight."

Aisley nodded happily. "Just make sure he eats lots of butter and ale. I like my Heroes fat." She laughed and lightly punched Jim on the shoulder. "Go have fun. I'll be done soon!"

Emma grabbed Jim's hand and led him towards the bonfire, towards the others. The flames were high and bright, the air crisp from the heat of the roaring pillar.

Prince, Bren, Belle, and Shell were watching as Bazzer attempted to juggle and recite some ancient poem. So far, he had four balls, two yellow and two green, rotating through the air, but stumbled on an awkward stanza and dramatically dropped to his knees. Everyone shared a laugh at his over-exaggerated tantrum. Even Bazzer laughed after he stomped his feet into the dry grass.

"That was impressive." Davey's voice grew closer as he walked towards the others. "Right until the end, at least." They all shared another brief round of laughter. "Now, I'd like to show you what I've been learning this month."

Davey pulled an instrument case from behind his back. Jim practically salivated at the sight of the small black box, fully aware of the item that lay inside. He had a similar case, held a similar instrument, so many years ago.

The box clicked open, and Davey pulled a lute from the velvet lining. The instrument was worn and scratched. A few of the pegs looked warped and the grooves of the frets had been worn flat. *Worn instruments always make the greatest songs.*

"Oi. Ya gonna serenade us?" Bren jovially lifted her mug in the air.

As an answer, Davey lifted the lute and strummed on its strings. The tune was a bit sour, so he turned a few of the pegs and attempted another strum. He repeated the short process, turning the pegs and testing the strings, until the sound of honey filled the camp.

"Jim," Davey said warmly, smiling and motioning for him to sit by the others.

Jim hadn't realized that he was the only one standing. He sat by Emma and felt embarrassment kissing at his cheeks. But the undesirable emotion was gone once the music began to sing.

The songs were simple and happy. They all sang of good times, or better times about to come. Mostly they were songs made for children to fall asleep listening to. But as the music continued, Jim allowed it to lift him.

His eyes closed, and he began to hum the familiar tunes, his fingers moving as he played along to each song. Emma's hand was resting on his arm, her grip becoming tight as the music steeped her into childhood memories. Then, the music ended. The world around them became clear and loud, and everyone clapped their hands and cheered for Davey.

Davey took a shallow bow, pride beaming on his face. "Thank you! Thank you! I'm afraid that's all I know, so there will be no encore." He chuckled from his belly. "If any of you have also taken up the lute, you're welcome to come impress me."

Emma's hand shot in the air. "I think Jim knows how to play."

Jim looked at the girl, confused. "What are you talking about?" he asked, wondering if music had ever come up or not in their conversations while traveling.

She whispered to the Hero, "Your fingers were dancing up and down my thigh." She winked mischievously. "You have a musician's touch."

Davey looked shocked. "Can you play, Jim? I know I'd love to hear one of the legendary songs sung in the streets of Paradise," he joked.

"Oh ya! Play us a Hero song, Jim!" Belle said, her hands clapping happily at the idea.

"Umm." Jim hesitated until he felt Emma's hand tighten on his arm. "Sure, I can play something. If it's alright that I use your instrument, Davey."

"Of course," Davey said merrily.

Jim tested his fingers along the neck of the lute. It had been so many years since he had held such a beautiful thing. His hands fell into place, feeling the rough wood that marked each fret. His fingers began to move, and the lute began to speak.

Time slowed, and the air grew still. The world outside of the music vanished as the notes flew higher and higher into the air. His fingers kept dancing along with his thoughts, telling a story that only music could tell. The notes came even and strong. They pushed through the ages and engulfed everything within their reverberations.

The story the music told was simple. A story of a boy lost in the woods, so cold and hungry. Death had threatened him many times in such a short period, and the boy was ready to give up. The tune grew warm as a stranger found the freezing Hero and wrapped him in the cloak from off his back.

The music spoke of a small cabin, used mostly for hunting by the aging stranger. The boy recovered quickly due to the kindness shared by the man. As months passed the boy and the man bonded and became family. The man taught the boy so much about hunting, and fishing, and killing. He showed the boy how to use a lute to make his hands strong and his movements deliberate.

The music continued, sharing the story of the adventures of the boy and the man. They survived the harsh winter together, leaning on each other during moments of great weakness. They knew that their strength together was stronger than the deepest threats of the woods.

Somber notes vibrated into the world, for somber became the story. *What do you do when you see a husk?* It was the first the boy had ever seen, and curiosity drove him to recklessness. The monster saw the boy, chased him through the woods, and buried itself into his back. The man had known to run, but he could not leave the boy. He dove at the creature and knocked the boy free from its awful grasp. *Run, Jim—I'm right behind you.* The music faded and so did the man.

The world appeared again as Jim's hands struck the damning final note. He breathed heavily and his eyes flickered between the faces that stared back. He found the comfortable green and rested there.

Davey sniffled and brushed a tear from his eye. "Thank you, Jim."

"Food's ready!" Aisley's voice broke the reverent air. "What did I miss?"

"You missed a Gods damned angel, Ais!" Prince shouted as he walked toward the stew.

Aisley saw what Jim held in his hand and pouted her lips. "Aww man! I always miss the good stuff." She whined and followed the others to dinner.

"I'm going to grab our guest a drink," Davey muttered softly, and he wandered alone towards his wagon.

Jim felt the familiar rumble of hunger in his stomach. He put the lute back into its case and set it where Davey had been standing. He started walking towards the others when Emma's hand caught him and forced him to stop.

"Can we wait a minute?" She asked softly. "I'm not ready for this moment to end."

Jim sat, and Emma rested her head on his shoulder. And, for the first time since he was a boy, he felt like he may have found family.

## 10: DANCING IN THE DARK

The stew was delicious. Bits of carrots and celery floated with chunks of venison, separating wonderfully on Jim's tongue as he spooned another bite into his mouth. This was his third bowl and, by the size of his distended belly, his last of the night.

Davey returned from his wagon with a brown and dusty bottle. "As is tradition," he said, uncorking the glass, "let's get drunk."

Everyone raised their cups high into the air and cheered as Davey drained the bottle of its liquid. Jim laughed and finished off the meager amount of ale that remained in his cup. The others drank along and quickly disseminated into varying stages of drunkenness.

Bazzer had pulled a wooden flute from his pocket and was loudly playing shrill notes while hopping in place. Bren was dancing to the high-pitched sound in such an elegant way that her brutish demeanor seemed to melt. Aisley only stared at her drunken lover while attempting to hide behind her hand in embarrassment. Prince was chewing on a whole hen while cheering at Bazzer in an attempt to have him play louder. Shell happily clapped at the foolish sight and began to sing a song as her own contribution to the night.

Belle forced Davey's lute into Jim's hand and demanded that he harmonize with the madness. Jim took the task to heart with a glossy-eyed smile and put his fingers to work. Davey's feet were too wobbly for him to stand, so he sat and hummed while Jim played.

And Emma, she was the most entertaining person of the night. She took the invitation to drink as an order and downed three ales in a matter of minutes. Jim had decided to cut himself off after she drank his remaining ale and nearly stumbled into the fire. He created a mission for his slightly-inebriated self, and spoke it aloud so he would remember,

"Don't let Emma die." He chanted his mission a few times, loud enough for Davey to hear him and join in his chanting. "Don't let Emma die." They chanted along with the tune that the lute produced.

Emma was a drunken whirlwind who would rush to dance with Bren and Bazzer and then fall in place next to Aisley to share in slurred philosophy. At once she jumped at Prince and demanded a piece of his hen and, when he refused, tackled him to the dirt and wrestled until Prince yielded. She also ran over to Davey, meat stuffed in her mouth, and pulled him to his feet to dance. Despite everything, she would always return to Jim's side, finish off another ale, and run to dance with Bazzer and Bren again.

Jim watched as the night folded to the alcohol's intoxication. Emma was first, falling asleep with her arm around Aisley. The kind girl covered Emma with a blanket and whispered something into Bren's ear. They left hand-in-hand a moment later. Jim heard the shrill recorder die and saw Bazzer and Prince snoring by the dwindling flames. Davey had his arm around Shell, and Jim helped them both safely to their wagon.

Jim became the only one conscious, and the camp grew eerily desolate.

"I'll take first watch," he whispered and sat on the outskirts of the fire, playing the lute softer than before.

□ □ □ □ □ □ □

Jim observed how some of the bugs whistling about the fire flew headfirst into its cackling timber. It was odd for him to realize that the thing the bugs wanted, the light of the fire, was the thing that inevitably killed them.

A rustling came from behind the log Jim sat upon. He turned and saw Davey hobbling from his wagon, rubbing his temples with the heel of his hand. Davey saw the Hero and joined him in his quiet observation.

They sat for a while, Jim picking at the lute's strings and Davey humming softly along with the melody. A perfection thrummed through the stars as the two men sat under them. Nevertheless, a deep part of Jim's mind felt uneasy hesitancy just before Davey started speaking.

"Should I trust you, Jim?"

Jim placed a hand over his instrument halting its sound. He allowed the silence to build while he thought. The question was so simple to ask but infinitely more complicated to answer. He thought about what question would be asked after each iteration of every answer he could give. But, he knew, trust was deep. Far deeper than friendship and fighting. Trust was thoughtless and damning and impossible and...

"Probably not." Jim kept his voice low, almost whispering his response.

A wall always stood between what Jim wished to say and what he needed to say. It was a confusing tangle of emotion that frustrated him.

Darkness swelled as Davey contemplated what to say next. Jim could feel the turmoil that spread through the man as he tried to speak with honesty.

"Heroes killed my family." Davey didn't look at Jim as he spoke. "My wife, my children, they're dead now. I see them every time I close my eyes, and each time I sleep I can hear their voices. And when I saw you, I heard them again. They were begging me to pull them from our burning house. Screaming as their lives turned to ash." Davey paused for a long while, his eyes wandering through the sky.

"They didn't even have the decency to leave the dead alone. Those Heroes, those pillaging murderers, placed every corpse in a pile on the courtyard stones." Anger percolated Jim's mind as Davey spoke. "I recognized my wife, because she was clutching my youngest in her arms. But, the rest of the bodies were so burnt, black and cracked, that we couldn't distinguish where one limb separated from the other. Two of my children were among the tangled charcoal. We were never able to pull apart the mass, never able to find my boys."

He looked towards Jim, the fire in his eyes roaring in the quiet night. "Their voices yelled at me when I saw you. They demanded I force your golden eyes closed and taste the copper in your blood." Davey released a breath and allowed his gaze to shift towards the forest before continuing. "I wanted to do it, Jim. I could feel the motion of my sword sliding through your neck. Part of me still wants to, more than anything. But...." He breathed slowly, forcing his calm collection towards the surface. "I blamed you. It was unfair; but, when it comes to family, thoughts aren't usually bent towards being fair."

The intensity of Davey's memories threated to overwhelm him and burst through his skin. The hatred for Heroes, for Jim, could melt ice from the peaks of the Eastern Mountains and freeze the fires that moved the world.

The guilt that built up inside Jim dwarfed that conviction. He could feel a force filling him, demanding a confession from the boy who had led to the death of this man's family.

Davey looked up at the stars twinkling across the speckled blackness. Clouds of purple and grey freely floated through paths of moonbeams. He watched the quiet and beautiful night, allowing silence to bond them once again.

But, for Jim, that silence was suffocating. The hint of acceptance that tickled his thoughts drove his self-resentment deeper into his chest.

Jim suddenly stood and walked a few paces away. "You're different from the people I grew up with, Davey. Where I grew up a person is convicted the moment they are born. Either they are right, or they are punished." The cold night air stabbed Jim's chest with each sharp breath he took. "I was claimed by perfection and reveled in the overpowering ideals of my upbringing. It took my sister's death for me to realize how corrupt that perfection is."

Jim turned towards the man whose family's blood stained his hands. "You should blame me. For everything."

A long moment passed as they each tried to anticipate what may come next. Davey rose to his feet and walked towards Jim. He reached out his hand, clasping the Hero's shoulder.

Davey hesitated before speaking. "It feels like your blame might be enough for both of us."

Everything inside of Jim seemed to rapidly cascade. So much confusion, so many thoughts all screaming for his immediate attention. Davey's foreign emotions joined in the chaos as a mixture of questions and forgiveness embraced within him. Warmth spread through his spine and tingled his fingertips.

"Why don't you get some rest?" Davey asked kindly. "I'll finish the watch tonight."

Jim left the man and the darkness, confused thoughts still roaming his consciousness. He found Emma, sprawled beneath a blanket by the fire. The Hero brushed a few twigs and pebbles from the spot next to the girl. He grinned at her disheveled hair and the small dribble coming from the corner of her mouth. And when he finally closed his eyes, he dreamed he was staring at a purple sky as the girl with emerald eyes sang beside him.

## 11: A MARE, A MAN, AND A MEMORY

Her world rocked back and forth in the slumbering eternity. Dreams and fantasies ran rampant throughout the landscape, colliding with the girl that wandered through its planes. Rocks rippled through the calm water and the girl stared in fascination as the ripples grew to waves. The perfect glassy surface needed more chaos. She threw another rock, targeting the heart of the ancient water.

She could almost hear a voice, and she shuddered. The waves grew, towering over the insignificant girl. The wall of foaming water crashed at her feet. It would never harm her, she knew that, but the sight was still magnificently terrifying. Her world shook again, and this time a voice was clear to her wandering mind. The world was trying to hide the high, familiar whispers. But the water called her back, had become so serene in her absence. It needed more chaos. She looked on the ground for another stone that she could use to break its still surface. Another shake, and this time she felt something grasp her shoulder.

"You snoring log!" Bren whispered, frustration heavy on her breath.

Emma blinked, and the un-real existence faded from her memory.

"Wha? Who wants?" Emma stumbled from sleep.

"Ah, finally." Bren breathed. "It's a miracle you haven't been killed in your sleep, Em, you know that. I've been shaking at you for a good while now."

Emma rubbed her eyes. Bren stood over her, sleepy frustration painted on her face. The sky hinted at dawn, the sun barely peaking over the Eastern Mountains. It was too early, and Bren knew how much the girl enjoyed her sleep.

Jim was lying next to Emma with an arm draped over her abdomen. His golden eyes rested shut, dashing side to side as he dreamt. He was gone to the world.

"Watchu want, Bren?" Emma muttered, her mouth feeling heavy.

Bren shook again. "I want you to hunt with me." She paused, and her eyes shifted, before adding, "There is a lot we need to talk about."

Bren was not the type to seek companionship. So, Emma begrudgingly rose to her feet, placed the Hero's hand gently on the ground, and walked towards Aisley's food-cart. After a breakfast of fresh fruit and cold oatmeal, the two stepped away from the camp and headed into the nearby forest.

□ □ □ □ □ □ □

A fat pheasant sat on a branch twenty feet away. Regardless of the obesity of the animal, it was a small and difficult shot from this distance. Emma's hand was steady, her fletching hovered over the feathered meal. She took in a breath, long and deep, and her arrow flew. The sharp steel pierced a branch's bark and the frightful bird took towards the sky.

Bren's arrow flew past Emma's ear, causing a force that pulled her loose strands of hair after its shaft. The arrowhead stuck into the bird's stomach, ending its escape. Emma tracked where the pheasant fell and retrieved it. She pulled the sticky arrow from the trophy, handing both to Bren.

"Glad you're here to pick up the slack," Emma said.

Bren nodded her head. "You're the best branch slayer I know, but I do prefer a warm, juicy meal over a tree's barky hide." She winked.

An embarrassed blush crept on to Emma's cheeks. "I'm sure Aisley could make a tree-branch stew that would change your mind."

"Yer damn right about that," Bren said with pride. "With just a few spices and her magic hands, of course, she would have people paying in gold for just a smell of that stew."

Emma raised an eyebrow. "Magic hands, huh? I guess that explains some of the noises you were making last night."

This time the embarrassment colored Bren's cheeks. "What can I say? She knows me. Inside and out."

Emma laughed at the rare sight of Bren's bashfulness. She moved towards her sister and, playfully, punched her shoulder.

"You're alright, you know that, Bren?" Emma said in between her laughs.

Bren smiled widely. "That's what I've been told."

The sisters drank in the happy moment. Neither wanted to preemptively end its natural course, as it wove through their smiles and lungs. They survived on moments like these. Times when Bren would shake Emma awake and beg her to talk. No matter the time of day, although Emma preferred the sun to be high in the sky, the two would walk away from the camp and release their problems upon the world. Emma didn't like to think about who she might have become without those moments.

The laughter dissipated. Their bellies heaved violently to recover from the much-needed cull of emotions.

Emma scanned the trees and took a step farther into the forest. "Come on. Last night you came back with a deer. Today, let's make it two."

"Alright," Bren said with hesitation and fell in stride with Emma.

Emma recognized that hesitation. Despite their sisterly bond, Bren rarely spoke about her own problems. She would sometimes seek a conversation and leave without saying a word. It was a language that Emma had been deciphering for years, and hesitation always meant unfinished.

"Talk." Emma stopped abruptly and stared at the archer.

Bren stopped, but she didn't talk. Not right away. She looked around, checking every piece of the forest that surrounded them. Her head swiveled, and she wore an intense gaze. Her brown eyes burned through the thick foliage before finally resting on Emma's emeralds. She took a breath, long and deep, choosing her words with precision.

"I've seen him before, Emma." She took another breath. "I know your Hero."

■ ■ ■ ■ ■ ■ ■ ■

Jim watched as Belle's hair flew in the wake of her mare's gallop. Her hips moved in tandem with the horse's clopping hooves. She looked so relaxed as she swept past the tall grass. A serene joy soaked her smile and shone like the sun beaming from the clouds. *There is no difference from a true rider and his mount. They become one the moment hand grasps reins.*

Jim never had the gift, or patience, required to train a steed, though he had many chances and his father had forced him into the stables as a boy. Horse-riding just never stuck. The vulnerabilities of Hero and beast always felt too overwhelming. His mobility was quick but so limited on the thousand-pound animals. So, the moment his father stepped out of sight he would flee from the stables and head to the arena. It was much better. Hero fought Hero with their weapon of choice, dulled on the edges of course, and whatever tactics they had. No horses, no holding back.

From behind he could hear Bazzer and Prince arguing about one thing or another. They looked nothing alike, but their constant bickering was definitive proof that they were brothers. Aisley was hustling near her cart, taking an inventory of their supplies and planning the day's meals accordingly. Shell and Davey were hammering at the wall of their wagon, and Bren and Emma had left hunting.

Jim started, having awakened after everyone else. It wasn't like him to doze while strangers around him yet breathed—other than Emma, that is. Things had changed ever since his run in with that dark…place…just before he met her.

He searched for Emma in the peculiarly warm air of the morning, until Davey informed him of the girl's whereabouts. She would be back by dusk. So, for now, there was nothing to do but relax. Jim had found a secluded spot by the outskirts of the camp to watch the sea of swaying yellow grass and the girl who rode on the waves above.

"Hey, Jim." Davey's voice interrupted. "Could we borrow you for a minute?"

"Of course." Jim rose and walked towards the couple and their wagon.

They had completely torn open the side of the wagon and a good chunk of its floor. Wood and canvas littered the ground and an arsenal of tools were neatly placed at Davey's side. Jim glanced inside. Where they had ripped the floor he could see the wagon's axle. A spiraling crack had spread from the base of the wheel, winding towards the center.

"Now, I'm no expert, but I'd guess you've got a broken axel," Jim teased.

Davey chuckled. "Shell thought the ride up here was a bit bumpy. I told her I'd give it a look and…well, you can see the mess we've made of it." He put a hand near his mouth and whispered, "If she ever asks you to help out with a project, run." Davey winked.

"Note taken." Jim smiled. "How can I help?"

"Ah, straight to business! I like it!" Davey fell to a crouch. "I need to saw off this portion and replace it with a new one. But, and here's where you come in, we will need to remove the wheel and take pressure off the supports. I need you to lift on either side of the wheel and hold it while I crawl under. It shouldn't take more than…," Davey looked up as he thought; "fifteen minutes. Can you do it?"

Jim remembered the last wagon he had lifted. It was upside down and filled with miscellaneous belongings. He was contracted to retrieve a painting from the wagon's owner, but when he tried to force the driver to stop the horses veered over a steep cliffside. It was a messy contract and ended in half-pay due to the tear that now covered the painting's center.

This wagon was empty, and he wouldn't need to lift it too high. He walked towards the wheel and tested the sturdy wood that his hands would grip.

He nodded his head. "Tell me when you're ready."

Davey pumped his fist in excitement and pushed a few tools below the wagon. "Okay. Now."

The Hero grunted in effort, and the wagon rose a few inches from the ground. Jim breathed deeply, allowing a cooling calm to obscure his senses so the pain in his side wouldn't cause him to collapse. Davey scuttled beneath and began frantically sawing. After a minute the wheel fell, and the broken axle was flung from below. Davey occasionally muttered under his breath as he worked.

"Shell, could you kick the wheel back to me? I need to get it into the socket before I re-bolt the axle." Shell moved at the task.

Jim closed his eyes, the strain from the action revitalizing his nearly-healed chest. A throbbing pain came with each heartbeat, so he dove deeper into his mind. An escape from the physical world was resting inside of his calm. A pool of black, so dark and consuming, drowned the inhibitions of reality. Jim sank into that pool and everything started to fade.

Calm became eternity, quiet and cool and warm. He sank into that eternity, breathing in the omnipotent emotion. This place was so wonderfully dark, so secluded from even the Hero that resided in its haven.

A hand gripped his shoulder and a voice from far away began to scream. His haven became hell, his warm dark erupting into freezing white. Snow. Snow and ice crystals hung from trees that lead to his village. Smoke rose from the distance and fire brightened the blue night.

He was running. So tired, exhausted, but he had to keep running. He had to find them. They were safe, they had to be safe. Inside the village walls, behind the barriers that kept out the husks. They were there; they were safe. He just had to run.

The path turned and twisted, the snow crunching beneath his tattered boots. Everything would be fine. He would take his wife and his children, and they would leave, denying the name of Ash if that's what it took to keep them safe. The Willows treated humans fairly—he would lead his family to them, find sanctuary and serve as payment. They would leave tonight, take the horse and ride through the moonlit world. It would be a cold trip, so he would take the wool blanket that hung above the fireplace. That would be perfect to wrap around....

The trees opened along the path, and the village beyond was only charcoal and fire. But he kept running. My house is near the back. They could have made it out before....

"JIM!" Aisley yelled.

Jim's arms were so tired, so heavy, and his chest burned in angry pain. Davey stood in front of him, tears running from the man's eyes. Jim placed the wagon onto the ground and looked at the faces of those who surrounded him.

"What in the hells just happened?" Aisley asked.

Jim didn't have an answer.

■ ■ ■ ■ ■ ■ ■ ■

"What do you mean, you know him?" Emma asked after finally finding her voice.

Bren shuffled her feet, her eyes never leaving the safety of the forest floor. "It's just…a memory. One I've tried to forget. A memory that's whispered to me every night since.…"

Emma knew the girl's story and the nightmares that plagued her. She had talked with Bren so many times about the night the Heroes ravaged her village and life. The tall warriors had burned most villages, and snow buried the coals left behind. The Heroes took control of Bren's town. They conquered and controlled her people, ransacked them, and made them wretched and despondent until the end of the Southern War. When the fighting finally ended, the Heroes left, taking the town's winter supplies.

The story that followed always led to Bren shaking. She would rub her arms, as if the frigid winter bit at her again. Her details were sparse: no food, a frozen well, strength fading. And then came death. Illness was just as dangerous as starvation, and both were prominent in her home.

Bren buried her mother first. A day later it was her sister. On the day she went to dig a grave for her brother, she found the corpses of her family. She thought animals had gnawed on them. She ran home and found her father with a mouthful of her brother's arm. Without thinking, she took a fire poker to her father's skull. And just like that, her family was dead.

She fled through the gates, hoping to find respite in the woods. She was only a child then, ten years old if Emma remembered correctly, and the deadly night treated her with ruthlessness. Once desperation took her again, she returned to her town, only to see the gates still open wide and the people inside dead. The husks had seen the vulnerable town, seen the gates that Bren had left open, and they feasted on her friends.

It was a story that haunted Bren and chilled Emma. Davey found the girl a week later, barely more than bones and breath. She was the first of his adopted children, the first of their new family.

"I found my people dead, Em. I've told you that. Saw the scraps of flesh that the husks left. And I was scared, so scared, but I couldn't leave. I didn't have anywhere else to go. I stayed. I went into my house and crawled beneath a blanket. I was ready to die. But then came the Heroes. The same bastards who had claimed my home before. I could hear their voices outside my window; I could see their faces in my mind."

Bren rubbed her arms while she spoke. "I had to kill them. It was the strangest feeling, but it warmed me enough to creep from beneath my covers and wander into the darkness. And, there they were. Laughing by a fire and eating charred meat inside my decimated village. I had the fire poker in my hand. I don't even know when I retrieved it from my father's head, but there it was, swinging towards one of my tormentors.

"I felt the sharp metal pierce that monster's skin, and his scream made me smile for the first time in so long." A malicious smile appeared on Bren's face as she reveled in the memory. "I even laughed when I saw his blood steaming in the light of the fire. It was marvelous, Em—so wonderful and beautiful and right.

"It was a short-lived joy, of course. A smack in the back from a child couldn't do much to a Hero. They had me on the ground in an instant and began kicking at my ribs. The pain they gave me warmed me even more, and the blood that dripped from that bastard's back forced me to laugh through the beating. And that really pissed them off." Her smile faded.

Bren turned away from Emma. "They tore my clothes. I kicked and screamed, but…the night was so cold. After a few minutes my skin was numb, my tears were freezing on my cheeks." She took a shuddering breath. "That must be what hell is like. There is no worse place, no worse feeling, I have ever known."

Emma took a step towards her sister. She had no words to contend with the immense memory. She placed a hand on Bren's shoulder. And, briefly the girl seemed to be rescued from her memories. She wiped her face with her cloak and cleared her throat before delving back into her nightmarish tale.

"I remember yelling, but I don't remember words. I don't even know if I made any sound. There was just silence and cold and gold. For so long, eternities, I stared at the face of the men who were meant to be my end. But then…there was blood again.

"I felt it long before I saw the red. It's an odd thing to remember, the feeling of the steaming droplets of life raining on to my exposed skin. And I know I should have been afraid still, but that warmth was…beautiful.

"I stared at the crimson pebbles that pooled across my body. I just stared at them, mesmerized. Blood continued to rain from above me, but my eyes never left those pools. My other senses didn't work, didn't register anything that was happening beyond that sticky pool. So, I just watched. I became that blood, that warm red. I felt something slap my face. The stinging was red as the rain. Another slap reminded me of the cold. And," Bren added, looking into Emma's eyes, "the third slap is when I saw Jim.

"I saw his gold, and my world turned into fear again. I tried to back away, but my arms couldn't move my weight. It wasn't until he offered me his hand, until I saw that beautiful color stained on his fingers, that I looked for those other Heroes. They were all at his feet, hacked in to wonderfully tiny pieces." Bren's eyes sparkled. "I decided to take his hand, to trust a Hero. He smiled before his fist found my jaw."

Emma jumped at the mention of the Hero's punch. Her mouth hung agape as she tried to find the words necessary to describe her confusion. Could that have truly been Jim, her Hero? She had only known him for a few days now, but there was no way that he would ever harm a freezing child. Would he?

Bren laughed at Emma's expression, her usual swaggered attitude returning. "The look on your face, Em." She laughed again. "He didn't kill me, obviously. And, as far as I know, he didn't' lay another finger on me. I woke up with a blasting headache, my clothes repaired and folded neatly beside me, three heavy cloaks draped over me, and a purse full of gold at my feet. He must have carried me into a nearby house, because my head rested on a feathered pillow and my feet were toasting by a fire." Her tone became serious. "But I was alone again. Alone in that town. He left me. And only a true monster would turn his back on someone in that situation." She shook her head. "A true monster."

The two girls stood quietly amongst the breeze. Emma's mind clenched in a knot. Her head pounded along with her heartbeat. The man that she knew - it didn't make sense.

"C'mon, Em." Bren poked Emma's nose with the tip of her bow. "Let's keep hunting. I really need to kill something."

■ ■ ■ ■ ■ ■ ■ ■ ■

Jim sat in solemn solitude. He had to think, try and make sense of whatever it was that just happened at the wagon. With all those people around him, he had felt so trapped. He had to get away, find seclusion. So, he left. Walked away from the camp until he was surely alone.

His mind was spinning with the memories that he had relived. He had felt them, feared inside of their immortal remembrance. But those were not his moments to remember. He had disappeared, traveled through Davey's touch, become a piece of the man whose life he had destroyed. It didn't make sense.

And now what would happen? He had left the first family he had known in so many years, fled from them the instant that something went wrong. Going back would be wrong, especially after hurting Davey the way he did. So, it was time to move on, forget those people, forget Emma, before he hurt them even more.

He rose to his feet. It was time to return to the things he knew. Those contracts to kill, his blades and his blood, his calm. His plan became clear and his path became determined. Forget how he came back from the dead. Forget falling and the curious man who asked questions in the abysmal purgatory. Forget Emma and the person she represented from the start. He began walking.

Floydd would be a problem, but he would be dealt with. His was a death that Jim could already feel and taste—that foul copper. He would go through the man's home, kill every guard that he had stationed inside. He'd go room to room leaving corpses where the living once stood. Then he would find Floydd. Jim began to run, his determination fueling each heavy step.

He would force that bastard to suffer. Cut through each of his muscles before granting his death by slicing his throat. It would be perfect. His rates would go up, and his contractors would agree with his new value. He had died after all. Died and returned to the land of the living again. He would be the most sought-after killer, and his victims would line the streets and flood the Life-Giving Lakes.

A horse cut abruptly in front of the sprinting Hero. His feet dug in to the soft ground, leaving a trail of uprooted grass behind him. Belle sat on the mighty beast, an angry look in her hazel eyes. She jumped from the mare and shoved a pointed finger into Jim's chest.

"Where do you think you're going?"

Jim blinked, "It's time for me to go. I don't want to hurt any of you...."

"No!" She cut the Hero off. "That's not how this works." She shoved him downwards. "Sit."

Her push wasn't forceful, but her words held weight. Jim sat as commanded. Belle snapped her fingers and her horse trotted next to the girl's side.

"Her name is William, and it was my father's name so don't you tell me it's improper." She patted William on her nose. "I call her Billy for short, but that's because she lets me. You see, she was very fond of my father, and when I asked her what her name should be, she told me that William would suit her perfectly."

Belle looked at Jim and he nodded his head. He didn't have any idea what the girl was saying, but he now knew the proper way to address her mount.

She continued; "It was just Billy and me for a long time. This is way before Davey, Jim. I'm talking years. And we would argue all the time. She would get mad when I wanted to stop for apples in the middle of the day, and I would snap at her when she woke me in the mornings. It was rough at first, but we grew together. She was all I had, my sole family member. She made me promise to make it. She made me swear that I would fight until I made it to a new home. And when Davey found us, she was so proud of me. That's when she told me I didn't have to call her William anymore. From then on it's just been Billy." Belle sat next to Jim, grasping his hand. "Do you understand what I'm saying?"

Jim clicked his tongue. "Not really."

Belle huffed in frustration. "You are William." She spoke slowly and waited for Jim to nod his head before continuing. "And my family is me, Belle." She gestured towards herself, and Jim nodded. "We are different, but we will grow together. You just can't give up. We will fight, and we will disagree, but we will get through this world together." Jim nodded again, and Belle seemed contented.

They sat together. She rested her head on his shoulder and stayed quiet while he thought. She stayed with him for hours as he absorbed her words. She offered him her wisdom, a beautiful wisdom that caused his eyes to water. He would stay, he would live, and they would do it together.

The sun began to fall through the sky before Jim finally decided to move. He helped Belle to her feet and patted William's head. Then, the three of them headed back towards camp.

■ ■ ■ ■ ■ ■ ■ ■

A wild boar scampered through the bushes, Bren's arrow lodged in its backside. They had been tracking this beast most of the day and had finally marked its hide with steel. It would bleed out soon, another hour maybe, so Emma and Bren devoutly stayed on its trail.

As she ran, Emma's mind wandered. So many conflicted thoughts tangled with one another. It was confusing and frustrating and sharp, a rose bush made of thorns that hid the beauty of the flower. The thoughts would collide and form painful possibilities that rattled through her consciousness. She became so distracted by her inner mind that she barely registered when Bren tackled her to the ground.

They hit the soil hard, Emma's shoulder bouncing off an ancient exposed tree root. Bren held a finger vertically across her mouth telling Emma to remain silent. The girl pointed her finger forward, motioning for her to look. And what she saw was terrifying.

Heroes, five of them. A full patrol this far through the woods. Patrols usually stayed near Paradise, protecting the Hero city's wall, so to find them here, near the edge of the forest, was peculiar.

"Ayy Brig, looks like we've got some good fortune." Emma heard the deep, familiar voice through the trees.

She glanced again at the patrol and saw Lumberjack holding her boar by its hind legs.

"Even a free arrow. Good steel too." He chuckled.

"Captain Blackthorne, please keep your voice lowered." Helmet's voice whispered harshly. "The Ash heir could be hiding behind any tree in this damned forest, and you're blabbering mouth could be the exact warning he would need to get away. This pig means someone's nearby."

Bren's eyes were wide when she looked at Emma. The two women stayed low to the ground and backed away slowly. If the patrol was this close to their camp, the danger was astronomical. Bren and Emma had to warn their family immediately. They crawled until their thighs burned and they could hear the Heroes no more. Then, they got to their feet and sprinted towards camp.

## 12: ONCE WE WERE DRAGONS

She drove her burning legs forward. Hero patrols were efficient, and they wouldn't spend time to rest for the night. There was only a small opening to evade the camp without notice, and the opening was closing fast. Bren's breath reached the nape of Emma's neck while the two pushed deeper in to the night.

A rustling bush drew Emma's attention. A flash of color rushed through the slim openings of the plants. A cloak? Hair? Imagination? She didn't have time to observe, because she had to keep moving. Faster.

The trees were thinning, growing smaller and lower as their need to grow for sunlight lessened at the forest's edge. The women were close, and soon the camp would be in sight. But, would they have enough time?

■ ■ ■ ■ ■ ■ ■ ■

Belle kept a hand on Jim's shoulder as they walked. Normally she was a girl of few words, but she always carried her emotions on the collar of her shirt. Through odd looks or a glance of her eye, Jim had learned to discern her thoughts. She stared past the looming campground. William nudged the girl's arm. The horse must have sensed ill feelings as well. Once the enormous nose brushed against her shoulder, however, Belle's concern faded and became reassurance.

Jim stared enviously at her, for she was one of them. With each step he took towards the camp, a certain doom permeated in his heart. Blood pounded throughout his head. The others would surely hate him or fear him at the least. They would ask questions, so many questions that he would have no way to answer. It would never be the same. The small acceptance that had blossomed between Hero and human would shrivel back into a cautious seed. And Davey....

He could see them all sitting around the fire. They were a few miles away, but if he concentrated, he could make out the smiling faces of Davey and Shell as Bazzer and Prince danced for their enjoyment. Those smiles would flee once they heard his footsteps. The dancing would stop, the fire would dim, all would grow dark. This was a mistake. They hadn't seen him yet, maybe he could turn back before his presence destroyed their happiness.

William nuzzled Jim's hand with her snout. The hot air from her nostrils spread a heat against his fingers. He shook his head, losing sight of the wagon and clearing all thoughts of running.

"Thanks, William." Jim patted the horse on her head.

Once Jim's hand fell back to his side, William trotted ahead happily. Jim would follow her, go into that camp and face the questions. He would apologize and leave it in the hands of fate. If worse came to worse, he would leave and never speak their names again.

The sun was falling through the darkening sky. Aisley would be starting on a dinner now, and Emma would be returning soon. It would be good to see her.

He concentrated on the camp again, hoping to see the girl's emerald eyes beginning to ease the woes of the day. But there was no fresh beast lying on the slaughter table, no sign of Bren, no Emma. Surely, they hadn't returned. He scanned the wall of trees besetting them, the forest that had swallowed Emma this morning, and....

"Belle," Jim said urgently. "Send William down the path to the forest."

The girl spoke no words to the Hero, only looked at the horse and asked, "Will you do as he said?"

The horse turned, peering in the same direction as Jim. Then, with a loud whinny, bolted towards the tree line. Jim swept Belle from her feet, placed her arms snuggly around his neck, and sprinted after William's tail.

He kept his eyes concentrated as he ran, kept his gaze glued at the tree line. Suddenly, Emma and Bren emerged from the thicket. He could feel the wrongness emanating from their direction, a sensation he had honed as an assassin, which grew stronger as their frantic feet drove them forward.

■■■■■■■■

*Thank the Gods Belle sent her horse.* Emma's drained arms snagged William's neck and dragged her on to the animal's saddle. Bren leaped on behind her, keeping Emma's form solid. They would reach the camp in minutes.

Emma watched as Jim reached the camp. Belle held tight to the Hero's neck, her hair disheveled and eyes wild. Jim shouted to alarm the camp. She saw Davey peer down the forest path. He waved his hands in distress, calling out a few orders. In no time a small contingent of the family, headed by Davey, grouped at the foot of the path.

"Heroes!" cried Emma, her breath fogging with dragon smoke as she yelled.

Jim and Davey exchanged understanding nods. Even through bleary eyes Emma could see the silent relief that washed over Jim, at that small show of comradery.

Jim. So many secrets, so much pain revolved around her Hero. What kind of monster was he before they met? She had to watch him; she knew that now. Had to make sure that no one else suffered because of him. But did that change who she believed him to be? The man she had fought with, who had nearly died protecting her, for seemingly no reason. Was that real, or was it just another lie that created the mask of a man?

It didn't matter now. Rather, for the sake of keeping her spirits high, it didn't matter *yet*.

Bren shouted, "A patrol is coming. Pack up!"

People became a blur of motion. Prince and Bazzer ran alongside Aisley, throwing their miscellaneous belongings into the back of her cart. Aisley yelled crude instructions, then she began the monotonous task of attaching her horses to their harness. Jim helped Davey and Shell pile tools and supplies into the back of their wagon. Belle busied herself by collecting and distributing weapons.

Emma found herself running towards Davey's wagon. Shell pulled her inside as the horses began to move, following Aisley's cart through the grassy plain.

She looked towards the front. Jim rode with Davey, his eyes fixed on the shielding trees. He clasped a dagger in each of his hands. They wouldn't be much use at this distance, but the sight of the weapons made Emma feel safe.

But the feeling of security was short lived when the Hero's eyes grew and he yelled, "Arrows!"

· · · · · · · · ·

Two bolts struck the side of Davey's wagon, causing splinters to fly from their punctures. Warning shots. It was protocol for the first shot to be a warning, an instruction for the target to stop. The next shot would be for blood.

Jim watched the patrol step from the trees. Two archers among them, only two bolts to avoid at a time. He offered thanks that this was a first wave patrol, carrying only lightweight bows instead of heavy snipers and other rifles. If the wagons had to evade a fusillade of bullets, their escape would have already ended. The Heroes pulled back on their draw-strings, and arrows flew again.

Jim calmed, all senses concentrating on the wood and metal that wished to bite at the flesh of this newfound family. The arrows would target the driver. That would be the easiest way to stop their fleeing prey.

Jim took in a breath, hearing the whistling of the bolts. His eyes were sharp as they brushed over the magnificent firmament until he spotted them. They were only dots, moving swiftly through the air. One was aimed at Davey, but the other would pierce the wagon's canvas.

"Heads down," Jim said, not waiting for a reply from those inside.

His hand shot out, his dagger cutting through the thick air. The arrow's steel tip bounced against his blade, harmlessly falling to the ground. Shell's gasp at the Hero's skillful display of coordination was interrupted when the second arrow cut through the canvas top and sank into the floorboards.

Jim looked again towards the Heroes. They saw their failed attack. They saw the Hero that denied their bloodshed. They took aim, and Jim knew he would be their primary target. Arrows flew.

He had to breathe, had to concentrate, as a barrage of metal rained from the heavens. At first, they came methodically, each archer taking their time only to have their careful darts thwarted in their paths by Jim's fluid blades. Then the darts began to fly rapidly, and Jim was forced to rely on instinct and reflex over his enhanced senses.

His daggers swept arrow after arrow from the sky, but they continued to fall anyway. The Heroes couldn't keep this up for much longer. The horses were moving quickly, and they would be beyond the range of the otherworldly archers soon. But still, the arrows fell.

Vibrations shook his muscles and undermined the sturdy grips that glued his hands to his weapons' hilts. He could feel the heat of the sparks that jumped when the metals collided and smell the molten scent that blacksmiths carried in their clothes. Sweat cooled his chest as he maneuvered among the sharp hail.

He couldn't see anymore, not in the way he usually saw. Everywhere around him was dark and blurry. Only the death that tried to strike at him stayed in focus. His world was a song of the whistling sky and the clanging sound of steel meeting steel. The song was growing louder, faster, as time passed, and so the dance forced his tempo into a flurry of frenetic flight that nearly caused him to hover in the air above his small perch at the driver's box. His heart tried to match the rhythm, beating forcefully through his overly-exerted arms.

And then the dance stopped.

The sky cleared. The danger quieted. The world grew around him again.

He focused on the patrol shrinking in the distance. They looked defeated by the lone man; their frustrated knuckles whitened on the wooden shafts of their weapons. Jim smiled in victory.

The large woman he had met before—Helmet, Emma had called her—cried angrily at her subordinates. She kicked one of the archers into the dirt and grabbed his bow. She had three arrows in her muscled hand, three more shots that Jim had to avoid.

In one motion Helmet released an arrow, then another, and another. Her arms moved so fast, pushing each of the deadly gifts into the clouds as one. Jim pushed into his calm again, focusing on where the arrows were going to strike.

The familiar whistling rang through his ears and his blades danced with their soaring opponents. One: his dagger cut the wooden shaft in half. The sharp arrowhead cut through his shirt and stuck into the boards at his feet. Two: the arrow's tip met the edge of his blade. Reverberations shook Jim's arm and shoulder as the dart was deflected towards the soft swaying grass. Three: his dagger flew across the sky and collided against...nothing.

No third presence met the end of his weapon. No final enemy flying at him from the vast sky. No third arrow.

*Pain.* He felt it, from somewhere. *Pain.* It was unusual, he had felt the familiar heat many times before, but this time felt...different. *Pain.* This was pain, yes, but it wasn't his. It came from somewhere else, that place inside that felt those foreign things. *Pain.*

Jim flashed into reality when the familiar sticky warmth of blood splashed against his hand. At his side he found the third arrow, lodged deep in Davey's throat.

"No." Jim's word made no sound as he fell to his knees.

His hands and his eyes met Davey's. He felt his pain, his regret, his sorrow. He could hear his own blood pumping on to the hard ground. And he felt cold. So cold.

Ice swallowed the man, torturing him and painting his eyes black. *You are right for this place.*

■■■■■■■■

So much blood. Jim was holding Davey, the Hero's torn shirt soaking the blood that poured from a pierced throat. Emma stared in shocked disbelief at the dying man. *This can't be real.* She exhaled, and her breath became smoke in the suddenly freezing air.

*Once, we were dragons.* Davey had told her that. *That's why sometimes we breathe smoke. It's our dragons reminding us that we are strong.* She spent that night breathing hard, trying to force flames from the dragon that lived inside her belly. Davey laughed so hard when a gnat flew into her opened mouth and gagged the fire-breathing child. *I guess your dragon was hungry.*

She watched Davey's nostrils, his shallow breaths smoking in the dusky light. This man had encouraged her to believe in dragons and love, had made her laugh even after her mother died. The man who became her family, her father, in a world that had stolen hers away. She watched, as his chest stopped rising and his smoke stopped flowing. And her world became empty.

## 13: THE PERSISTANT MAN

The wagon felt slow. The horses kept their galloping pace, but through Jim's eyes they moved through water. Each step, each beat of their hooves, was drawn through time in a heavy and uneven rhythm.

Dark clouds hid the moon and the stars, causing the deep night to become as black as pitch. They had traveled far enough. No Hero could catch them without mounts of their own, but Jim forced the small caravan to go just a little farther. *There is a safety in distance.*

His eyes burned from somber exhaustion. Hidden in the shadows of the covering, Shell and Emma didn't make a sound. They ought to be sleeping, but Jim knew no rest would come for the shattered family. Not tonight.

And Emma...She refused to look into his eyes when he gently placed the body at her feet. Her eyes locked in on the man's still features. A ferocity welled inside her. Anger and pain and emptiness consumed her. He had to leave her alone before his guilt fed her growing monster. So, he sat now, steering the horses into a clearing between trees that would serve as their sanctuary for the night.

Light beamed from above, illuminating an area of purple flowers and tall green grass. It was the only place blessed by the moon's bright touch in the harsh night. This place would offer them safety. The wagon slowed to a stop, Aisley's cart beside it, and their torturous escape was over.

Jim jumped from his perch and went about releasing the horses from their harnesses. It was a mundane task and a needed distraction. But, for now, the horses would save him. Afterwards he would need to build a fire and search for a meal. He was sure he could help in one of

Shell's projects or carve one of Bren's fresh kills. There was a plethora of necessities that needed completion before...

"Jim?" It was Aisley's voice.

He looked up from his task and met her gaze. She didn't know yet; her life was still whole. But as her eyes wandered down from his face, saw the blood, *his* blood, her expression contorted to the question that Jim feared most.

"What happened?"

Jim looked at the ground and said, "Davey..." But he couldn't say more. The name was thick in his mouth. It felt cold and wrong when said aloud.

Aisley's scared expression told Jim that she didn't need to hear more. She ran towards the wagon, towards the rest of her family, and beheld the awful truth that sat inside.

Jim took a step forward before an intense wave of sadness knocked him to the ground. He stayed sitting in the tall grass, hiding from the mourning family. Their guilt and their terror blurred his vision, causing spots to appear in his peripherals.

He stood suddenly, frantically looking for a reprieve from his nightmare. A grove of trees sat outside of the moonlit meadow. It was dark there, concealing. He moved towards the gnarled limbs. Each step took him away from those foreign emotions of the family. Each step brought relief.

He walked as deep into the trees as he could. The people behind still existed, still radiated their somber stories at him. But it was smaller here, leaving room for his own mind to dispel its pain.

He pulled his dagger from its sheath. The whining leather shook the reverent grove, another wonderful distraction from the screams of his inner voices. He stared at the blade. *This blade failed me. It killed...*

No.

Jim swung the dagger at the trunk of the nearest tree. It bit wood hungrily as chunks of bark flew from the base.

He swung again, forcing the steel halfway into the soft insides of the tree. Sap spewed from its wound. *Bleeding, the tree is bleeding from its throat. Staining your soul for your...*

No.

The tree fell from his final attack. The crackling sound of branches breaking and the thunderous thud as the giant fell silenced his thoughts. It was a temporary quiet, only lasting long enough for the small woods to settle and the world to calm. Then the voice spoke again. Spoke its guilty lies and unaccepted realities.

Jim felled another tree.

■ ■ ■ ■ ■ ■ ■ ■

Davey's body sat in the middle of the family. It was so odd to see his features stay still, stony in expression, instead of his usual warm smile. It was just an empty vessel that lay in their midst. So why couldn't she speak? Why did it feel like shadowy walls were closing in around her? Why was it becoming so hard to breathe in this suffocating stillness?

Emma couldn't stand it. The silence, the sadness, it was becoming too much. She had to break it, move past it, somehow. But she felt restricted. She was bound in immobile chains, forced to live in this place where he lay.

Dead. He was dead. And she didn't help him. She couldn't, but she should have. Instead she had left his life in the hands of that Hero. Her Hero, she had thought. But who was he really? What was his intent in pretending to save the humans that surrounded him? Maybe he was also just a vessel, a husk that held the hands of death and released them on the vulnerable.

The stories all pointed towards that truth. He had caused the death of her first family, and now he was striking at her second. He would run rampant over those she loved if she didn't stop him. The body in front of her was proof.

Shell spoke. "You know, Davey asked me to marry him only a week after we met. Bren, Bazzer, you were there. Although you were so young at the time, so you might not remember. I told him 'no'. Not for lack of feeling, but my beliefs tell of one, and only one, forever bond." She stopped for a breath to compose. "I thought that my late husband held that bond, but Davey was so relentless. He kept asking me, day after day, and I kept telling him 'no'.

"He wrote me poems and picked me bouquets of wild-flowers, such a silly man. But he fractured my denial, made me remember what it was like when love begins to grow. Then he got that lute, that damned lute." She let out a small laugh echoed by several of her children. "All he did was pound at its strings and play sour songs from sun up until sun down. He didn't' have a musical bone in his body in those first days.

"My head was pounding at day three, and I demanded his silence on the fourth. But when the music stopped my heart began to sink. I tried to live with the quiet, but I couldn't last an hour. The look on that man's face when I asked for a song...." Shell choked on her words. "He won. I was in love. And although we never married, I know he is my forever bond."

Shell fell into silence and the darkness returned, driving Emma towards madness. She wished for Jim's presence. Wished that he was here to comfort her, stop the emotion from clenching her throat. But no, of course he wasn't here when she needed him. He disappeared the instant he made trouble. The damn moronic Hero. The man who forced himself into her life only to tear it all apart. The man....

Prince killed the silence with his story. It was a tale of a boy learning how to wield a knife from the man who missed his sons. Prince told of how frustrating it became when the blade refused to do as his mind wished. He spent hours working on his stances and trying to change his technique into one that suited him best. But he could never get the hang of it.

One day it all felt like too much. Prince fell to the ground and wallowed in his failure. He stuck the tip of his knife into the dirt to quench his anger. It was something he always did to relax. He would try and focus on an image in his head that expressed what he was feeling. Then, he would trace that image into the dirt, thrusting it out of his mind and into the ground.

It wasn't until he had finished his drawing and finally calmed down that he noticed Davey standing over his shoulder. The man was awestruck at Prince's creation and exclaimed, "No wonder you're no good with a knife! Your hands are meant to create, not destroy!" The next day Davey used all the money he had to buy Prince a glistening canvas and a few tattered brushes.

Prince was in tears as his story ended, and Emma feared the silence that was sure to return. But before doom took hold, Aisley spoke her memory.

Her tale had Emma laughing, though hot tears still ran from her eyes. She spoke of when she had caught Davey and Bren trying to surprise her with a cake for her birthday. They had made a royal mess of her inventory and burned the pastry to ashes. They then sang the loudest celebratory song they could manage and watched as Aisley took a bite. It was the best birthday she ever had. But, when she saw the destruction that they had left in their wake, she swore and made them promise to never cook again.

It was a brief story, but it was perfect. It was what everyone needed in that moment. A little laughter that fought for purchase inside of them.

Belle talked next. She talked of the day Davey found her and William. William insisted the man ride her after only an hour of traveling. It was an odd request from the horse, but William always got what she wanted. Davey rode ahead and spoke sweetly to the mount, and when they returned, she insisted that he call her Billy.

"Can you believe that?" Belle said, exasperated. "It only took a day for her to allow Davey to call her Billy! It took me months! Sometimes I think she's more of an ass than a horse," Belle muttered, and William whinnied behind her.

Bazzer said how kind Davey always was. He would always volunteer to be the first to watch a performance or rate him on an act that he was practicing. When others had wished for Bazzer's silence, Davey demanded he continue and gave an uproarious applause at the conclusion.

Then there were only two who remained quiet. Emma still couldn't make a sound. Her mouth was dry, and her voice was elusive. The looming walls were returning as she fought to speak. Bren stepped forward and knelt next to Davey's body.

She placed a hand on his cheek and spoke so softly that Emma struggled to hear. "You found me, Davey. And you saved me. I will never forget you."

Black crashed into Emma. She couldn't catch her breath. She couldn't see. She couldn't feel anything. She turned and ran towards the trees.

■ ■ ■ ■ ■ ■ ■ ■ ■

A pyre built by the heir to a great Hero house. That is what Jim created from the splintered trees. He placed each branch carefully, hoping to honor the man who had accepted him as family. It was all he could do with his rage and guilt. He piled them high and planned to set them aflame and release them from his mind.

A powerful, strange emotion appeared from behind. It was filled with an empty, angry sorrow that Jim felt in his entirety. It came closer and closer, crashing through the brush with reckless intent. The possibilities of what it could be only occurred to Jim when Emma stepped into view and her emeralds finally met his gold. She needed to release her emotions. She needed to hurt someone else the way that she was hurting. And she found her perfect target.

She said, "How could you just leave? We were all together, the last time we will all be together. And you just left? Is that who you are, Jim?" Her anger grew. "A runner? A coward who flees from the people who need you most? That's it, right? That's who you are. You ran tonight just like you ran from Ellie. Didn't you, Jim?"

He stumbled backwards. She didn't mean what she was saying. She couldn't. But the results of her attack hit Jim harder than anything he'd experienced.

"That's all you do, Jim. You leave those who need you. You left your family, your home. You left Bren all alone. You left him…." She cut her words off sharply. "You should have left me too."

Emma's rage burned white on her visage. It took all Jim had to force his retaliation into submission. He had known that anger before, unleashed it on those who didn't deserve his hatred. And, somehow, he needed to stop hers before her fire consumed everything she knew.

Jim reached towards the center of the pyre and pulled two sticks from its belly. They were light and green and about the length of his arm. These would do.

"So, this is what you were doing?" Emma continued, "building the stage for his final moments. What were you going to do, watch the flames from the shadows before you left forever? Or were you at least going to look at the man you killed one last...."

Jim's branch slapped hard across Emma's jaw. The girl fell to the ground, shock stinging her as much as the red that marked her face.

He threw the second stick at her feet and said, "Hit me."

Her anger flared again after the shock. "Hit you? That's your answer? You think that will make me forgive you for...."

He smacked her again, knocking the girl to her back. She pushed herself up and grabbed the stick at her feet.

Their weapons whipped through the air. He matched the pace she set, forcing her to focus on catching his branch. Her rage still flared, but with each collision of their sticks he felt it dissipate. Emma moved faster, and Jim did the same. She winced when he caught her on the arm and pushed herself into fiercer attacks.

"He was a father to you, wasn't he, Emma?" Jim asked as he swung at her neck.

"Shut up!" She caught his branch easily and retaliated with a flurry of strikes.

Jim continued to match her blows and push back with an equal attack. She stumbled on the foliage and Jim delivered her a sharp crack on her thigh.

"He's gone now, Emma. You have to accept it, or it will swallow you whole."

Her rage exploded. "No!" She yelled and pushed the Hero back with a quick succession of strikes.

Her thoughts were clearing, he could feel. But she rose in intensity while they fought. Jim pushed himself to meet her pace, struggling to match the speed and flow of his opponent. She landed a hit on his elbow, then another across his chest. She continued a barrage, fueled by anger and loss, and forced the Hero to retreat.

She reeled her arms back and put all her strength into an attack aimed at Jim's cheek. His branch shattered, and her sharp wood knocked him to the ground.

Jim sat stunned, Emma glaring down upon him. They stayed like that for minutes, each gazing at the other but neither knowing what came next. Blood ran from Jim's lacerated cheek. He could feel its warmth drip down his arm.

"I'm sorry, Emma." Tears ran from his eyes, and his regret made a clear impression on her.

She offered her hand to the fallen man, and he felt relief due to her simple acceptance. But she didn't pull him up. The moment his hand met hers, she fell into the Hero. Her arms wrapped around his neck and they embraced entirely.

She looked into his eyes and spoke. "I'm so sorry, Jim. I don't know what to do. I don't know who I am. I feel so lost. Please forgive me." She sobbed. "What I said…I didn't mean it, but I just needed to…."

Jim's lips found hers. And she knew that everything was going to be alright.

• • • • • • • • •

The pyre burned hot and brightened the dark night. They all stood around the flames, watching as the man who brought them together turned to ash. Jim stood at Emma's side, his hand protectively resting on her hip.

It was time.

"I never had a father," Emma said. "My mother told me he was an evil man and wanted nothing to do with him, so it was just me and her for as long as I can remember. So, when Davey found me, I was careful. It took him days to convince me to come back with him, meet the family that he found. But he was persistent. He saw how much help I wanted. He saw that he could be the man that I needed, the father that I never had. And he was. Thank you, Davey. I'm going to miss you."

Jim's hand tightened comfortably around her, and an accepting silence surrounded the family. Emma watched the smoke rise from her father's fire. And, as her eyes found the sky, she could swear that she saw a dragon rise towards the heavens.

## 14: THE WILLOW CITY

The road to Salix was well traveled. The rutted paths swallowed the cart's wooden wheels, pulling it towards the large city. The towering walls stood in the distance, draping the eastern plains in an ever-growing shadow. A light breeze carried the smell of smoke as the day waned and a chill swept the land. Thousands of small fires were kindled to combat the frigid cold of night and light the sleepless streets.

The gates would close the moment the sun vanished. Travelers and traders would be trapped outside the safe city and forced to fend off the monsters who hunted the vulnerable few. Each night, hundreds of people were left under the moon's gaze, and by morning, less than a dozen would remain standing.

Jim rode with his hood drawn over his head, keeping the dropping temperature from biting his ears, and hiding his face from curious onlookers. Emma sat at his side drawing aimless circles across his thigh with the tip of her fingers. Bren and Aisley dozed in the spice-filled cart, exhausted from the day of travel.

Shell had taken Prince and Bazzer with her that morning. She planned to travel East, to Indrasmos for the night, then towards the base of the Eastern Mountains until they gathered again. Belle departed too, giving Jim an awkward hug before climbing onto William and galloping South. Her plans were unknown, which, Emma told him, was not unusual.

Aisley hoped to sell some of her expiring goods and stock up on the rare ingredients offered in Salix. So, here they sat. The remainder of the fractured family, heading towards the largest city in the Willow territory. They would make it by nightfall, only just, and stay in the slums until tomorrow.

A bed, that's all Jim really wanted. A feather pillow and fluffy mattress would ease the burden caused by so much extended travel. He smiled at the thought of Emma sleeping beside him, carefree for the first time since they met. *True paradise rests in the eyes of a lover.*

There was only one more obstacle that blocked a restful evening: the guards of the gate. They would have been informed to watch for a Hero on the run by now. They would surely speak of his presence to their superiors. But he had a plan.

They were nearing the gate. He would need to split from the cart before watchful eyes observed his secretive movements.

Jim tapped Emma on her shoulder. "There is a tavern in the Low District, The Silver Nail. I will meet you there by sun-up." He whispered and handed her the reins.

She gave a look of concern but nodded at his instruction. "Just...be careful."

Jim smiled at the blush that painted her cheeks. "Of course."

He jumped from the cart and ducked below the tall grass that lined Salix's exterior. He would meet her in the safety of the city. He would rest his hand upon hers and fall into the world of dreams in a soft, warm bed. But first, he would find the man that he needed to kill.

□ □ □ □ □ □ □

A crack ran up the corner of the Eastern wall. He had noticed it the last time he visited Salix, noted the small weakness in its protection for the next time he wished to visit undetected. Night had conquered the bright day, giving Jim the shadowy cover that he required. He placed one hand into the coarse stone and began to climb.

Exhilaration flooded Jim's stomach as he rose from the ground. He always felt free while climbing. He would scale the walls in Paradise as a child, peer over the lands that his people swore to protect. A warm breeze would flow past his ear and carry his hair through its current.

His mother scolded him, somehow knowing that he had made the dangerous ascent. *There is nothing worth dying for that lies beyond those heights. If you fall...not even one of us could survive.* He had fallen, only once. Landed among the trees in a frozen winter. And he never looked back.

This climb was different from those of his memory. The wall felt more fragile than the guardian of the Heroes. He stumbled, twice, due to handholds that crumbled to dust when his fingers gripped their edges. And the breeze was cold as it pulled at his hair and nipped the tips of his ears. But still, he felt free.

The top of the wall came quicker than expected. The taut muscles in his arms and hands began to warm up when his fingers brushed the smooth wood that lined the inner wall. He dropped below the stone and waited for the guards to make their rounds.

He looked back while he waited. Though the night was dark, the beauty of the land still dazzled in Jim's irises. Different shades of dark purple and blue formed the cascading landscape that stretched into the forest. The trees held no individual shape. They all meshed together as one large fog with a looming obelisk standing in its center. Paradise.

Jim forced his eyes from the monumental city. He could barely make out the silhouette of the Eastern Mountains from this distance. The ever-snowy peaks reached towards the sky, brushing the clouds and grasping at the stars.

That is where Shell was heading. But why? Jim had hiked the trails that lead to the mountain's perilous peaks. He swam in the warm spring that bubbled from the snows. Did Shell intend to climb, or was Elodin, the city at the base, her only destination?

"...pulled her right from the grave. I saw it m'self!" said a slurring voice. "I don't know if he's a man of the Gods, or the blasted devil!"

Another voice intervened, getting closer as the conversation continued. "I've been to his sermon. He spoke too soft for me to hear, but I could see light dancing around his head." This voice was high in pitch, whiny almost. "Brought tears to my eyes when I saw him. He couldn't be a devil!"

"T'was a figure of speech." The slurring voice again. "I know he ain't no devil. A blind man could see that!"

"But blind men can't see."

The voices started to move away, "I know they can't see! T'was another figure of speech!"

"You need to clarify what you say, Lez. I've known you my whole life and I still don't know what you mean most of the time." The voices faded as they passed.

Jim stayed still, silent, as he waited. He breathed lightly and listened to the crumbling wall. Nothing. It was time. Jim placed his hands above the wall's edge and pushed through the wooden scaffolding.

Burning torches ran along the creaky walkway. Jim felt exposed in their flickering light, a fox amongst hens. He crouched quickly and looked for his route out of the light.

The sleeping city was dark and quiet. The vague textures of slated rooftops and bricked, smoking chimneys invited Jim to their perches from below. The drop from this height would be loud—not to mention it would probably shatter most of the bones in his legs. So, he continued his search.

Multiple guard towers connected the wooden path, each with a winding staircase that opened at the base of the wall. But the pile of dead guards that he left in his wake would make his arrival apparent to everyone within earshot of the night watchmen's alarm, and Jim only wanted to spill one man's blood tonight.

Salix was always Floydd's favorite city. *The women are cheap, and the drinks are loose. Or was it the other way?* Jim's contracts usually took him to the Angeloak and Northtree territories, leaving the Willow contracts for Floydd's grimy fingers. He was sure to have an apartment or a favorite establishment somewhere within this city's walls. And Jim knew how to find those things that left a man vulnerable.

To Jim's right he saw the shrinking figures of the men that had passed him. He stayed crouched and stalked after them. Maybe he could use these men. They already proved to be God-fearing, maybe Hero-fearing as well. He pulled a knife from his belt and silently sped towards the unsuspecting guards.

As he came near, the figures took form. One of the men was short and pudgy; he had oiled-down hair that tangled tightly on his head. The other was a thin man who looked sickly next to his fat companion, and he walked with a small limp as if he was partly lame in his right hip. Their conversation became clear as the Hero stepped closer.

"So, if fire eats, then it must be alive?" said the thin man.

"Exactly, Brume! Are ye finally coming around to seeing my side?" asked the pudgy man.

"Lez, you get dumber as you drink. And you must have drunk a lot tonight," said Brume.

"You just don understand a good philosophy, Bru...."

Jim grabbed the pudgy man by his throat and placed the tip of his knife on the belly of the other. He made sure the terrified men saw his eyes, knew what it was that held them hostage in the night. The fat man, Lez, whimpered as Jim's hold tightened.

"Wha...what do you want?" asked Brume shakily.

"Do you know who I am?" Jim snarled.

"N...no," said the frightened man.

Lez grabbed frantically at the arm that held him in a vice. He tried to speak, but words couldn't escape the Hero's hold. The man's face had turned a dark purple and his eyes began to bulge.

"Do you have a guess? It seems your friend's life may rely on an answer," Jim boasted.

"Are you...are you a Northtree?"

Jim nodded.

"And you're here to meet with that Willow Captain?" Brume continued.

Jim nodded again, loosening his hold around Lez's throat.

"You weren't supposed to be here for another week. I'm sorry for our inept behaviors. There is a room below, in the Hero District, set aside just for you. I could go tell my commander now, and we can take you there right away!" Brume rambled apologetically.

"No, that won't be necessary," Jim said, releasing the fat man. "As far as the city is concerned, and this includes your commander, I will not be here for six more days." Jim sighed inwardly at his stroke of luck. "But I have use of you two."

The two men shot to rigid attention. Fearful sweat coated their foreheads, but Jim waited until they found the courage to meet his gaze. Then his lies began again.

"I will be monitoring the guards of this city. We have come to the realization that Salix is very under-protected, and the possibilities of a human coup are in the works. I have been following you two all night, and I have determined that you would never betray our people's trust. Am I wrong to assume that?" Jim asked.

"Of course not, sir!" Said Brume and Lez in tandem.

"Good. Now, this is where I need you. To get up here tonight I took... precarious measures. You will not find the bodies that I had to make, but you will note that I made it up here undiscovered." The men's eyes grew wide. "I wish to keep it this way. You will clear that tower of all men," Jim pointed at the nearest tower, "and ensure its vacancy until the announcement of my official arrival. Understood?"

Only Lez spoke this time. "Umm, yessir. But, how do you expect we get 'em all out?"

"Hmm." Jim said. "Perhaps I have the wrong men, after all." He reached towards the hilt of his dagger.

"Wait, sir!" Brume interrupted, "We can handle it! You have the perfect men for the job! Only one week? We can do that, right, Lez?"

Lez nodded weakly.

Jim smiled. "Good. How long will it take you tonight?"

Brume and Lez looked at each other and spoke quietly. Together they discussed possible routes of evacuation, the amount of men that were currently inside the tower, and the best way to keep the tower empty for an entire week. It was a daunting task, but the two seemed determined to impress the *Northtree* Hero.

"Give us...an hour. We'll have guards gone and the streets cleared below," Brume said impressively.

"An hour it is," Jim said happily. "And remember, Brume, I am not here."

Brume nodded and the pair ran towards the tower.

▫ ▫ ▫ ▫ ▫ ▫ ▫

Jim crept down the vacant tower. Bowls of steaming soup and half eaten bread littered the interior of its stone walls. Dripping candles plumed smoke throughout the freshly emptied rooms. No guards, no eyes, no informants. Jim raised his hood over his head and opened the large, wooden door that led to the outside.

An eerie silence captured the barren streets. In Salix there was always movement, no matter the depth of the dark. But tonight, here, Jim was alone.

Jim shook paranoia from his shoulder. In the true depths of solitude, the unseen eyes were his greatest enemy. If he was the only being walking through the night, he would be truly exposed. Therefore, he moved, blending with the shadows that ran along the winding roads, a raven darting behind bricks and chimneys. He cut through alleys and scaled over the low bars that separated the rich districts from the poor, keeping his senses sharp and frequently looking behind him to ease his suspicious nature.

As the streets grew dirty and cracked, they also grew busy. Life bloomed, slowly at first, but erupted into an anthill of chaos as he traversed the thinning streets of the Lower District. People here didn't have the luxury of leaving the streets. Hundreds were homeless and even more held grueling jobs that required their presence at all hours of the night.

Jim seamlessly joined the crowds of bustling people, hiding his eyes behind his hood. The poor never took kindly to Heroes. Everything about the other-worldly race spoke of wealth and power, the envy of the low. And envy led to drastic hatred.

Once, he had made the mistake of trusting the desperate: his first official contract, the first money that he would earn with the spilling of blood. The job took him to Hollow, the Angeloak's city of learning. Students were desperate for money, and for the first time Jim had gold to spare. He offered payment for the services of a few desperate men. They agreed to unlock the latch on a window that led to the third-floor library. They would then post themselves at the library's entrance while he extracted information from his target before his execution. It was a simple plan. Well thought out and intricately timed with the stations of the patrolling guards. But those desperate men saw an opportunity to gain.

They had left the window unlocked. But when the Hero stepped amongst the city of books, betrayal was clear. Half a dozen guards met Jim inside, not waiting for an explanation before attacking. He disbanded the men and found his target, cowering between the shelves. His time was up, his opportunity for information had ended. He killed the man as the sound of rushing boots filled the exterior hallways. Jim had fulfilled his kill, but he lost half of his bounty when he failed to deliver the location of his target's research.

A humiliating failure. Jim made sure never to relive that mistake. He only trusted those who had proved their worth, through trials and weeks of observed behavior. That day made Jim a distrusting man, and a much better assassin. The men who betrayed him were found a while later, their limbs strung about the very same library they had promised to post. Jim always repaid deception with detachment.

So he stayed hidden on the streets, just another citizen busily wandering to his predetermined destination. He felt grateful to his hood for blocking the frigid night. He wanted to put food on the table and provide a bed for his family. He was a human, just like everyone else.

Few people traveled the route that he chose. Many were leaving, but only a sparse amount headed toward the den of the city's crime. Here, no alley was safe, no coin purse was off limits. It was the place that bred thieves and created murderers. And in its center sat Waggon Wheel.

The rickety bar held the city's worst. The lowest of the low drank and schemed and gambled their earnings away. Middlemen auctioned contracts to the up-and-coming scum. They settled territory disputes within this haven of villainy. This was the place where violent actors came to truce for information bought and sold.

The small bar pulled on Jim's thread of direction, nagging at his inner compass. He took a breath before dawning the mask of the relentless Hero assassin and stepped through the double-doors. The Waggon Wheel would lead him to Floydd.

## 15: THE CONTRACT

Every city had a place like Waggon Wheel. Indrasmos had The Boiled Ham, Ketch had Everly Flight, even Paradise had The Burning Log. They came with many different names and offered a variety of different drinks and dishes. But they were all the same.

Gambling tables were always in the front, housing the suspicious figures with promises of winnings and friendly banter. A bar lined the side, empty seats cushioned for the illusion of a welcoming drink. Tables were placed in a large circle, perfect for betting on fights that would take place each hour. And the contractors sat in the back by the large metal doors that led to sound-proof rooms.

Jim headed towards the contractors, ignoring the deviously inviting smile that the card dealer gave while offering to buy him in for a round. A fight had recently ended, and victors were boasting merrily over their pot of prizes while losers moped and ordered large drinks. Jim stepped past the contrasting group, planting his eyes on the face of the nearest contractor.

The man's bald head shown in the nearby torchlight. His gaping mouth showed more holes bedded in his gums than teeth. He wore fine, jeweled rings on each of his fingers and thumbs, and sparkling earrings stuck through his lobes. A man willing to show his wealth in a place like this meant a man with power, or powerful friends. Either way, he would have what Jim wanted.

"Buying or selling tonight?" The man's voice oozed from between his teeth.

"Buying. Information, not contracts," Jim replied.

The man raised an eyebrow. "Ahh. And what sort of information are you searching for?" he asked deviously.

"I'd rather discuss that in private, Mister...?" Jim asked.

"Robert. Robert Still," the man said and motioned at the nearest door.

Jim began to move, following the bald contractor towards his secluded room. Robert kept his sinister smile painted on his round face. He knew the stories of Heroes and their piles of wealth, and he would use all his nasty tricks to squeeze every bit of gold from Jim's pockets.

"You're really going to trust a man named Robert?" A familiar voice spoke from behind Jim. "I mean, his name is literally rob and steal. I thought a Hero would be smarter than that."

Jim turned to the man. He was just under Jim's height with a large, beakish nose. He had an agile build supported by tight and toned muscles. The man wore tight-fitting clothing, but the Hero's trained eye spotted the indications of pistols and knives plastered closely to the man's body. Colter.

Colter winked at the Hero. "You could go with Robby tonight. Have all your questions sold to the next sack of coin that waltzes in. Or," Colter added as he walked towards the farthest room, "you could get the dead-man's discount with me. Your choice, Hero." His words snuffed as the door closed behind him.

Jim acknowledged Rob with a nod, then joined Colter in the padded room. Rob cursed.

□ □ □ □ □ □ □

"Took your time getting here." Colter said, offering Jim a glass of wine from the flask in the room's center.

"I had a few complications." Jim replied, his tone making it obvious that further prodding would lead nowhere.

"Fair enough." Colter sat and sipped at his drink. "There's a lot of talk about you, everywhere. Floydd hasn't been quiet about his...victory."

"I'll have to shut him up then."

"That you will."

"So," Jim asked, carefully keeping his voice steady, "where can I find him?"

"I...I don't know." Colter admitted. "But I know who does know. It's just..."

"At a price?" Jim asked.

Colter nodded. "I need to meet with him, but...for the meeting to even happen I need you to kill someone."

"A contract?"

Colter nodded again. "It's his terms. A meeting and a favor for a prepaid job."

"Just one kill?" Jim asked. "What's the catch?"

The smile of a trusted negotiator protruded from Colter's face. "You will need to complete it tonight. My information gets sketchy once the sun rises. And the seller was very specific about the state of the target's head. Namely, it must be removed."

Jim thought over the conditions. It would be a rushed job, but it would give him access to the answers he desired. And decapitation...it would be messy.

"Do you accept?" Colter asked the necessary question and extended his hand.

Jim reached forward and shook. "I accept."

The deal was made. A bond between contractor and assassin held tighter than the blood of family. Failure to complete his assignment would mean a failure to gain access to Floydd.

Colter quickly gave Jim the instructions he needed to find his target. He would be in the High-Born District, hopping from bar to brothel until the night was over. Tall man, purple cloak, cropped black hair, soon to be headless.

Jim rose from his velvet seat and moved to exit the room, but Colter's voice interrupted again. "This contract comes from...powerful people." He spoke to the Hero's back. "It's a death that may inspire significant retribution...So, be careful."

The echoed words radiated through Jim's mind. A promise to friend and the whisperings from a woman. Coincidental warnings often led to an eventful night.

The Hero stepped through the metal door, and his hunt began.

◦ ◦ ◦ ◦ ◦ ◦ ◦

Mason Gray was just as tall, and just as drunk, as Colter said he'd be. Jim had been watching the man for hours, learning his stumbling pattern as he bounced from drink to drink and lover to lover on the brightly lit streets of the High-Born District. And the man was loud. Laughing hysterically from his own comments, bragging boisterously to every barmaid about his large wealth and power, singing slurry songs at the starry-eyed and exhausted people that wandered passed him in the night; by the gods he was loud. But, very soon, the voice would sing its final stanza and fall into eternal silence.

The light didn't reach Jim's perch on the slated, clay rooftops from which he observed his foolish prey. He knew when to strike. It would be after Mason's time in the next bar and before his adventure to the brothel. The drunkard would wander into an isolated alley to relieve himself and leave his back to the watchful streets. It would be an easy execution, except for Mason's level of noise. With this boisterous but traceable prey, Jim had to loosely play it by ear.

As if on cue Mason emerged, new liquor warming his belly, and Jim moved. The Hero sprinted across the clay shingles of adjacent rooftops, leaping the small distances that separated one house from the other. He stayed behind his target, far enough that an accidental misstep or dropped shingle would go unnoticed by the babbling man.

And then he saw the sign. Mason's head tilted from side to side, checking for a private place to piss. He stumbled towards the nearest wall, leaning his entire weight on to his outstretched hand. The wall guided him to a separation, a small, dimly-lit alleyway.

Mason hummed to himself, shouting occasional words of a song, as he went about his business. Jim descended from the rooftop; the stones of the alley were solid below his padded feet. He drew a dagger from his side, the sharp steel glinting from the gas-powered lamps that lined everywhere in the rich districts. He pulled his arm backwards and swung a powerful arch towards the man's neck.

Before blade bit body, Mason moved. He ducked, quickly, dropping to his belly and rolling to a low crouch. The drunkenness from his eyes was gone in an instant as he reached for the pistol faintly outlined underneath his shirt. A gun would change things. Bullets would fly faster and hit harder than anything in the arsenal on Jim's body. He had to strike again, before Mason drew his weapon.

Jim pushed forward with another sweeping strike, letting fly, with his opposite hand, a knife from its holster. Mason ducked to avoid the obvious swing, his pistol clutched tightly in his hand. The Hero's thrown knife pierced the flesh under Mason's hip, however.

The man cried in pain and shakily shot his gun where he expected his killer to be. The deafening bang rang through Jim's ears and the heat from a bullet grazed past his cheek. Jim dropped to a roll, still advancing on the bleeding man. Mason readied another shot, his finger hugging the tight trigger. But Jim was upon him.

The Hero's roll ended, placing Jim face-to-face with the future corpse. His dagger's edge cut the soft flesh of Mason's forearm, and the gun clacked on to the pavement. When Mason saw the face of his attacker, saw the Hero that would seal his fate, his face grew…peculiar.

Jim saw the strange expression. Fear? Recognition? Prayer? They all felt right, but the unusual sight fueled an uneasy feeling in the Hero's chest. Jim inhaled; time felt slower in his calm place. He studied Mason's face, his eyes, his fear, consuming him entirely in the elongated breath. But the moment needed to end, the humanity that emerged from Jim would be quelled, and the man who caused it would fall. He exhaled, his blade soared, and blood rained from the sky.

The Hero turned his back, hearing a thump as his target's head fell from the heavens. His job was done, his contract fulfilled. But a piece of it felt…wrong.

He reached for the disarmed gun, turning the intricate weapon in his hands. It was bright with shiny silver and wooden handgrips. Some skilled artisan sketched rose bushes and vines, intricately entwined, around a fallen tree. It was beautiful, an artful weapon made by a master craftsman.

Jim turned the weapon over, looking for the makers mark, and his anger grew. He knew the mark, an ancient oak with branches lined with winged women and children. The mark of the Angeloaks. A weapon with this mark was only awarded to those born within the Angeloak lineage. And if this man really was a human, that meant....

Jim placed the gun on his belt and went to examine Mason's body. It would be on his arm, if Jim's horrors were correct, one of the brands of the Hero family. Each child was awarded a brand on their tenth year, burning a permanent promise into their flesh for the world to see. It was an honor to most, but a shame to Jim.

As an heir, Jim gained the brands of all four of the 'guardian' families. He remembered the blistering burn that marked his arm and crisped the air. It had caused an incredible pain that shook through his spine and left him bed-ridden for days. But he was so proud to hold the binding promise that kept the four houses strong. The pain was almost worse the day he removed the brand with his own molted knife, but at least it was warm.

Jim lifted the headless body's sleeve, and his stomach sank when he saw the same brand that marked the gun. Mason was an Angeloak, a Hero-born human bastardized by the beliefs of the backwards people. He would have been expelled from Paradise, like all bastard Heroes when they came of age. A distinct slash had been added to the brand, marking Mason as a Fault. A Hero in birth but not in body.

*She can be marked, but it will be different from yours, Jim. Do you understand why?*

Rage frothed in Jim's throat. He screamed angrily at the black sky, forcing his fury from his lungs. He got to his feet. If Colter knew...

The Hero, dripping in blood, walked back to the Waggon Wheel.

▫ ▫ ▫ ▫ ▫ ▫ ▫

"Jim?"

Colter's voice seemed far away as the Hero threw him into the private room. Colter slammed against the wall, slumping on to the carpeted floor. He staggered to his feet, but Jim was upon him again. He gripped the man by his neck and pinned him to the wall.

A knife brandished in Jim's hand. He didn't remember unsheathing the blade, but it was welcome to the Hero's throbbing peripherals. The pressure of a gun barrel pressed into his stomach. Colter must have drawn it when he was lying on the ground.

Jim stopped his assault. He needed to be alive to find revenge, to find the reason why the contract had been targeting a Fault. He took a calming breath and stared through Colter's eyes.

"Don't think I won't shoot you, Jim. If it comes to it, I'll...."

"Who was he?" Anger seethed from Jim's voice.

"Ah, using your words now. Very professional of you, Jim." Colter struggled through his restricted throat. "Why don't you put me down and we can talk."

"Who?" Jim yelled.

Colter glanced away. It was a brief moment, a subtle movement, a tell. The glance was his way of saying that he knew more than he was willing to disclose. Jim tightened his grip, his message clear.

"I can't...tell you, Jim...there are rules..." Colter gasped.

"Damn the rules!" Jim dropped Colter at his feet.

The man collapsed, breathing heavily and rubbing his throat. Jim pulled the fine blade of his knife across his palm. Crimson pooled in his hand and dripped down his arm. Jim knelt and smeared his blood across Colter's face. The humiliated man froze.

"I ought to slit your throat from ear to ear," Jim said.

Colter's eyes grew wide. "Just like that? You'd be willing to end this, kill me, over a contract?"

Jim stared at the man. His unblinking eyes burning through his friend, gazing into the alley where Mason lay dead. Colter was trying to appeal to Jim's friendship, but Jim's spurned memories far outweighed that of kin.

"Fine then, Jim. Do it." Colter spat. "I can't tell you who ordered the kill. I am bound by my promises."

Jim stayed quiet for a long moment. Crusty blood caused his skin to itch. The stinging in his hand pulsed with his heartbeat. *I won't kill Colter, unless he knew* . Jim pulled Mason's gun from his belt and tossed it to his friend.

Colter admired the gun, bringing it close to his face to examine the beautiful carvings. Then he turned it over, saw the mark, and understanding flooded him.

"I didn't know," Colter whispered. "But I still can't tell you. I...there's more going on and...Ears where sound ought to be ignored."

"Fine. I'll take the payment you owe and collect another name later." Jim resigned.

Colter nodded. "Let me gather the information. And we should meet somewhere less...listening. Tomorrow?"

"Tomorrow," Jim agreed. "And I know just the place."

■ ■ ■ ■ ■ ■ ■ ■ ■

A creak disturbed Emma's light slumber. The Silver Nail was filled with creaks and groans, but in her fragile paranoia she had to make sure that nothing was amiss. She cracked open her eyes and peered over the dark room.

Bren and Aisley sprawled on the bed, deep in the safety of sleep. Emma swept her gaze across the room. There were many dark corners and crooked boards, but nothing was out of place. Then her eyes found the open window and the man that sat in its moonlight.

Jim was covered in dry blood. He was rubbing at his forearm, staring at the scarring that covered his flesh. His contemplation contorted his face, his breathing was deep and deliberate, and his pupils were dilated to near blackness.

It was a sight that made Emma gasp. He looked so rabid in his distraught state, a feral animal trapped in a looping cage. Perhaps she could alleviate him from himself.

Emma rose to her feet, her blankets wrapped tightly around her. She fell to her knees next to the Hero and stared intently into his eyes.

At first, he fought to look away, but recognition of her compassion stole him from himself. He blinked rapidly as he regained himself and opened his mouth to speak.

"Em...."

Emma pushed her mouth against his and pulled his head onto her chest, holding him tight.

"Sleep now. We will talk in the morning," she whispered.

And her Hero slept.

## 16: ANOTHER'S KNOWLEDGE

Jim sat in the dark, empty guard tower. An isolated paradise in the large city of noise. Colter would join him soon, tell him all the wrathful secrets that fueled the Hero's revenge. Today he would learn, plan, and set the dominos of death toppling towards Floydd.

The morning was odd. Emma had started some...uncomfortable conversations, tried prying into the pieces of Jim that were best left undisturbed. His only thought was seclusion, so he left and wandered the brightening streets until his thoughts drove him towards the lonely building that allowed him to think.

His thoughts were scattered. He remembered the words from the Divine Priests that frequented him in his youth. *Faults are bastards that are barely worth our attention. If the heavenly lords already denied them position within our ranks, why should we offer them patronage in Paradise? This holy city was made by Heroes and should remain a sanctuary only to we who are transcended.*

Outcries followed the preacher's unjust and hateful words. *Blood is what matters;* his father told the Priests. *This is a place of family. Just because some few don't share our golden marks doesn't mean they deserve banishment. All our houses have birthed humans, even the purest of our high-four. Right, Northtree?* The Ash house was strong then, filled with those who swore to protect unconditionally. They outnumbered the Willows and Angeloaks combined. But that was long ago, and now only Jim remained.

Three knocks sounded from the door before Colter entered. He wore his usual dark, tight clothing which hid the staggeringly large number of weapons strapped to his torso and limbs. Colter's left eye was bruised, and one side of his lip was swollen from being tossed around the night before. The man squinted in the dimly lit room, not noticing Jim until he blinked his eyes and adjusted to the darkness.

"Are we alone?" Colter asked while glancing around.

"Yes," Jim replied.

"Good."

Colter took the pack from his back and emptied its contents onto the table. Stacks of paper covered in intricate writings scattered. They were cyphered, Jim knew, in a language Colter had invented. But the Hero knew what the papers would say, and whose death they would gift.

"Alright, Colt," Jim said. "Give me Floydd."

■ ■ ■ ■ ■ ■ ■ ■

Emma stared out the window that decorated the wall of her little room. The day outside was bright. People walked briskly and chattered in jovial conversation. But, for her, the day felt gloomy.

Her Hero, the damned fool of a man. All she did was ask a question. *What happened last night?* His eyes got so shifty and he wouldn't sit still. He mumbled about a climb and some guards, then fell silent. Of course, she pushed further, what kind of person wouldn't have? *The blood on you is from the guards?* A shake of his head. *Then whose blood is it, Jim?* More mumbling, his answer just a spiraling mumble of babbling uncertainty. Then he left. His eyes darted from the window to the door the entire time he spoke. He left without waiting for Aisley to return from her cart with breakfast.

She didn't go after him, only stared in disbelief at the arrogant fool who sped past her shoulder. He would tell her eventually what bothered him, she hoped. Whatever fractured him last night, he would tell her. It must have been something significant, so tormenting that he couldn't conceal it behind his golden eyes. She couldn't lose anyone else; she wouldn't allow Jim to be consumed by himself. When he returned, they would talk, even if she had to smack him with every stick from a handmade pyre.

Behind Emma, the door swung open and Aisley stepped into the warm room. A heavy leather pack filled with various spices and marinated meats was strung around her back. In her hands, she held two steaming bowls of porridge. She looked around the room, confused to see only the solidary figure of her sister sitting in the sunlight. Her eyebrow scrunched in question, and Emma shrugged her shoulders in response.

Aisley plopped down next to Emma and handed her a bowl. She spooned a bite into her mouth and was pleasantly surprised by the hint of cinnamon on her taste buds. She greedily swallowed another bite, feeling the warmth from the food filling her empty stomach. She polished the wooden bowl, running a finger along its bottom and sides and licked off the remaining contents. *The world is less awful with a full belly.*

Aisley placed an arm around Emma's shoulder. "I've got a full pack and an empty purse. But, by the end of the day, I'd like to have a full purse and empty pack. I could use your help, if you would like the distraction," she said merrily.

Emma thought for a moment before replying. Her thoughts repeated with questions and worries she couldn't quell. Roaming through her imagination were golden eyes and cracking dry blood.

She shook her head. "A distraction would be good."

■ ■ ■ ■ ■ ■ ■

There was a lot of information hidden on the sheets scattered on the table. Days' worth of study and weeks' worth of stalking were written in black scratches of ink in Colter's enigmatic writing. Lofts and sanctuaries, frequently visited bars and brothels, houses of the higher-ups that owed favors to a crooked man: all delicately placed for the Hero to learn.

As the information grew and expanded, no weaknesses manifested. Floydd was as careful as he was despicable, always traveling with numerous bodyguards and hidden henchmen. His multitude of safe rooms were built like bunkers. Metal doors and sparse, bar-lined windows kept out the uninvited, and many heavily muscled men patted down the lucky few who had an invitation.

A sniper shot would be the easiest way to fell the man, but the plan was scrapped once Jim told Colter of the lightening belt. The belt was a reminder of Floydd's many friends. He had contractors and leaders who owed him personal favors. He could own cities and sell souls with the wealth and contracts he had made. He was frustratingly well-known throughout each of the Hero houses and all the human cities. But, with notoriety came enemies. Maybe that was the way to lead to his downfall.

"Who does he associate with most? Is there anyone we could buy?" Jim asked.

Colter shuffled through some papers and scratched the geometrical tattoo that lined him from wrist to shoulder. "No one obvious. Looks like he keeps in frequent contact with the nobility here in Salix. He visits a priest after each contract, and an orphanage in the Low-Born District, but there's no loyalty in religion or children. Floydd knows that." He fingered through a few more papers. "He owns half the city already. There isn't a bakery or bar that doesn't owe him favor in one way or another. Buying people is not a viable option. Perhaps we could set-up a fake contract and strike when he's outside these walls. What do you think?"

Jim hadn't heard the question. Something Colter had said tickled a piece of memory, surfacing in his consciousness. It was a time when Jim first met Floydd. He was only a naïve Hero, willing to trust whichever man his contractor chose. A well-earned lesson.

The mission was a complicated thievery. An old religious piece, a painting depicting Dom, the man who killed Death and brought about the Ages of Prosperity. Jim marveled at the beautiful, and ancient, drawing. But when Floydd saw it he scoffed and said. *Gods are a silly thing, and those who believe deserve whatever ill fortunes befall them.*

It ended in bloodshed. Somehow the sleeping owners had stirred and saw the two strange men carrying their prized possession. The contract was one filled with secrets, meaning they could leave no witnesses. The contractor congratulated them on a job well done. It hadn't gone according to plan, but nothing ever did when Floydd was around.

Colter was still speaking, naming off a list of people who owed their lives to Floydd. The list was long, but the names had all fallen on deaf ears. Jim cleared his throat, causing Colter to quiet.

"I want to know about the priest," Jim said.

"The priest?" Colter asked. "Alright." He searched through a few papers. "I don't have much on him. Floydd visits with him twice per week, when he's in town. Each Sabbath and a few days later for a personal communion. The meetings are a few hours long, but nothing unusual. The priest is squeaky, Jim. He talks a lot about Heroes, and seems to love The Time Before, but most of the religious folk do."

"Where can I find him?" Jim asked.

"Umm...I have a note here that the priest gives a sermon each day at noon. But, Jim, I really don't think he is our in."

Jim rose to his feet and headed towards the door. "Floydd hates God more than Heroes hate humans, Colt. Keep digging here. I'll meet you tomorrow."

Colter nodded, and Jim left the tower.

■ ■ ■ ■ ■ ■ ■ ■ ■

Carts filled with merchandise lined the overly crowded walkways. Merchants shouted their discounted prices. Customers bargained haughtily over everything from food to cloth. Jewelers and smiths boasted of superior products. And, most of all, money was exchanged. Patrons hoisted heavy coin purses to and from the marketplace. Baskets of bread and cheese filled empty hands with a week's worth of food. Patchy pants and ripped cloaks were exchanged for discounted prices on newer clothes. All around were hectic screams from hundreds of voices, and Emma heard them all.

She kept a wary watch on the multitude of people, guarding Aisley with her observations. A sneaky thief or a starving man would see the chaos of the streets as an opportunity for easy gains. It was a haven of potential wealth.

Bren walked beside them, replying to the light conversation that Aisley and Emma happily shared. Emma always thought their pairing was odd. They were entirely different in most ways but came together in a binding unity of love. *There are opposites everywhere, Em. The world needs opposition to balance out our lives: Night and day, snow and fire, valleys and mountains,* humans and Heroes.

"We need thread," Aisley said, "and cloth. Any color will do, but if they have a green that is fairly priced, get a bundle!"

"Alright," Bren said. "I'll be back in a moment." She stepped towards the motion of people and disappeared in the crowd.

"From you," Aisley said, turning towards Emma, "we need a new whetstone. And the sharpest carving knife you can find. Make sure it's a quality steel—they had painted brass last time I visited Salix. Tried to tell me it was sharper and stronger than any knife I had ever owned." She laughed. "So test it against your sword."

Emma nodded. "Should I wait for Bren to return? I don't want anyone seeing you alone."

Aisley laughed again. "This is my battleground, Em." She winked. "I'll be fine."

Emma hesitated, but when Aisley's look became stern she left towards the blacksmiths.

Lining one side of the street were half a dozen weapon racks. The weapons were organized in a pleasing manner, keeping the smallest on one side, knives and arrowheads, and graduating towards the largest on the other side, maces and iron shields. Emma sauntered past the shining metals, eyeing a few blades that would fit well with her rapier.

A large man stood amidst the racks. He had a bald head and wore the leather apron of a blacksmith. Soot was smudged on his face, obscuring his cheekbones and chin. He stood in a proud stance, daring any to question him about the quality of his work.

"I need a whetstone," Emma told the man.

He grunted in acknowledgement and walked towards one end of his makeshift shop. "'Ow big?" he asked with a thick northern accent.

"Knives mostly," she said.

He crouched, reached towards the bottom of a rack, and pulled out a whetstone a bit larger than his outstretched hand. He tossed it to Emma for examination. She ran her nail across its base. It was a trick she had learned from her mother: *if your nail leaves a mark in the stone it won't be hard enough for your steel*. No marking trailed her fingernail; the whetstone would work.

"Anythin' else?" the blacksmith asked.

"A knife. The best you have to carve a deer," she said.

He grunted again and walked a few paces down. Dozens of knives lined the racks. Most of the blades would be best to carry, but the variety of throwing and carving knives was impressive. The smith scratched at his naked chin, thinking, before he chose a knife from among the rack and handing it to his customer.

The blade was simple, silver steel with a leather hilt. "Can I test it?" Emma asked.

He nodded, and Emma unsheathed her rapier. She smacked the knife with her sword, causing a ringing to reverberate through the racks. She observed the edge of the knife and was pleased to see only a small dulled edge where her sword had landed. She put away her weapon with a content smile.

"What do I owe you?" she asked.

Instead of a price the blacksmith asked an awkward question. "Ye a fighter?"

He used a tone that conveyed neither mockery nor an attempt to dissuade, but simple curiosity.

"I suppose," she said hesitantly.

"Excellent." The blacksmith sounded pleased.

He walked towards the opposite end of the shop and stopped when he came to a wooden table. He reached below the table and pulled out a leather-bound package about the length of Emma's forearm. He gently placed the package onto the table and unfurled its contents. Four daggers reflected the sunlight on their polished blades. But, the rippling brown colors of the blade told Emma they were not made of steel, nor any metal that she had ever seen.

"Wood originally." The blacksmith answered Emma's unasked question. "I've been testin' a new technique. Normally petrified wood is brittle, too brittle ta be useful. But I've always been fond of wood, loved the circles that live inside 'em. So, I experimented, and these are my successes."

As he spoke, Emma lifted one of the weapons in marveled examination. The grips were lined with pewter dyed leather. The edge looked sharp enough to cut with only a look. But a weapon made of wood seemed dangerous in a world of metal and fire.

"It's a pretty dagger, but I don't think I'll—" she began, but the blacksmith cut her off.

"A test then." He grabbed the dagger and the carving knife from her hands and smashed them together.

A spark flew as the blades met, but the wood dagger held strong. The smith handed the weapons back to Emma, a proud smirk on his oily face. The wooden blade had no markings on its edge, but the carving knife's fine edge was now dented with a nasty looking gouge.

"How much?" Emma asked.

"The wood is a gold. For the other items…three silver."

"If you throw in a sheath for the dagger and a new knife, of course, I'll give you a gold for the lot." Even bewildered as she was, Emma still knew how to barter. "I'm not sure I want to spend more than that on a weapon you whittled."

The man scratched his chin in thought, calculating the price. "I can do that, but you ave' ta send any who ask 'bout it to me. And brag about the wood, eh?"

Emma smiled and tossed him his gold. "I will, mister…?"

"Elk," he said.

"Thank you, Mr. Elk," Emma said, and she exited his shop.

The new blade bounced against her thigh. The leather sheath felt awkward as she searched the streets for Aisley. Soon it would feel natural to her, another extension of herself resting against her leg. But for now it would draw her conscious attention.

The feeling of a new weapon always elated her. A new piece of protection against all those who wished her harm. Her gaze drifted through the crowd, looking for an excuse to brag about her newly acquired dagger, but what she saw caused her to stop.

Surrounded by a group of guards stood a Hero. He was heavily muscled with a pudgy face and a large, double-sided ax strapped to his back. Lumberjack.

Emma ducked into the crowd, blending perfectly with the waves of rushing humans. He was oblivious to her presence, but she knew that one glimpse of her could be her end. The Hero was moving, walking lazily through the parting people. Those who were foolish enough to stand in his way were berated by the guards and thrown to the ground to be trampled.

Emma followed, keeping a safe distance. Lumberjack wandered towards a building with a spire that reached for the heavens. Hundreds of people stood outside the building's doors, waiting. The Hero stopped when he reached the edge of the crowd, just as the noon bells began to chime.

The building's doors flew open, and from the dark interior stepped a priest.

■ ■ ■ ■ ■ ■ ■ ■

Jim peered down at the large congregation from a rooftop. Hundreds of heads below him hungrily watched in wonderment as the holy man reached a podium. The noon bells were on their final chime, quieting the crowd and allowing the priest his moment of speech.

The priest was dressed in white robes with silver accents. In his hand he held a large, leather-bound book with golden inscriptions upon its cover. Disheveled, shaggy hair fell from his head and mingled with a large curly beard that populated his chin. The robes he wore covered his feet, causing his movement to look more like a glide than a strut, as he moved from place to place.

"My family," the man gently sang, "my friends, my curious onlookers. Do not be dissuaded by the doubts that surely plague your minds. I come before you today, not to tell you to believe, but to ask you to try. There are questions in this world, so many questions. And answers only come to those who are willing to subject themselves to the ethereal beings of our world.

"I was once like many of you. A man without answers. A man without hope. The world crashed over my ambitions and I broke. Desperation is a familiar enemy. As is Death." The priest looked towards the sky and the sunlight glinted from his eyes.

"I know the answer to the question that many of you may ask. It is a timeless question, one that haunts many and engulfs lives with fear and falsities. I know what happens when it is our time to die."

The crowd hushed over the man's proclamation. It was a bold claim, and many of the people began to disperse after hearing what must be the ramblings of the unwell. But Jim stayed. His curiosity in the priest's statement prodded the memory of his own death.

"I see," the priest continued, "many of you are cautious of my words. That is understandable. You have no reason to trust me, no reason to become a believer. But I know this answer because I have been to the world which Death rules. It is a world made of shadow; a world populated by smoke. And when you scream the dead swallow your voice. But, this dark place, is where your next life may begin."

An intense recognition flooded through Jim. Had the priest fallen through that same world? Had he spoken with the man whose skin had been clothed by smoke?

"The Sabbath is the day after tomorrow. We will meet then, as a family. We will discuss the questions that plague us all. You will hear my story, and the story of those whom I have helped to become reborn. Whether you are human or Hero, rich or homeless, all are welcome to join my folds. We are all a family, living under Dom's gaze."

The priest bowed his head and sat silent for minutes. No one in the crowd spoke, no one moved; the atmosphere was thick with reverent acknowledgement. When the priest looked up once again, when the sun shone in his eyes, quiet overwhelmed the world for a breath.

When he finally spoke again it was to one man specifically. "Ryan Blackthorne, I will meet with you now." Then he left the podium and entered his sanctuary.

The people began to disperse, slowly returning to their tasks of the day. Only one man continued towards the church. A Hero who carried a double-sided ax walked up the stairs and entered behind the priest. Captain Ryan Blackthorne, Lumberjack.

Jim's mind filled with confused questions. The priest had known something that Jim thought may have been only a bad dream. He had been to the place ruled by Death. He knew something, and Jim needed to find out what.

■ ■ ■ ■ ■ ■ ■ ■

After the priest's speech, Emma had retreated to her little room. Bren and Aisley would be back soon, but for now she needed to breathe. There were so many people devouring the priest's words. So many nodding heads and mumbles of agreement. And then Lumberjack....

Something felt wrong to Emma. She was never one to associate with religion, though she wasn't opposed to the idea behind God. But to see so many people blindly accepting his words as truth was disturbing. There was something bigger that she couldn't see. The priest was claiming to know the answer to death, and he had taken a Hero Captain into his holy house for some kind of personal matter.

Her curiosity was as big a factor as her doubt. She decided to visit the priest's church on the coming Sabbath. But to go alone would be...painful. To subject herself to the beliefs of the blind would surely anger her and bitter her mood further. Maybe she could convince Jim to come. Her Hero had been so distant; maybe a bit of religion would remind him of the multiple lives that cared for his worries.

As if he felt her thoughts searching for him, Jim entered the room. His clothes were dirty from a full day and his boots were caked with dirt from the Lower District streets. His face was stern in thought and his eyes seemed far away. He was still troubled by something, still beating himself up over some small incident, Emma was sure.

It took him a moment to realize her presence. Once his gaze found her, his shoulders relaxed, and his focus gleamed closer. He dropped to the floor and put his arm protectively around Emma.

Together they sat, pondering the questions of their individual minds. It was a pleasant time, each enjoying the warmth from the other.

"I've missed you," Emma said.

Jim seemed shocked. His grip tightened around Emma's shoulder with a comfortable strength. It was an action that caused her flesh to prickle and her stomach to knot.

"There's a lot I need to tell you," Jim whispered.

"I'd like that." She rested her head on his shoulder.

The loud giggles from Aisley could be heard before she and Bren entered the room. The pack on her back bounced lightly from her shoulders and her coin purse jingled happily at her hip. She smiled widely, and her eyes grew merry when she spotted Jim and Emma.

"I've found the most wonderful thing!" Aisley exclaimed. "There's a man in Salix, a man like no other! He says that he knows what happens after death, and you could feel the energy radiate from his body! It was amazing." She stopped talking to catch her breath. "He is meeting this Sabbath, and I intend to join his flock! He is a wise man, you could tell from his beautifully composed words. There is much that he can teach us!"

Emma froze when she heard Aisley's enthusiasm. Of course, she would have believed the words of a new religion and wished to seek out more truths. But it still felt so wrong. Emma looked towards Jim, hoping to read the Hero's expressions and determine his thoughts towards religion. His eyes were glued on Aisley, stunned almost by her happy invitation. It was an odd sight to see, the mixture of shock and denial. And it was surprising when the Hero's mouth began to move, and he spoke a few strange words.

"I'd like to join you."

## 17: THE NAME IN THE BLACK CIRCLE

The rain pattered rhythmically against the small glass window. The moon and stars had been covered by the heavy black clouds that soaked the Willow city, making the night thick with darkness. The weather reflected calm serenity and silent secrets. This was the Hero's preferred time. Everything would hide him, and no one would be listening to the things that he needed to say. Only she would know.

Jim brushed Emma's hair with his fingers, gently raising her from the clutches of sleep. The girl groaned and spat the small strands of hair from her lips that had wandered onto her face while she dreamt. If he gave her a moment, she would collapse and re-enter the imaginary world where dreams spoke truer than reality. He reached his hand towards her again but hesitated at his action's implications. By waking her he would be forcing himself to tell, to speak as she had been wanting. But if sleep took her again....

"Emma," Jim whispered, "get your boots on and follow me."

Jim climbed from the window and scurried up the clay tiles of The Silver Nail's roof. From the room he could hear the clumsy movements of the exhausted girl. He suppressed a laugh when he heard her fall and curse loudly in the Hero's name. Eventually, she joined him on the slanted rooftop. They each wore their hood, their cloaks hugging tightly to their bodies in the frigid rain.

They would have to travel by rooftop, in the rain. It was the only sure way to traverse the city. The streets were organized in a manner that funneled running water from stone pavements of the rich districts and towards the dirt roads of the poor. The waters flowed like a river and gathered at the Southern Gate. By morning, a small lake of brown water would accumulate, only to be drained by the gate's opening at dawn.

Jim extended his hand to the girl and pulled her close, his forehead resting against hers. He didn't know what to say. There weren't any words he could use that would convey the vulnerability that he was going to reveal. But he could show her.

He released her hand and jumped towards the nearest roof. She followed easily, and together they hopped across the slick shingles at a quickening pace.

■ ■ ■ ■ ■ ■ ■

The rain drenched every inch of Emma's body. The small waterproofing from her cloak had only lasted the first minutes of the journey. Jumping above the city streets, water now clung heavily to her goose-prickling skin. Even her boots had gathered a small amount of water in their soles, causing her toes to numb from the cold and exertion.

But she wouldn't complain. Jim's air of uncertainty was enough for her to trust in tonight's importance. Somehow, she could feel the Hero's dread as they came closer to the unknown destination.

The buildings and rooftops had slowly evolved as they neared the richer parts of Salix. Instead of plain clay tiles, the roofs were shingled in intricate patterns of varying colors with boasting brass chimneys blowing smoke into the sky. The charred wood of the Low-Born District was replaced with stone and metal houses that reeked with numerous flowers hanging from every window.

The houses grew farther apart, causing each jump to feel more treacherous as she bounded across alleyways. Once, Emma slipped, knocking her chin hard against the shingles and shattering one with her elbow. Jim slowed and watched her with careful eyes, but he didn't stop. She pushed herself up with a grunt and sped to follow her Hero through the night.

Below, a metal gate barred entrance from the street. It was spiked on top and plated in gold. A plaque above the gate read *Hero District* .

From a near rooftop, Emma careened over a gap that made her stomach churn. She jumped and landed in a clumsy roll on the adjacent side. She rose to her feet, preparing to sprint and throw herself after Jim, but she was surprised to find him stopped.

He stared at the cluster of houses that resided inside the gated area. There were twenty of them, each beautifully designed with large metal doors and windows showing, at least three stories of rooms. They sat in a rectangular formation. In front of each house stood a tree, each differing from the others in shape and size. The trees showed signs of expert pruning. The beds in which they sat were meticulously weeded of all unwanted growths.

Jim sighed deeply and jumped on to the cobbled street that led to the houses. Emma followed, her legs shaky as they met the solid ground.

This area was brightly lit by a multitude of gas lamps that lined the street every few feet. She felt exposed in the contrasting light, but Jim walked in a casual and uncaring saunter as he neared the mansions. He had a building in mind, his feet pointing him towards the Southern row, the center house.

Emma squinted towards the house. It opposed the normal order that every other mansion seemed to follow. The grass outside was wiry and unkempt, the tree that lay in front grew wildly with twiggy branches and dying leaves. The stone walls were flaky, the doors rusted at the hinges, and the glass from each of the windows was broken inward by stone or storm. Altogether, the worn-down building looked like a husk of its companions.

Jim walked up the building's stairs and pushed the creaky door open. The inside was just as ruined as the outside. The ground had missing or splintered floorboards, the walls were covered in a thick sheen of dust and grime. Markedly cleaner spots showed where rugs once laid and pictures once hung until outsiders carried them away. The rooms looked stark and naked. A broken banister led up the crumbling staircase, and a shattered chandelier was swept into a corner by the door.

Emma pursued Jim through the dilapidated house, passed its many rooms, and through a door that led to the cellar. He began down the rickety stairs, ducking his head before it smacked against the landing above. The light from the streets couldn't reach far into the house, so he was swallowed by shadows as he descended.

Emma took a weary step. She could hear Jim's breathing and the floor groaning beneath him, but where he stood was a mystery to the blind girl. She trusted her feet to lead her safely down, keeping a hand in front of her head to avoid any stray hangings. She nearly screamed when Jim's hand reached in front of her chest, barring her from moving forward.

A spark illuminated the room, then another, as Jim struck at a piece of flint with his knife. The sparks landed on a torch the Hero was holding, hungrily consuming the oil-soaked cloth and lighting the room with a warm glow. The heat of the torch reached Emma before she registered its light. She leaned towards the fire, her hands shaking and shivering. Jim allowed her to take the torch, though his eyes stayed planted on the room's walls.

As feeling returned to Emma's fingertips, she absorbed the room in a long gaze. Shock forced her mouth to gape and her eyes to widen. It took her minutes to realize that she was holding her breath, her vision darkening when a gasp finally forced its way into her lungs.

Along the walls were thousands of carvings, each depicting a name and a crest. The names were all tangled together with lines that split and branched towards the others. Often a name would end, all lines leading towards that name never moving further. But mostly the names led to other names, spreading over each wall in the large room.

Emma placed a finger over a carving and followed its rough line across the wall. She reverently traced each symbol, each name, that interrupted her finger's path as she made her way towards the center. Some carvings looked newer than others, and many felt shallow in the walls grain. A sparse few black marks lay on the path, the names and symbols charred beyond recognition.

Finally, Emma's finger reached the center. Each line led back to one name and one solitary symbol, *Quill Ash*. She traced the name over and over, feeling an odd gratitude from the name and a dark history from the symbol.

A single tear ran from down her cheek. Emma had no idea where her melancholy emotions were coming from, but they crashed through her entirety like a wave beating against a cliffside. A lump in her throat caused her breaths to come in shaky and uneven gulps. This room, it's power, was something she had only read about in books and heard from in ancient stories.

With blurry eyes Emma searched for her Hero, finding him still standing in the center of the room. He watched her with careful expression, the look of caution buried beneath his, otherwise, soft gaze.

"What is this?" Her voice sounded boisterous in the quiet room.

Jim stepped towards her, his hand resting on top of hers and tracing along with the symbol.

"Quill Ash," Jim whispered, "The first Ash. Do you know the story of the First Four?"

"No," Emma said, with barely a breath.

"The first Hero was nameless. No script or story has ever recalled the name that the Hero was given, and the only description that anyone can settle on were the Hero's golden eyes. They lived in the Time Before, side by side with the Killer of Death, if the stories are truthful. The Unnamed watched as the world burned and humanity edged towards extinction. They wandered the globe, and where they stepped, life began to flourish. They spread their life through all that was touched. Lush, green forests bloomed where they walked. They reminded the birds to sing and taught them new songs as they journeyed. Their presence alone was enough to heal every human that saw their glory. They walked for a thousand years, spreading life through every field and city.

"But, when the Hero returned to the place it was born, it was greeted only by Death. The life that they had once brought had sunk deep into the Earth, leaving the creatures above to suffer and die. The Unnamed spoke with Death, asked how they could prevent this from happening in all the wonderful places that they had seen. Death thought for days and saw an opportunity to take the life from the one being who still evaded him.

"A crooked smile shone on Death's face as he told the Hero of his plan. *Life leaves unless you are near. So, you must be more.* The Hero saw Death's wisdom, though they also saw his devious intent. The world was growing sick once more. The Hero had been missing for too long, time was growing short. So, the Hero agreed, asking Death what would be done.

"*Your life for four. Immortal no longer, but ageless they'll remain.* The Hero took Death's hand into their own, and with a shake the Unnamed Hero was broken in to four pieces and given to four trees. An Ash, a Willow, an Oak, and an Elm: the trees that would become the First Four.

"It took centuries for the trees to birth the Heroes. But one day they emerged. Golden eyes and ageless bodies stepped upon the soil. And where they walked, life spread once more."

Jim paused, feeling the carving's fine detail. "Quill was born from the Ash. Jonathan was born from the Willow. Vanessa was born from the Oak. And Maria was born from the Elm. They walked in four directions, maintaining the life vicariously for the first and nameless Hero.

"Though they remained ageless, they were still mortal. The sword could kill them. They could freeze in the winters and burn in the deserts. They could poison themselves, nurse disease. If they did not feed, they would whither into nothingness. And if they died, so would the world.

"No one taught them the value of their lives, and they never learned themselves. Seeing the potential of Death's dirty trick, they began to breed; expanding their names and their families and protecting the lands which they had claimed. As their lines expanded so did their names. The Oaks grew into Angeloak, Bur, and Chestnut. The Ash name stayed, but the line was filled with Griffiths, Blues, Blackthornes, and Firs. The Elms spread themselves thin, becoming Dogwood, Vine, Maple, and Ilex. Eventually they would reunite, each keeping their name but identifying only as Northtree. The Willows did not spread their name. They stayed pure in the beliefs of Jonathan and decided to keep his name throughout the generations.

"The names, and the Heroes, became many, and territory became contested. As is common, a war spread like wildfire through the world. Heroes fought with humans for their right to protect their homes, and Heroes fought with humans for the right to spread their ideals and beliefs. And the soil became wet with blood.

"When the fighting ended, life was sparse. An unintended consequence of the war made Death strong and life weak. All that remained of man and Hero-kind was forced to band together in one city. A city which became strong. A city called Paradise.

"This is the part that you may recognize," Jim said to Emma, his breath brushing against her ear, "A leader was chosen, and she placed guardians over each of the four directions. Eventually, the city became strong enough that spreading was an option. The four guardian families were tasked with spreading in each direction and keeping the life that grew under their watchful eye.

"The world we live in now is a result of the first Leader's choices. We've spread as far as we can. Our task to protect life is one that is sacred, but one that has been muddied by time." Jim finished.

The room filled with a tangible silence. Emma had never heard the story before, and she doubted any human alive ever had. It was a piece of Hero legend and, from the way Jim had told it, the Heroes believed it to be true.

"So," Emma said. "Quill was the first Ash."

"Yes," Jim replied.

"And his line in spread over these walls?"

"Only those who kept his name. Each of the mansions are for a Hero house, and each tells the story of their lineage."

Emma dragged her finger down the line until she came across a charred spot. "And these?" she asked.

"Names that are best left forgotten."

There were so many names across the walls, so many generations. It was marvelous that the Hero history was remembered enough to carve each name into the wood.

"Do you know these Heroes, the stories of the ones who are worth remembering?" she asked, circling names as she walked.

"Yes."

Emma stopped walking. "Every one?"

"Yes," Jim said again.

She looked at the name her finger rested on. "Tell me about Lilly Ash."

Jim looked at the name and the symbol beneath it. "Lily was the first to leave the forest that surrounded Paradise. She set up colonies just beyond the tree line where humans could live and farm. She died at three hundred and five after falling from a tree while collecting feathers. She had…three children. I think."

"Hmm." Emma moved down the line. "And Seth Ash? Tell me about him."

Jim's eyes brightened at the name. "Seth was one of my favorites as a boy. He domesticated a wolf and became the leader of his own pack. He roamed through the forest in the dead of night and only fed on those who had a guilty conscience. Wolves can sense a person's guilt, so Seth used them as his judge. He had no children and died at seventy-one…."

"Seventy-one?" Emma asked, surprised by the low number. "What did he die of?"

Jim smiled. "A wolf bite." He laughed.

Emma laughed with him as her finger found another name. "Tell me about Parker."

"His is not a funny story, quite tragic really." Jim said this and his smile faded. "Parker volunteered to travel to the Misted Forest, the forest that lies on the Southern border, just beyond the Savior Wall. Many had entered before, but none had ever returned. He, and twenty of his chosen Heroes, rode to the forest on horseback to expand our territory. The expedition was supposed to take three days but, after five, no word had been given of the scouts' whereabouts. It was ten full days before three horses galloped from the trees with three riders on their backs. One rider was dead, but the other two survived, Parker and his friend Gavin Chestnut. He spoke of a temple that was protected by a dragon and monsters that buried themselves until the sun sank in the sky. Humanoid creatures with claws that dragged through the ground and could cut through flesh like a knife through water."

"Husks," Emma said in a hush.

Jim nodded. "He had one child. Parker died at one hundred and seventeen, days after the attack. Blood loss from the first documented husk."

The history of these names astonished Emma. Each carving held so many legends, so many pieces of the present. And the Hero knew them all.

"Sam Ash," Emma said.

"Sam was the General of the Undead War. He led the charge of Broken Hill that pushed the husks back into the trees. He died in the charge. Because of him, the lands of Ash were protected long enough for the Savior Wall to be constructed. He died at age four hundred twelve. He had two daughters."

"His daughter's story is good too, Erin Ash." Jim continued. "She was the Hero who had wisdom enough to expand the Savior Wall. She used her cunning, and the many favors her father had earned, to get the resources and men necessary for expansion. She designed the wall to reach all the way to the Eastern Mountains and into the Western Shores. Because of her, when the hoard of husks returned, we were ready. She has had four children, a marvel for a Hero, and is still alive. She serves as one of the Leader's Twenty-Four, at three hundred sixty years old."

She traced Erin's name. A legendary Hero who was still alive? Heroes' lives were something that amazed Emma. Something able to live longer than trees and stone, it was a marvel in itself, let alone their amazing life feats.

The carving was coming to an end, only a few names remained for her finger to trace. "Steven Ash. Who's he?"

"Ah, I remember his story well." Jim said in a satirical tone. "He's a man who is not known for his deeds, but for his politics. He served as Leader for twenty-seven years and nearly erased the gap between Hero and human by claiming that we are all bred from the same life. He was removed as Leader when his son slaughtered the Dogwood heir and began the Southern War."

Emma stared at Jim in disbelief. "Your father?" she asked.

"Yes," Jim said quietly.

"Then that means...." Emma moved her finger down the line, but she did not continue speaking.

Instead of a name there was a charred black circle. His carving was removed from the lineage, his name to be forgotten by time.

Anger boiled Emma's blood. Her vision flicked with red and she bit her tongue to keep from screaming. She pulled her arm back and punched at the wall with all her strength.

She winced when she felt her knuckle split against the charred wood, but she couldn't stop herself from punching again. Her blood covered the place where his name should be. She punched again, feeling another knuckle split. But it still wasn't enough. She pulled back again and sent her fist flying towards the black circle.

But it never reached the wood a fourth time. Jim's hand stopped her bleeding knuckles from smashing against its target again. His grip was firm on her fist. Furious tears were streaming down her face and her breaths came in ragged frequency.

"Steven had one child," Jim said calmly. "Or, that's what the lineage will say."

He pulled her fist with his along a carved line. This one was different, shallower and squigglier. The careful precision of a master carpenter was missing from the jagged carving that read the name *Ellie Ash*.

"I carved this when she was born. My father sent me all over the territories when he was Leader, to practice politics and grow my knowledge. I was twelve when I came here, and she was two and her name was missing from the wall. So, I added it. Owen, my companion and caretaker, was furious when he saw what I did. I got whipped bloody and was washed with saltwater to ensure I never disgraced the sacred lineage again." Jim laughed at Emma's horrified expression. "But I never really understood. When I told my father what I had done he cleared the room and sat me on his lap. He said that even though she was our family, our people would deny her in our history. It was something that he was trying to mend, a right he was trying to wrong, but it was the way our world worked."

Jim placed his hand over Ellie's crude carving. Emma's blood coated the name, but the Hero didn't seem to mind. He looked longingly at the name, reliving memories of when his sister still spoke.

"She died at thirteen. Internal bleeding, most likely, but the healers were unsure." His eyes stayed glued to her name.

"Why would your people deny her a place in history?" Emma asked.

"Because," Jim said simply, "she was human."

"A Fault?" Emma asked, shocked.

She'd heard of Faults before—every human had. Hero children that resembled humans more than their own race. They were spoken of as mere stories, half-breeds that bore a Hero's name and brand but walked seamlessly among their human counterparts.

"I didn't know they were real," Emma whispered.

Jim looked at the girl. "They're real. But the Northtrees have been hunting them for generations. It's a grey practice that no one has successfully fought. The Northtrees are too powerful. Their ideals are so backwards, but no one can persuade them to change. It doesn't help that their namesake, Lye Northtree, is the current Leader. It's only made them more obvious in their barbaric practices."

Emma thought she understood. There was a reason Jim had brought her to this place, more of a reason than history and stories. There was something here, something hidden in his words. Some kind of terrorizing secret that held beneath his skin. He wanted to tell her, she could feel it, but something was stopping him. Some hatred for himself that fed from this torture, and if he told, its fuel would lessen.

"Tell me," She demanded, softly.

He looked into her eyes, his gold reflecting the shade of her emerald. And then he spoke. He told her of the night they entered Salix. He told her of the friend he found, the contract he took, the Fault he killed. He told her everything that had dug deep inside of him and clung to his ribs and refused to let go until he talked. And when he was done, he waited, anticipated a new wave of hatred to flow from her and into him.

But the hatred never came. Instead, Emma finally understood. This wasn't about Mason Grey, it wasn't about a contract or a kill. It was about a girl, a Fault that he had loved and whose love now ate him alive.

Jim refused to look at Emma when she spoke. "You didn't know what he was," she said plainly.

He stared at the ground. "And that makes it alright?"

"It makes it less wrong. And Jim," she started to say when his gaze lifted. She waited for his eyes to meet hers again. "It wasn't her."

He looked at the crimson-soaked name. He didn't speak, not for some time. They both stood in silence, looking at the name that he carved and the blood that she spread. It was a silence that radiated warmth through Emma and caused Jim to shudder. She didn't know what it meant, but it felt...right.

After a time, she moved to her Hero and took his hand. She longed to have his lips touch hers, and she rose to her tiptoes to tell the Hero of her lust. He read her body language with heart-filled acceptance and leaned down to meet her mouth. He stopped, his lips a hair's breadth from hers, teasing her eager desire for a moment longer than she could stand. Then, he pressed against her, uniting them in calm perfection.

By the time they pulled apart, she was forced to gasp, and her lips had surely turned blue. Her breath came back to her slowly, her pride stung from her forced reaction.

Jim laughed at her dramatic suffocation. "The way you're acting, you'd think I held you against...."

"I love you, Jim!" The words burst from Emma's mouth, needing to leave her and enter the Hero.

He stood in shock, blinking stupidly. Of course, he wouldn't say anything back. He was a Hero. She was idiotic for even thinking of love. Afterall, it was probably more of a childish crush, or lust, and neither of them were to be trusted. And yet, he still stood there, fighting with himself. That's how they both were. Foolish idiots who could never truly love each other. It was more of a fantasy, had to be only pieces of a dream that would never actually reach the light of day.

She would take it back. Apologize for saying the awkward phrase and building a new barrier for them to break. Maybe she would get lucky and break her neck on their way back home, that way neither of them would have to live with the....

"I love you too, Emma," Jim said, his mouth finding hers again.

She pulled him to the ground, tearing at his cloak and shirt. She flung her boots across the room and loosened the cinch of her pants before Jim took over. Together they lay and explored, holding tightly to one another in an explosive embrace.

The sun rose and fell while they lay under a blanket of their own clothes. It wasn't until the night returned, and the frigid darkness bit at their revealed skin, that they decided to dress and return to The Silver Nail. Wonderful exhaustion collided with Emma the moment her head met her pillow.

And she dreamt while lying in her lover's arms.

## 18: THE SABBATH

Hundreds of people sat, packed in the cathedral's pews and chattering about the week's events. Everyone wore a smile and their cleanest clothes, not wanting to offend the man who spoke for the God he knew. Children ran around irreverently only to receive a scolding from their parents who eventually caught them.

It was strange to see the different classes of people all gathered together. Proper noblewomen held their noses as they shuffled past the reeking homeless and found their seats at the front. Jolly bakers passed small loaves of bread to any who asked. Laborers, who had surely worked the night before, dozed quietly while they waited for the church's scheduled meeting to begin. Sure, there were segregated sections for the rich and the poor, but the amalgamation of different classes all gathered in the same room was a rare and progressive sight to behold.

Jim and Emma found the seat which Aisley had saved for them, a few rows from the back, and squeezed through the crowd to reach them. Bren sat next to Aisley, a bored look on her stern face. Aisley sat on her hands, excitedly flitting her eyes about the wooden podium at the front of the room and humming a happy tune.

Jim was about to explain the reason for their tardiness when the noon-bells began to chime. The reverberations from the bells shook the large cathedral and quieted the congregation immediately. The large wooden doors, that served as an entrance, closed tightly, denying access to all who remained outside and dimming the interior with a lack of sunlight.

Large velvet curtains dropped to the floor from ropes on the walls, exposing colorful windows that lined the church's body and shone magnificently amongst the people. The windows depicted different scenes from religious stories: A snake wrapped tightly around an apple, Death bowing to the form of a man, a buck with golden antlers in a wooded grove, even the rainbow throne that the Hero Leader sat upon. Jim stared in amazement at the finely crafted glass, wondering how many years of expertise it took to make the intricate depictions.

A door opened from the front of the room, interrupting the silence for a moment, and through it walked the priest. He glided towards the dark podium, his hands folded kindly across his chest. He was dressed in the same white robes that Jim had seen him in days before, but now wore a brilliantly jeweled necklace around his smooth neck. His hair was brushed neatly, and his beard was braided in tight knots.

When he reached the podium, he looked over the hushed crowd. His eyes lingered on every face, absorbing their images into his memory. When the man's blue eyes found Jim, he paused and nodded pleasantly. The priest's eyes seemed to shine and reflect the colorful glass as he stared through the Hero and continued his gaze towards the others. It was a process that took minutes, and throughout, no one dared speak.

Finally, the priest looked down. He pulled a large leather book from beneath the podium and began to finger through the fragile pages. He stopped on a page, his eyes darting across the small words, but shook his head and continued his process of flipping through the book.

Jim watched with a careful concentration. *Meticulous men have a great meaning in everything they do. A simple action can tell you their full intent, if you are willing to watch.* The priest stopped on another page, moistened his lips, and smiled at the congregation.

"Brothers and sisters," his song-filled voice spoke, "I wish you a warm welcome on this, the most beautiful of days. I am happy to see some new faces among my flock." Jim could have sworn the priest winked at him. "And I hope you find the answers, that plague you, within my words.

"There are many sacred texts, and many differing gods that serve as each religion's foundation. But here, the books are not sacred, and the god we love was merely a man. The purpose, and my true belief, of gathering together is to speak of death and to become reborn through it."

The priest held the book over his head, showing the audience its pages. "This book is not of some historical God. It does not tell of aging stories or the birth of existence. This book," he said, placing it back on the podium, "is a journal of the life that I have lived and the lives that I remember."

A whispered chatter waved through the congregation. Questions of the priest's legitimacy, or the meaning of his statement, held heavy on the people's tongues. Aisley loosed a few questions of her own towards Jim, but his eyes stayed transfixed on the priest.

"Please, brothers and sisters," The priest said, holding up a hand to quiet the crowd. "I will explain, I promise. When I was young, a boy of only twenty-two, I was traveling along the Stone Road. I had wished to visit every city that was built along the road's path, a dream since my youth. But Death had another plan for my destination.

"I left Forge and was a day's walk from the Twin Cities, when my path crossed the Heroes. These were wicked, angry men, and they foamed violence from between their teeth. They demanded I pay a fee to continue forward. Their price was a silver, not the treasure of a wealthy man but still a price that I could not pay. They threw me to the ground and emptied my pockets of the few trinkets that I had taken to remember my journey through the world. Worthless garbage to their golden eyes, and a fee that would go unpaid.

"They allowed me to stand. I thought I would be free to travel unhindered. I gathered my few trinkets and tried to put the Heroes behind me. I heard one of them hurry after me, saying that I had forgotten one of my possessions. I turned to thank the man.

"He was holding a spear in his hands, and nothing else. Before I could ask after my missing item, he thrust his spear through my heart. That was the first time that I died, and it was the start of my first rebirth."

An outburst of noise erupted from the congregation. People flung their accusations at the holy man, calling him a liar and a thief who was trying to play them as fools. Many rose to their feet and began shuffling through the pews. But the priest stood calmly and raised his hand into the air again.

Using his other hand, he began to unclip the buttons that lined his silk robe. He stretched his shoulders and sent the robe tumbling to the ground. The congregation stilled, and Jim's eyes widened.

Over the priest's heart stretched an angry white scar. The jagged edges of the wound spread over his pectoral, shaped like a many-pointed star. The priest turned and showed another scar on his back that surely connected through his body.

"An impressive mark, isn't it?" The priest said kindly. "My story is one of truth. I know there are many who use religion to gain wealth and power, but I only wish to gain and give knowledge. So, if you would allow, I will tell you of my truths."

The priest waited patiently as people found their seats. He waved his arm, and six people from the congregation stood and joined him at the podium. They stood behind him, three men and three women, stoically waiting for some unknown cue.

"Once the Hero pierced my heart, I died within a minute. I had never feared death, never ran from the eventuality that all things must end. But where I found myself made me shiver. It was a world with no sun, no light at all. There were shadows and there was darkness and there were shapes. It was a terrifying reality that I found myself wandering. But, as I wandered, the world revealed itself to me.

"The cities that I had visited, the walls which protect us all, even the Stone Road were all there, encased in blackness. It was like living in a reflection…no, more like a blind imitation, of the world that all of you know. I was alone in the strange world, but I knew that I was wrong for that place. I was not meant to die, not meant to leave the bright world behind. I begged the heavens, tried to plead with the devils, and I screamed at the lonely existence which became my everything.

"It was after one of my outbursts that I saw the form of a man walking towards me. He was misted in smoke and silently offered me his hand. Fear was unknown to me in the desperate place, so I reached for him. When our hands met my rebirth began.

"The man whispered an offer. He would give me the pieces that had been his life, if I lived through his death and took his name." The priest paused and gestured to the people who stood behind him. "I gave the same choice to each of them. And I will give the choice to each of you."

One of the men stepped forward and spoke. "I took another's death so that I could live again. The man who found me was mauled by a bear, beyond the Eastern Mountains. My name was Connor but is now Evan."

Another stepped forward, a woman this time. "The death I took was from a husk. It clawed through my leg and fed on my blood as I died. My name was Skylar but is now Hazel."

Another woman stepped forward, "My death was at the hands of my beloved. He found me in the bed of his enemy and unloaded a scattergun through our chests. My name was Violet but is now Zoe."

One by one the remaining stepped forward and told their stories. Their deaths came in many different varieties and their names seemed to span the restrictions of time. The congregation gasped as each death was foretold and each name was accepted. They cried from both faith and disbelief as the stories of the devout inspired them to openly praise the great plan of rebirth. If death was no longer a permanent state, it would no longer be feared.

Once the six were all standing next to the priest, he raised his arms and shouted at the ceiling. "I died at the feet of the man who killed Death! The Savior spoke to me as I drew my final breath! My name before is one that I will not speak, for I have accepted the name Marcus!"

An uproarious applause exploded from the crowd. Shouts of wonder and teary-eyed cheers filled the large and echoey room. They began to chant the priest's accepted name, while he stood at the podium with his arms still raised.

Jim watched the ecstatic people, which Aisley had enthusiastically joined. Emma and Bren sat still, their faces full of disbelief and doubt. Jim knew of the world where the priest had screamed, knew of the figures that floated there, but could the rest be true? An opportunity to live again by accepting the death of another. Had he done so to return after the fall?

"Please," Marcus spoke again. "Please quiet yourselves." He waited for a beat. "You will all have the opportunity to be reborn. But it is a tedious process and is quite taxing on the body. If you are a man who must labor for his family, or a woman who must care for her young, I would advise you wait until your life is in a slower state. I invite ten people each week to accept another's death and be reborn with a new name. Those individuals have already been chosen for this week, but next week the opportunity will arise again."

Hands shot in the air and questions were shouted at the man.

"I must rest, brothers and sisters. My devout will help you with your questions. May Dom bless you with his guidance."

The priest, Marcus, after finishing these final words, took a small bow and glided back to the door. Before he left, he looked over the crowd once more and stared into Jim's eyes. He winked, the sun glinting from his iris, and mouthed the word *Ash*. Then, he closed the door behind him and left the questions that had just sprung up in Jim unanswered.

## 19: WELCOMING OF HEROES

The streets were unusually calm. Instead of crowds of hurrying people, Jim and Emma observed only a sparse number of yawning workers. Empty shops lined the walkways, even a few with 'closed' signs still sitting in the windows. An eerie quiet loomed in the air.

A tugging came from Jim's cloak and a small voice whispered, "Excuse me, sir."

Jim looked down. A young boy stared bright eyed at the Hero. He wore rags so dirty and filled with holes that a swift breeze would blow them to dust. He danced excitedly on his bare, mud-caked, feet.

Jim cocked an eyebrow. The boy continued to stare, unsure of the question that lay heavy on his mind.

Emma crouched low. "Go on, speak," she said kindly.

"Umm…" the nervous boy said shakily. "My…my mother told me that the Heroes would be handing out g…gold at their welcoming. S…she asked me to do my best t…to catch some, but I lost my way. Are you with the Northtree Warriors?"

"Northtree Warriors?" Jim asked.

"Yes, sir," the boy said with a look of admiration. "The greatest fighters in the Hero realm. They have killed hordes of husks upon the plains, even traveled South of the Savior Wall to kill more. Each of them wields a blade made of blood and can shoot a coin with a rifle from ten miles away. When I grow up, my mother says I can train and fight with them."

"And which gate will they be entering through?" Jim asked.

"The North Gate, of course," said the boy. "It would be improper for a Northtree to enter through one of the Lesser Gates."

"Of course," said Jim.

He reached into his coin purse and pulled out three gold pieces. The boy's eyes grew bright as Jim placed them firmly into his hand.

"You are with them! The Northtrees are the most generous of all Heroes! Thank you, sir!" the boy said jovially.

"You get those coins to your mother, right away," Jim demanded. "You will miss the welcoming, but I don't want you to lose that gold."

The boy nodded and ran off.

"Why would the Northtree Warriors be coming here?" Emma asked once the boy was out of earshot.

"Why don't' we find out," Jim said, and headed towards the North Gate.

· · · · · · · ·

Emma elbowed her way through the crowd. She held Jim's hand tightly, not wanting to lose her Hero amongst the multitude. People moved from the rude girl's jabs, eventually relenting their spots to her ministrations.

Slowly they made their way closer to the gates. Excited noise hummed from all around. People chatted loudly over one another, their questions and joys blending and adding to the deafening noise.

Emma tried to move closer, but Jim's grip pulled her back. The gate was a few yards away but easily within eyesight. He glared at the open barriers, seeing much farther than she ever could.

A booming voice cut through the ruckus. "Off the street! You'll be able to see the warriors from the walkway, and they won't stop if you are in their path."

People pushed and cramped closer, trying to evacuate the paved tiles where the Heroes would ride. Emma was squished close to Jim, her body fitting into his arms like a sword to a sheath. He was unmoved by the throng's bustling, standing strongly as the river of people pushed against him. But still, he stared past the gate at the Northtrees that only he could see.

He craned his head down, his lips brushing against Emma's ear. "Here they come." His soft voice and touch drowned out all other noise.

Forty men and women on horseback strode into Salix. Their pristine cloaks and polished boots made the city, and the people within, seem dirty and unruled. They each sat tall in their saddles with smiles that boosted their bravado. Their eyes never met the faces of the people who cheered for them along the streets, but their hands waved from side to side in greetings. *Many of our people hate humans but still see their necessity. And it's easier to rule them when they revere us in their stories.*

At the lead, rode a majestic looking man. His white hair flowed to his shoulders, bouncing with each of his horse's trots. On his back, peeking from each end of his crimson cloak, sat a large broadsword, its sheath the color of a blacksmith's fire. His chest was covered in shiny chainmail that bore divots of battle upon its rings. His gloved hands held only his reins, never making any intention to wave or greet the city he entered.

"Bastion Northtree," Jim began to say, "leader of the Northtree Warriors and heir to the Northtree house. He fought in the Undead War when he was only twelve, and helped his father convince the Northern houses to join their names. He's obsessed with the Time Before and has killed more husks than any other Hero alive. The stories that give him acclaim are almost as numerous as the stories of the Unnamed Hero."

Two Heroes rode closely behind Bastion. The first was a stunning looking woman. Dark hair curled loosely down her back. A small nose rested among her freckled cheeks. The white of her teeth shone brightly under her smiling, red lips. A rifle rested comfortably on her lap. The second rider was a younger looking man. His face was the spitting image of Bastion, but he wore his blonde hair shorter and bore a long scar on his lip that parted his mouth awkwardly as he smiled.

"Bastion's daughter, Faye, and son, Kole," said Jim. "They banned together centuries ago to form the Northtree Warriors. Over the years other members have come and gone, but the three have always remained together."

Kole reached into his pocket and flung coins at the mass of people. The rest of the Heroes did the same, showering the small metal bits on the heads of the inferior. Arms reached frantically for the money, and bodies began to shove against each other for the meager pay. Cheers became louder as more coins were tossed and the Heroes rode by.

Emma watched the group ride down the streets where a lone figure stood: Lumberjack. He waved at the new arrivals and walked alongside Bastion as they made their way to the Hero-District.

The crowd dispersed slowly once the Heroes were out of sight. The regular routines of the day beckoned from the exciting morning. But Jim kept watching, glaring at where the Heroes must be, through buildings and blocks to the mansions that were gated from humans.

He suddenly began to move. Pulling Emma towards an alley with large, purposeful steps, his eyes darted around to determine if they were truly alone.

His gold rested on Emma, and he placed a tender kiss upon her lips. "I'm going to follow them," he said, a hair's breadth from her mouth. "Go back to The Silver Nail. I'll meet you there tonight."

Another lingering kiss wetted her lips. Then, her Hero was gone.

■ ■ ■ ■ ■ ■ ■ ■

The Hero mansions looked even more glorious in the bright daylight. The horses pranced freely in the gated section, grazing on the green grass and colorful flowers. Each of the northern houses showed signs of life, whether movement from a wandering Hero or light from illuminating chandeliers.

Tonight, the houses would come alive with drinking and songs. But, for now, a resting hush hung over the district. After days of traveling, the Heroes would be dormant, regaining their stamina and resting their heavy eyes.

Jim moved quickly, darting behind the Willow mansions to remain unseen from a distance. He needed to reach the center house; that is where Bastion would stay. Blackthorne would be with him now, speaking of the Ash heir that he let slip through his fingers. It was a conversation that Jim needed to hear.

He crouched low and rolled to the side of a northern house. He peered around the corner to see desolate gardens and empty fields of grass. He sprinted past the remaining houses, his footsteps silent in the soft soil.

The center house was a floor taller than its brothers. Jim looked at the slick stone sides and the windows that were placed precariously out of reach, his way inside. He jumped and his fingers gripped tightly to a wooden windowsill and pulled himself up to peer through the glass. He saw an empty room, but light from the hallway danced with a shadow. He slid his knife beneath the window and silently pried it open.

A large bed was against one wall, its blankets tucked taut into the mattress. Painted on the wall was a beautiful depiction of Paradise. The mural must have taken months to paint, the accuracy was astounding. A dark wooden door with golden hinges was open wide. Light from the hallway beamed in through the doorway.

Jim crouched against the door and used the reflection from his dagger to check the hall. The light came from the chandelier that illuminated the floor below. The hall remained empty of Heroes but was populated by packs and chainmail that were tossed lazily to the floor. He could hear a murmur of voices too far to make out.

Jim crawled down the hallway, passing a few closed doors and empty rooms, and stopped where the stairs led down. The voices were clear here, carried through the painted walls and up the staircase.

"...sixteen husks this time." Jim recognized the deep tone of Bastion's voice. "Must've climbed over the Savior Wall without the Dogwoods noticing."

Blackthorne's voice spoke next. "They wouldn't notice if an entire horde were banging beneath their feet. It's a good thing you were nearby to clean up their mess."

"They won't be so lucky next time." Bastion said, "We were only down there to campaign for new recruits and listen to the rumors about rebel groups. Next time they let this happen, those Dogwoods are going to lose a few men."

"Did you learn anything about the rebels?" asked Blackthorne.

"Only the usual," a third voice said. Jim assumed it must be Kole, "stories of bandits attacking lonesome Heroes, rifles gone missing, bullets being manufactured, secret tunnels beneath the mountains, the name *Iris* . It's all just dribble, no good information from any of the humans that we paid."

"We were on our way to check the Angeloaks when your news reached us," said Bastion. "The heir is still alive after being shot through a window. Typical of an Ash, never dying when it's obviously beaten."

"That's not all," Blackthorne said. "I've two guards who say he's here. Bunking in some lodge in the Lower-District."

"You're sure?" Kole interjected.

"Yes," Blackthorne said cockily. "The human he was traveling with tried to follow me the day I met with Marcus. I had her followed by one of my men and he swears that he saw Jim enter through a window. We can move on them at any time."

Jim held his breath in surprised fear. The Silver Nail was compromised, his whereabouts revealed. He would have to leave and get the others out of Salix. Today if possible. He began to crawl away when Bastion's voice rose again and froze him in place.

"Is the laboratory all that we hoped?"

"More. Much more," Blackthorne said, fascination edging his voice. "Marcus showed me…everything. The devices, the husks, it's all as he claimed through his letters."

"When will we meet him?" Kole asked.

"He's a busy man. But I'm sure he would be willing…"

"Tonight," Bastion said, cutting off Blackthorne's response. "We will meet tonight."

"Yes, sir," said Blackthorne. "I will inform him of the meeting."

Heavy footsteps came from below, and Jim sunk lower as Blackthorne's figure came into view. He reached for the front door and had it open a crack before Bastion spoke.

"Excellent work, Captain Blackthorne. You will be leaving the Willow woman and joining my ranks once we leave Salix behind."

"Thank you, sir." Blackthorne said and left the mansion.

Jim moved, heading towards the room that he had entered through. He tiptoed over the discarded armor and almost reached the room through the hallway when the shaking of a doorknob halted him. The door swung open and revealed a groggy Hero. She was rubbing sleep from her golden eyes, and her hair was in tangled heaps, but Faye Northtree still looked beautiful.

Faye's eyes widened in recognition and confusion. She opened her mouth to scream or ask about the intruder's intentions, but Jim slapped his hand over her lips before a noise could be made. He pushed her into her room and punched at her belly. She jumped back, fully awake, and kicked at Jim's leg. He stepped over the kick easily and attacked, his knee finding the hard bone of her sternum.

Faye gasped loudly, only to be interrupted again by Jim's hand covering her mouth. He punched at her ribs and spun her around. He flexed his arm over her neck, choking Faye while she grunted and flailed her arms at his face.

Jim counted in his head, knowing the appropriate amount of time it would take a Hero to faint from lack of oxygen. Faye's fist found Jim's nose and hot blood fell from his face, but his grip held tight. She pounded her feet against the floorboards, trying to draw attention. Jim pulled her backwards by her neck and lifted her from the ground. Her feet dangled and kicked but landed uselessly against Jim's shins.

The time was nearing its end. Faye's attacks came slower and with less vigor. Finally, her arms fell limp and her eyes closed. Jim stayed choking for a few extra seconds, just to be sure she wasn't pretending, but Faye stayed still. He wiped the blood from his nose and placed her on the bed. If someone were to peer in, all they would see was a sleeping woman.

Jim took a moment to catch his breath, but time was a luxury that he didn't have. He opened Faye's window and jumped to the grass below. His legs carried him through the Hero District in a frantic run. He had to get Emma out of Salix.

## 20: AN UNKNOWN PLACE

The streets were too busy for the Hero's pace, so he moved to the rooftops. He bounded from roof to roof, flying over the Willow's largest city. The districts passed beneath him in a blur of colorful motion. Wind whistled in his ears, drowning the noise of the world from his senses and silencing the voice that kept him sane.

■■■■■■■

Emma had just returned to the little room inside The Silver Nail. Bren and Aisley were napping in each other's arms, peacefully snoozing in the warm glow of the afternoon sun. She stretched her arms, a yawn escaping her lips. A nap sounded wonderful.

Suddenly, Jim crashed through the window, shattering glass throughout the room and startling Bren and Aisley awake. In his eyes was something Emma had never seen before: fear. In a paranoid manner he ran to the door and checked the hallway for onlookers. His breathing was heavy and incessant and sweat glistened on his brow, giving him the look of a feral animal.

He reached for Emma's pack and pulled her waterskin from its leather. He drank deeply, droplets streaming from the corners of his mouth. It was strange how afraid she could be of the man who usually made her feel safe.

Jim put the waterskin back into her pack and tossed it to Emma. "Pack up," he said in between breaths. "We need to leave."

Emma stood there, pack in hand, and said, "What's going on Jim?"

"The Northtrees," he began to explain, "know I'm here…they know we're here."

Bren and Aisley went to work, packing their things tightly together. Emma grabbed her extra clothes and few possessions, stuffing them messily into her pack.

"What's the plan?" she asked her Hero.

"You three will go to the horses and leave through the Eastern Gate. There isn't much daylight left, so try and get a safe distance away before stopping to camp," he said in one breath.

"And you?" she asked, suspicious of his answer.

"There are a few things I have to clean up. But I will meet you in a day if you keep traveling East." Jim avoided Emma's gaze as he spoke.

She could feel his guilt, his secrets piling inside of him. There was something that he wasn't telling her, something that held too much importance for him to worry about alone. But he would never ask for help; the man was too stubborn to see when he was overwhelmed.

"One day?" she asked.

"Yes. Just keep going East." Jim said this with relief.

Emma pulled him close, his body enveloping hers completely. He planted a kiss on her forehead while she listened to the strong thump of his heart. It was a moment that needed to last forever but ended in less than a minute.

Emma stepped through the door, following in Bren and Aisley's footsteps, and left her Hero behind.

Their horses and cart were stored only a few blocks away. Bren and Aisley had already reined the horses and were preparing to leave by the time Emma reached them. She threw her pack inside the cart and went to speak with her sisters.

"The plan is East," she said plainly. "Jim and I will meet you in a day."

The three embraced and the cart sped through the streets, leaving Emma in its shadow.

■ ■ ■ ■ ■ ■ ■ ■ ■

Night took Salix. Jim sat, his silhouette masked by a brick chimney that sprouted from his perch. The church stood out in the darkness, a large outline reaching for the stars and heavens. He breathed deeply, the crisp air flowed through his nostrils and burned in his waiting lungs.

It was time to move, enter the church before the Northtrees arrived to meet with Marcus. Jim had only observed one obvious entrance, a window near the top of the steeple. The tower was framed with wood and brick, and it would be an easy climb for his expert fingers, but to get to the top unseen required precision timing.

Jim jumped from his perch and scrambled up the church's slanted roof. His hands found purchase on the steeple and pulled him from the clay tiles. The brick scraped at his fingernails and the old wood stung him with tiny splinters, but his ascent was unhindered.

Halfway to the window, a rotting plank ripped from Jim's grasp and tumbled noisily to the street below. He stayed still, pushing his body flat against the cold tower until he was sure no one was coming to investigate. The rest of his climb was uneventful, though by the time he reached the window his fingers had bloodied and the muscles in his hands burned with aggravation.

The window slid open effortlessly and Jim pulled himself into the dusty attic. He stayed motionless, breathing in shallow and slow breaths, listening for any indication of movement. Quiet creaks came from the warped boards many floors down, moving back and forth in a pacing pattern. Otherwise, the church remained silent.

Jim crouched through the room, leaving billowing footprints in the undisturbed dust. A door rested in the floor near the center of the room. It pulled open on rusty hinges, sending a pillar of light through the dark below.

A winding, rug-covered staircase ran through the steeple's interior. Gas lanterns shone brightly at each landing, illuminating wooden doors that led to unknown rooms. At the bottom sat a velvet couch with leather-bound books piled in knee-high stacks all around.

Jim dropped from the trap door, landing on his toes on the padded floor. He stalked down the stairs, reaching the first door. It opened, and the room housed moth-eaten silk robes and cobweb covered slippers. Another flight down, the room showed various instruments with broken strings and cracked necks.

The third room was locked. Jim pulled a slim piece of metal from his boot and jostled it in the lock until he heard a soft click. The room housed a desk, papers littered across its surface. A candle flickered near the wall, smoke spiraling towards the rafters. A cloth chair was tucked at one edge, the mark of a buttocks imprinted on its seat.

Jim snuck into the room, closing the door behind him. He reached for one of the scattered papers on the desk, bringing it close to his eyes to read in the limited light. The letter was unremarkable, a letter of gratitude from one of the priest's subjects, dripping with affection.

Jim glanced over the other papers, and a signature caught his eye.

Marcus,

*If your experiments are yielding no progress with the Faults, then they will no longer receive our compensation. Do not think that we will pay into another religious scheme. There are promises that you must keep.*

Bastion Northtree

He searched through the papers until he found another.

Marcus,

*The items you have uncovered may have value in a world beyond your gospel. The implications of changing a human into a creature is beyond curious. We have captured a few Faults from the Dogwood cities, and they will be the subject of your experiments moving forward. If the amulet works like you claim, the Leader himself will exalt you.*

Bastion Northtree

Faults? Amulet? Something strange was beginning to form in Jim's mind. A picture of twisted torture, with Marcus lying in its epicenter, manifested.

M.

*I can't believe you got the door open! We've been trying for decades, but you were the one to crack it. We will be heading there after our meeting at the Savior Wall.*

F. N.

Piles of letters described different pieces of vague experiments. The Northtree signatures lay at the bottom of each one, guiding Marcus through their plans and directing him on what to test next. The next letter that caught Jim's eye made his blood turn furiously to ice.

Marcus,

A belt for an heir was an expensive price, but from what our rumors say it was an effective incentive. Send your killer to Ketch next, for there is a defector there that will be perfect to test the gauntlet on. He must be alive, husks don't like dead flesh.

I will be visiting the dark plains when I arrive. I expect you to have your problems resolved before my arrival. My name will be from the Four that you have located. I will accept nothing less.

Bastion Northtree

Jim reread the letter and the confirmation of his planned death. If Marcus was behind his contract, it was ordered with the Northtrees' blessing. He should have killed Faye when he had the chance, lowering the number of enemies that now resided so near to him.

A shadow obscured the light from under the doorway. Someone walked closer to the room, their feet distinctly marked from the bright hallway. Jim slunk to a corner, hiding where the door would open.

The door inched open, and gloved fingers wrapped around its side. A head was visible, scanning the dark room before the person entered fully. A hood covered the person's head and a dark handkerchief covered their mouth. They took a hesitant step towards the desk, and Jim struck.

He kicked at the person's knees, buckling them to a kneel. The person dropped farther and rolled to face their attacker. Jim jabbed with his dagger, but the figure caught it easily on their own blade, its brown color shining oddly from the hallway. Jim recoiled and lunged towards the person's abdomen. The unknown person twisted gracefully and pulled a thin sword from behind her back, a rapier.

Jim stopped. "Emma?" he asked the figure.

Emma pulled the mask from her mouth, a devious smile shinning from her beautiful lips. She pulled a finger to her mouth and pointed towards the voices that now rose from the floor below. The Northtrees were here.

Jim moved close to her, keeping his voice at barely a whisper. "What are you doing here?"

She whispered back, her breath warm on the Hero's neck, "I couldn't let you have all the fun." She pulled away with a wink and moved towards the staircase.

Jim stepped in front of her and reached for his belt. He pulled the shiny Angeloak pistol from his holster and thrust it into Emma's grasp. It was too late to debate whether she should be here. If Heroes attacked; the girl would need an advantage.

"There are only eight shots," Jim whispered.

Emma looked at the weapon with a childlike amazement. Most humans never got to touch a firearm and would only see them on the backs of passing Heroes. She tucked the gun snuggly in her waistband, next to her dazzling brown blade, and followed Jim down the stairs.

"You'll have to tell me about that dagger once we're done here," Jim said, curiosity heavy on his breath.

Together they reached the bottom floor. Jim stuck his ear against the door, listening to the muffled voices that came from the other side. He could hear multiple tones, but they spoke in hushed reverence, too quiet for the Hero to understand. He risked cracking the door and peering into the large room.

The recognizable chapel, where the congregation had met the day before, spread out in pews before him. The pews were mostly empty, making the room seem much larger than it did when bodies had stuffed every seat. The podium stood a few yards away, close enough for Jim to see the shelf that held Marcus' journal underneath.

In the center of the room stood four men: Marcus, Bastion, Kole, and Ryan Blackthorne. They sauntered from the double doors that served as an entrance, talking nonchalantly about the ride they had taken to Salix.

The priest yawned mightily. "Apologies, sirs," he was saying. "I have yet to recover from my rebirths this afternoon. It takes a lot from me, drains me within an hour."

"No apologies necessary," said Blackthorne. "We are honored that you could make time for us in this late evening."

The Northtrees stayed quiet, but Kole nodded his head in agreement. They stopped when they reached the podium, and Marcus lifted his journal to the crook of his armpit. He slunk below the podium again, reaching towards the back. A loud click echoed through the room, and a grinding sound emanated as the podium slid across the tiles.

A ladder peaked from a hole in the floor. Marcus said, "I have a few guests in the bed chambers, but they should be sound asleep until the morning. The rooms are built to keep out noise, so there is no need to speak in hushed voices." The men climbed down the ladder.

One by one the men disappeared through the hole. Jim waited as their voices sank into silence. The metallic bang from metal on metal resonated from the hole, but otherwise, all was quiet.

He pushed the door open and looked at where the men had disappeared. A wooden ladder stretched downwards, going as deep as the steeple was tall. At its base was a dirt floor, compacted by trampled footprints. A tunnel led beyond what Jim could see.

Jim grabbed the top rung but stopped when Emma touched his shoulder. "Are you sure?" she asked. "There's no easy way out if things get messy."

"There are answers here, Em. I need to find them." He climbed down the ladder.

The tunnel was long, and the ceiling was too low for Jim to stand upright. He ducked his head and traversed through the underground path. The claustrophobic walls were made of crumbling dirt and wooden support beams every few feet. Roots from buried plants spiderwebbed from above, scratching at the back of Jim's neck as he walked.

The tunnel twisted left and right, going a mile before it opened into a wide room. Torches burned on the walls, their light stretching upward but was eaten by shadows before they reached the ceiling. At the opposite end sat a door and a green pad, buried in the wall at the door's side, about the size of a hand. The door was made of thick metal and had sharp tongs on its edge. It was a door made for protection, a barrier to keep out all unwanted intruders. But despite its unwelcome appearance, it hung open.

The room beyond the door was unlike anything Jim had ever seen. Metallic, grated tiles lined the floor. Light shone from glass tubes that were implanted in the ceiling, the source of its flame unseen. The decorators had hung plaques behind glass containers lining the walls.

Jim entered, Emma at his heel. He read the first plaque. *Project: External Imitation – Failure*. Spectacles rested in the glass case, their frames covered by different colored lenses. When he bent down to peer through the lens, Jim saw warped and swirling patterns where the wall was blank before.

The next plaque read *Project: Cure End – Testing*. The size of the case above the plaque was the size of a small shield. The glass walls were broken, and no object sat within.

Jim continued to read as he wandered down the halls. Half of the cases were whole and held a variety of ordinary looking items. Gloves sat over the name *Adhesive Accelerator*. Underneath a metal helmet the sign read *Gravitational Limiter* . A shiny vest read *Electromagnetic repulse 1*. The other cases were broken. Plaques read of things like *Incinerator, Genome Enhancement,* and *Life Harness,* but these items within had also been stolen from the glass protectors.

Metal doors lined the sides of the room, green pads soldered to the walls beside them. When Jim placed a finger on the pad, it lit up and numbers brightly displayed on its surface. After touching a few of the numbers, the pad flashed red and went dark.

Voices shouted from farther ahead, startling the curious Hero. He snuck deeper through the room, towards the voice's location. A hallway split in two directions, the doors on either side open wide. He began to wander towards the left room when another shout came from ahead.

Forward, the walls expanded, opening into a room as large as a city block. Jim looked up in wonderment at the shiny silver walls. Glass cylinders filled with bubbling liquids were placed one every few feet. When Jim pressed his face to the glass, he saw an oddly shaped figure floating inside.

"I just don't think I could pull you back," Marcus' voice said from the other side of the room.

Emma grabbed Jim and hid behind the container. Marcus and the Heroes entered from a doorway across the room. Sweat glistened from Marcus' forehead and a frustrated look was glowering from Kole's face.

"This is unacceptable. After all we've done for you, you choose to give this gift to humans instead of their betters. I know you're a Lesser, but a I didn't expect you to sympathize with the...."

"How long do you require?" Bastion said, cutting his son's exclamation short.

"One night. Just...let me sleep. I should regain enough energy by the morning to help one of you transcend," Marcus said.

"We will meet again, at this time tomorrow. Will you be able to transcend both of us then?" Bastion asked.

Marcus thought for a moment before speaking, "I think so. It is very taxing, but...I should be strong enough by then."

Bastion clapped Marcus on the shoulder. "You have proven yourself a worthy investment. Now, take us to the surface. Our men will be waiting to toast in our honor."

"Yes, sir. Thank you, sir!" Marcus said and began walking in Jim's direction.

As the men came closer, Jim and Emma pivoted around the container, staying out of sight. The heavy fall of the men's boots echoed loudly through the metal chamber and quietly crunched when they reached the floor of dirt. After a few minutes, Jim heard a scraping sound of the podium hiding the entrance to the tunnel.

Emma let out a breath and gasped for another. Jim relaxed the muscles in his neck and released the hilt of a knife that he had absentmindedly grabbed. They exited from behind their hiding place, free to explore the secrets of the strange place.

They entered the room that the Northtrees had exited. It had the same metallic walls as the large room but was roughly the size of an ordinary bed chamber. A chair was bolted to the floor in the center, locks for arms and legs built in to the cushioned rests. A hook hung from the ceiling, too high for Jim to reach without jumping. The room reeked with the copper scent of blood. A golden gauntlet sat at the side of the chair, the insignia of a phoenix rising from flames branded into its palm. Jim went to reach for the gauntlet. Nausea emanated from the armor piece with each step that the Hero took. As he reached to touch the metal, Emma's hand grabbed his elbow.

"Don't," she said seriously. "Something feels...wrong."

Her warning was all Jim needed to validate his one sense of foreboding. He backed away and exited the room, relief flooding his chest.

"We need to leave, Jim. This place...it's...I don't' know. It's unnatural. My head started aching the moment we entered."

Jim closed his eyes to think. Why was it so hard to think here? His head throbbed with each beat of his heart, causing flashes of light to dance on his eyelids. Emma was right, for there was clearly something wrong about this place.

"Let's go," Jim whispered, though his voice felt booming to his throbbing head.

They started down the chamber, passing the broken glass cases and plaques. But, when they came to the cross in the hallways, Jim stopped. He felt something here. Something familiar yet foreign. It was coming from the left, an open door that invited the Hero.

The feeling pulled him towards it, calling to him through an unknown void. Emma said something, but her voice was only muttered nonsense to the Hero's mesmerized mind. His feet marched through the doorway, as Emma pulled tightly against his will.

The room was long but not very wide. Barred cages were stacked on both sides, from one end of the room to the other. Inside each cage hunched a husk.

The creatures screamed when they saw the Hero, slashing wildly at the metal bars with their elongated claws. Foam dripped from their mouths and splashed on Jim's face when they shook their frantic heads. Sparks flew where claw met metal, but the bars remained unmarked from the numerous attacks.

"We need to go!" Emma yelled over the furious monsters.

Jim shook his head and tried to respond to the girl's exclamation, but the familiar feeling pulled at him again. It was coming from one of the cages, in the center of the room. He stepped towards the cage, each step amplifying the intensity of the familiar unknown.

Inside the cage, much like the others, stood a husk. It was cowering in the corner, its claws covering its rabid face. Fresh cuts gaped on the creature's stomach and a burn was brandished around its neck. But somehow Jim knew the monster. The familiar aura was flooding from its cowering form, and the geometrical tattoo that lined one of its arms sang of an old friend.

"Colter?" Jim whispered.

The creature froze and uncovered its face. Colter's dark eyes stared into Jim, a look of recognition contorting its disfigured mouth. Then, as if a switch flipped it from human to monster, it lunged at the Hero. Razor claws grazed Jim's cheek. He was too shaken to move, too petrified of the husk that couldn't possibly be the man it resembled.

Emma's fingers brushed Jim's neck. "We have to...." She fell silent, her weight falling completely against Jim.

Jim felt sluggish when he moved to catch the falling girl. His arms wrapped around her before she smashed against the floor. A dart was lodged in her neck. He plucked the spike from her and smelled its tip. *Tranquilizer.*

"Well, Jimmy," a disgusting voice began to say, "looks like you're harder to kill than I thought."

Floydd stood in the doorway, a rifle pointed at the Hero's chest. Jim jumped towards the man but caught a dart in his neck the moment he rose to his feet. His tongue tingled, his muscles trembled, but he still managed to take a step forward. Floydd split the difference in distance by taking a step, then punched Jim to the floor.

## 21: A HERO'S DEMISE

Her head throbbed in substantial, stabbing frequency. Her eyes felt so heavy and fought against her effort to open them. The vague awareness of pain came from her wrists and shoulders. Her eyelids parted slowly, revealing blurry reality made from still shapes with fractured lines. She blinked, her fuzzy vision clearing as her head bobbed. Nausea rattled in her empty stomach, the taste of bile rising from her throat. She tried to spit, but the muscles in her mouth were too weak and her saliva only dribbled from her lips.

The air here smelt of tobacco and curls of smoke flitted towards the iridescent light that shone from above.

She felt fear when she saw her hands bound to a metal hook jutting from the ceiling. Her eyes wandered down her body to find her clothes had been removed, a large shirt the only thing covering her nakedness from chilly air.

A small grunt came from somewhere in the room, though to the girl the sound felt far away. She inched her head in the direction of the noise and saw a figure sitting in the shadowy corner, the light from a rolled cigarette illuminating his sharp cheekbones and nose. He stared into her eyes as another plume of smoke rose from his parted lips.

Her eyes wanted so badly to close, and her head fell in protest. Through her half-closed eyes, she saw a metal grated floor that her bare feet dangled above. Beside her, there was a bolted chair with a Hero in its clutches. Emma's mind jolted awake at the sight of Jim. She tried to call his name and raise him from his sleep, but her voice came out as a raspy wheeze.

"The tranquilizer acts like a paralytic for a time," the man in the corner said, standing and walking towards her. "Your vocal cords will be one of the last things to work again." He placed a hand on her foot and began trailing his finger up her leg.

Her flesh prickled at his touch, but she had no strength to pull away. His finger stopped at the hem of the shirt. Instead of climbing farther, his finger glided in tiny circles over her thigh. He breathed deeply as his eyes wandered up her barely covered form and reached her gaze.

"The transformation would have ruined your clothes." He smirked. "I took the liberty of saving them from such a dreadful fate."

While holding her gaze, the man's circles moved beneath the shirt. A sudden power rippled to her leg and she struck. Her knee contacted the man's face, forcing him to take a step backward. Her chest heaved from effort, and her eyes glared with rage.

The man rubbed his jaw and looked up in crazed elation. The smile that parted his cracked lip exterminated her heat. She shivered against her will. He moved closer and grasped her chin firmly. His head was only inches below hers, his breath warm against her neck as he forced her to look at him.

"Once the priest is here with his amulet, we will wake your Hero. He will watch as you are disfigured beyond all recognition. Your mind will stay for a time, long enough for you to watch as he is disintegrated and banished from this world." He looked over her body again. "It's a shame to lose something so precious as a beautiful woman."

He planted his revolting mouth onto her lips, but she couldn't pull away. He held her tightly against him, her nausea growing unbearable with every moment. Then, he released her and walked out of the room, whistling merrily.

□ □ □ □ □ □ □

It was some time before Jim awoke, his eyes groggily assessing his captured state before finding Emma. Her voice was a scratchy whisper and she wiggled her fingers and toes in an attempt to loosen her bounds. The chords that bound her wrists tunneled through her flesh and a light trickle of blood ran down her body and pooled to the floor.

She didn't speak to Jim, but there was nothing she could say that the Hero hadn't realized. Instead, she gazed in his eyes, finding hope deep inside his gold. The truth, that this would be her final place of living, had settled on her while Jim slept. It hit her with a deep depression before manifesting as rage. Now, she allowed a small piece of hope to transform it into acceptance. If she were to die, at least Jim would be near.

Footsteps clanged against the tiles, coming towards the captured duo. Marcus entered, with the sharp-faced man at his heel, and inspected his guests. He looked in wonderment at Jim, who stared with fire in return. Then, he walked towards Emma, stepping in the blood that had accumulated on the floor.

"Her restraints may be a bit tight," Marcus sang. "Is she unharmed, otherwise?"

"Yes," the other man said.

"Good. She will be an excellent specimen." He went to Jim again and rubbed his thumb across the Hero's face. "The heir of Ash," he said reverently. "I must say, it is an unexpected honor to hold you here."

Jim shot his head towards the priest, but his restraints kept him an inch from smashing the man's nose. Marcus was unmoved by the attack, and he reached for his hip and pulled a curved blade from behind his robes. Keeping his face near the Hero, he slid the blade easily through Jim's side.

Emma could see the flashes of pain erupt from her Hero, but he didn't move from his position. The priest gave an impressed whistle and stepped back, keeping his knife lodged in Jim's side. Anger and fear contracted inside of Emma as she saw her Hero's blood spill from the wound.

"You Ash Heroes are a stubborn group. We give you the South, and you make it the strongest territory. We banish your heir, and you become the most renowned killer in the human world. We shoot you, throw you from a building, kill you in all rights...and you crawl your way from Hell."

Jim fell against the chair, his muscles finally relenting. He looked at Emma, his eyes stung with pain and regret. She stared back, unconsciously trying to transfer the little power she had left.

"Floydd said he found you with the husks," Marcus began, "in front of a specific husk actually: Colter." Jim's eyes snapped to the priest in hot fury. "He spoke of you before he turned, Jim. He cried for you to come to his aid, said that you were always the one to pull him from a doomed situation. But…you never came. Not until Colter was gone, and only his shell remained."

Marcus inched towards Jim and whispered loudly into his ear, "Do you want to know how I did it?" Marcus twisted the knife in Jim's side, causing the Hero to finally twitch and grunt in pain. "It's hard to explain, but…I could show you."

Marcus reached for his collar, pulling a golden amulet from around his neck. The amulet was made of thin chain and had a large ruby with the image of a radiant personage carved on its visage. He walked towards Emma, the jewelry dangling from his callused hand.

"You see, it doesn't work on Heroes. Something about our genes, our code, makes the necklace think we are already perfect. But humans," he continued, taking another step towards Emma, "have many, many flaws." He slipped the amulet around her neck.

Pain seared from Emma's flesh. Her skin, where the necklace touched, sizzled and blistered, and the smell of burning meat filled the room. Her eyes rolled to the back of her skull, but the pain didn't stop. She shook fiercely and could feel foaming blood as it spilled from her mouth. She screamed, spraying the wall with acrid liquid. Something pushed against her mind, trying to dominate her very being. When she fought against it, the presence snarled and caused the amulet to burn hotter. She began to lose consciousness, but the beastly thing attacked her until she woke. It would not let her sleep until she gave it control. The amulet grew hotter, still.

■ ■ ■ ■ ■ ■ ■ ■

Horror filled Jim as Emma screamed. The amulet around her neck sent billowing smoke from her blackened skin. Her face was contorted, her mouth foaming, making her look like a rabid animal, ready to bite.

Jim pulled against his restraints, arching his back with effort. The knife in his side fell to the ground with a crash, but the leather straps that held him didn't budge. A roar of curses burst from his lungs, tearing through his throat.

"Now Jimmy," Floydd oozed. "Are those the last words you want your woman to hear?"

He relaxed his muscles and stared daggers through Floydd. He put all his anger, all of the vile hatred that he held in his heart and pushed it through his gaze. Floydd's eye twitched, his expression turning from one of psychopathic joy, to one of unwholly dread. He fell to his knees, a puddle of urine spreading where he knelt.

"Floydd?" Marcus said with concern. "What are you doing?"

Floydd looked at the priest with a sniveling expression. He pulled a pistol from the holster at his side and placed the barrel to his temple.

"I can't...," Floydd said and pulled the trigger.

Red and pink matter covered Marcus's silk white robes. The man stared in awe at his partner's body, then rose and met the heir of Ash's eyes. He frantically reached for the gauntlet that sat on the table next to Emma's dangling form and placed it snuggly on his hand.

The phoenix on the gauntlet's palm began to glow, then a beam of white particles erupted from its surface. Marcus grunted from exertion as he hoisted the beam towards Jim. The particles collided with Jim's foot, disintegrating it instantly.

"I was going to savor this moment," Marcus said as the beam traveled up Jim's legs. "But it seems Dom has blessed you more than I imagined." There was no pain from where his body vanished, only the sense of butterflies. "When you get there, tell Blackthorne I'm sorry I wasn't strong enough to pull him out."

The beam moved to Jim's chest and his breath left him. He turned his head, trying to find the emeralds that would allow him to die in peace. But, instead of green, white eyes of riling pain stared blankly.

His head was consumed by light, and his world became dark.

## 22: FROM PLACE TO PLACE

His body was weightless, floating amongst a sea of smoky clouds and consuming black. His eyes still fixated on the spot where Emma had hung, dying from an ancient magic that charred through her flesh. Nothing was there now. Only a corner of concentrated darkness so thick and heavy that it pulled at his conscious mind.

What if he sank through the dark depths? What if he allowed himself to fade and become a piece of his surroundings? Would that be so bad?

His abdomen still ached with phantom stabs. His shirt was soaked with chilled blood, irritatingly sticking around the hole in his body. Even now, he could feel the sinews and muscle pulling itself back together, attempting to heal the Hero's reminder of failure. But his body refused to stand.

It had been an hour, maybe two. Time was difficult to comprehend in the indistinct place, but it was long enough for Marcus to have won. Even if Jim had the ability to return to the bright world that he knew, it would be too late to change fate. So he stared and floated in the unknown place. If he moved, so would reality. It would become an existence that traveled past the things that he could not accept.

*"You talked before."* A light, melodic voice whispered in Jim's ear.

He tried to look at the figure who spoke, but his eyes refused to move. He could feel the presence's gaze on his horizontal form, feel the uncomfortable observation of the stranger. It made no sound, but the air seemed to shift as the image of a human shadow inched through his line of vision.

The figure was smaller than the one he had talked to before. If Jim were standing, the place where a head should be would only reach the lower section of his chest. It held its thin arms behind its back as it hovered back and forth in front of the Hero's face. Tendrils of smoke trailed behind as the figure moved, latching towards pockets of clouds.

"*Last time, you were wrong for this place too. So why return...*" The voice paused. "*Jim. Yes. You are Jim.*" The feminine voice was pleased with her recollection. "*I saw you before. I was drawn to you, like so many others, and that is rude. I do not like to be with them. But I did feel the pulling, and I had to go.*"

Jim's eyes twitched and shifted at the small figure's head. His body reluctantly responded to the movement, but he forced himself to find the ground. Like before, his feet met an invisible, solid surface when he transitioned to a standing position.

If he began to walk now, what would he find? Jim remembered the priest's recollection of visiting this place. *A blind imitation.* The world here reflected the world he knew, so this place…

Jim took a few steps forward, his fingers reaching outward. They brushed against a slick surface, the metal wall that he had felt before. He reached down and he found the grated surface of the tiles that lined the room where he had…died? He walked around the room, keeping his hand on the wall. Eventually, he felt the indication of a door's hinges and handle. But, no matter how hard he pushed and pulled against the door, it refused to budge.

Jim pounded on the door, the sound of his frustration ringing through the silent dark. He kicked and threw his body against the stubborn object; but, no matter how hard he attacked, it stayed firmly in place. In frustrated resignation, he threw his hands into the air and screamed at the ceiling.

The small shadow flew above him in a frantic motion. "*Shush!*" She spoke harshly. "*Do not call the others!*"

He quieted. The fear in the shadow's voice spread contagiously. Her words held power and ice, forcing Jim's vocal cords to stop.

"What others?" Jim asked.

"*All of them.*" said the shadow. "*They will come, and they will force you to take them towards the surface. It is a fate that they will not live through, and neither will you. But they cannot stop themselves. The call is too tempting.*"

Jim pondered on her words and a thought struck him. "How would they get in here? The room is sealed."

"The room is not sealed, only the door is closed. But this is not a place for doors, not even a place for walking and running." She sounded dazed. "Maybe for flying. I like to...fly. But to leave here, you cannot fly. You just have to leave."

"Okay..." Jim started to say, no closer to an answer than before; "and, how would I leave?"

"Oh! I know that one!" The shadow said with excitement in her voice and movements, "Can you think?"

"Yes."

"Hard." She insisted, "Can you think very, very hard?"

"I...I think so," Jim said, confused.

"Where did you think? It can't be here, or you will be here."

"Where did I..." Jim stopped.

It couldn't be that simple. He closed his eyes and drew an image in his head, a place. One that he knew from his days spent in the Celestial Grove. The same place where he had taken Emma the night they first met. Once the image was formed completely, he opened his eyes.

The shape of a familiar camp greeted the Hero. Though there was no color, the obvious signs of the natural wall, where trees had grown close together, and an opening formed by two large boulders, told him of his location. In the camp's center were the featureless remains of an old fire that scattered under Jim's step.

"Where is this?" the light voice whispered, startling Jim.

He turned to face the shadow. "A place I used to call home."

"Oh! It's small. But you are large." She said, gliding around the shelter. "But home is a wonderful place.

"Yes, it is. How did you know to travel here?"

"Luna," said the shadow.

"What?"

"My name is Luna. Please ask a question for Luna."

"Alright. How did you know to travel here, Luna?" Jim asked, emphasizing her name.

"*Thank you, Jim. It is very polite to use the name. That way, I know you are the one who is asking the question, and not...*" She trailed off and cupped her head in her hands.

She spoke in soft mumblings. Her tone shifted constantly, becoming harsh and sharp or shy and subservient. But the meaning in her conversation was indistinguishable.

For minutes she rambled and held her head. Jim took a hesitant step towards Luna. He stretched out his arm, intending to place a hand on her shoulder to rouse her from her trance. But, as his fingers neared her swirling form, she snapped away and faced his direction.

"*Do not touch,*" she said firmly. "*I will not go back, not even with you.*" She spun her head around and waited for Jim to retract his hand before speaking again. "*Oh, yes!*" she exclaimed merrily. "*Your question. I forgot for a second, but I remembered now. You are easy to find, easy to follow. You are wrong for this place, so I must look past everything that is right. Then, I find you. Easy.*"

"So, I can go anywhere with just a thought?" Jim asked.

"*Yep ,*" Luna said happily.

Jim closed his eyes and formed an image in his head. Before he opened his eyes, he could feel that he had traveled. The air moved freely through the Hero's outstretched arms, the sound of wind rustling, light rain rapping against millions of leaves, the smell of snow and pine clearing his sinuses.

When his eyes finally opened, he saw a familiar scene. The dark shapes of trees stood on one side of him. Looking towards the inky horizon, he could see the outlines of all the Willow cities, their walls obscuring the shapes of the houses that resided within. He had seen the view before, climbed the Eastern Mountains and peered over the protected lands of the Heroes. The beauty of the colorful lands was lost in this place, but the majesty of the magnificent landscape radiated proudly through the obsidian and onyx view.

Jim was vaguely aware of Luna hovering to his right, but she stayed silent on the overlooking peak. In the distance, the tiny shape of Paradise rose from the black ring of the Celestial Grove.

He kept his eyes open this time, as he thought of his old home. The world around him seemed to melt. The trees and boulders that jutted from the mountain fell into pools of murky water before tangling together to form a new place.

Buildings and pleasant gardens rose from the liquid, the shapes of the Ever-Flowing Fountain marking the city's center. The ground below changed from rough dirt to cobbled stone and silky grass. The tower that marked the Leader's home stretched for the sky, a black pillar that sat only a few feet lower than the wall.

"Oh! Paradise!" Luna marveled. "I nearly forgot about this place. You know, I lived here...or...under here. It was before. Now we would have to live in the trees or by a river, I think. But rivers move much faster than I prefer. Maybe a stream, or a brook. Why is it that brooks always babble?" She held her face inches away from Jim.

"I'm not sure, Luna." he replied, and began walking through the streets of his old home.

"I think they are merely infants in the water world. Streams can speak, but they are usually nonsensical. Rivers roar so loud because they are the oldest of their kin. But brooks are still learning, babbling as they grow." Luna stopped in front of Jim and twirled between the houses. "That must be it! You are a wise companion, Jim!"

His surroundings distracted Jim far beyond care for such conversation.

It had been years since he last left Paradise, a lifetime. This place was nothing like the home that he had once known. Tall towers lined the walkways, ladders reaching toward the fortified top. Jim climbed one tower and found the shapes of four rifles leaning against a wall, though they did not move at his touch. From the tower he could easily see the peaks of six identical towers, all surrounding the small living area.

As he continued down the street, he was stopped by the form of a chain fence that reached the roof of the two surrounding buildings. On its top sat curling razor wire that twisted through the chains. Jim bounded over the obstruction, but the sight troubled him. He remembered, vividly, running through these streets, chasing the other children through the curving passages. Each street was safe and free, no fences, no towers, only Paradise to protect them.

Jim didn't comprehend where his feet were leading him, until he saw the ancient tree that marked his childhood home. A rickety rope swing hung from the lower, mangled branches, swaying uninterrupted by the surrounding still. Behind the tree sat the homely cottage his mother had lived in while his father ruled the city. Memories of climbing the old ash and rolling over the sweet-smelling grass flashed through Jim's mind. These memories triggered emotions that lapped at his heart like a faithful tide touching the beach. From a distant thought he could hear his mother's voice, calling him for supper or chastising him for setting a careless example for Ellie.

"It's happy here," said Luna soberly. "You, I mean. You are happy here. It's an odd feeling from you, one that you haven't shared with me before."

Jim looked quizzically at Luna. "How do you know what I feel?"

Luna shrugged and wandered towards the tree. She hovered above the swing before sitting atop it and joining in the object's swaying. She laughed giddily, and her feet kicked with each motion.

"You share; it's nothing I do. It's just like how He can share, the one that touched you. He can feel everything here and make everything feel him, and you are part him. That's what happens when we give those who are wrong a piece of us: we both live again, together. It sounds wonderful, but I have already been too many people. I prefer to just be me."

Jim's face must have conveyed his confusion, because Luna continued to explain. "You see, the man who touched you is...omnipotent. He's god here, Jim. But he is not ruling, and he is not spiteful. No. He is only curious. He was furious but is now curious. That's fun!" Luna laughed, repeating the words "curious" and "furious" over and over.

"So, when he touched me," Jim began, interrupting Luna's delighted repetition, "he gave me part of himself?"

"Yep."

"And he was powerful, so now I am too?"

"Yeppy!" Luna jumped from the swing and stepped in front of Jim. "I doubt you can do everything, but you can definitely share. Try it on me. What am I thinking?"

"What do you...." Jim started.

"*Shush!*" Luna cut him off. "*Concentrate, Jim. What am I thinking?*"

Jim closed his eyes and thought of the shadow girl. At first, he felt nothing, saw nothing but the back of his eyelids. But a feeling began to manifest, radiating from where Luna stood. It was faint and fleeting, but it was definitely an emotion that was emanating from outside of himself. He dove towards the feeling, allowing it to flutter around him and slip into his memory. The harder he concentrated the more distinct and consuming the emotion became. Then, the feeling morphed, began to take shape, color in the otherwise black world.

He and she saw the blinding green grass that itched at her feet. Gnarled roots crawled from the dirt below, from the apple tree that held her prize. On the upper branches she could see the ruby apple that called to her, beckoning that the small girl taste its juicy insides. She began to climb, and it wasn't easy, for she was only a child and restricted to her few measly abilities. But she would have that apple, feel its juices run down her chin and make her cheeks sticky.

It was just out of reach, mocking her useless attempts to satiate her lust. She moved farther along the thinning branch, feeling the heavy sway that her body caused on the weak limb. But alas, her fingers wrapped around the fat fruit and, as she brought it towards her mouth, the branch cracked.

The ground approached at a terrifying speed. A blur of branches sped past her flailing arms and grasping fingertips. Then, the ugly root which tainted the beautiful grass collided with her head.

The world was black for a moment, then it became different swirls of color. A trickle of blood poured from her forehead, the red almost as wonderful as the apple which sat beside her. She reached for her tasty treat.

"You do not want the apple," a voice whispered.

She looked around but could not find the source of the voice. She reached again for her prize.

"STOP! STOP! STOP! STOP!" came another voice.

"No!" she yelled back and took a bite into the fruit.

Instead of the tart taste she was prepared for, her teeth clacked against the rock that she held in her hand. She looked at the rock, angry that it had betrayed her, and threw it against the trunk.

"I said to stop."

"You should have listened."

"You do not know better."

"The apple was poison."

"The grass should serve as a proper punishment."

"Your head is bleeding; perhaps it can be undone."

She reached towards the wound in her head, overwhelmed by the sound of the multiple voices. When her fingers brushed against the angry gash, she could feel a thread that wound down her skin. She pulled at the thread, unweaving the mask that she wore and releasing the truth that hid beneath.

"Yes, remove it all."

"You will be much happier when it is off."

"Don't stop at the mask. Remove it all."

She pulled at the thread, extending the hole that would allow her to breath. She concentrated on her single task, her tongue licking at her clenched lips. The shouts of a woman fell upon her distant ears, but it was a voice that was quiet compared to those which urged her to continue.

Her hand was pulled away from her mask, the grip of her mother's hand tight on her wrist. She stared at her mother's face, and a scared expression stared back.

"What have you done?" her mother asked.

The world around Jim formed again, showing him the tree and the shadow, which stood in front of him. He shook his head, trying to clear his distorted mind. Luna danced in front of him, tilting her head back and forth while she hummed.

"So?" she asked. "What was I thinking of?"

"I saw a tree, and...an apple." Jim's voice portrayed his confusion.

"Yeppy!" Luna shouted. "That's exactly what I was thinking of! A wonderful apple!" She spun in a circle as she spoke. "I knew you could do it! What do you want to t...."

Luna dispersed in an amalgamation of clouds and dust. The sudden silence startled Jim, and he reached towards the empty sheath that sat on his hip. He spun in a circle, looking for the cause of Luna's disappearance, but he saw only smoke and shadows. He ducked low and pushed himself against the wall of a nearby building.

"*You are a funny one to watch, Jim,*" said a familiar, all-encompassing voice. "*I've been waiting for you to return, because we have much to discuss.*"

From behind the tree appeared a man clad in shadow everywhere except his face. A face that was distorted and blistering, a face that held ever-staring eyes and a crooked smile, a face that had forced Jim to burn.

The shadow man walked towards the Hero and placed a hand on his shoulder. The world of Paradise melted away, leaving the two surrounded by blackness.

## 23: A MIND'S DELIGHT

Everything hurt. Each breath sent burning red pulses through Emma's vision. The smell of bile and smoldering flesh stung her nostrils and forced her to gasp and spit with each panting breath. But all her pain, all her meager discomforts, drowned in waves of attacking temptation from the presence that whispered through her consciousness.

It had started as snarls and growls but slowly took the form of shrill words and promises. It told her she could sleep, be through with the endless pain that she experienced, if she allowed the presence to consume her. The offer had seemed preposterous at first, but now the ability to stop the pain was beyond enticing.

Her only respite were the small moments when the presence needed to rest. The moments came in fractioned seconds, most of the time lasting less than a heartbeat. They allowed the tortured girl to remain strong enough to defend her inner inhibitions. During these times, Emma was able to return from her mind and observe the chamber with her overwhelmed senses. She heard pieces of words or shuffled steps, could smell the shifts in the musky air as people entered and exited the room. She saw blurry silhouettes standing in front of her. But before she could blink away the blur, her mind would come under assault again. It was a repetitious and exhausting pattern that gave no sign of ever ending.

Once, she had heard her name, mumbled between the distinct voices of two different men. Fingers brushed against her forehead and pried open her sealed eyelids. But the face that was revealed filled her with confusion. Blue eyes, a ring of copper circling the irises, stared from the darkness. Crow's feet wrinkled the edges of each eye, causing the man's kind expression to sing of aged joy. His white teeth shone with a bright and warm smile, one of happiness and love. It was the face, the smile, the eyes, the love, of Davey.

Hot tears watered her eyes when his soft hand cupped her cheek. There was so much that she needed to say, but her words caught in her throat and came out as a wet sob. Davey responded by pulling Emma towards him in a strong embrace. Her hands found his protective shoulders and held to him with all the strength she had left.

"You need to sleep, Em," Davey whispered.

Emma's voice was scratchy when she replied. "I'm so tired, Davey."

Davey pushed his head away and stared into his daughter's face. His look became serious, still retaining the kindness in his eyes. He studied her tattered features with a paternal gaze, a father finding the best way to help his child.

"Let it consume you," he said softly.

The air grew cold. Davey's form backed away slowly. When she tried to follow, Emma found her wrists bound and feet unable to reach the floor. Her heart beat in terror as her father faded from her vision, leaving a bare metal wall as her only comfort. The amulet that hung from her neck oscillated hotter and heavier, forcing her to pull back to her mind. The presence cackled as it saw her deteriorating consciousness retreat to her inner sanctum. It thrashed towards her, taunting her and laughing uproariously at her torment.

She tried to drown out the obnoxious being, tried to push it away from her and leave her to wallow in her depression. But her struggles only emboldened its attempts. It struck at her over and over, louder and louder, each attack causing her to shrink and fracture.

"You must sleep!" it screamed. "You must allow me in!"

The presence grew larger as she shrunk, towering over the cowering girl. She could feel it all around her, biting into her neck and boiling her blood. It was so strong, too strong, too overwhelming. Maybe...maybe she could let it win. She could sleep, join Davey in whatever haven he had prepared. It would be so easy...and painless.

*Emma.* Her mother's voice spoke through her. *What's wrong, Emma?*

Emma looked around. She had fallen from her horse, a wild stallion that she had been trying to break for the last three days. The stallion threw erratic kicks each time she sat upon his haunches. The palms of her hands had blistered from her desperate grip. Tears streamed down her cheeks, and her nose sniffled from her latest failed attempt at the beast. In this state her mother found her.

Steady arms lifted Emma to her feet, and a calloused hand patted her head. When she looked up, her mother's benevolent face peered back. Her mother crouched low, matching her daughter's height.

*Are you going to let him win?* The voice didn't come from her mother's mouth, but it resonated through her touch. *You are strong. You've kept us alive for all these years, and you are going to let some brute beat you?* Her mother gestured towards the horse.

When Emma looked towards the field, she no longer saw the beast. Instead stood a man draped in white robes, a grin on his twisted face. She blinked, thinking her vision was fooling her, but the man remained.

Her mother took her hand and led Emma toward the man. *When I took you hunting and you missed that buck, did you stop hunting?*

"No," Emma whispered.

The man's eyes were glued on the duo as they approached. *When the crops froze over the short winter, did you allow us to starve?*

"No," Emma again said, finding strength returning to her voice.

They stood a step away from the priest. *When the Heroes came, when they took me from our bed, when my blood muddied the path to our home, did you let them take you to your father? Did you surrender yourself to the will of those who thought they had domain over you?*

Her mother pushed the hilt of a knife into Emma's hand. Her grip felt comfortable on the worn weapon's handle. The priest continued to stare at them, though his grin had fled and left him looking concerned.

Her mother pointed at the priest, then motioned to the knife. *So, will he be the one that you let win?*

"No!" Emma thrust the knife into the priest's belly.

The presence screamed in agony as Emma attacked. She forced her entirety against the opponent, blasting through its overwhelming façade. As her attacks grew fiercer, the presence fled and cowered towards the amulet and forced it to grow as hot as she could endure.

Emma laughed, a miserable laugh, and screamed at the burning pain. But, when the torture grew to an astounding boil, she found that unconsciousness would finally be allowed.

Her world fell away, her mind hiding the pain from her conscious self. It was the most perfect nothing that Emma had ever experienced, a paradise inside a volcanic chaos. From somewhere, far away, she could hear the confused words of people speaking in the room. But what they said was not important. Her mind was hers again, and she could sleep.

## 24: TO KILL DEATH

Jim blinked rapidly, his eyes moving over the pure and unending blackness. There were no formations to break the single shade, no familiar shapes to help him distinguish his surroundings. All that remained was the suffocating darkness, which promised the Hero madness if he were left exposed.

When he stepped forward, the floor evaded his prodding foot. He fell backwards, his leg hanging from an invisible crevasse, and he tried to slow his frantic breathing. The air around him moved, a breeze that betrayed the location's size and chilled his lungs as he inhaled. A shiver ran through his torso, magnifying the eerie feeling that had begun to creep from behind.

Jim tried to leave, think of a comforting place and travel there as Luna had explained. But, after multifarious efforts, he remained stuck. This dark place would not yield to the images of his homes and havens.

"Why try and leave?" A deep voice rumbled through Jim's body. "I have brought you here for a purpose. It is important to realize when a purpose is greater than yourself. But you, Heir, are perfect for this place."

Jim stood. "And where is this?" he asked, gesturing blindly in every direction.

"Oh. Can you not see?"

Jim blinked again, the scene before him remaining dark, and shook his head.

"That is...curious." The voice paused in contemplation, mumbling secret words to itself as it thought. "Only once, before you that is, have I touched a being. Well...that is not quite right. Only once has the recipient of my touch decided to ascend again, thereby not falling into madness by my hand. Most times the dead stay dead, only listening to the calls of the living. But you,

Jim, you rose. You did not heed to your chosen fate. You took my touch, took my death, and decided to live. It was an encounter that I did not expect."

The words of Marcus' sermon resounded in Jim's head. The priest spoke of taking deaths and exchanging names, just as the invisible being was speaking. He had, unknowingly, lived through the religious man's preaching, by experiencing the death of another, and his name....

"Who was I before I died?" Jim asked, afraid of his identity's fragility.

The voice hummed, a single and monotonous note for a long while before it responded, *"Before I touched you, you mean?"*

Jim nodded.

*"You have been listening to too many preachers, Jim. There are so many who speak of me as a deity or a devil. They speak of this place with the same reverence as they would a celestial world. Humans become blind when they search for meaning. They look past the obvious prison which holds me and call it a possible heaven. They see the hungry souls, feel the deaths that have trapped them here, and call it rebirth. Why would any believe that the name of a deceased is anything but tragic? Can they not see that the meaning that they so desperately hunt is not complex wonder but simple irony?"*

The voice gained in strength as it spoke, sending tremors through Jim's feet and legs. The voice recognized its crescendo, so it took a few seconds to calm down, mumbling and emphasizing calm breaths.

When it spoke again, the voice was hushed and collected. *"I did not give you my name, Jim. It would hang over you, curse you with knowledge so great and terrible that you would collapse from my guilt. I only gave you my death, or what I assume was death."*

"I don't understand. How was I able to live again, just from seeing your death?" Jim asked.

The voice laughed. *"Understanding is a frustrating thing, especially when speaking of spiritual matters. Yours is a question I have asked many times, but the answer has proven to be...astounding. Do you know of the Time Before? When death did not exist?"* He asked.

"Only what little information my father taught me. It was a time of prosperity. No disease, no famine, no murder. They are only stories to our people."

"Ahh," the voice breathed. "Most of them are only stories, or, at least, misunderstood recollections. Those days were pleasant. Discoveries revolutionized each day, men and women held no struggles or worries, time was no longer an issue that loomed over mortal minds, and speculation created new gods.

"I was there at first, when the cure overtook humanity and promised salvation to all. Those times seemed miraculous. But a pattern formed as the years of serenity became centuries of prosperity, and the centuries formed a millennium of stagnant stupidity. It was a frustrating reality.

"Then, it toppled. The man who had killed Death revived him, and the world began to burn. The process took months to become a public realization. Stories of sickness evolved into eulogies that splattered pages. The new gods proved their folly as their followers fell beneath the thrust of a man. They cried to me, begged me, promised me objects of desire and lust, but those tangible absurdities were nothing compared to the death that I longed for, and all the answers that it would bring.

"Imagine my surprise when I woke in this hell of shadow. The fleeting answers I put faith in yielded only more impossible questions. I was alone for years, or what I thought to be years, until another personage entered my prison. They were drawn to me, as a moth is drawn to fire. One placed a hand upon my brow. She forced her memories through my thoughts, forced me to see through her eyes the life that had belonged to her. Then, once her blood began to fall from my throat, she left.

"Do you see, Jim? Do you understand as I did that day?" The voice paused long enough for Jim's silence to resonate his lack of clarity. "We are all connected." The voice chuckled madly.

"You see? Surely you see. I gave you my perceptions when I gave you my death. It was the piece of me that I thought necessary for you to understand and utilize. Above, the connections are faint but tangible if you know how to look. They can allow us to perceive and manipulate all those around us.

"Memories are no longer private, not for us, nor are they perfect. Our knowledge of the connection gives us dominion over all who breathe. You can enter the minds of any who cross your path, push your will on the belligerent. Through Floydd, I can see that you have used this connection. Forced him to take his life through…anger. Interesting."

Jim was shocked at the mention of Floydd's name. Words tumbled from his mouth in utters of nonsense as he attempted to gather his thoughts. The voice hardly noticed Jim's fluster, as it continued to rant over the connections that link every living thing. The questions that were building up in Jim's mind began to violently shake through him, demanding he release them to the shadows. So, as the voice was rambling about the trees speaking to the birds, Jim interrupted.

"How is that, any of it, possible? I saw the terror in Floydd before he pulled the trigger. He did not want to die. So, why did he do it?"

"Because of the connection, Jim. You dove through the differences between you and him, became singular in your mind and thoughts, and then your will overpowered his."

"So, he died."

"Yes, he died. It is what you wanted, needed, at that time. Your anger was beyond fury. Floydd's entire being became death and fear. It was quite...disturbing to experience," the voice projected with a shudder.

The implications of this connection soared through Jim. The power he could wield, the will that he could force, made his possibilities of strength immeasurable. None of his enemies would dare stand in his way; whether Hero or human, all would bow at his feet.

"I can feel your intentions, Jim. I will warn you, we are not omnipotent. Our control is only as powerful as our targets are weak. If you wish to manipulate the perceptions of the powerful, you will be the one who suffers. These connections belong to everything, they are not ours alone to control alone. There are those who walk in your world, old and ancient people, who have realized the same things that I have told you.

"But," the voice began to say abruptly, "warnings and wonders are not why I tell you of these connections. I tell you, so that you will see. Go through yourself and find me, then see the things that I look upon."

The room felt larger as the voice fell mute. A sharp ringing filled Jim's ears, his mind not accepting the silence as a true possibility. He closed his eyes and thought on the words the voice had spoken. He searched inside his mind, scanning every piece of himself for a connection to an outside source of life. But it was difficult.

Images of green eyes and bleeding wrists filled his mind. The sight of Emma hanging from a hook, the grin of Marcus's face as she screamed, disrupted his senses and distorted his time with impressions of urgency. He needed to make it back, needed to cut the binds from Emma's wrists and kill the bastard who had forced him here.

"*Calm,*" the voice demanded near his ear. "*Do not let memories overtake you. Not here. Be calm.*"

Jim took a breath and pushed the torturous images away. His breathing became deep and methodic. He pushed towards the calm places of his mind, the places that drove him towards success when killing or stalking. He dove towards a deep pool of serenity and drank the cool water that poured from his unconsciousness. He allowed the water to immerse him entirely and sank towards the smooth stones that formed the bed, and he stayed still at the bottom.

Then, he felt...something. A faint flutter of consciousness that seemed different from his own. He reached his hand towards the obscurity, but it danced away in playful circles. He swam towards it, determined to feel the odd presence with the tips of his fingers. As the object grew closer, it also grew in size. Soon, it felt as large as himself, then bigger. Before long, the presence towered over the Hero's consciousness, but he still swam forward. The moment his finger brushed against the oddity, it swallowed him entirely.

"*Now,*" the voice said softly. "*Open our eyes.*"

Jim slowly opened his eyes. Instead of the shadowy world that he had come to know, a room lightly revealed itself. The room seemed to stretch beyond what his eyes could see. The walls were lined with shelves overflowing with books of varying size and color. The wooden floor was grained in pleasing patterns, a golden trimmed rug covering its cold exterior. On the ceiling, brass and crystal chandeliers shone brightly every few feet. The room resonated with richness and royalty, from the carved brass doorknobs to the freshly dusted corners. The world of black had given way to a plethora of muted color, then the vibrance continued to grow inexorably, revealing the majesty of this place.

As his gaze wandered towards the center of the room, his eyes widened, and he forced himself to blink. Standing, in the center of the shaggy rug was himself. His eyes had closed tight in concentration, and strain crinkled his nose. He could see the sticky patch of clothing that gripped his abdomen, dark patches of blood splotching his pants and boots. An empty sheath dangled from his belt, barely revealed from the hidden safety of his cloak. It was without a doubt him standing in the room, frozen in thought. Yet, somehow, he was also floating and observing his concentrated form.

Jim's head felt dizzy, and the room began to flash in and out of existence, darkness taking its place. A wave of nausea churned through him, though he had no substance to vomit, which might have alleviated him. He brought his hands to his head and clutched his temples, trying to comprehend the impossible image. But the hands that grabbed at his face were not the scarred and familiar hands that he had always known. Gnarled, bony digits with translucent skin flexed in his vision. Rings decorated his large knucklebones and accentuated his trimmed fingernails. The pads of his fingers and palms were soft and malleable, the hands of a poet or inventor, not a fighter.

"Do you understand?" His mouth moved against his will, emanating the deep voice through his chest and throat.

What was happening, though it seemed impossible, was beginning to become clear. Somehow, he was looking through the eyes of another. He had some control over the actions and senses of this body, though he felt obvious limitations when he tried to prod through the being's mind. He was an observer to another's reality, a passenger looking through the windows of a carriage as it carried him to an unknown destination.

"I think so." Jim watched in fascination as his mouth moved and he spoke from where he stood in the center of the room. "But I don't know how."

"It is likely you never will." The voice boomed through his body. "But now, you can see."

The color of the room flickered, leaving shapes and outlines in place of the shelves and chandeliers. The flicker only lasted a few seconds before the color and light returned to the majestic room. But, in the small amount of time that had passed, the room had drastically changed.

The covers of the books kept their brilliant colors, but now bore splotchy stains of brown and black. Many pages were ripped from the covers and laid in crumpled piles at the base of the shaggy rug. The chandeliers still shone brilliantly, but many of the dazzling crystals that reflected their light were cracked or missing. The clear and clean colors of the carpet were now scarred by the impressions of boot prints and a worn rut from pacing feet.

The room flashed black again and the scene continuing to disintegrate. One of the shelves had toppled, leaning diagonally across the room. Many books were scattered on the floor, ripped and dogeared pages laid bare. A chandelier lay crashed in the center of the carpet, wires sparking in a composition of buzzing light. The floor acted like a mirror, reflecting the light and chaos in a perfect, upside down image. It took Jim a moment to realize why. A shallow pool of water had accumulated across the floor. The water barely reached the bottom layer of books and had soaked the rug, giving it a puffy look.

"This is more than just a place," the voice began, "for it is where I am and where I was. This is where I decided to die."

The darkness flickered, and when light returned the entire room was underwater. Books floated in a suspension of space. Dangerous flashes of lightning surged from each of the brilliant chandeliers, leaving boiling bubbles where they trailed. Jim's instincts screamed at him to hold his breath, but the body he inhabited refused to acquiesce and continued to breathe unhindered.

"It was beautiful here once, long before the world burned. Now...." The room flashed black again, revealing the room as it had been originally. "it is only beautiful in my memory."

Jim felt a large force push against his consciousness. He tried to push back, but the force was so great that he trembled and fell beneath its weight. He felt the sensation of flipping and twisting through the air, before colliding with a familiar gravity. He gasped deeply and fell to his hands and knees, coughing. The world was dark again, the solid void uncluttered by the shelves and chandeliers that he knew were hiding.

"It is a disorienting feeling, being ejected from a consciousness. Eventually, you will become intricate in the way of control. But for now, you must be careful."

Jim realized that the deep voice was no longer coming from a mouth that he could feel. Instead, it rumbled through him, from a source beyond himself. He felt his hands and face, recognizing the familiar features that he had always possessed. He was back in his body.

"Be careful of what?" he asked, disoriented by the nearness of his own voice.

"Anyone who is more powerful than you. Mostly Heroes, I would assume, but some humans hold wills stronger than the most stubborn of your brethren."

Jim thought for a minute, leaving a palpable silence lingering in the shadows, before asking, "Why did you want me to see this place?"

"Oh!" the voice exclaimed. "A silly thing for me not to explain. It is so important that I nearly lost myself in presentation! This place, though you cannot see it now, is real. It's real here, and that means that it is real in the place where you belong, Above. Though, technically your world is not higher than this—they are equal in height and space. But it is easier to call yours 'Above' and mine 'Below', do you agree?"

"Umm...sure," Jim said.

"Excellent! So, you must come here, but Above, and you must kill me."

"What? What do you mean, kill you? You're here, aren't you? Which means you are dead already."

"Well yes, and no. Like you, I am wrong for this place, but unlike you, I cannot leave. I am the foundation of this world, the reason that it exists at all. Because of me, millions are trapped, forced to walk in the shadows eternally or join with the souls of those who came here by mistake and worship. Without me, this world will collapse and fade to dust. I did not foresee my role in this nightmare, but it was a consequence of my hasty decision.

"I'm not sure how, but I am alive. I can feel it as clear as I can feel the connection between us. But I am unable to return to myself, unable to end my life the way that I should have. So, I'm asking you to do it for me. Will you do this for me, Jim? Will you destroy this prison and allow me to explore the existence that comes next?"

Shock petrified Jim. For the life of one person to create an entire world, to hold within it the multitudes of dead that now roam in darkness, seemed impossible. The request that the voice had made seemed too simple. How could he believe it? But, how could he say no? He couldn't allow the doom of the dead to remain intact when he had a chance to be their salvation, when Ellie might still be lost—and Emma.

"I'll do it." Jim said plainly, though his mind still reeled with hesitation.

"*Thank you, Jim,*" the voice said, quivering with gratitude.

"Tell me," Jim said, "why you have chosen me."

"Because you were unknown to many, and almost to me, and this is the work of a shade!"

The answer seemed logical enough, though Jim suspected there was far more to know. "Where do I find this place?"

"*I will show you.*"

Jim's feet rose from the solid ground with a lurch. He lifted through the air, rapidly flying at the invisible celling that he had seen in the voice's memories. But he did not encounter any resistance as he neared the top, only felt a tingling sensation through his torso and limbs as he passed through an invisible barrier. Somehow, the world seemed darker than before, but the air still rushed past his ears and through his open mouth. Then, he broke through the ground, and the darkness evaporated.

Color did not return, but the darkness shattered into many different shades and variety. The outlines of coal colored buildings and tall trees fell beneath his feet. In the distance he could see the tall, familiar shape of the wall that kept Paradise safe. But still he flew, rising beyond where birds dared soar, in the air that would have frozen him if he had not already been dead. Then, with a violent deceleration, he stopped, suspended above the world. To his side he saw the shadowy figure of the man who he had been blindly speaking to for so long. The man gestured downward, pointing to the distant shape of Paradise, miles below their feet.

"*The Heroes have held a secret, protected and trusted only by the Leader and the Twenty-Four. It gives the reasons why Paradise has flourished beyond* any other city, and it reveals the source of its dominant power. This secret is also what has stopped humanity from spreading beyond the small, safe space that you all now occupy. Jim, I am that secret.

"The great tower, which houses only the most important members of your race, sits atop my home. It serves to hide me from the worries and prying eyes of the world, and it serves as the only entrance to where I reside."

"You want me to break in to Paradise, the most well-guarded city in the world?" Jim asked.

"Yes."

"And then, you want me to infiltrate the great tower, the most powerful stronghold that the Heroes have ever built?"

"Yes."

"Then, you want me to find the entrance to the greatest secret to ever have existed, and then kill you?"

"In your era, yes. To kill me, yes again."

"Sounds like the perfect contract," Jim said, adrenaline coursing through his blood. "Consider it done."

Instead of replying, the voice only laughed. It was a hardy chuckle that reminded Jim of thunder and earthquakes. Then, the man snapped his fingers, and Jim began to fall.

## 25: A FEAR OF WAKING

Emma slept. Her dreams projected a sapphire blue sky, trees that swayed on a lazy breeze, the chirps of small birds that harmonized with the babble of a nearby brook. No pain emanated from her flesh. This place felt safe, though it was a fragile safety, doomed to end when she was forced to wake.

Somewhere, behind her acknowledged perception, she could feel intimations of the awful presence prodding at her mind. If she gave it too much concentration, the presence would flee and leave her to the created desires of her dreams. Once she became preoccupied, it would begin its search again. There were also the sounds of voices and shuffling footsteps that interrupted her fantasies from time to time. But these noises were easy to ignore and easy to forget.

Now, she sat on the beach that lined the Endless Ocean, sand tickling the soles of her feet. The smell of salt mixed with the aroma of pine, clashing in her nostrils with potent pleasure. Four-eyed crabs snipped at screaming seagulls that mistook them for helpless meals. The crabs scuttled towards piles of seaweed, hunting for the small creatures that would prove to be prey to their mighty claws.

A waft of smoke distorted the water, smelling of seasoned fish and baked clams. Emma peered at the source, seeing Aisley fussing over three hot pans, screaming orders at Bren as she cooked. Jim was laying shirtless behind them, admiring the cloudless sky and warm feeling of the sun on his body. His head tilted as he sensed her gaze, and a smile parted his lips. He spoke, though his words never reached Emma's ears. She contorted her face, informing him that she did not hear what he had said. Instead of repeating his phrase, he rose to his feet and walked in her direction.

Jim wore no boots, the legs of his pants rolled to mid-calf, perfect for wading in the cool tide. The tight muscles in his chest and abdomen flexed with each step. The strong definition in his shoulders tightened when he saw her wandering eyes, causing them to bulge and causing her eyes to linger longer. She remembered the wonderful hardness of his muscles under her touch, remembered tracing each of his scars with the tip of her finger, admiring the sculpture that he had become through each of his adversities.

Emma could feel her cheeks flush and knew that red fluster now marked her face. She shook her head, trying to clear indelicate thoughts from her mind and return her composure. But, as the Hero neared, and she smelled his virile scent, her mind cleared of all thought beyond her Hero's lips, wishing nothing more than to press them against her own and unite in embrace.

Jim reached out his hand and lifted Emma to her feet in one smooth pull. She placed her arms around his neck and closed her eyes in anticipation. His lips parted as their mouths neared, but the kiss that she wished for never came. Instead, a voice broke through her reality, shattering the beach and the waves and leaving her holding Jim in darkness.

"How long has she been like this?" a soft, feminine voice asked.

A woman, average in height with dark hair and a small nose, stepped from the darkness. Faye Northtree. She was staring at Emma, studying everything about her form. The woman looked to her left and a man joined her from the shadows. His white hair was slicked behind his ears and a powerful smile shone from his red lips. Bastion Northtree.

A response came to Faye's question, though the voice that spoke was too quiet for Emma to hear. She saw as Faye nodded and looked back at her with an impressed expression.

Then Bastion spoke, "Before her, what was the longest a human resisted the transformation?"

Marcus emerged from the inky shadows, his blue eyes glaring with a sense of wonderment. "Sixteen hours," he replied.

"Jim…" Emma said.

She looked into her Hero's eyes, trying to find comfort in his golden irises. But she found no hope, no comfort, no love, only a blank stare as his pupils began to grow. Black enveloped his eyes and he fell away, exploding into a puff of smoke once he hit the ground.

"Jim!" Emma screamed.

"What is she saying?" Faye asked.

"The name of the Ash boy," Marcus said. "She has been saying his name, and nothing else, for two days."

"Can she feel him? Is that why she has the strength to speak?" Bastion asked, his voice filled with curiosity and envy.

"It is...possible," said Marcus. "Though, a human having the capabilities of the Nexus is unheard of."

"But possible?" Bastion asked again.

"Yes," Marcus confirmed. "There is much we do not know about Dom's tools. I have been studying them for many lifetimes, and I have barely grasped any form of understanding."

"We've noticed," murmured Faye.

From the distance, far behind where the three spoke, Emma saw a dozen figures take form. They began to near, moving in rapid, stuttering steps. Their features were shrouded in shadow, but the distinct shape of claws jutted from each of their fingers. The shapes sent shivers through Emma's spine as she recognized the husks. She took a step backwards, pivoting on one leg, and sprinted towards the darkness.

Ravenous snarls echoed from behind, growing closer with each of the girl's frantic steps. Her muscles stiffened and her running began to feel slow and unnatural, as if she ran in a world filled with rice pudding. Each time her foot fell, it rose with increased difficulty and effort. The husks were nipping at her neck, slicing deep gouges in the muscles around her throat and breastbone.

"The amulet is still fuming," a male voice said from somewhere behind her.

"Yes," came a cool reply. "It's hot enough that the moment we pour water over her, it steams and boils."

A girl stood before Emma, facing away. Flowing blonde locks reached down to her mid-back, swaying as she moved her head to the tune she was humming. The girl was oblivious to the voices that spoke and the husks that would devour her as soon as they finished ripping the marrow from Emma's bones.

Emma tried to yell, warn the naïve girl of the danger, but her voice halted in her throat as pain seared from the husks' claws. The form of the girl drifted closer, not moving in steps or hops, but hovering lightly in Emma's direction, until she stood within Emma's reach. With the last of her remaining strength, Emma broke her arm from the grasp of the monsters and held tightly to the girl's shoulder. When the girl turned, to feel who was disturbing her song, Emma saw the familiar hazel eyes of Belle.

Belle stared at Emma, confusion twisting her face and scrunching the skin beneath her hairline. She took Emma's desperate hand, placing it between her soft palms, and knelt, pulling Emma to do the same. When her knees met the invisible ground, the pain around her throat lessened to a dull thrum of remembrance, the snarls and growls from the husks silenced, and the voices from the Heroes faded.

Emma stared at her sister, tears welling in her beaten eyes, and whispered, "Help."

Belle acknowledged her plea with a nod and a simple, but intense, smile, and kissed Emma on her brow. Then, she closed her eyes and disappeared in a wisp of smoke.

Emma cracked her crusted eyelids open, seeing the metallic room that served as her prison. Her wrists burned, though the coarse ropes had been replaced with a soft cloth binding. Everything hurt and her lips cracked when she tried to move them. She would have cried, but no moisture remained to wet her cheeks and sting her eyes. Her neck hurt too badly to observe her surroundings, so she stared. Looked deep into a dark corner of the room, wishing for sleep to take her once again.

## 26: THE DEATH OF ANOTHER

"*Hello,*" a light, happy voice whispered by Jim's ear.

A grunt was the only reply Jim offered. His head ached fiercely, sending a flash of pain with each beat of his heart. Opening his eyes revealed the dark world that had become a familiar plane of his existence. The shapes of trees and large boulders surrounded the fallen Hero. To his side, the lone outline of a small cabin obscured the otherwise natural landscape.

After blinking his blurry eyes, Jim saw a shadow drifting back and forth in front of him. The pacing seemed awkward on a being with no feet to pace upon, but the action was a familiar indicator of unsure anxiety. The shadow turned its head, seeing movement from the Hero's form.

"*Hello,*" the voice said again.

This time, Jim recognized the light, breezy tones that came from the shadow. "Luna?" he asked.

"*Yes. I'm Luna. I already told you.*" She danced on her invisible feet, swirling as she spoke. "*I heard you and then I saw you in the sky. You are not supposed to be in the sky, Jim. You are not made with feathers, nor are you made of air. You belong in the sky the same as a rock or a fish. Falling was inevitable. You should have asked me before trying. If a rock had asked, I would have told it to stay put—stay in the dirt, you silly rock!*" Luna drifted close, the tendrils of her smoke breaking against Jim's arm. "*Next time ask before you fly.*"

"Alright."

Rising to his feet revealed sharp pains from each of his joints. Audible cracks and pops echoed through the darkness and vibrated through his bones. Jim stretched his neck and stared upwards, imagining his fall and remembering the rushing wind that tore through his mouth and ears.

"How am I alive?" he wondered to himself.

"*You are not,*" Luna answered. "*Nothing here is, Jim. This is a place where Death cannot watch, for his duties are complete. He abandoned us here, allowing the gods of torment and torture to prod us with their cruelties, when they care to show. Here,*" Luna twirled, "*we will suffer. Forever.*"

A multitude of religions filled the Hero territories. Each of them had different variations of the afterlife, ranging from gross to subtle. The Creed of the Immense believed all life resides in the stomach of a giant, and upon death it is digested and absorbed into the giant's mind to become one with the gargantuan being. The Sect of Halthos worshipped a Hero who taught of invisible worlds that a person's consciousness would fall through once his body died—these worlds were all defined as stages of bliss which grew in intensity depending on the standing of one's life. However, Jim had never before heard mention of a world made from darkness, where no sun would shine and shadows remained as the singular population, in any of the world's diverse teachings.

Jim looked down to see the shadowy figure sauntering lazily through the nearby trees. "Luna, do we all come here, people I mean, when we die?"

For a long while, the shadow stilled. Her lilting hums abruptly ceased, allowing silence to join in her still contemplation. Jim considered reaching for the connection that stood between them. This way he could see what made her hesitate. But, before he could extend himself through their faint connection, she sat and motioned for Jim to join her by the trees. Though his muscles and joints still protested movement, he walked towards Luna and sat beside her.

Luna's voice was soft and unsure, all hint of song replaced by poignant philosophy. "*No…or…I don't think so. Many do, so, so many. But, many do not. I've been in this place for…*" she paused as she thought, "*forever I think, but I have never met my mother, nor Alexander, my greatest friend, in this place. My father I have met, four times now, but no matter how hard I have looked, I cannot find my mother. I even tried calling her name, but that only caused me to become lost with the others."* Her form shivered from the memory and her voice faltered.

*"There is a piece of me, I can feel deep inside, that wanted to come here. I think each of us, trapped in this place, have a similar piece. Even you."* Her head tilted towards the Hero. *"I think it is the familiarity that draws us to this dark world and forces us to stay. Not you though. You do not have to stay. Not yet. Because you are wrong, for you are dead but also alive."*

Quiet emotion resonated from her thoughts. Together, they sat, Jim immersed in thought and Luna softly humming a leisurely lullaby.

"So," Jim started, "how do I leave?"

Luna's hum perked in an excited tune. *"I know that!"* She rose to her feet and began to sway and spin. *"You need to take another's life and live their death."*

"How...do I do that?"

*"I can show you! First, and this is important, you have to decide where you want to emerge."*

"What do you mean?"

*"Where do you want to be...when you leave this place?"*

Images of a metal room filled with Emma's screams flashed through Jim's mind. That room would be the place that he needed to be. Jim blinked his eyes and the forest melted and reformed into a solid, dark shape. A moment later, Luna appeared beside him.

*"It is rude to leave me behind, Jim,"* she said. *"You are easy to find, but still you should not wander."* She glanced around, seeing the new environment. *"Is this the place you wish to live again?"*

"Yes," Jim said.

*"Good."* Her hands clapped together, though no sound came when they collided. *"Now, call for a life."*

"What?"

*"Call for a life."* Luna said, louder. *"Inside, you will feel the closest lives. Just call for them, inside and out. Then, they will touch you and you will live their death and take their life."*

Jim closed his eyes. At first, he remained alone, floating through the pool of his mind. After he concentrated, sparks of differing consciousness began to form around him. One was closer than the others, so he reached for it and called towards it, asking if he could take the being's life. From the being, elated emotions emanated so strong that it forced Jim backwards and caused his eyes to open.

Jim found himself on the dark floor, breathing heavily. Luna stared at him, her head tilted in curious observation.

"Today has been special, Jim," she said sweetly. "I am pleased that you were born from my failures. It was lovely to meet you."

Before Jim could reply, the form of another shadow burst from the wall and lunged towards him. Jim rolled and jumped to his feet, instinctually reaching for a weapon but finding only his empty scabbard. Again, the shadow lunged. Jim braced himself, ready to break his attacker's wrist and throw it to the ground. But, when Jim reached, the shadow's arm went through his grasping fingers and collided with his forehead. His eyes became wide when the shadow's hand touched his bare flesh, and he became one with the being.

◦ ◦ ◦ ◦ ◦ ◦ ◦

*My name is Naal. Though I am of no notable birth, I reside within the tribe of Elm and carry the title of 'Hero' and 'Killer of the Ancients'. My wife, who's name I will not give, is one who has eyes of a varying shade, blue, like that of the sky and the Life-Giving Lakes. Many in my tribe disagree with the bonding, though the members of the Twenty and Four have blessed our union under the name of Dom and the blood from the sword-handed beasts.*

*Still, contention has risen from our marriage. I have sought the approval of my family, of my father and his father, to leave the walled city and build a fortification beyond Paradise. They say I must go North, for that is the way that my family watches. Many have left, but few have returned.*

*Today I shall leave. My wife is heavy with my child, but the venomous glances and whispered warnings from those around us are growing bolder each day, so we must leave. My pack is heavy on my back, and the mules have been tied with the provisions we will need for a month of survival.*

*The Golden Gates lift, just enough for us to slip beneath and exit our protected home. The world that greets us is bright and green. The sword-hands do not hunt under the sun, because its light is too mighty for the evil in their* hearts. The thick trees could still hide dangers, so we must leave the forest before nightfall.

Days of travel have led us to the tower, built by our oldest ancestors who defeated Death and lived in peace. The tower reaches towards the sky, nearly as high as the walls of Paradise. The frame is made from twisted steel and translucent glass. The building's metal doors open with a loud creak. I explore the tower and find no danger. This is where we will live, where my son will be born.

My days are spent hunting and fetching buckets of fresh water. I dig a trench from the small stream a few miles from our new home, to make the gathering of water easier. My wife tends to our garden and has begun to build a stone structure around the tower. We are happy here.

The nurse-maids in Paradise had instructed me on assisting with birth, but when the time comes, their instruction fails to properly prepare me. The birth goes well, but instead of being a comfort to my wife in her time of need, she comforts me. I feel foolish, though the feeling only lasts moments. When I hear the cries of the newborn babe, my heart swells with love and excitement. It is a boy, just as the elders predicted, and we name him after the founder of the Western tribe. I send a raven to my father, informing him of the boy's health and strength and naming.

The boy grows strong as the years pass. He has the eyes of the powerful and, therefore, will be given the title of 'Hero' if we ever return to Paradise. I give it to him anyway. He proves brave in the nights when the beasts wander near our tower.

Our bellies are full of the boar that I hunted this morning. Tomorrow, the boy will be ten and he will have to provide a meal for my wife and me, as is tradition. The size of the beast will predict how great of a man he will become. Knowing the boy's tenacity, I know he will return with an antlered buck or a forest wolf. He will make me a proud father.

The sound of shattering glass wakes me from my slumber. My wife is awake, a knife in her small hand and an arm over our son. I rise to my feet and release my sword from its sheath. I sneak down the quiet hallway to find the source of our disturbance. I find the broken window, but there is no indication as to what had caused it to break. I search and stalk through the tower for an hour but find nothing.

Sleep beckons to me as I make my way back to the room. When I get inside, I see my wife writhing on the ground. I run to her and lift her head to my lap. Foam falls from her mouth and her eyes are a sheen of white. I whisper her name, but my words fall on deaf ears.

A muffled scream catches my attention, coming from the dark wall at the edge of the room. There stands my father, my son held tightly in his arms. He hits the boy in the temple with the hilt of a dagger and the boy falls limp. He steps forward, tossing my son over his shoulder.

"Tell me what you are doing," I demand, but he does not answer. "Did you do this? Did you poison her?" I scream, and he raises his eyebrow.

He is close enough to touch as he bends down and unleashes the clasp of a bracelet from my wife's arm. Where the item once sat, her skin is blistered and black. My father slips the bracelet into his pocket and wanders towards the door.

I leap after him but in a smooth motion he slaps me across the face, and I fall to the floor. The door slams behind him and I can hear a rattle as he places an iron chain around the handle. I push at the door, but the chain will not break. My father is gone. My son is gone. My wife....

I turn towards my wife. Her breathing has become ragged and labored. I run to her side and place a hand upon her chest. Her heart beats furiously and her skin burns with angry fire. Her breathing escalates as she vomits blood and foam on to the ground. Then, she goes still.

I can no longer feel her heart beat. Her chest no longer rises and falls with the movements of breath. She is dead, and my son is gone.

I rise in a frenzied state and bash my shoulder against the door. Over and over I run against the chain. It will break and I will have my revenge. I feel my shoulder crack as it collides against the metal, but my fervor forces me to continue.

I only stop when I hear breathing coming from my back. I turn sharply and see the empty space where my wife had perished. Then, I see...her.

Her eyes are the only indication that remains of my wife, blue like that of the sky and the Life-Giving Lakes. Her body is now covered in graying flesh and her mouth is agape and filled with jagged teeth. But her hands are what cause me to scream. Instead of her small and beautiful hands, long claws jut from each of her fingers. The blistering skin from the bracelet catches my eye, because now a white scar that contrasts her dark skin has replaced it.

*She lets out a howl of fury and leaps at me, slashing at my neck. I am too slow to stop the attack and feel the hot sting of her claws ripping through my throat. I fall to the ground. My wife, or what was left of my wife, howls again and digs her teeth into the soft flesh of my leg. I can feel her gnaw until she reaches hard bone, and then my world goes black. All I can see are shadows and darkness.*

## 27: ENDING TORMENT

Emma stared at the dark corner where the metal walls met. Beside her she could hear the familiar sound of a blade sliding against a whetstone. Light, methodic breaths, with occasional purrs of admiration, came from Faye as her blade gleamed and glinted with a fine edge.

Emma's eyes began to sting, their dryness forcing her to blink. The action took effort, and the muscles around her eyes began to burn and groan. Slowly they closed, only to crack open again and stare at the empty corner.

The shadows seemed to be dancing. Specs of darkness circled together in a whirlwind of hallucinated motion. Many hallucinations had entered her hanging life, but they mostly came in the shape of loved ones and whispers, so Emma enjoyed the simple movement and forced her eyes to stare longer than normal.

After a few minutes of admiration, she gave in to closing her eyes again. But she could not sleep, would not allow the pain to force her into an unconscious state that would be torn from her the moment she felt peace. Each time she slept, her energy waned. So, with momentous effort, she forced her eyes to open again and stare at the empty corner. This time, no hallucinations occupied the corner, but it was not empty.

Hidden deep inside the shadows stood Jim, his golden eyes shone as he met Emma's gaze.

■ ■ ■ ■ ■ ■ ■

A wave of nausea and dizziness passed over Naal. No. That wasn't right. Not Naal, not anymore. His name was...is...Jim. Jim's hand reached for the gash in his neck, from where the husk had felled him. But only smooth skin acknowledged his touch: the wound wasn't his either. He looked around the room, trying to find the monster that his wife had become, but saw new surroundings.

He was in a small metal room. A crude looking chair, with leather straps on the arms and leg rests, decorated the center, and a long, wooden table sat against one wall. Leaning against the table, with her back turned towards him, stood a woman with locks of black hair falling to the middle of her back. The muscles in her arms and shoulder blades were moving with practiced rhythm as she sharpened a silver knife against a flat stone. Closer to him, hanging by her arms from a large metal hook, stared a green-eyed girl. Her eyes stared into his, never blinking or breaking away. She looked at him with familiar eyes so beautiful that he was forced to take a step towards her. Her mouth moved as she silently spoke, forming one word on her cracked and bloodied lips, *Jim*.

A stream of memory flooded through Jim's mind and caused him to halt. This room, this world, this woman: they were all things that he knew and had fought to return to. Emma. Her name was Emma. The girl who had fought with him in the forest. The girl who had allowed him to join her family. The girl who had exclaimed her love at him while they stood beneath his family home. Emma.

Jim crouched low and strode towards the dark-haired woman, now recognizing her as Faye Northtree. She would not expect an attack from behind. Who would in her situation? So, he made his steps quick instead of silent. His foot scraped against the loud serrated tiles, causing Faye to perk and stop her repeated motions.

"So," sang her smoky voice. "You have found the strength to continue fighting?"

Faye began to turn towards Emma, but, before her rotation was complete, Jim was upon her.

"Wha!" Faye exclaimed as Jim grabbed her head and slammed it against the wooden table.

Her head bounced with an audible thud, but no other noise came from the Hero. A trickle of blood seeped from her temple, but her chest still rose and fell with life. When she woke, she would feel a screaming headache, but that would not be for many hours.

Jim grabbed the silver knife from the table and moved towards Emma. How long had she been hanging? What kind of hell had the Northtrees forced upon her? Whatever her torment, it was over now. He cut the binds from Emma's unstaunched wrists and caught her as she fell. He laid her lightly on the ground and examined the many scrapes and cuts that adorned her body. None of them seemed life-threatening, except for the blistered burns beneath the amulet.

Wafts of sizzling smoke still rose from the amulet, boiling Jim's blood in fury. He grabbed the large jewel, wincing as the ornate depiction of a radiant man burned his palm. But he did not allow his pain to overcome him and drop the jewelry. He persisted in his task, lifting the necklace over Emma's head and off her body.

The moment the amulet left her, Emma sighed with resounding relief. Her emerald eyes shimmered, though no tears streamed down her bruised cheeks. She locked her gaze with his and blinked slowly. Jim tenderly kissed Emma's forehead. When he pulled away, she was asleep. Jim lifted the slumbering girl and exited the room.

The room beyond was large and square. The ceiling reached high into the air and shone with cylinders of glass and fire. Scattered throughout the room, and along the expansive walls, were tubes filled with green, bubbling liquid. In a few of the tubes, figures floated, varying in shapes and size. And, standing in the center of the room, a tray of food in his hands, stood Marcus.

Marcus's mouth hung agape as he stared at Jim. He tried to speak but could not find the words that conveyed his astonishment.

Hatred and anger emanated from Jim as he gingerly sat Emma on the ground, leaning her against the door from which they had exited. He stepped towards the shocked priest.

Finally, the blue-eyed man found his words and said in a quivering voice, "How?"

Jim stayed silent, keeping a steady stride. The tray fell from Marcus's hands. A finely-made ceramic piece, it shattered on the floor.

"What is your new name?" Marcus asked in a voice that was filled with both curiosity and fear.

Jim thrust his fist against Marcus's face, using as much strength as he could muster. The strike would have killed most humans, concaved the face and left the victim with nothing but a shattered skull. But Jim was surprised to see Marcus still standing, a maniacal laugh erupting from his throat and, when he looked up, one of his eyes sparkling in a golden color.

Marcus blinked rapidly, the shade of his eye reverting back to brilliant blue. "Humans would never trust a Hero, Jim. You know that better than most."

Marcus's fist flew at Jim's abdomen. Jim took a quick step backwards and kicked at Marcus's front leg. The strike landed, and Marcus fell to a kneel.

"What is your new name?" Marcus demanded, reaching for a weapon that was hidden beneath his robes.

Jim jumped forward and twisted Marcus's wrist until it snapped. A yowl escaped the priest's mouth, but Jim struck again. This time, his knee met the underside of Marcus's chin, clacking his teeth together and forcing his eyes at the ceiling.

"Are you Dom?" Marcus asked, his voice weakening.

Jim grabbed Marcus by his hair and leg and threw him against one of the glass tubes. A large crack spiderwebbed from where the priest impacted. Jim did not let up. He advanced on the priests stunned form and shoved his head against the tube over and over. Marcus's face became a bloody pulp of flesh and bone, but still he spoke.

"Was it one of the Four? Or the man who controls the shadows?"

The crack grew as Jim bashed Marcus's face against it. A drop of the green liquid splashed against Jim's arm, burning and sizzling on his skin.

"Who...are...you?" Marcus groaned.

Jim forced Marcus's face through the weakened glass, feeling the tips of his fingers singe on the foul-smelling liquid. Marcus screamed and pulled at Jim's grip, but Jim held firm until the priest grew still. He pulled his hand from the corpse, inspecting the blistered skin on the back of his hands and knuckles. Then he retrieved Emma and raced down the hallway.

One of the many doors along the hallway's walls was left open. Inside, Jim found the arsenal of his and Emma's weapons as well as the various items of Emma's clothing. He placed his many blades in the sheaths that adorned his body and wrapped Emma tightly in her cloak. Jim placed the rest of Emma's clothes and her few weapons into a cloth sack and tied it at his waist.

The Hero ducked through the dirt tunnel and found the ladder that led to the church. The climb was awkward but became easier when Jim draped Emma over his shoulder and freed the arm that she had occupied. He pushed the podium from the tunnel's entrance and was greeted by the dimly lit room where Marcus had once preached.

From the door to his right, Jim could hear multiple footsteps descending the many flights of stairs that ran through the church's steeple. He moved quickly, taking long strides to reach the double-doors that would lead to the outside of Salix. As he reached the brass doorknobs, the door behind him flew open and the merry voices of Bastion and Kole Northtree echoed off of the pews and walls. Jim stood still, hoping that the two Heroes would neglect to see his still shape; but his plan was folly. Bastion and Kole turned to exit from the church, and their conversation ended as they saw the man who blocked their path. Without words, Kole sprinted towards Jim, a short-sword in his muscled hand, and Bastion pulled a pistol from his belt. Jim kicked the doors open and darted to the dirty cobbles of the Middle District.

The Eastern Gate was the closest route of escape from the Willow city, so that is where Jim ran. The sky was growing dark, dusk heavy on the darkening clouds, telling Jim that the gates would be closing any minute. He had to make it, had to leave the evils of this place before they caught him and forced him to bow.

Though he was encumbered by the weight of Emma and her belongings, he was still able to keep ahead of Kole and his father. The steady pace of the large Heroes' footsteps sounded distantly but never disappeared through the many turns that Jim incorporated in his route. The wall loomed overhead and, only a few blocks away, the thick wooden gate peered over the tops of houses and shops.

"Close the gates!" Bastion's voice boomed through the streets.

The gate began to lower, and dread doused Jim's hopes. The only other way to exit the city would be the same way he had entered. He changed his course, drifting toward the vacant guard tower that had served him many times.

The winding paths ended in a long, straight passage that led toward the tower. Jim pushed his legs forward, the extra weight he carried drastically lowering his stamina.

The sound of a sword leaving its sheath whined in Jim's ear, right at his back. He grabbed a dagger from his belt and spun, intercepting Kole's short-sword with his gleaming metal. Without missing his stride, Jim twisted his wrist and slashed through the chainmail on Kole's thigh, causing the Hero to scream and clutch at the wound. Jim turned and closed the gap between him and the tower, shouldering through the wooden door.

Jim took a breath to recuperate and observe the place where he had last seen Colter. Papers still sat, littering the table and floor where they had met and discussed. But, one note looked new. It was sealed in wax and marked with the insignia that Colter brandished on his wrist and weapons. Jim grabbed the letter, shoving it into his pocket, and made his way up through the tower.

The view from atop the wall was breathtaking, even in the darkness of night. Heavy steps from the tower's lower floors dissuaded Jim from admiring the sight, so he ran along the wall's top, trying to find a suitable place to descend. He made it a quarter way over the eastern side, not liking the few options that had presented themselves, when guards flooded from the tower ahead of him, congesting the narrow walkway. Jim turned, hoping to move to the northern end, but his path was blocked by Bastion Northtree, his pistol pointed at Jim's head.

"A valiant effort, James, but you are caught. Bested above the city of Salix." Bastion's voice was strong and unlabored, despite the chase that Jim had forced upon him. "You must tell me about the World of Shadow. Though, there will be plenty of time for talk later. For now, you will drop the girl and fall to your knees, or I will shoot you and leave your body for the husks and wolves."

Jim glanced around, looking for a way out of Bastion's victory. The wall here would be difficult to scale, even more so with Emma draped over him, and the guards behind were too many for Jim to defeat. Bastion had won.

He moved to lower Emma but stopped. Deep in his mind something stirred, trying to gain entrance to his consciousness. Jim barred his mind and thrust against the invading force.

Bastion's eyes went wide. "You know?" he asked.

Jim didn't answer. Instead, he attacked the foreign presence and overwhelmed it with all the will he could attain. His consciousness surrounded the invader, and, for a moment, he saw himself through the eyes of Bastion. Then, he was attacked by a force so powerful and overwhelming that his entire being trembled.

Jim fought against the force, holding on to the small piece of Bastion that he still had under his control, and demanded, "Stop!"

The force did not retreat, but it stopped attacking. Jim opened his eyes, unaware of when they had closed, and looked at the shaking form of the Northtree. Bastion's arm fell to the ground, pointing the pistol at the beams by his boots. The muscles in his arm and hand were twitching, trying to fight against the command that Jim had forced upon the man. The pistol was inching upward with incredulous effort, and Jim knew he had to move. There would not be much time until Bastion fought through their connection and had his facilities back under control.

Seeing no other choice, Jim grabbed the dagger from his waist and jumped from Salix's wall. He stabbed the dagger into the crumbling stone, slowing his descent to a manageable speed. The ground was approaching fast, and he prepared his legs for impact. From above, Jim heard the deafening sound of a gun releasing its bullet and, a moment later, felt the bite of the projectile as it tore through his hand. The shot forced him to release his grip on the dagger, and he plunged the final few feet to the grass below.

Jim landed with a grunt and heard Emma land beside him. The pain in his hand flared when he pushed himself up, but he could not afford to wallow in his injury. He had to keep moving.

As he picked Emma up, he heard the groan of wood as the Eastern Gate began to open. Dozens of soldiers would exit from Salix, most on horseback, and soon be on Jim's heels. His best chance would be to flee to the southern territory, where trees and brush densely packed the unhindered lands. But the nearest clump of trees was miles away, and if the soldiers had horses.... Jim ran.

His breaths began to burn in his chest, but still he ran. The howls of wolves and beast of the night rang from ahead of him. Arrows flew from the sky, cutting through his cloak and piercing the soft soil ahead of him. He ran continuously, but when four horses galloped ahead of him, their riders holding long pikes and crossbows, he fought.

First, he threw his knife, catching one of the men in the throat. Blood bubbled from his punctured airway as he clawed at the wound, but soon he fell from his mount and fell from the world of life. The next guard shot the bolt from his crossbow, but the sack filled with Emma's belongings absorbed the attack. Jim tore the pike from the third guard and thrust it through the chest of the second, before that guard could unload another bolt. The third guard frantically reached for the sword on his back, but Jim moved first. He cut through the strap on the man's saddle, causing it to lose grip and fall from the fifteen-hand horse. The horse lurched forward, stepping on the man's abdomen and causing him to scream in agony. The fourth man swung his pike at Jim before trying to flee. Jim ducked the attack and scrambled to the second man's crossbow, unleashing a bolt into the fleeing man's back. The man fell from his horse as it galloped through the night.

Jim started down the path, hearing more guards riding from the distance. He didn't know how much further he could go before he collapsed and was captured by his pursuers. Even as a contract killer, he had never worked himself this hard, nor had he ever used such mysterious means of killing. Emma, draped over his shoulder, winced with each step Jim took, though she remained semiconscious. Safety, he had to get Emma to safety and treat the many wounds that had lacerated her body.

Ahead, the whinny of a horse cut through the brisk air. He prepared to attack but stopped when he saw the riderless mare. The horse was tall and dark, and it approached Jim with dutiful demeanor. The horse was only a few feet away when Jim recognized the animal's chocolate coat and the patches of white that splotched over her nose and ear.

"William?" he asked, looking for the shape of her rider among the distant trees. "Where is Belle?"

William nudged Jim's arm with her nose and turned to face the way she had come. Jim didn't question the horse's offer. He gently placed Emma in the saddle and climbed behind her. Once Jim's feet found the stirrups, William moved.

The horse galloped faster than any animal Jim had ever ridden before. Soon, tall trees surrounded them and the sounds from the Salix soldiers became nothing more than distant shouts, and the Willow city became nothing but a nightmarish memory.

## 28: THE WHISPERING WOODS

Dawn kissed the horizon before William began to slow. The change in speed surprised Jim, causing him to take further note of his surroundings instead of focusing on the path ahead and the danger behind. What he saw was...familiar.

Massive trees reached towards the heavens, their green and yellow leaves dancing in the clouds. The roaring sound of rivers flowing and crashing against stones and shores, just beyond the cover of foliage, soothed the warrior. He saw small hints of abandoned cabins and hunting houses built so perfectly that the untrained eye would only see the natural and untamed forest. Even the dirt on the muddy path had the familiar tint of reds and greens that he remembered from his childhood travels and later adventures. It had been years since his contracts had taken Jim to the South, but it still felt like home. Still felt like family.

*The forests here are unlike anywhere else in the known world. A power resides here, so uncontrollable and wild that it drives most men toward insanity. Only we Ashes have had the discipline to stay, and it has not been through conquering. We have stayed because we have become part of this place.*

Originally the land had been named after those who protected it, *The Ashen Forest*. But, after the Undead War ravaged through the trees it had been given the name *The Forest of Corpses* or *The Whispering Woods*. Hundreds of Heroes and humans had died beneath the ancient trees. It had taken months to burn all the bodies. Scars from the battles could be seen on all but the youngest plants.

As an Ash, Jim was intimate with the histories of each battle and life that had been claimed in his territory, and The Forest of Corpses held the names of many. But not all names had come from wars. The first people to suffer from the claws of husks lived in the South. Wild packs of wolves and rabid bears saw the forest as their home and preyed on whomever crossed into their territory. Even giant eagles and swift falcons had gouged at the throats of unlucky travelers. But still, this place was the home that Jim had always loved.

*It takes a special breed of person to live here. The nights are frigid, and the days are filled with the bloodshot eyes of beasts. But it is our duty, our privilege, to protect these lands. And not just the people! The trees, the animals, the Savior Wall: they all survive under our constant gaze. Without us, Paradise would fall in a matter of months.*

Jim ducked as William trotted under a low-hanging branch. Emma winced at the movement, but, otherwise, lay still. She had refused to wake, no matter his ministrations. But she was breathing, and the wounds around her neck showed no signs of infection, so Jim allowed her to stay in her stubborn state of semiconsciousness. She would wake when she needed, whether it be for food or drink or a need to return to the world of thought.

William's hooves clopped loudly as she passed over a bridge made of grey and black cobblestones. The river beneath flowed with a deafening roar and rumble that vibrated through the horse and numbed Jim's legs and back. But the bridge held strong against the water that was gradually eroded its holdings.

As the pathway lead to the deeper reserves of the forest, the natural beauty of The Whispering Woods began to show. It started with flecks of colorful flowers, sparse at first but eventually erupting into fields of blue and red and purple. The trees grew larger and thicker as they traveled through the heart of the forest, reaching so high that Jim had to crane his neck straight up to see the canopy. Then came the sounds of the birds and insects that populated the bushes and branches. Everything sang and shouted, whether in warning or a ritual of mating - Jim was unsure - in a choir of chaotic voices that pleased the Hero's listening ears.

Jim had always loved the gust of sound that came from such small creatures. *The voices of the day* , his father had called them. A sound that informed the listeners of safety or danger. His father had told him of the sounds to listen for, which meant warning and which meant peace. But he had also mentioned another voice. *The whispers of the night*, he called it, but would only speak of the voice in brief and hushed sentences, and always finishing by saying, *I hope you never have to hear them yourself.*

It took nearly four years, but Jim had heard the whispers. A buck he had been hunting sprinted through the brush, Jim's arrow imbedded in its thigh. Jim had followed the trail of blood and broken branches for miles, not realizing the amount of time that had passed as he traveled. When he spared a glance at the sky a cold fear absorbed him, for it was not the blue sky of day that had greeted him, but the orange sky of a dying sun. Never had he been out of a village wall beyond dusk, and traveling back would force him to wander the woods in the pitch of night. His father had warned him never to travel at night, unless he was dying or being pursued, and to find a high branch to perch upon until the sun returned above the Eastern Mountains.

In an instant he forgot about the buck and scaled the nearest tree he could find. The branch he chose was thick enough around for Jim to lie on but would require him to sleep perfectly still lest he roll off and fall while he dreamt. But, sleep never came.

He sat, with his cloak wrapped around his shaking shoulders, as the night plunged the world into darkness. Then came the whispers. They were faint but distinct, foreign but human, serene but wrathful, and they spoke to him. What they said was unclear, mumbles and groans that distorted all meaning from the understanding of the frightened boy. But, one word was unmistakable, and was said with increasing frequency: *release.*

As the night progressed, the whispers grew in speed and volume until they were screaming. Jim shoved his hands against his ears, trying to quiet the frantic world but only succeeding in muffling the raging chorus. Then, with a flash of light, the voices stopped, and the sun rose in the distance.

In less than an hour he had sprinted back to the village where Owen, his caretaker, was waiting. When Jim told Owen what he heard, the caretaker ended their travels and they returned to Paradise. His father's face when Jim told him about the whispers was one of the few times that surprise had painted his features. *The voices are from those who are lost, in death and life, and cannot find the sanctuary that they were promised,* his father had said. *They speak to us because we are their protectors and we must do everything we can to give them peace. They spoke my name once too, but...that was long before you were born.*

No matter how much Jim pressed, that was all his father said on the whispers. Only once since then had Jim heard the voices, heard them call to him and scream his name. But fear was far from his mind on that night and the blood of the Dogwood heir distracted him from rationality.

The path traveled alongside a river, twisting and curving with the watery companion. In a few miles the river would join Galian, one of the eight Life Giving Lakes, and the path would lead to Adok, a small fishing village that profited from the lake. Jim had spent a few days in Adok, mingling with his people and learning the pieces of their history. The village was always clean but suffered frequent chills from the breeze that swept over the lake.

William trotted around a bend, bringing Adok in sight. The village, like most of the South, had been affected by the Southern War. From the distance Jim could see charred marks along the simple wooden wall. All that remained of the docks were a few floating splinters, and the gate had been torn from its pulleys and now lay covered in mud and moss. The lack of movement from the once lively village told Jim that it had been abandoned for some time, left to succumb to the elements and creatures of the forest. But, Adok is where William wanted to go.

Jim pulled against the horse's reins, not wanting to face the destruction that hid behind the walls, but William was persistent. She fought against her bit, whipping her head back and forth against Jim's administrations, ambling into the village of Adok.

The houses here were simple and small, wooden walls with clay shingles and shutters instead of glass over each window. Most of the houses were missing walls and doors or had holes in the roofs from where trebuchets had flung boulders through them. Many lay in heaps of charred rubble or were nothing more than dilapidated foundations that had fallen against its neighbor. The few houses that remained whole stood covered in vines and mud, but were proud amongst the destruction.

William pointed her nose towards the edge of the village, weaving through narrow streets and alleys. She knew the best route to take to get to the far corners of Adok, traveling with practiced steps over fallen beams and crumbling boulders. Her destination became clear after a few minutes, a house that stood almost whole, a trough built by the front supports. And sitting on a swing made from rope and cloth was Belle.

Belle stared at the sky, distracted by some unknown idea. William whinnied and quickened her pace, causing Belle to jump from the sudden exclamation. She rose from her swing and opened her arms wide, embracing William's snout and rubbing her cheek against the horse's forehead.

"You have to tell me about your journey," Belle said. "It was quiet here without you, but not so quiet as to be lonely. But still, next time run faster. Okay, Billy?"

William nudged against Belle's chest and nickered softly into her shirt.

"I missed you, too," Belle whispered.

Jim raised his leg from the horse's back and jumped to the soft dirt below. He grabbed Emma's arm and lifted her from the saddle, cradling her in his arms as he moved to greet Belle.

"There's a bed up the stairs," Belle said, tightening her grip on William.

Jim nodded and moved towards the house.

The house's interior reflected its simple style. A thin rug wove through the hallway, its colors wearing from use; the walls were covered in white and blue paper; the dining table was made of a grainy oak and held platters and bowls made from clay and silvery candlesticks which spit smoke from wicks that had recently been snuffed. The hall was lined with three rooms and ended with a staircase that led to the next floor.

Jim carried Emma up the stairs. Only two rooms were on the upper floor, both with beds covered in wool blankets and cotton pillows. The first bedroom was obviously taken; the sheets were in shambles, the pillow rested at an awkward angle against the bedpost, and various items of clothing were strewn about the floor and hanging from the wardrobes and windowsill. The second room was tidy, the blankets pulled taut over the mattress.

As Jim laid Emma on the bed, Belle's footsteps tromped towards the room. She stood in the doorway holding a leather sack. She tossed the sack at Jim as she entered.

"Billy told me Emma was burned," Belle said.

Jim opened the sack and pulled out a glass jar filled with a purple paste. He scooped the contents with a finger, bringing the salve to his nose. It smelled sweet, a mixture of lilac and...

"Lavender," Belle said, studying the Hero's actions. "Shell told me lavender would seep the sting from a burn. She knows about my fondness for fire and made me promise to carry that with me, everywhere I go." She pointed at the jar.

Jim began to apply the salve to the skin around Emma's neck. She winced as his calloused fingers rubbed against her blisters. Her skin looked splotchy, deep blue and yellow bruises connecting the draining blisters to complete a circuit around her once-smooth neck. But the worst wound was in the center of her chest, where the jewel had rested. The skin there was black with an angry red outline radiating from the diamond shaped mark. Jim slathered an obscene amount of the salve on the mark, hoping to give her as much relief as he could manage.

He pulled away, his hand smelling of the flowery paste, and examined the rest of Emma's wounds. Small cuts and bruises covered her arms and legs. Jim reached into one of the many pockets of his cloak and retrieved a small needle and a spool of sheep-gut thread. He proceeded to sew up the larger cuts with fine, steady stitches. The worst of her wounds, excluding her burns, was a four-inch laceration below her navel. The wound was deep and still seeping her crimson blood. Jim left the stitches there loose—the scar the wound left would be much more prominent, but allowing the wound to drain would hopefully stave off an infection.

Closing Emma took a few hours. It was a meticulous process that had Jim's back groaning from his awkward pose by the time he finished. Belle sat beside him, watching silently as he worked, only leaving to fetch a few candles when the sun began to dim. When he was satisfied, all that remained of the sheep-gut was a length of thread the size of his little finger. But Emma would be okay. She would sleep and regain her strength. She would wake in the morning and demand a large, well-cooked meal. She would be...

"She'll be okay, Jim," Belle whispered.

Jim looked at the girl. "Yes."

"Are...are you okay?" Belle asked, sounding timid for the first time since Jim had met her.

Exhaustion beat through Jim's veins as he processed the question, and the hole in his hand throbbed with angry healing. Was he okay? So many things had happened, so many awful things: Emma, the world of smoke and shadows, Marcus, Floydd, Colter.... Oh gods, Colter.

Jim reached in to his pocket and pulled out the crumpled letter. The seal, Colter's seal, was pressed in black wax and was unbroken from travel or trespasser. Jim snapped the hard wax and opened the wrinkled paper. The message was short and written in Colter's distinct handwriting.

*Jim,*

*You missed our meeting today, but I have some news that you must hear. I write to you in case you return in the night or before I do tomorrow morning. The man responsible for your Fault Contract was Lye Northtree. His son is coming to Salix tomorrow, so I will be busy through the morning getting my eyes in order. I will start in the Hero District and work block-by-block until I reach the church. Meet me if you read this before I return. The Northtrees have been making plays larger than I suspected. Larger than any of us suspected. We have to take down Floydd soon, and then we need to strike against them.*

*Tomorrow we will plan.*

*Colt*

Jim drifted the corner of the letter over a candle's flame, watching as the paper turned black and the words flew as ash. The killing-calm percolated his mind, consuming his emotion and causing his peripheral vision to cloud and darken. Vaguely, somewhere deep beyond his consciousness, he was aware of an outside presence peeking into his thoughts. He sent a wave of rage towards the presence, causing it to flee and causing Belle to recoil and gasp.

"I'm okay, Belle," Jim said, locking her eyes in his gaze. "I'm just angry."

## 29: AN ISLAND AND A WORLD

Jim woke in a panicked sweat and raced to don his belt. He sprinted towards the stairs, taking them two at a time, and took a breath as he reached the front door. How had he fallen asleep without fixing the gate? How could he be so foolish? Now, the streets would surely be swarmed by blood-hungry husks, ready to make him their latest meal. As he exhaled, Jim opened the door and was greeted by...nothing.

Vacant streets, a light breeze, a brightening sky, but no husks. The only sign of life came from William as she trotted towards the frantic Hero, snickering and nudging at his arm until he patted her head. Jim stayed on edge, listening for any sign that the peaceful morning would be interrupted, but the only unusual sound came from the house as Belle exited behind him. She was rubbing the sleep from her eyes, her hair a nest of untidy silk. She looked towards Jim, then at William, an annoyed look in her bloodshot eyes.

"It's impolite to wake so early," Belle grumbled. "I could've slept until the sun burned away the dawn, but no. You come out here and worry William half-to-death, just so you could...what? Get an early start? Chat as we watch the sky?" She walked until she faced Jim. "Why would any sane person choose to get up at this hour?"

Jim kept his eyes darting to each dark corner of the small village. The husks would surely have heard Belle and would come running towards their prey. Any second now they would burst through the narrow corridors and kill the ones who were marked with life. Jim's hand twitched on his hilt. Any second....Belle snapped her fingers in the Hero's face, an action that made Jim jump and crouch in anticipation of attack.

"What's wrong with you?" Belle asked, cocking an eyebrow.

Jim allowed the silence to remain for a heartbeat, continuing in his practiced listening, before he spoke.

"Husks," he whispered. "The gate was open."

"Husks?" Belle repeated loudly. "Jim, there haven't been husks here in…" she paused, looking up as she searched her memories, "…about seven years."

"What?" Jim asked. "How is that…" He trailed off as thought overwhelmed his speech.

Seven years. Adok, a village in the center of the Southern territory had been husk free for seven years. That wasn't possible. The South had held the largest population of wandering husks in all the Hero territories. The Whispering Woods were their preferred hunting grounds. So, to be rid of husks in the thick of the forest was…had to be impossible.

"Are you sure?" Jim asked, his mind racing with questions and improbabilities.

"Of course," Belle said sternly. "Shortly after Adok was attacked and abandoned, they stopped coming. At first it was just inside the walls, but now they don't even enter the trees near here. There are miles of empty woods all around us, husk free."

"How do you know?" Jim asked, curious as to how Belle had scouted such a large area of the woodland.

"Because I can't feel them. You don't have to believe me, just feel for yourself. The nearest one was far beyond the Savior Wall when I checked last night. Way too far to make the travel while we slept."

Jim shook his head, trying to make sense of Belle's statements. She could *feel* the husks? And not just feel them, know the location and number of husks that resided around them. He thought through the limited knowledge of the connection that the shadow-man had taught him and remembered Luna's lesson in reaching towards the consciousness of distant beings. Perhaps that is how Belle knew, perhaps…

"Exactly!" Belle exclaimed. "I knew that you knew! I knew it!"

"What?" Jim asked, startled at the girl's exclamation.

"We are all connected, Jim! So few people understand, but I knew that you knew!" Belle hopped excitedly as she spoke. "I thought I could feel you when Emma first brought you to camp, but those feelings were only whispers. But last night I knew. I felt you so strong, so much more powerful than anything I've felt before. It was...scary...but invigorating to know."

"I know...pieces," Jim admitted, causing Belle to happily squeal and giggle. "But I don't know much."

"Hmm." Belle tried to control her joy. "Have you practiced?"

"Practiced?"

"Oh, Jim," Belle huffed. "You have to practice for adequacy. No wonder you were so worried this morning. You need to learn how to feel, and then practice feeling until it becomes as natural as breathing." She thought for a moment, rubbing her chin with an overly large sleeve. "Practice with me, right now." She went quiet again, closing her eyes. "There is a squirrel, behind the house to your left. Do you see it?"

Jim looked left. "All I see is the house."

Belle peeked open her eye, then huffed again. "Not see with your eyes. Feel for the squirrel. Close your eyes. It's too hidden to see with them anyway."

Jim did as he was commanded, closing his eyes and looking for any hint of distant consciousness. Slowly, a flicker of life crept from ahead of him, a soft joy radiating from its center. He moved himself towards the joy, allowing it to enter a piece of his mind and fill him with emotion.

"I said the squirrel, not me." Belle giggled. "Look a little farther."

Jim backed away from the happy intrusion and searched harder. Behind Belle he found another consciousness filled with a leisurely whinny, informing him it was William who he felt. But, beyond the horse there was only darkness. Darkness for miles of empty space. Still, he searched. Hours past, maybe days, before a glint of light scurried through the darkness. Jim reached towards the light, grasping it with his mind and delving towards its center. Before he could consume it entirely, he was stopped by the feeling of joy that he had felt before. Belle.

"Yes!" she proclaimed.

Jim opened his eyes and looked towards the sky. The sun had moved but only across a small portion, indicating that only a few minutes had passed. A sheen of sweat had accumulated on his brow, and he felt the need to sit and catch his breath.

"Oh," Belle said when she saw the Hero's quick breathing. "You are very new. Hmm...I have an idea." She grabbed Jim's hand, pulling him to his feet, and began to wander towards Galian.

The lake was immense, a smooth silver landscape that reached until the distant trees were no larger than Jim's outstretched finger. The shore around the lake was covered in fine, black sand and pebbles that had been rubbed shiny by the ever-coming tides. A small island, less than a mile in diameter, rested in the lake's center.

Belle pulled Jim to what remained of the shattered dock. A row-boat was tied to the pier, lazily bobbing up and down on the rippling waves. They moved over the slippery wooden dock, Belle staring at the distant island.

"I was there when... My family was at home, but I was there. It was silly. I was praying because my mom and I had an argument—I don't even remember what about, but we were yelling and slamming doors and my father had had enough. He was a large man, always ducking through doorways and lifting logs as if they were tinder. He grabbed me by my collar and dragged me to the boat. He told me to go there," she pointed at the island, "and pray until I was calm enough to talk.

"I prayed for hours to Brun, the dragon who sleeps at the bottom of the lake. I prayed, and I calmed myself, and I listened, and I searched, and then I felt. I felt the bugs and the plants that were all around me, I felt the fish that swam through the hollowed caves far beneath the lake. I felt the birds that were hunting over the water, and I felt the people of my village as they ran and screamed and died. I searched for my family, my father, but their light had gone out. And I was there."

Belle squeezed Jim's hand, as if to offer comfort to the Hero. "You should go there too, I think. It's a good place to think and to feel. It's...safe."

She stepped away, leaving Jim alone, staring at the distant island. He felt startled by her abrasive story, but he calmed himself and took her words to heart. A quiet place to think and *feel*. He took a step forward. It would be nice think, nice to banish himself to serene singularity and rest his tired thoughts. He stepped again, feeling the shallow water soak against his boot.

"Take the boat!" Belle shouted from behind him. "It will be much faster than swimming!"

□ □ □ □ □ □ □

The island felt smaller than it had looked from the shores. In only a few minutes of a leisurely walk, Jim had traversed its perimeter, staring deeply into the dark waters that surrounded him. An air emanated from the island, blowing through the breeze and rustling the leaves, an air of reverence and calm. He felt his mind relax as he breathed in the crisp air and listened to the rhythmic waves.

A small grove of trees circled the island, thick enough to hide its contents from wandering eyes while still leaving paths for travelers to walk through. Bright yellow and orange bushes sat on either side of pebbled pathways, all reaching towards the center. Hummingbirds drank from patches of red and purple flowers, flitting around dramatically from blossom to blossom.

Jim's footsteps sounded like thunder as he walked over the loose gravel. It only took him a minute to reach the center and see what was hidden in the island's heart.

An opening in the grove's canopy allowed a beam of light to shine brightly through the trees. A wooden platform sat in the grove's center, overlooking a garden of flowers and sweet-smelling vines. Each of the pathways led to the platform's base, leaving a circle of stones surrounding the blue and grey wood. To the side of his path, lying beneath a cluster of closely-grown trees, were indicators for three graves.

Jim walked towards the indicators, careful not to disturb any of the plants or fallen leaves. The graves were piled with black and white stones, each placed particularly to create a clean, round surface. At the heads were the indicators, planks of wood tied meticulously with lengths of rope to form a cross, and, on each of the planks, a name was carved elegantly into the grain. *Elena, Gent,* and...*William. All that remains of Belle's family.*

Jim rested his hand on the graves, picking a few stray pieces of grass that had begun to grow between the stones. He brushed off the speckling of dirt on the indicators. He silently stood, then returned to the pathway.

This was Belle's place, her home, her safety. Here, she had lived and buried her family. Here, she had prayed and searched and found the connection that binds each living thing. Jim walked to the platform and sat upon the wood. The smell of mildew rose from the wet planks. This place was special, not because of tradition or heroism, but because of loss. Jim closed his eyes and allowed his mind to wander.

Specks of light danced in the surrounding darkness. Many flew in rapid trajectories, never staying still or settling on an invisible perch. Jim focused on one of the specks, pulling it close to his consciousness and entering the light.

Through hundreds of eyes he saw the world around him. Everything was large, abstract compared to his usual sight, but the world was the same. Through instincts that belonged to the beetle, Jim saw in every direction and knew to watch for predators and prey. The experience was disorienting, and he pulled from the bug's mind after a few seconds.

Jim expanded his mind, enveloping the island entirely. The specks grew in size and brightness, becoming birds and lizards that dwarfed the light of the minuscule insects. Dim light shone from each of the plants, outlining the darkness in familiar but obscure shapes and patterns. When Jim tried to focus on one of the trees his mind was filled with sensations and scents that his senses could not comprehend. He pulled away from the tree as nausea began to bubble in his belly from the disorientation.

He delved through Galian, searching for the mind of the ancient dragon that was rumored to be slumbering beneath the wake. The minds of thousands of fish caressed against Jim, but no sign of Brun. The largest being he could find inside the Life-Giving Lake was an eel that snaked through the deep banks and caverns, swallowing arm-length trout and salmon in its massive maw.

Beyond Galian, Jim found Belle's happy mind. It flashed in recognition, brightening as Jim brushed against her. He searched for Emma but found only an obsidian wall blocking the sleeping girl's thoughts. When he tried to prod, Jim was blasted with a spark of fury and felt the obsidian grow thicker. He did not pry after that.

Jim's mind soared through the forest, feeling the deer that sprinted through the trees. He stumbled on a pack of wolves that slept in a nearby hollow, their ears perking as his presence brushed against theirs. He even found a group of travelers, their mule heavily burdened by the large packs and pots of the weary men. But, through the multitudes of light and life, no husk pressed against his mind. Belle was right. The forest was free of the undead monsters.

He moved his mind South, searching for the Savior Wall, the place where Belle had seen the husk last night. Finding the wall was difficult, due to its lack of life, but he eventually found it due to the vines and lichen that outlined its surface. But on top of the wall, where Heroes were supposed to patrol, was lifeless. Sentinels should have been stationed there day and night, dozens of the golden-eyed soldiers watching for any sign of the husks; but now there were none.

Jim inspected the wall, from the edge that pushed against the Eastern Mountains to the overhang that tilted above the Western Shores, but the wall remained unkempt. He moved back over the wall, looking closer and examining each mile of the silent protector: still no Heroes, but what he did find chilled the air in his lungs.

A section of the wall, large enough for Adok to fit between, was gone. The lichen grew in ragged patterns on either side of the large gap, patterns that Jim suspected had been caused by explosives and picks. The wall was broken, but not by the claws of husks. The break was made by the hands of the living.

The light of people formed in a semi-circle around the Northern end of the gap. The light was brighter than the humans he had seen before, radiating in near-blinding pulses from the depth of the darkness. Perhaps the people were Heroes. Jim moved closer but stopped when he felt another presence on the Southern end of the wall. The presence was dark, darker than the black that this world was made from, so dark that it pulled at him, calling at his mind to be consumed by its invitation. Jim heeded to the temptation for a moment before fear caused him to stop. The presence continued its call, a song that played in uneven intervals and jumpy tones, but Jim did not answer. Instead, he moved to one of the soldiers, a Hero he now assumed, since it stared down such a force. He melded its mind with his own.

The world was bright and colorful, though blurry from the distant Hero's eyes. Jim watched in fervor as the husk clambered through the Savior Wall's breach. Even after the hundreds of husks this Hero had encountered, fear climbed through her throat and caused her breaths to become shaky and sharp at this one. Halfway through the wall, the husk spotted them. It stopped, bending its backward knees as it prepared to dash at them. A howl escaped its mouth, and it moved with the speed of the supernatural. But it did not get far.

Before the husk could reach the end of the breach, a net made of chain and barbs snapped from the foliage and tangled the monster inside. The husk continued to howl and scream as the Heroes inched forward. One moved faster than the others, and with far less hesitation. The man had a strip of blond hair on top of his head, but the sides were shaved and covered in scabbed nicks and scars. He carried a longsword on his hip, but all he held in his hands was a silver necklace with an emerald in its center.

The Hero slipped the necklace around the husks neck, causing it to yowl and thrash angrily in its net. After a minute, plumes of smoke rose from the husks flesh, wafting into the air and dissipating after a few feet. The husk tried to grab at its throat, but the metal net stopped its claws from moving upward. Finally, after over five minutes of rabid thrashing, the husk went still. The Hero nodded his head then clapped once, and the net fell from around the monster.

The husk took a step forward but made no move to attack the Hero. The others cheered and moved towards the Hero, clapping him on the back and giving him praise. A few even stood near the husk, examining its features and poking at its flesh. The one whom Jim possessed stayed back, uneasy by the sight of the husk, even though it was under their control.

A hand grasped her shoulder and spun her around. The face of the Captain looked upon Jim, his gold eyes staring deep into his own. The Captain was heavily muscled and wore jeweled rings on each of his fingers. The face was familiar....

"Jacqueline," the Captain said with a deep Northern accent. "It seems you are not alone."

"Sir?" Jim felt his mouth ask, a light voice fluttering from his lips.

"There is another looking through you, even as we speak." He placed his hand on Jacqueline's temple. "Focus with me. Clear your mind and push out the invader."

"Yes, sir."

Jim felt another presence enter his consciousness. The presence was massive, towering over his own and drowning out the world around him. The presence moved towards him, pushing and jabbing at his mind with beams of force and power. The presence was overwhelming, surrounding Jim's entirety, pushing and attacking and relentlessly roaring. Finally, Jim was forced to retreat, pulling his mind back with as much force as he could summon.

Jim's eyes opened and the beautiful island greeted him, tinted with the orange sky of a dying day. He rose, shakily, to his feet and ventured down the pebbled path. Rowing was difficult, for he felt exhausted and his muscles felt heavy and sore.

Sleep. He needed to sleep. But tomorrow, he would need to travel.

## 30: DOWN THE PATH

Yellow light shone from the cracked shutters, directing torrents of light toward Emma's eyes. She squinted, not accepting the fact that wakefulness had finally pulled her from the wonders of sleep. Hunger grumbled in her stomach, helping her awaken. If there was anything she loved more than sleep, it was food.

Begrudgingly, she rose and, for the first time, realized she recognized the room that she had slept in. The white walls had only one window, with yellow drapes and simple wooden shutters. The floor comprised of wooden planks, though a hexagon-shaped rug covered its majority. The bed was soft, covered in woolen blankets and cotton pillows. Jim was deep in the wallows of sleep, facing away from the impression that her sleeping form had created. This room was familiar, homely, as if made for the single task of greeting guests with warm welcomes.

A quick inspection of her body revealed sore muscles and healing wounds. Tan stitches held her skin together in a dozen places, and cloth bandages were wrapped around her wrists. Emma knew that she must look awful, a corpse walking on borrowed time, but she felt surprisingly good. Her head pounded, but softly. Her joints ached, though her movements were unhindered. Her skin was sensitive, as if covered in a sunburn, but she was alive. Not only alive, but awake and near her Hero, the man who made her safe.

Emma's stomach grumbled again, demanding she provide sustenance. She exited the room and crept through the narrow hallway and down the twisting stairs. In the nearest room sat a table, a clay bowl filled with apples and pears resting on its top. Emma greedily snatched a pear and devoured it with a few bites. Juice dripped from her chin and stung at the broken blisters that decorated her neck, but hunger demanded she eat another. After four pears and one green apple, she was satisfied. A pail filled with cool water sat near the window. Emma used a ladle and drank her fill of the crystal liquid and used a handful to wipe the sticky juice from her face.

A shrill tone stunned Emma, coming from just outside the front door. She tiptoed to a window and saw Belle berating William, her hands on her hips and her head shaking. Emma pulled open the front door and walked to her sister. Belle did not notice the extra presence until Emma's hand grasped her shoulder. Belle jumped forward and yelped, reaching for a knife that she kept beneath her linens, but stopped short when she saw her sister.

"Oh!" Belle said. "Sorry, I...I didn't feel you coming."

Emma smiled. "Good to see you too."

Belle took Emma's hands in her own and pulled her close. "William came as soon as she could. I tried to find a faster way, but...I'm glad your awake."

Emma nodded her head, unsure of what Belle was talking about, and smiled. She was glad to be awake, glad to be here, glad that the pain was gone.

·········

The sun was in the center of the sky when Jim awoke. He had slept through an entire night, and into half of a day, a sign that his excursions the day before had been more taxing than he initially thought. Jim got to his feet, testing the movement in his arms and legs and brushing the hair from his face.

The bed beside him was empty, though its scent informed Jim that Emma had left recently. That was a good sign. She was up and moving, able to leave the bed without assistance. From the floor below he heard her laugh, and his skin prickled from the joy her musical tones gave him. *She is going to be okay.*

Jim's pack sat in the corner of the room, bulging with supplies that he would need for his journey to the Savior Wall. He did an inventory in his head: two days' worth of dried fruit and salted meat, three days' worth of water, flint, steel, sharpening stones, oil, bandages, and what remained of his sheep gut sutures. The food and water would take him to the wall, but on his trip back he would be forced to hunt and boil water from local ponds and puddles. If his prey or his water remained elusive, he would just have to fast for an extra day or two, nothing he hadn't done before.

The pack rested heavily on his back, settling between his shoulders and collarbone. The extra bulk forced Jim to exit the door fully before turning in the narrow hallway and down the stairs. Emma and Belle's voices grew louder and more distinct with each step Jim took. They were talking, reminiscing about the last time Emma had visited this place.

Belle was talking in between her frequent giggles, "...and when you pulled the line from the water, it was a pile of kelp as long as you were! You had been fighting a plant for over an hour. Your face was," she gasped for air, "priceless!" Belle slapped her thigh.

"Hey!" Emma retorted. "It was still the biggest catch of the day!"

"I guess, but...hi Jim...not even Aisley could figure out a good way to cook it up!" Belle said as Jim entered the doorway.

Emma turned quickly, and Jim devoured her with his gaze. To see her smile. He had longed to see happiness return to her features.

"Good morning, sleepy head!" Belle said jovially.

Emma just stared, her expression going from joy to discontent in an instant. Her eyes fell to the ground and she blinked in slow but frequent intervals.

"How are you feeling, Emma?" Jim asked, but Emma stayed quiet. "You slept for nearly three days. For a minute we thought you were...."

"You're leaving," Emma said flatly, looking at the floor.

Jim took a step back. Emma's tone had gone cold and soft, but the power in her words burned like melted wax.

"Yes. I need to go, but I shouldn't be more than a week. I'll be back before...."

"No," Emma said sternly.

Jim quieted. Emma was shaking now, her fists clenched in tight balls. Her shoulders were hunched in a protective manner, and she acted as though she would flee at any moment. This behavior was wrong for her. She looked like a caged animal, or a dying man, hopeless and fearful of an uncertain fate.

Jim stepped towards her and nudged her chin until she met his gaze.

"Don't," Emma whispered.

"I have to, Em. There is someone that I saw, someone that I knew, and I have to find out what he is doing at the Savior Wall."

Jim pulled his hand away and turned to leave the room. Before he made it through the doorway, Emma's hand caught his, her grip like iron.

"Don't leave me," Emma pleaded.

Her words were filled with anger and fear, and her grip tightened as she spoke. But her eyes...her eyes filled with a devastating torment. She locked her gaze with his, transferring everything she couldn't bring herself to say with the single, crushing look. *But she will be okay.*

Jim kept his eyes on her emeralds. "Alright," he said, placing a hand on top of hers and squeezing comfortably. "Grab your pack."

■ ■ ■ ■ ■ ■ ■ ■ ■

After two hours of walking through the trampled forest, Emma's body was burning. She wasn't ready for another adventure, wasn't back to her full strength, but she couldn't let Jim leave her behind. With him around she felt stronger, more capable, safe. Having to rely on him for her independence felt wrong, a reliance that she had never given to anyone before; but...he had saved her from a fate worse than death. In some ways, too, it felt right.

Still, the acceptance of her reliance didn't take away from the fact that her muscles protested with each step she took. Jim seemed to notice her discomfort, but he wouldn't stop. Emma didn't expect him to, for she knew what choice she had made, what choice she had forced upon her Hero, and she would journey with him without complaint.

But, when Jim pulled the pack from Emma's back and strapped it to himself, with no noticeable effort, she nearly cried with relief.

Wordlessly they traveled, Jim matching Emma's pace with the ease of his kind. Miles passed through The Whispering Woods, with the only sound coming from chatting creatures and tweeting birds. Once, an unobservant hare darted across the path in front of them, nearly colliding with Emma's calf as it sprinted for the safety of a blueberry bush. The incident received a yelp from Emma and a small chuckle from Jim. But, otherwise, their conversation was a silent one. A conversation of acceptance and quiet admiration of her partner's determination.

A rock caught Emma's toe, causing her to stumble a single step. Before her foot landed, Jim's hand supported her hip, ensuring that she stayed standing. His grip felt hesitant, yet firm, the kind of grip she had used when clipping the feathers from a bird's wings. Once she had regained her balance, he removed his hand.

Strange. Jim had been acting so different since she had awakened. His face stayed soft when he looked into her eyes. He kept his voice low and monotone, his touches sparse. When he touched her, he did so with that same hesitating grip. He was testing her, seeing how fragile, how broken, she had become. Seeing how long it would take for her to recover and overcome her beating. But maybe there was more. More to his looks and hesitations, more to his quiet demeanor and lack of touch. Maybe, he was broken too.

The thought made Emma look at her Hero, stare at the contours of his face and the side of his golden eye. His eyebrows twitched and the corner of his mouth moved, as if he were speaking to an invisible god. His face had the look that he used so frequently when he thought too much and debated every little choice that he had ever made deep within his mind. There was more going on than he would ever say outright. She had learned that a few times. The only way to get him to confess his inner turmoil was to beat around in conversation until he was ready to speak. But she loved him, loved him more than she had ever loved before. He was her Hero, and she would take care of him, as he had taken care of her.

So, after hours of silent contemplations, she spoke.

"Why the Savior Wall?" Emma hated how meek her voice sounded.

Jim cleared his throat and looked at her for a moment before replying, "There's something going on there. Heroes capturing husks and...."

"And what?" Emma asked softly.

"And I saw someone, a man from my past. A dead man."

"So, you want to find this man and talk with him?"

"No. I'm going to kill him."

When Jim spoke, his eyes held regret and sympathy. The expression was troubling, something that he hardly understood and was trying to make sense of. This was what he had been thinking about, the broken puzzle that refused to come together in his thoughts.

"You don't want to kill him?" Emma asked, though she knew his reply.

"No."

"Then why?" she continued.

"I...there was something wrong." His words were unsure as he spoke. "He felt like...someone else, I think. I need to make sure."

"Oh."

Emma couldn't think of anything else to say. She didn't know how to quell his turmoil or how to make sense of his feelings. His thoughts scattered but felt determined. All he knew was that killing this man was somehow right.

They walked quietly for another mile, both thinking about what Jim had said. Then, it was Jim's turn to break the silence.

"I died, Emma."

"What?" She blurted out.

"I died." Jim took in a breath. "Twice now. That's why I was in the woods the day we met, when we fought. I didn't understand, still don't really, but I had taken a shot through the chest and had fallen from the top of a tower." Jim looked at Emma, and she met his gaze, prompting him to go on, to trust her. "Then in Salix, Marcus disintegrated me while you were...the necklace." Emma nodded, appreciating his sensitivity around her torture.

"You died?" she asked, not unkindly.

"Yes." Jim answered with confidence.

"Where did you go? When you died, I mean, what did you see?"

"That's...complicated. It doesn't all make sense, but I think it's just a shadow of this world. A place where many are trapped and wander." Jim shook his head.

Emma grabbed Jim's hand, interlacing her fingers and his. "Go on." She squeezed.

"I met...people. I think they were people, but I don't know what they are now. They knew things, showed me pieces of this world and memories of The Time Before, and they told me about how all life shares a connection. It sounds crazy, I know, but I've felt it. I've felt the connection and I've used it and...it's powerful. With it I can enter people's thoughts and manipulate their minds. I can...."

"Show them things that aren't real." Emma remembered the presence that had haunted her from the amulet.

"Yes," Jim confirmed.

"And with this...connection, you saw the man, the dead man, at the Savior Wall? There was something wrong with him?"

"Yes."

"And now you need to kill him, because of...whatever you felt."

"Basically. But...it's weird. The need is different this time. It's not something that I want or something that I was told, it's just...there. Driving me and pushing me to confront him and end whatever it is that he has become. It's...frustrating." Jim went quiet.

"Alright," Emma said.

Only a minute passed before Jim said, "Oh, Marcus was a Hero."

Emma looked at Jim, his golden eyes light and smiling. "A Hero? I guess that explains why the Northtrees were talking to him. Is he...?"

"Dead." Jim said. "Drowned in a foul-smelling liquid."

"Good," Emma said, and the silence returned to guide them once again.

■■■■■■■■

That night, they slept beneath the branches of an old oak. The canopy full, light from the twinkling stars still found their way through the dense leaves. Jim and Emma ate a meal of salted meat and berries from a bush nearby. Then it was time for sleep.

Jim closed his eyes and scouted the surrounding forest, checking for any source of life that may be a threat to their unconscious selves. A wolf pack hunted a few miles away, but the light of their fire would keep them at bay. No husks, no people, only the small creatures of the Earth and the two exhausted travelers.

Emma was deep within the embrace of sleep by the time Jim opened his eyes. Traveling was difficult for her, he could feel it in their unconscious connection. Each step was a struggle, each breath burned in her lungs, but she was persistent. She never mentioned her aching body or her tired mind. But sleep had found her with the speed of an arrow and the weight of stone. Her arm was twisted above her head, her mouth gaping and blowing dragon smoke as she snored, drool dribbled down her cheek. She was beautiful.

With a smile, Jim propped his back against the giant tree, and drifted in to dreams.

□ □ □ □ □ □ □

A sting, and the cold familiarity of metal, cut at Jim's throat. His eyes sprang open, but he did not move, did not want to cause the blade to slip farther into his flesh. Keeping his breathing calm, he stared at Emma, her rapier in her outstretched hand. Its tip pressed firmly against his neck. But her eyes were closed.

Emma mouthed something unintelligible and placed more pressure on her deadly weapon. Her eyes were moving rapidly beneath her eyelids as if she were...dreaming.

She's asleep, Jim realized, keeping his breathing calm and collected as he tried to find a way to repel Emma's blade. But, even in the swells of sleep, she had chosen her footing well and her stance was sensitive.

"Emma," Jim whispered, trying not to startle her with a sudden voice.

Emma paused, her mumbling stopping as she heard his voice.

"Emma," Jim said louder, the cold metal sinking deeper as his throat bobbed.

Emma stayed still and her shoulders relaxed, causing the pressure from her rapier to lessen.

"Wake up, Em," Jim said with gentle sternness.

Emma's eyes peeked open, reflecting the light from the fire in her groggy gaze. When she saw what she was doing, what she was holding, her eyes flew open and she jumped back. Tears flowed as she stumbled over words of apology and concern and regret. Her rapier fell to the ground with a clank, and she dropped to her knees, covering her face to hide her sobs.

Jim reached for his neck, feeling the small laceration that trickled hot blood onto his shirt. The cut was small, but deep. It stung each time he swallowed, but it was far from life-threatening.

Jim looked at Emma. She was shaking, her hands trembling over her wet eyes. What happened? What had she dreamt about that had caused such a visceral action? He stood and knelt beside her, tentatively placing a hand on her shoulder. Emma collapsed against him, her arms desperately grasping his shoulders.

"I'm so sorry. So…so sorry," she repeated, her voice muffled against his shirt.

Jim wrapped his arms around her, patting her head with his hand. "I know, Em." He whispered, "I know."

She stayed in his arms for a half hour before her shaking finally stopped and she drifted back to sleep. Jim continued to hold her, protect her from whatever haunted her dreams, until the sun rose above the Eastern Mountains and the sky filled with the songs of birds and the chatter of squirrels. And, as he held her against his steady heart, he hoped she would be okay.

## 31: THE CARETAKER

The next day was filled with small talk, awkward apologies, and travel. Jim continued to practice scouting with the connection, always looking ahead for danger or unforeseen circumstances, and Emma trudged on with her sore muscles and achy skin. By the time the sun fell and the moon illuminated the forest in blue light, the Savior Wall was within walking distance. They made good time, unhindered by distraction and lack of motivation, but their difficulties had just begun.

Jim searched ahead, finding the gap within the wall and the soldiers that camped around it. There were twenty-seven, all Heroes watching the Southern gap with proficient intent. Just beyond the wall, Jim could feel the dark lullaby of a husk, slowly hobbling towards their trap. At the head of the Heroes, the Captain's consciousness flared, radiating light in pulses, grasping towards the husk and gauging its distance.

The rest of the camp was sparse. Only four Heroes stood as sentinels, lazily watching the tree-line for ambush. Jim could sneak by them easily. Jim determined he had to move, now.

Emma was sitting on a stump, unlacing her boots and preparing to rest. She would likely collapse if he forced her to continue, but a chance like this, a Hero camp left in such poor condition, was a rare opportunity that Jim could not overlook it.

Jim placed his pack on the ground, concealing it within the dense leaves of a bush, and signaled for Emma to stop. Emma squinted and sighed, her shoulders rising then falling with unspoken contempt.

"We're going in, aren't we?" she asked, and starting retying her laces.

Jim nodded, his mind focusing on the location of the sentinels and the level of each of the guards' focuses. The Eastern-most guard continuously glanced towards the Southern group, a longing in his stare that caused his eyes to linger for copious amounts of time. Jim would enter under his watch, the gap, caused by the sentinel's daydream.

Jim waved his hand at Emma and said, keeping his voice low, "Follow me." Then, he moved towards the East.

· · · · · · · · ·

The Savior Wall was magnificent, towering high above the clouds and stretching farther than Emma's eyes could see. Bards sang about the structure. It was spoken about in stories, all filled with a stoic reverence. For one seeing it in person was…breathtaking. The old stone had patches of algae and lichen, giving it a flecked, almost natural look. In places, the bricks had cracked or fallen out, but diligent masons had since filled the fractures in the wall with silver mortar that shone in the moonlight.

Emma watched the Savior Wall as she drew closer, admiring the old giant as she carefully stepped over crumbling leaves and snapping twigs. She could have stared for hours at the archaic wall, listening to the songs that each stone sang, but her admirations would have to wait.

Jim moved ahead of her with the speed and grace of an elk, bounding past saplings and cicadas until he stopped suddenly at a predetermined location. There, he crouched, Emma emulating his movement until she ducked beside him. The Hero stared attentively at the camp, waiting patiently for a sign that remained invisible to Emma. His hand rested gently on her knee, tapping with each beat of his heart. With a deep exhale Jim stood and sprinted into the open field towards the Hero camp. Emma did the same, acting as his shadow, though struggling to match his inhuman speed, until the walls of canvas tents hid her from unknown eyes.

Jim stopped with her, concealing his form in the shadows, and winked. A smile crested his lips. He allowed Emma to catch her breath and slow the pace of her rapid heart, then he crouched low and darted through the camp.

Emma's heart beat loudly in her ears as she crept. Her senses reached hyper-aware states as she noted any movement or sound that would betray her stealth. Dancing shadows from flickering torches caused her moments of hesitation, but Jim ignored them with the ease of a veteran thief.

Then, the Captain's tent was before them. A large red canopy towering above the surrounding structures. Gold tassels and embroidery decorated the outside flaps of the tent's entrance, showing the wealth and power of the man who would sleep within. Emma gulped as Jim entered silently through the flaps and waited for a heartbeat before he emerged and waved her forward.

The inside of the tent was just as glorious as the out. Golden candlesticks illuminated an ornate desk which was cluttered with papers and heavy wax seals. Silver platters with fruits and fresh meat were displayed on various pieces of furniture and the soft cushioned seats. The bed was the largest that Emma had ever seen, taking up a full quarter of the tent's interior, shining with crimson silk sheets. A trunk was at the bed's foot, a pantleg stuck in its closed jaw.

Jim stood near Emma and whispered, "Sit there," then gestured to a dark corner of the tent, "and have your pistol ready."

Emma pulled a chair into the dark corner and placed the shiny pistol on her lap. Jim sat at the desk, the candles shadowing his features in a devious manner. Then, they waited.

Outside the sound of a small scuffle disrupted the quiet, but it was over after a few minutes. Cheering erupted shortly after, and then the sound of footsteps echoed through the camp. Jim's attention peaked as someone brushed aside the flap of the tent and three Heroes entered.

At the lead was, Emma assumed, the Captain. He wore a stunning white cloak and had a scar that ran from his left eye to his chin. The other two Heroes wore red cloaks, one with spiked black hair and a quiver over his shoulder, and the other with cropped blonde hair and a hatchet at his waist. The three men stopped when they saw Jim, but none moved for their arms. The Captain stared at his intruder, recognition on his scarred face.

With a large, ringed hand, the Captain waved at his guards and said, "Leave." He had a deep and grizzled voice.

"Sir?" the dark-haired Hero said.

"Now," the Captain said, his words holding the power of a gunshot.

The two guards gave a short bow before swiftly exiting the tent.

The Captain waited until the movement his guards vanished in the night, then he acknowledged his intruder with a nod and said, "James."

Jim stared back at the Captain, never breaking eye-contact under the authoritative gaze, and said, "Owen."

■ ■ ■ ■ ■ ■ ■ ■ ■

The sight of his old Caretaker had childhood memories flooding back into Jim's mind. Owen had been assigned to Jim as Caretaker once his father was appointed as Hero Leader and, as Caretaker, Owen needed to teach Jim the ways of the Ash people. The man who had taught him to hunt, how to wield a sword and shoot a gun, the man who had traveled by his side as he visited each of the Hero cities, was standing here now, as Captain of a Northtree encampment. It felt like a betrayal, seeing Owen donned in Northtree white and crimson. But for Owen, betrayal was expected.

"Why are you here, James?" Owen asked, a pained look on his battle-hardened face.

"I think you know," Jim replied, his voice filled with malice.

"I see."

Owen slowly moved to his bedside table and pulled out two crystal glasses and a decanter of whiskey. He filled the glasses with the copper liquid before stopping the decanter and returning the bottle to its drawer. He returned to the desk, glasses in hand, but nearly spilled them when he saw Emma sitting in the dark corner. Owen placed one of the glasses in front of Jim then pulled a stool to the desk to sit across from him.

"Cloakers are rare, boy. You'd best hold on to that one," Owen said, taking a long sip of the liquor.

"Cloakers?" Jim asked.

"Aye. At least, that's what I call them." Owen cocked an eyebrow. "The kind who can hide their presence from even the most skilled Seer."

Jim stayed quiet, though he saw Emma slightly shift in the corner of his eye.

"The gun won't be necessary, will it?" Owen asked. "Even if things get...out of hand, wouldn't you rather settle this between us?"

"If it comes to it."

Owen sighed. "Once I finish my drink then?"

Jim nodded.

Owen took another drink. "It isn't poisoned. I'm no coward." He tilted his hand towards Jim's glass. "Drink with me."

Jim lifted his glass and sipped at the whiskey. The foul taste burned his throat and heated his belly. Owen was many things, but not even he would turn to poison to rid himself of a nuisance, so Jim drank again.

Owen seemed satisfied. He crossed his leg over his knee and relaxed his muscled shoulders.

"It was you that I felt, the other night. Poor Jacqueline had to be...relieved of duty because of you. Can't have malleable minds under my rule, now can I?" Owen used leisure tones.

"It was me," Jim said, taking a large mouthful of the whiskey.

"Ahh. How'd you die?" Owen asked, light glinting in his curious eyes.

"Which time?" Jim said, allowing a small smile to part his lips.

That caught Owen off guard. The Captain's eyes went large, and he blinked rapidly before a loud chuckle broke through his surprise.

"Which time!" Owen repeated. "James, you curious creature! How many times then? Tell me what happened."

Jim kept the smile on his face. "Twice," he said. "Once by falling and once by...it's hard to explain."

"Many things are nowadays," Owen agreed.

"And you?"

"How did I return, you mean? I assume you remember how I died," Owen said.

Jim nodded slowly, draining the remainder of whiskey from his glass.

"Well, I woke up in...the place." He looked carefully at Jim to make sure he understood. "And the shadows all swarmed around, like a whirlwind. I tried to scream for help, but that only made the shadows angry. They came closer and closer until I shut my mouth. I didn't want those damned things touching me, so I stayed quiet until they left. It felt like it took days for them to grow bored, but I didn't have anywhere to go, being dead. But after they left, I was alone.

"Days, months, years, I don't know how long I wandered in the dark. There were…things there, in the deep crevasses of hell. Things that petrified me and left me screaming with a silent voice." Owen shuddered. "I did not sleep while there, did not eat or drink, never having to use my body in the way that God intended. I was dead, but somehow, I wasn't.

"Then, one day, I heard a voice. A hallucination, I thought, but it was a persistent phantom. It spoke in a soft voice, coming from all directions but always growing closer. Then I saw him. A priest, emerging from the shadows. His arm was glowing, showing me color for the first time in a lifetime, and he smiled when I bowed at his feet. He patted me on the shoulder and offered his glowing hand to me, asking, 'would you like to come home?' More than anything I did. He told me how, how to take a name and take a life, and he promised to guide me through the torment.

"My new name was Jonathan. Not of the First-Four, mind you, but a Willow boy who grew up under his grandfather, as an heir in Paradise."

*Son?*

"With Jonathan as my name, I came back to a church in the middle of Forge. The priest dressed and bathed me, made sure my mind remained whole, and then asked about my ventures in the place he called 'Below'. I had an…understanding that not many return with. An understanding of the connection, of the amulets, and of husks. These were all things that Jonathan had taught me in our brief duality, but still I could hear him whisper and guide me as I learned how to control that unknown power. When Lye Northtree heard of my ability, we met. He tested me against his might. I felt dwarfed in comparison, but he assured me that I compared with the great. He offered me a title and his family, and together we devised a plan to use husks as our servants."

Owen drank again, leaving only a mouthful of liquor in his glass. "And that's about it, I think."

"The priest," Jim said. "Marcus?"

"Ahh. So, you know him. He's a genius of a man. Too smart for the world that he...."

"He's dead," Emma said from the corner.

Owen gave Emma a brief glance and brushed her comment off with a wave of his hand. "I very much doubt that."

"It's true," Jim confirmed. "I killed him myself."

"Well, James, you once killed me, did you not? And yet, here I am." Owen spread his arms as he talked. "Did you take his name?"

"What?" Jim asked.

"Did you take Marcus's name when you *killed* him?"

"No," Jim said softly.

"Then he is not dead." Owen chuckled and sloshed the liquid in his cup. "Now, I think we should...."

"The amulets," Jim started to say, trying to keep the curiosity in his voice hidden, "what do they do?"

Owen raised an eyebrow and smiled. "Powerful things, but they have only a few uses. The stones inside can hold a fragment of a soul, or something along those lines. If you are strong enough, as Heroes are, these fragments cannot find purchase inside of you. But for humans and husks the result is the same. We can use the gems to put a piece of ourselves inside and overtake the will of the creatures, making them subservient to whomever the soul belongs. I've done so with fourteen husks. Five of which I have commanded to lay dormant in the outlies of this very camp."

"And humans?" Jim asked, his eyes darting to Emma.

"Humans are...imperfect. If another soul is placed inside, it twists their mind and body until they become strong enough to contain them. They become husks, James."

The world around Jim seemed to slow as he thought about the implications of Owen's statement. The creatures that haunted the deepest nights and the antagonist in bedtime stories, they came from humanity.

"Why the curiosity?" Owen asked.

Jim couldn't stop his eyes from flicking to Emma and staring at the scabs around her neck. Owen saw the movement and turned, studying the girl who sat in the shadows. His face seared with delight as he turned back to Jim.

"I see," he said in a taunting voice, "but you don't."

Jim stayed quiet.

"The amulets transform humans, boy. There is no getting past it. Which means, your Cloaker is no human. She is a Fault."

Jim's jaw fell, and he saw Emma stand at Owen's proclamation. A Fault? But how? Who? He had heard her speak about her mother, felt certain of her humanity—but her father. Had Emma ever mentioned her father? Did she know?

"Who...," Jim started, but Owen silenced him with a gesture of his hand.

"My drink is empty," he said plainly.

"But...." Jim tried, but Owen threw his glass at Jim's face and unsheathed the sword from his belt, its length a hand-and-a-half.

Owen lunged forward, the tip of his weapon imbedding in the wooden chair where Jim sat just a moment ago. Jim grabbed the dagger at his side and deflected Owen's sword as it whistled through the air again. Jim kicked at the desk, sending it sliding at Owen's legs. The Captain jumped, landing on the table and taking the opportunity to slash downward at the Ash heir. The sharp metal grazed Jim's cheek, cutting deeply into his flesh and nicking against his jawbone. Emma moved forward, raising her pistol but Jim raised his hand at her, shaking his head to keep her from interfering.

Jim fell to the floor, rolling under the desk and slamming his back against the wood. With a thud the desk flipped, sending Owen somersaulting through the air and landing with a crash against a silver platter filled with grapes and strawberries. The Caretaker looked stunned, but before Jim could strike, he lifted the platter and flung it at him. Jim sidestepped the silver disk. Owen was upon him, never letting Jim breath or find an opportunity to attack.

Dagger met sword, steel sparking against steel, bringing Jim and Owen face to face in a match of strength. Jim began to crumble beneath his old Caretaker's might, slowly bending at the knee. After a full minute, Jim stumbled backward, falling towards the ground where

Owen would defeat him. But, as he neared the ground, Jim threw his hand back and kicked his legs at Owen's chest catching the Captain off-guard and sending him staggering backwards.

Jim jumped on to his feet in an instant, grabbing his second dagger in his off-hand. With a flurry of unstoppable swipes, Jim let his daggers fly. Owen parried with his sword and blocked with the metal greave on his forearm, but Jim remained relentless. Blood splattered from cuts and punctures that found purchase on Owen's arms and hands, and the Captain's expression changed from one of power to one of concern and fear.

With a flick, Jim's dagger tore Owen's sword from his palm and removed the first finger and thumb from his right hand. Owen grabbed at his missing digits and stared at the blood-hungry Hero that towered above him.

"James...," Owen begged.

With a smooth motion, Jim stabbed through Owen's left eye, silencing the Caretaker's pleas.

Jim stood over the dead Captain, breathing heavily and shaking with adrenaline. This time, he would stay dead. This time...*his name*.

Jim reached for the connection and found the place where Owen knelt. The life there was faint and cowering. Jim pulled at the small light, bringing it as close to him as possible before surrounding it with his consciousness and tearing inside.

Then, all went white.

□ □ □ □ □ □ □

*My name is Owen Northtree, although I was Owen Ash for most of my life. My family was small, one of the lesser Ash houses, but well-versed in the histories and teachings of our people. Imagine my surprise when the Hero Leader, I cannot give a name for it is not mine to give, asked me to become the Caretaker of his only son. My mother burst ecstatically, for such was my honor.*

*The boy, who's name was...oh, his name is now mine, was a troublesome boy. He was very mischievous and too smart to control. So, instead of a teacher, I became a friend. We travelled the world, telling jokes and stories growing in our friendship. Plenty of times teaching arose, but with him it never felt like work or chore. I felt inseparable from him.*

*The day the Hero Leader declared his new position on Faults, everything changed. The boy, always so influenced by his father, consumed everything the man said, taking it as gospel. It never made sense to me, to care for Faults. Not until that night in Salix.*

*The boy desecrated the walls of our ancestors, defiling them with the name of his unknown sister, a Fault. We punished him fairly, and from that moment on I sought a way to break him from his father's teachings. But he was as stubborn as his father and never saw the truth of my words.*

*It was a day between travel, a day inside the walls of Paradise, when I saw the Dogwood heir. I had heard his views on Faults in years past, but now I had some information to give. I told him about the boy's sister, the Fault that would play on the swing outside the Hero Leader's house, and he went to see for himself.*

*When I found the Ash boy, I spoke of the awful things that the Dogwood boy had told me, his cruel heart and how he knew of the boy's little sister. The Ash boy ran, but I did not think he would kill. I had no intention to have things escalate to murder. To have her killed, to cause the suffering of any Hero, I did not intend, but the dominoes tumbled.*

*I hunted with the search parties for weeks, trying to find the escaped Ash heir and give him the unfair trial that I knew the Twenty-Four had waiting for him. But he ghosted in the night, just as I had trained him to do. After two months in the coldest winter of my lifetime, we gave up and returned to greet our new Hero Leader who's name then was Lye Northtree.*

*The South was in shambles for years. I stood as a revolutionary figure, one of the first to deny the Ash name and seek out a new family to join, but none would have me. I decided to leave Paradise until the war that had bloomed ended. I found myself in the Northern city of Anvil, one of the twin desert cities, where I continued my education on the properties of metalwork.*

*Six years I was there. Ignoring the problems of our people, forgetting my race, forgetting the boy. I found out the hard way that the past is never far behind us.*

*When he found me, I knew he wanted blood. Jim. We fought, and I was much slower, using a hammer I held as my only form of weapon. The boy toyed* with me, using the techniques that I had taught him, breaking my form and leaving a cut running down my face. He tried to have me confess, but I never did, and that made him angry. The boy's knife pierced my heart, and he spat on my crippled form before leaving me to die in a pool of my own blood.

But perhaps I deserved it.

The rest I told you. I was reborn, given a new name, promoted by our Leader, and then you found me again. I don't think I had wanted to apologize, but it was nice to drink with you before I died. As you found me through the life-connection, I felt afraid. But no longer. My life has gone from one of learning to one of pain, and then to learning again. All I see are shadows and darkness, but even those change.

■ ■ ■ ■ ■ ■ ■ ■ ■

Jim went still. Emma moved to him and placed a hand on his shoulder, trying to wake him from whatever trance had captivated him, but Jim refused to move. Outside men began to scream. Panic drowned in the sound of swords unsheathing and clashing against an unknown foe. Emma shook again, receiving a small gasp from Jim as he opened his eyes.

Jim looked around, confused until he saw her, a smile erupting on his face. The two guards from before ran into the tent, blood dripping from lacerations on various parts of each of their bodies.

"Captain!" the first man yelled, his eyes finding the fallen form of Owen.

"You bastard!" The second man seethed, pointing his hatchet at Jim. "You've killed us all!"

Jim crouched, readying himself for an attack, but Emma was faster. The Angeloak pistol rose in her hand as she pulled the trigger, causing the second man to crumple from the hole in his head. She turned the gun to the first man, her finger heavy on the trigger. But, before she could pull, a husk dove in from the outside, sinking its claws into the first man's neck.

Jim grabbed Emma's hand and ran backwards. He cut through the canvas tent with one smooth motion, and they darted into the night.

Bodies and blood littered the sacked camp. Jim seemed unfazed as he pulled her through the obstacles towards the tree line. Behind them Emma could hear the ever-disquieting sound of screams and battle cries. But one sound was louder than the rest, the howl of the husk that chased them through the campsite.

## 32: THE FAULT AND THE HERO

The husk was close, gaining on Jim and Emma as they bounded through the forest. Any minute now it would overtake them, sink its grizzly talons through their flesh and feast on their marrow. Emma knew they would have to turn and fight, but they needed more distance from the campsite. The other husks would be listening for fleeing prey.

Emma spared a glance at Jim running beside her, sweat dripping down his cheeks. His fight with Owen had taken a lot from him, and whatever trance he had been swallowed by had sapped him of his usual vigor. But she had also been affected by the dead Captain. His revelations bruised her as much as any blow from a fist or boot. She was a Fault. Everything that she knew about herself was wrong, a fallacy created by the woman who called herself mother. It simply felt true. It made sense. How else could she have followed Jim this far? This, on top of Emma's broken body, made the fight that would inevitably crash upon her seem even more daunting.

Jim's golden eyes flicked to meet hers, and Emma knew it was time. If they continued to run their energy would be drained and the husk would kill them immediately. But even now, Emma was unsure if they could kill the beast.

Emma gave a short nod of her head and, together, they stopped.

Jim crouched low, his blood-stained daggers in hand. Emma unsheathed her rapier, standing tall at Jim's back, peering over his powerful stance. It would be her duty to kill the husk. Jim would be too busy fending off its attacks. Her Hero was counting on her, trusting her to have the skill necessary to remove the husk's head from its shoulders.

With a crash, the husk barreled through the brush, never braking pace as it collided with Jim's blades. The Hero was swift, catching each of its claws with his daggers and matching its furious swipes. Blade and claw rang together in a blurry succession, but Jim held.

Emma struck her sword over Jim's head, aiming for the soft flesh below the husks' chin. With a flash of movement, the husk caught her sword in its razor claws, protecting its neck but leaving an opening for Jim to strike at its belly. Steaming blood dripped from a gash where the husk's kidney should have been, but the beast didn't seem to acknowledge the devastating hit.

This time, the husk swiped at Emma, forcing her to jump back a step before retaliating with a stab of her needle-like blade. Her steel punctured the husk's shoulder, but Emma stumbled when the husk writhed, pulling her rapier with its rapid movements. Jim shot his dagger upwards, dislodging Emma's sword and leaving a long laceration up the husk's arm in the same strike, but also leaving his right side vulnerable to attack. The husk saw the opening and struck. Emma's sword was too far away to block the attack, so she kicked at the monster's claw just as it sank into Jim's side. The Hero shivered, but Emma's foot forced the boney claws back enough for him to pull free.

The husk struck again, and Emma parried the blow. Jim's blades flew, catching the husk in its sternum. Jim then twisted his blade and arced it towards the creature's neck. With unnatural speed the husk jumped back, raising its claws above its head to strike with its entire force on Jim's head. Emma vaulted over Jim's shoulder, catching both of the monster's claws on her thin sword. The attack knocked her breath away, and she grunted, her muscles quivering from overexertion.

Jim ducked around the husk's side, burying his blades in the beast's neck. The husk turned to fend off Jim, but Emma saw an opportunity and struck in the gaping wound that the Hero had just landed. She felt her rapier sever bone and sinew and heard a satisfying slurp as her blade removed the head. The husk wobbled on unsteady legs, frantically flailing its arms, before falling to the ground.

Emma breathed hard, her arms trembling in a defensive stance. Jim was beside her, his daggers shaking as he wiped the dark blood on his cloak and sheathed them at his belt. He turned to Emma, gore speckling his exhausted face, and smiled. Together they had killed a monster of nightmares. Together, they were unbeatable. Emma smiled back and laughed. There were songs about legendary Heroes who had killed husks and escaped with their lives. But never had there been a song written about a Fault who managed to do the same. *Someone would write one now.*

Jim put his hands on his knees and spat a clot of blood on the ground. Emma looked at his side, saw the three punctures that had pierced it.

"You're hurt," she said, her voice quiet and raspy.

"It will heal," Jim replied, standing and walking to her side. "Let's keep moving. The others will soon wander this way."

Jim put his arm around Emma's shoulder, leaning a great deal of his weight upon her. And together, they stumbled through the forest.

■ ■ ■ ■ ■ ■ ■ ■

Jim could feel four husks walking in the distance. Their minds were dormant, the terrifying lullaby slowly coaxing them onward. But at any moment they could catch the scent of Jim's blood, or hear a crack from the echoing twigs, and their minds would flare, and they would hunt the wounded prey. The only safe action was to keep moving, stay ahead of them until sunrise, when the husks would burry themselves deep within the dark soil. But morning was a long way away.

The wound in his side seeped hot blood onto Emma's shirt, but she stayed close, supporting him as they slowly traversed the dark woodland. Sleep would help the punctures to heal faster, but until then Jim had no choice but to persevere. He knew that Emma was exhausted too, though she never showed it. She was stronger than anyone he had ever met before, or maybe just more stubborn. Still, she astounded him.

But, he realized, a part of her strength was due to her race. A piece of her blood was the same as his, Hero, though her outward appearance hid it well. A Fault, human in all but name.

"Did you know?" Jim asked, keeping his voice low as to not disturb the sleeping wildlife.

"No," Emma said, knowing immediately what he meant. "My mother always said my father was a powerful man. I thought she meant the head of a province, or a great hunter, but...a Hero? Sometimes you dream, think of yourself as more than you were born to be, but I never thought those dreams would be real."

"And, your mother?" Jim asked.

"She was human. I think."

Jim nodded, placing his arm around Emma's shoulder in silent comfort.

"Are you...?" Jim started, hating the simplicity of the question.

"I'm okay." She sounded somber. "There's just...it's a lot."

"It's a lot," Jim agreed.

Clouds covered the moon and stars, forcing the shadows to grow denser and obscure the small details of the world. A trickle of rain poured from the weeping night sky. The rainfall was light, not unpleasant, and the cool water felt wonderful against Jim's side. Once his boots filled with water though, he felt sure he would curse the dreary weather.

"What about you? Did you know, about the husks?" Emma asked.

"No. The Twenty-Four would never have allowed the weaponizing of husks. They fear them too much to even consider it."

"So, the Northtree men were acting alone?"

"I doubt it," Jim said, remembering Owen's words. "Lye Northtree must have gone behind the council's back. He worked with Owen. He knew."

"Then, by Hero laws, that's...illegal?"

"It's treason." Jim stared ahead blankly. "He could be banished because of it."

"We have to tell the council."

Tell the council? The Twenty-Four would oblige an audience with any Hero, regardless of their standing. But, if Jim returned, they would force him to stand trial once their audience concluded. He would be declared guilty of murder and sentenced to banishment. The council would never bloody their hands by ordering the death of a Hero, not directly, but banishment was just as deadly. Jim would leave to the

Southern side of the Savior Wall and never come back. He would either die from husks or starvation, neither of which sounded appealing.

"Emma, I..." Jim started.

"Someone has to tell them."

"But if I go back..." Jim started again.

"He's the reason for Marcus's experiments," Emma said, her voice breaking as she spoke.

Emma rubbed the scaly skin around her neck. The amulets, the humans, the husks: she was right. Without the authority of 'Hero Leader,' Lye would never have had the power to conduct the cruel experimentation. Heroes would not capture and use husks as weapons. Humans, *Colter*, would never have been transformed into a monster. And Emma...

"Alright," Jim said, regretting the single word, but seeing no other option. "Tonight, we find a place to sleep."

"And tomorrow?" Emma asked.

"We go to Paradise."

## 33: INSIDE THE HERO CITY

It took four days to travel from the Savior Wall to Paradise, four days made longer due to foraging for food and boiling water. But in those few days Jim taught Emma everything he could about the Hero court.

Six representatives from each of the Hero territories oversaw the court. These four groups came together, creating the Twenty-Four, and judged the interpretations of Hero law. To be chosen meant a lifetime of service in the golden city of Paradise, an honor unmet by any other title.

The court took place in the bottom level of the Leader's Tower, in a chamber known as *Arbitration* . Inside the great chamber the Twenty-Four would sit around their subject and listen to cases before commenting and asking questions. Occasionally, the Hero Leader would attend these meetings, sitting in the Rainbow Throne at the head of the Twenty-Four, but he would not speak unless asked a direct question.

Then would come their verdict. Each of the 'directions', as Jim called them, would declare their sentencing. This was done by one representative from each territory standing and declaring, "The North sees fit...", or "The West will allow...", depending on their judgments.

Once a Hero requested an audience with the Twenty-Four, the council would have twelve hours to grant the request and listen to the Hero's words. Sometimes the court would last days and sometimes it would only take a few hours, but, before the meeting adjourned, the Twenty-Four would form a sentence. And whatever the Twenty-Four declared was law.

"We put our fate in the hands of the court and live with their ruling," Jim said, as Paradise's wall peeked over the treetops.

The wall was the oldest in all of the territories, and the tallest next to the Savior Wall. It was made of marbled stone that reflected the sun's light, giving it a golden hue that forced Emma and Jim to squint their eyes. Along the wall there were four gates, one pointing in each direction, and a patrol of Heroes constantly watching from above. The gates were made of steel and brass with depictions of trees and ancient beings carved across their scratched surfaces.

Jim pushed his legs forward, knowing that if he stopped moving, he would likely turn back. This would be the first time he had returned, the first time he stepped foot inside the ancient city since he started a civil war between his people. *The heir of Ash returns for his retribution.*

"If anything happens," Jim said, thinking about the court that would declare his fate as well as the Hero Leader's, "take care of yourself first."

Before Emma could reply, the Southern Gate came into view.

Four Heroes stood guard outside the Southern Gate, each holding spears and dressed in gold-plated armor. They raised their weapons, pointing them in the direction of the travelers.

One man, with red feathers decorated on his helm, stepped forward and demanded, "State your business."

Jim continued walking, dropping the hood from his head, and said, "My name is James Ash. I seek council with the Twenty-Four."

The man raised his spear, shock evident on his face, then said in an unsure voice, "Of course. We will escort you immediately."

Three of the guards moved forward, surrounding Jim and Emma, then escorted them through the gate and into Paradise.

■ ■ ■ ■ ■ ■ ■ ■ ■

Emma had never seen so much beauty in one place. There was so much gold and green everywhere she looked, and everything was clean. The houses were made of a stone so polished that they looked porcelain. Ornate symbols were carved in each of the doorways, some Emma recognized as the religious markings of the Vlour, meaning *hope* and *protection*. Others were unreadable, except probably to those educated in the religion's script. Children played and laughed in patches of trimmed grass, throwing a leather sack, filled with hay and leaves, to one another and tackling each other for fun. This place truly was a paradise, a haven in the world filled with poverty and death.

As they neared the tower Emma heard the torrent of cascading water, and she knew what it had to be. They rounded a corner and the Ever-Flowing Fountain came into view. Emma recalled dozens of reverent songs sung about the mystical fountain. A source of water so pure that everything around it blossomed with life and fortune, the reason the Heroes had chosen this location in the time after The Fall. And here it was, a geyser that shot through the air, higher than every building but the Leader's Tower, raining droplets of diamonds on the people below. Emma could have stayed for hours, basking in the cool mist that the fountain produced, but the Heroes behind her urged her forward.

Up ahead loomed the Leader's Tower, a building so tall that clouds burst upon its upper floors. The tower was comprised of shining metal and glass windows. It sat in the center of Paradise, a beacon for all the city's citizens to look upon in their times of questioning and doubt. The doors bore the crest of the First-Four, a tree with four roots connecting to the back of an unknown figure.

The first guard moved ahead, opening the door, and the group entered the Leader's Tower.

A woman sat inside, her feet resting on a black desk and a blue-covered book in her hands. She peered over the book's pages and gestured for Jim to walk towards her, leaving Emma with the guards by the door.

"Weapons on the table," she said.

Wordlessly, Jim began to remove his various weapons, pulling dozens of knives from hidden places on his form and finishing by removing the pair of daggers that he kept at his belt. The woman's eyes moved to Emma, and she waved the girl forward.

"Weapons on the table," she stated again.

It felt wrong to unarm herself, but Emma didn't have a choice. She pulled off her belt of knives, the holster for the Angeloak pistol; then she placed her wooden dagger on the table, and finally she removed her rapier. The woman marveled at the wooden weapon, then nodded. Emma stepped back.

"Inspect," the woman said.

The three guards moved towards Emma and Jim and began to pat down their clothes in search of hidden weapons. Once satisfied, the guards stepped away, and the woman waved for Jim and Emma to walk back towards the table.

"You may take one with you." She said, pointing at the pile of weapons. "No guns, no poisoned blades, no explosives."

Emma grabbed her rapier, hating how naked she had felt without her trusted blade. Jim hesitated over his decision. After a full minute of contemplation, he grabbed Emma's wooden dagger, testing its heft in his grip. With a nod, he buckled her blade at his hip, and they moved away.

"Mine were always better as a pair," Jim whispered to Emma with a wink.

"The Twenty-Four will see you," the woman said, and a set of double-doors opened at the far end of the room.

Jim walked forward, Emma hesitant at his heels, and together they entered the chamber known as Arbitration.

· · · · · · · ·

Jim looked around the large chamber. He had been inside this room once before, the day his father was chosen to become the Hero Leader. But that was long ago. Now, in the brightly lit room, he would know what fate had in store for him, what sentence and punishment the council wished to proclaim. But not until he said what he needed to say.

The Twenty-Four sat in the shape of a horseshoe, each facing Jim. Each of them wore robes of their family colors and had golden-handled knives at their belts. The knives were an honor that came with the title of 'Twenty-Four', only ever forged when a new member of the council replaced an old one. At the head sat the Rainbow Throne, a seat made of colored glass that caught light from every angle, shining rainbows on every surface of the room. And, in the colorful throne, sat Lye Northtree.

Lye was a large man. Not overly muscled, his lean body advertised speed and grace. He had a neatly trimmed beard beneath his crooked nose, and wore a platinum circlet on his head, marking him as the Hero Leader. Lye wore robes of red and white and a ruby amulet around his neck. The man sat with authority, always looking down on those who surrounded him, and only smiled a devious smile once, when Jim entered the chamber.

Each of the twenty-five Heroes glared at Jim, their golden-eyes unblinking as the scorned heir cleared his throat to speak.

"Council," Jim began, his heart beating loudly in his chest, "I come to accuse Lye Northtree of grievous crimes. I name him unfit to rule the people of the protected world. Will you hear me?"

The Twenty-Four looked at each other, whispering barely audible words amongst themselves.

After a few seconds of discussion, a man dressed in Green stood. "The West will hear you," he said, then sat.

A woman with black hair, her robes yellow and brown, stood. "The North will listen," she declared.

A man with an eye-patch over his left eye and dressed in blue and grey robes stood. "The South will hear the words of our fallen heir," he said, then sat.

And finally, a bald man stood, his robes a light shade of purple, "The East hears you, heir of house Ash," his words sang before he sat.

Jim took a long breath, closing his eyes to focus on his words, then he spoke. The things he said were strong and damning as he recounted his stories. The Twenty-Four listened intently to each of his declarations, only responding with understanding nods and cautious blinks. Jim spoke of the metal chamber beneath Salix and the tortures performed by Marcus with the Northtree's permission. He told the Twenty-Four of the breach in the Savior Wall, a testament that had three members of the council gasp and turn to the Hero Leader to see his reaction. When Jim told them how Heroes could control and weaponize husks, many of the councilors' eyes grew wide, and a look of shock twisted their faces. His final claim mentioned Floydd and the contract that the Northtrees had placed upon Jim's head, paying the human mercenary a lightning belt in advance to ensure his success.

When Jim finished the chamber fell silent and he stepped backward, informing the Twenty-Four that he had nothing more to say. He found Emma by his side, her small hand grasping against his bicep and squeezing comfortably to help calm his nerves. He had said all that he could; now his fate, and the fate of the Hero Leader, rested in the hands of the Twenty-Four.

Whispers filled the chamber as the councilors debated amongst themselves. Before long the whispers grew louder, and accusations flew from the lips of the revered Heroes. Jim could only make out a few words here and there, *traitor* and *treason* among the most common. But, for the most part, words drowned in a sea of voices. The Twenty-Four continued their debates for fifteen minutes before the voices began to decrease and only a few whispers continued. Then, after another ten minutes, all was silent.

The woman with black hair stood, her yellow and brown robes bouncing with her movement. "Heir of Ash," she started, her voice surprisingly kind, "what you claim is…disturbing. If found true, then we will declare our Leader a traitor and banish him beyond the same wall that you claim he has broken. But your words cannot be trusted alone. The man who you accuse will have an opportunity to speak. If we declare him innocent, we will hold you in contempt and place another crime upon your head. Still, to come here, knowing what your fate will be before you leave, gives the council confidence in your statements. Thank you for placing the needs of the Heroes over the needs of yourself." She bowed her head to Jim, a gesture that spoke of her respect louder than any word ever could. "Now," she continued, "we will give Lye Northtree an opportunity to speak." She took her seat once again.

The smile on Lye's face was terrifying. He stood with confidence, peering into the faces of each of the councilors, then settled his gaze on Jim.

"The Fault," Lye said, nodding to Emma, "what is her name?"

Jim opened his mouth to speak, but Emma interrupted.

"My name is Emma," she said beside him.

Lye raised an eyebrow and nodded. "Welcome, Emma. And Jim, I welcome you home. Even as my accuser, it is good to see you here, in the place of your birth, after so many years. A son of Paradise returning is always a happy occasion, my prodigal son."

Lye turned back to the councilors. "I have been accused of many horrendous things," he continued to say. "Though, I suppose horrendous is a matter of opinion, depending on each of our individual beliefs. But I have some accusations of my own, not to Jim, but to all of you, too blind to see beyond your fearful traditions. I accuse you all of cowardice and deem each of you unfit to bear the name of Hero. I accuse you all of hiding your eyes beneath your woolen blankets and trembling at the creatures who rule the night. I accuse you of blatant neglect and halting the movement of our race, our people, towards a hopeful and expansive future. And, I declare you all guilty of my many accusations, just as I confess my guilt of the Ash boy's claims."

An uproar of voices erupted from the Twenty-Four. Many of them stood, waving their fists towards the Hero Leader and screaming their disapprovals and disdain. But Lye continued to smile as he turned and sat on his glorious throne.

Lye raised his hand. "Quiet," he commanded, and each of the voices silenced.

The quiet was sudden and unnatural. Many of the Twenty-Four grabbed at their mouths and throat, as if their voices had left against their will. In a panic, two of the councilors stood and tried to run from the chambers, but Lye spoke again.

"Sit," he demanded, and the councilors all returned to their seats.

Beside him, Emma unsheathed her rapier, keeping her eyes glued to the Hero Leader. But, as much as he tried, Jim was unable to move his arms to grip at his dagger. He was frozen, surrounded by a presence much greater than himself. He screamed and raged in his mind, but the outside consciousness refused to budge, only radiating a small feeling of amusement at his effort, the same amusement that Lye held on his face.

"What shall be the punishment for the councilors' cowardice?" Lye asked in a bemused voice. "Banishment? Imprisonment? No. I think death is best suited for them. What do you think, Jim?"

Jim didn't know if he could talk, didn't even try. He just stared at the Leader, helpless to fight against the power that the man displayed.

"Hmm. No opinion?" Lye said. "Then I think my decision is sound. Council members, please unsheathe those knives and drive them through your hearts!"

In unison the Twenty-Four grasped their blades, their hands trembling as they tried to fight the command. But all opposition was useless. One-by-one their steel sank through their clothing, staining their shirts with crimson. Many still breathed, though their breaths grew shallow as the seconds became minutes and, eventually, their hearts refused to beat.

They were dead. All of the Twenty-Four, slaughtered in an instant.

"I can feel you waiting," Lye said to the far wall. "Enter."

The doors behind Jim flew open, and Bastion, Faye, and Kole Northtree entered the chamber. Faye and Kole stayed behind Jim, their weapons sheathed but their eyes sharp and keen. Bastion moved forward, stepping past Jim and through the pool of blood that had filled the chamber's floor. He bowed at Lye's feet, hanging his head low.

"Son," Lye said, and Bastion stood.

"Father," Bastion said in a respectful voice. "You called for us?"

"I did. Are we prepared to act today?"

Bastion hesitated for a moment, thinking through some unknown plans. "Yes," he said flatly. "Though more will survive than we anticipated."

"That is fine," Lye said. "We will start now. I will join you when I am finished with the boy."

With a short bow, Bastion turned and left the chamber.

Turning his attention back to Jim, Lye asked, "Was your father ashamed of your sister?"

The presence which held Jim dove through his memories, finding every interaction he could remember between his father and sister. The memories came forward, exploding into vivid images and becoming all that Jim could think about.

The presence, Lye, prompted Jim to speak, pushing the memories towards his mouth until, through clenched teeth, he said, "No."

"Ahh," Lye sighed. "He was a better father than I would have been. My wife saw that, something that I have been trying to redeem myself for…for twenty-three years. You see, now that we have the privacy that I desire, I will tell you my biggest failure. Some would call it sin, some tradition, but to me, it truly is failure.

"I was gifted a son, Bastion, when I was still quite young. A boy who has grown and conquered and become everything that I could have hoped for. You've met him, recently even, and I'm sure you admired him in your youth. Who wouldn't? He is a marvelous man, an accomplished heir. But…for so long, he was my only child.

"Though we tried for centuries, my wife remained barren of more children. We had nearly given up hope on extending our lineage, when her belly began to swell, and the physicians told us she was pregnant. The pregnancy was difficult for her and, by extension, difficult for me. But the true pain came when the baby was born.

"You see, as an insult from every god and ancestor, our child was a Fault. I was heartbroken, disgusted, furious. Nothing could have given me greater shame, nothing more damning than fathering a child cursed with impure blood. So, I decided to take action into my own hands and euthanize the infant. I spared my family of making the same decision. I left, to breathe the cool night air and to grab the tools I would need for a painless execution. But, when I returned, my wife had left. I didn't know where she went. I had men scouting for days, weeks, with no success. She had taken my child and vanished in the night.

"It took four months for my wife to return, but she returned alone. When I asked what happened to our child, she refused to answer, but I knew the baby lived. My wife was put before this very council and banished from our lands for kidnapping and marital abuse. So, in just a few months, my family had fallen from four to two.

"In the lonesome hours of the night, I writhed and dreamt of the child. I woke up breathless, sweat drenching my sheets, for the failure that I had allowed. But, as time moved forward, my failure began to gnaw upon me and change my inner-most self. I realized that the true failure came in denying my blood the rights of my patronage. The child, even as a Fault, was mine, my responsibility to raise and protect. She was my daughter."

Lye stood and stepped towards Jim and Emma. "When Marcus told me of the Fault he had found, I thought nothing of it until he mentioned the girl's green eyes. Then he told me of the power that he felt inside her, and I knew…I knew he had found the Fault that I had failed." Lye extended his arm and cupped Emma's cheek in his hand. "My daughter."

With the fastest strike that Jim had ever see, Emma let her sword fly. Lye twisted to the side, allowing her blade to cut his cheek. He wiped the blood on his hand and held it out for Emma to see.

"This blood is mine, just as it is yours," he said.

Emma struck again, yelling, "NO!" as her blade fell.

Lye danced around Emma's swings, never allowing her metal to come close to his flesh. His movements were fast and delicate, for he predicted each of Emma's attacks with the eye of a veteran swordsman. In a mighty arc, Emma tried to behead the Leader, but he ducked and darted his hand out, catching her hand in his.

"You will need time, I understand," Lye said, wrenching the rapier from Emma's hands.

Emma fell to her knees, wild sobs wetting her eyes and cheeks. Jim wanted to rush to her side, wanted to kill the Hero Leader, stop his lies, feel his blood spill to the floor. But the vice around his consciousness tightened, and his body refused to move.

"I will not leave you again," Lye said, wiping his blood on Emma's cloak, "Faye, Kole, please escort Emma to my carriage. Do not let her out of your sight, and do not allow any harm to befall her."

"Yes, sir," Faye said, moving forward with Kole and grasping Emma by her shoulders.

Together, the two Heroes dragged Emma to her feet, and pulled her away from the chamber.

"Family is a tricky business," Lye said to Jim when the others had left. "As are names." Lye walked over to Jim, putting his arm around the captive's shoulder. "Come with me."

And, without permission from his mind, Jim followed Lye Northtree.

## 34: EMMA

Emma was in a daze. Nothing made sense, nothing mattered. Her whole life she had wondered who her father was, but Lye Northtree...? No. It couldn't be true, had to be a lie that he spewed just to break her spirit. But...somehow, she knew he was right.

Emma Northtree: the name felt like bile on her tongue. She wished to rid herself of her name, rip it from her mind and splinter it beneath her boot. And now she was being dragged by...by her niece and nephew, to a destination that her father had decided. Faye stopped to gather Emma's few weapons, placing them in a satchel on her back before moving towards the exit. The Heroes' strong hands pulled her easily through the doors of the chamber and towards the streets of Paradise.

From outside Emma could hear screams and panic, growing in ferocity. And, when the doors parted, the Hero City revealed itself, not as a place of beauty, but as a nightmare.

Husks. Hundreds of husks ran throughout the streets. Blood decorated the cobblestones and soaked through the grass. Bodies of Heroes, young and old, laid massacred, many missing limbs and showing a pattern of bite marks on their necks and faces. One Hero stood in midst of the Ever-Flowing Fountain, his broadsword parrying and blocking attacks from three different husks. He was only successful for a second before the monsters broke through, filleting him and leaving his body to bloat in the fountain's water.

They traveled North, quickly passing the carnage that had contaminated Paradise. As they neared the exterior of the city, Faye and Kole turned to observe the scene behind them. The screams had grown louder and farther apart, a sign that the husks had spread, finding targets in the outskirts of the Hero city.

Emma's eyes shook. To see the oasis of beauty, the center of the civilized world, filled with so much death and fear, felt wrong. Tears flowed freely down Emma's cheeks, and she sniffled as she watched.

Then, in a broken voice, she asked, "Why?"

Faye was quiet, as if she had been asking the same question of herself, but Kole turned with a boastful grin and said, "To rebuild our people from the ashes of our ancestors. Just as Dom did in The Time Before."

Faye's grip loosened on Emma's shoulder as they escorted her towards the Northern Gate. There was something about the black-haired Hero that seemed different to Emma, a hesitation that existed in her touch and pace.

A husk bounded down the path towards them, causing Emma to flinch. Kole and Faye remained unfazed, keeping their pace steadily pointed North. As the husk neared, it slowed and tilted its head. Then, it turned, running towards the nearby houses, as if the three wanderers didn't exist. *They are being controlled.*

The Northern Gate was open. On the road that led outwards sat a wooden carriage with four brown horses waiting patiently for an order to run. Faye and Kole pulled Emma forward, opening the door to the carriage and tossing her inside like a sack filled with apples. Faye went to check on the horses and prepare them for their travels. Kole stayed to watch Emma.

"Lye will treat you well," Kole said. "I have heard, many times, his ramblings of regret for the daughter that he had lost. I think you will make him very happy. It will be good for him to have a famil…"

A silver sword pierced through Kole's mouth, splattering droplets of blood across Emma's face. Kole fell forward, sliding from the blade with a sickening slurp, and crumpling to the ground. Faye stood above her brother, wiping his blood from her elegant sword.

"This…" Faye started to say, her eyes darting to the chaotic world behind her, "…I did not want this."

Emma sat in shock, not knowing how to react or respond to Faye's actions and words. The look on the Hero's face was mournful, a genuine sorrow that threatened to burst from her throat. Emma put her hand out, silently asking for Faye to help her from the carriage. Faye obliged and, when Emma stood, she turned towards two horses that Faye had saddled and disconnected from the carriage.

Faye offered one of the reins to Emma and said, "Will you ride with me?"

Emma took the reins but looked back at the Leader's Tower. Jim was in there, alone. She couldn't leave him, abandon him, to the wicked doings of the insane Leader. *Father.* She dropped her reins, taking a step towards the towering obelisk.

"You want to help Jim?" Faye asked.

"I have to," Emma said, taking another step.

Faye moved in front of Emma, dragging the horses with her and forcing the reins back into Emma's hands. "Then leave. If you go back, Lye will capture you, and he will never give you chance to escape again. Jim will live. I don't know how, but I know he will. Jim's always been a stubborn bastard." Faye climbed into the saddle of her horse. "Ride with me, Emma. There is nothing we can do, not now." Faye kicked at the belly of her steed and galloped through the gate.

Emma stared longingly at the Leader's Tower, at the Hero, *her Hero*, that was alone inside its walls. *If anything happens...* Faye was right. There was nothing that Emma could do, not now. So, she bowed her head, praying to whichever god would listen to her desperate plea. Then, she mounted her horse and followed Faye into the forest.

## 35: JIM

Lye had led Jim through the Leader's Tower, commenting on each of the historical artifacts that had been gifted to the various Leaders. The display would be an envy to any who loved the Heroes' history or wished to gain gold through stories or thievery, but to Jim the items seemed hollow. Nothing that Lye thought precious held value in his eyes, nothing but the girl who had emerald eyes.

Lye stopped suddenly at one end of a long hallway. A set of double-doors sat against one wall, and Jim recognized them immediately as the doors to an elevator shaft. Lye pressed a button on a panel next to the doors, and Jim was awestruck when a small light illuminated a picture of an arrow pointing towards the floor. Even more awe took Jim when the elevator doors opened with a ding and a tiny room appeared in the shaft. Lye walked in to the room, forcing Jim to follow, and the doors closed. A moment later, Jim's stomach lurched as the elevator descended with a loud whirring sound.

"I can feel your discomfort," Lye said. "But please, try to calm yourself. We are perfectly safe."

The whirring continued for a few minutes, before the elevator doors opened once again, revealing a new floor. The walls here resembled the mining tunnels that the Northtrees used to excavate metals and gems in their territory. The grey stone was damp, narrow, and barely tall enough for Jim to stand in without crouching. Lye moved forward towards a thick stone door that blocked the end of the hallway. With a noticeable effort, Lye shoved the door open.

The deafening roar of a waterfall emanated from the room beyond, and a wave of humidity clashed with the Heroes. Jim's jaw dropped when he entered the room. A colossal cave loomed beyond the door, its walls and ceiling hidden in dark shadows that Jim's eyes could not pierce. The cave easily stretched as tall as the Leader's Tower and was large enough to fit the entirety of Salix within it. But, the most striking thing about the room was the building that sat in its center, a torrent of water crashing around it. A spark of lightning shot through the water, filling the cave with a sizzling sound and making the hair on Jim's arms rise to attention.

"There is no source to the water," Lye yelled over the noise. "As far as I can tell, the building creates it. Through it, the building has sprouted the Ever-Flowing Fountain, and, through underground tunnels, it has also created the Life-Giving Lakes. All drinkable water in our known world comes from right here." He spread his arms wide and basked in the mist of the torrent.

Jim just stared, not believing the sight that his eyes showed him. He had seen many things that he thought impossible, but this...this was grander than any dream his mind had created. A building in an underground cave that spat water from its sides was something a madman or priest would claim to have seen. But he wasn't crazy, nor was he inherently religious, and yet he beheld the impossible sight.

"I'm going to tell you a story, Jim," Lye shouted. "And it's important that you listen, really listen to what I'm going to say.

"A long time ago, when my father was still alive and I just a boy, my mother took me through our territories. There is a Life-Giving Lake, Maximus, in the center of the North, and we stopped there for a full day to play and fish. My mother encouraged play, said it was good for a growing boy. So, when I asked her if we could return to Maximus on our ventures back, she said yes, of course, and, after a few months of travel, we stopped at the Life-Giving Lake's shores once again.

"I was near the center of the lake, swimming in the dark waters when something pulled me under. I swear to you that I do not lie, not about this. The thing that pulled me under was a dragon. Not a dragon from the storybooks that flies and breathes flames, but a dragon of the sea, long and swift with fangs as sharp as arrowheads. The dragon sunk its teeth through my calf and pulled me down. I struggled, fought harder than I've ever fought before, but I was no match for the enormous creature. So, deep beneath the waters of Maximus, I died."

Water drenched Lye, his hair sticking to his forehead in clumps, when he turned to face Jim. "But, you and I know that death is not truly an end. I found myself in a world of black, with all the pain from the many wounds that the dragon had torn through me. But a voice whispered at me to be quiet, then it commanded me to stand and follow a path through the shadows that I could not have found alone. The thing that the voice belonged to was terrifying. A man with no flesh and robes made of shadows. He beckoned for me to look, so I looked, and what I saw astounded me.

"He showed me lamps that glowed without flame, doors that opened on their own, carriages that flew through the sky and blew smoke into the air, like storybook dragons. He showed me The Time Before. Then, he asked for help. He told me of how his world had died, how he had burned it to the ground, but that the mistakes that he made had caused him overwhelming regret and suffering. I told him I would help in any way that I could. He reached out his hand, to formalize our agreement, with a handshake I presumed, but when our hands collided, he showed me...everything.

"I relived a life so grand and filled with miracles that I lost myself in memory. I saw the world burn and then grow due to my advances. I saw the people become fat and flawed, using my creations to further their own interests. I saw people praise gods invented rapidly day by day and the erasure of important ones. And I realized a simple truth: humans needed to die. I promised myself that I would fulfill this duty, ending the plague of humanity. And, when the memories ended, I received the name of the man who had created and ended the world."

Lye laughed maniacally, screaming his lunacy at the ceiling. "Do you see, Jim? Do you understand? This is the same man who touched you. I could feel it the moment that you entered my courtroom! We are vessels, given a purpose singular in design and duty. We are brothers, no...closer than brothers, for we are the same, two pieces of a prophetic whole! He has not given you the same things that he has given me, but he will. All you must do is ask it of him, ask the man to give you his name, ask the man to give you his memories, ask for his power. Then, when you become whole, as I am, we will rule over a reborn world, free of human and husk and hardship. Together we will be as our creator! Together, we will share the name of the man who touched us. Together we will be DOM!"

Lye placed his hands on Jim's shoulders. "But first, you must die and find our creator. And I see no better death for you than to drown as I did, as a boy."

Jim moved forward, toward the torrent of water in the center of the cave. He fought against the power that held his mind. It was sturdy, a wall of ice so thick and slippery that finding purchase in its flesh proved impossible. But, along the crystalline consciousness, Jim found a crack. It was small but fragile. A crack that stared at Jim with green eyes and a smile that sang to his heart. Jim pried at the crack, expanding it until it was large enough for him to crawl through and free himself from the ice-cold clamp of Lye Northtree.

The moment Jim broke free from the consciousness, he found his body under his control. Jim grabbed the dagger at his side, Emma's dagger, and turned to face the Hero Leader. Lye stood, a few paces behind him, with a grin on his bearded face.

"You wish to fight destiny?" he asked, drawing his sword from its scabbard. "You wish to fight me?"

Jim crouched low, readying his stance to either dash forward and attack or fall back and defend. Lye's eyes were unreadable as he slowly moved closer, his blade dragging on the ground. Then, his left foot twitched, and Lye leapt at Jim.

Jim barely moved fast enough to catch Lye's blade as it neared his stomach. Jim ducked to the left, wanting to stay near the Hero Leader to give his dagger the advantage over Lye's sword. Jim shot out his blade, cutting through the air where Lye's thigh was a moment ago. A whistle came from above, and Jim's dagger flew upwards to catch an arcing attack. With his free hand, Jim punched forward, hitting Lye's chin. The Leader sank backwards, rubbing his boney chin with the palm of his hand. His smile grew wider as he spat a glob of blood onto the wet stone.

In an instant, Lye's attacks started again, but this time they came in rapid succession and delivered devastating force with each blow. Jim matched the Leader's attacks but could not find an opening to attack. He struggled as his blade bounced off Lye's sword, sending violent vibrations through his wrist and shoulder. Then he saw the opening, a hesitation as Lye changed from an arcing sweep to a vertical stab. *Yes, see my weakness.* Jim's dagger flew, perfectly navigating the hole in Lye's stance, nearing the soft flesh beneath the Leader's armpit. But his dagger never reached its mark.

Lye's sword sank into the flesh of Jim's neck, imbedding deep into his airpipe. Jim fell back, blood flowing freely from his severed artery. His hands grasped at his neck, trying to staunch the wound, but finding little success. Jim gasped. Air refused to enter his lungs, and his head was growing light from lack of blood. His body was growing cold, so cold.

"A dirty trick, heir of Ash," Lye said with remorse. "I'm sorry I had to use it to best you. Make you see a fault that wasn't there. But this fight was too important to lose." Lye grabbed Jim by his hair, dragging the bleeding boy towards the flowing water. "When you see Dom, tell him how I have reshaped his world. Just as he wished."

Lye shoved Jim's head into the water. Jim tried to struggle, but he couldn't find strength enough to shake his head. This was it. Jim had lost. He had tried, fought with everything he had, but it still wasn't enough.

So, beneath the broken city of Paradise, Jim bled and drowned in the ancient waters that fueled the Ever-Flowing Fountain. And, when his eyes could see once again, all that greeted him were shadows and silence.

# THE DAY AFTER

Belle could feel the death that tore through the land. She saw the lights of hundreds of Heroes extinguished in a matter of minutes. She felt the fear and heard the screams of fleeing people ringing through her head as loudly as they would have rung through her ears with physical proximity. She jumped on William and darted to the East.

That was yesterday. Twenty-seven hours ago, to be exact, and in that time William's gallop had not slowed. She could feel the horse's exhaustion as they rode through the narrow canyon that marked the entrance to the Eastern Mountains. *Only a little farther now.*

William stopped when Belle spotted the black stone that marked the entrance to the secret place. She jumped from the horse's back, patting her lovingly on the snout, and tapped on the wall eight times with the hilt of her knife.

The entire canyon seemed to rumble, as a chunk of stone was lifted from the wall, revealing a passageway that twisted through the mountain. Two guards, each holding short swords and shields, stepped from the entrance. They wore ugly scowls on their faces, but their expressions softened when they saw Belle.

"Good evening," one of the men said in a pleasant voice. "Been a long time since we saw you around these parts."

Belle nodded to the man. "Good evening. May we enter?" she asked.

"Of course." The man bowed and moved aside for Belle and William to enter.

"Go to the stables, get some food, and then sleep. I will bring you anything you need after I speak with her," Belle said to William, causing the two guards to look at each other in confusion.

William nodded her head and trotted through the cavern.

"Is she up or down?" Belle asked the men.

"Up," they said in unison.

Belle followed the twisting path through the mountain, always following the splitting pathways upward as she moved. She passed dining halls and barracks filled with hundreds of soldiers and civilians, all chattering in loud and uproarious voices. Her stomach rumbled at the smell of food, but her needs would have to wait. *Just a little while longer.*

The path upwards twisted in a steep slope as Belle neared the highest room. A single guard posted outside the wooden door, a woman with grey eyes and a rifle at her side. When the guard saw Belle approaching, she raised a hand and commanded that Belle halt.

"What business do you…," the woman said before recognition filled her face. "Belle? Is that you?"

"Hello, Marjory," Belle said kindly. "May I enter?"

Marjory hesitantly looked at the door. "She's in a right-foul mood today. Her head has been pounding for near-a-week now. If what you have to say isn't…."

"It's important," Belle interrupted.

"Right," Marjory said, knocking on the door three times. "Go ahead."

The uppermost room was beautiful. Books and desks lined three walls, and on the fourth was a large window that oversaw miles of beautiful land. Three cushioned couches sat before the window to give place to observe the mountain's magnificent view. Upon one of the couches, a steaming cup of tea in her hand, sat Shell.

Shell looked towards her intruder, a pained smile filling her lips when she saw her daughter. "Belle, what brings you here?" she asked, her voice filled with evidence of her bursting head.

Belle walked forward, standing in front of Shell, and said, "Paradise has fallen."

End of Book 1

CPSIA information can be obtained
at www.ICGtesting.com
Printed in the USA
LVHW090151110221
679023LV00009B/106

9 781649 695529